To John,
Your sanity was parked here ➡

(and thanks so much for that wonderful paste job during the Healey Summer!)

A Potside Companion

BEING A COLLECTION OF SHORT STORIES, TALL TALES, FAVORITE COLUMNS,
FOND MEMORIES, WILD RUMORS, OUTRIGHT LIES, A LITTLE POETRY,
A SWELL CHICKEN RECIPE AND ASSORTED MOTORING DISASTERS
IDEALLY SUITED TO THE MOST IMPORTANT ROOM IN THE HOUSE
(NEXT TO THE GARAGE, THAT IS!)

A Potside Companion

WRITTEN, PRODUCED, AND DIRECTED BY
Burt "BS" Levy

MARVELOUS COVER ART AND ORIGINAL CARTOONS BY
Greg Petrolati

ART DIRECTION AND COLOR SECTION BY
Olga Lindsay

TIRELESS EDITING, FACT CHECKING, AND PROOFREADING BY
Bill Siegfriedt
Karen Miller & Tara Treacy

ORIGINAL "PC" LOGOS AND INVALUABLE GRAPHICS ASSISTANCE BY
Art Eastman

TRANSCRIBING AND DATA ENTRY ASSISTANCE BY
Glen Stuffers and WordSpeed

WEBSITE (WWW.LASTOPENROAD.COM) AND CEASELESS CYBER-JOCKEYING BY
Dick Carlson

MORE HELP IN MORE WAYS THAN YOU COULD EVER IMAGINE FROM
Carol Levy & Karen Miller

SPECIAL THANKS TO:
EDITORS DAVE DESTLER AND GARY ANDERSON OF *BRITISH CAR MAGAZINE*
EDITORS ART EASTMAN AND D. RANDY RIGGS OF *VINTAGE MOTORSPORT*
DIRECTOR JAN NATHAN OF THE *PUBLISHERS MARKETING ASSOCIATION*
EDITOR BOB WOODWARD OF THE *MONOPOSTO REGISTER NEWSLETTER*

THINK FAST INK L..L..C.
OAK PARK, ILLINOIS
-2001-

COPYRIGHT 2001 BY BURT S. LEVY

PUBLISHED BY:
THINK FAST INK L.L.C.
1010 LAKE STREET
OAK PARK, ILLINOIS
60301
WWW.LASTOPENROAD.COM
E-MAIL: THINKFAST@MINDSPRING.COM

WRITTEN AND MANUFACTURED IN THE UNITED STATES OF AMERICA

FIRST EDITION:
APRIL 1ST, 2001

LIBRARY OF CONGRESS CATALOGING IN PUBLICATION DATA:
LEVY, BURT S., 1945–
A POTSIDE COMPANION
1. LITERATURE 2. MOTOR RACING 3. TITLE
LIBRARY OF CONGRESS CATALOG CARD NUMBER: 00-092886

ISBN#: 0-9642107-3-8

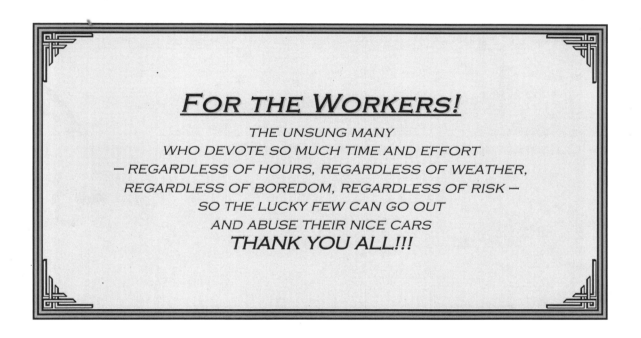

FOR THE WORKERS!

THE UNSUNG MANY
WHO DEVOTE SO MUCH TIME AND EFFORT
— REGARDLESS OF HOURS, REGARDLESS OF WEATHER,
REGARDLESS OF BOREDOM, REGARDLESS OF RISK —
SO THE LUCKY FEW CAN GO OUT
AND ABUSE THEIR NICE CARS
THANK YOU ALL!!!

The stories, essays, memories, and poems in this book represent a large part of a life happily squandered on the daily adventure of doing things I dearly love to do and being with people whose sensibilities I share and whose company I cherish. Some are new to the printed page and others have either appeared as or been developed out of columns, articles, stories and race reports previously published in various magazines and newsletters. Most of these tales are purportedly true, but perhaps seen through the narrow crack and dim, rose-colored light of hindsight. I hope they entertain and do not offend. And I wish to thank you, the people who read and enjoy my work, for providing the reason, opportunities, and rewards for all I've been blessed to do.

Table of Contents

The Lift from Hell.. 1
The Nature of Bravery...9
The Purloined Rolls-Royce... 15
Big Moments, Bad Moments...37
Surviving the Snake Pit...47
First Times, Grizzled Gurus, and Confessions of a Wild Man.......53
Brilliant Chrome and Bug Splat Radius................................69
From Blackpool to Biloxi...75
Elvis and Me..85
Dreams on the Chopping Block...93
Of Repair and Replace..99
Rolling Your Own...107
Body and Soul..117
The Ecstasy of the Agony...127
The Car that Never Was...137

– Gallery Catalogue Section –

Death of the Dip...151
Going for the Golden Jugular..157
A Greed for Speed..163
The Percy W. Dovetonsils Memorial Poetry Pages.................183
Screwed but not Kissed...189
Going Fourth...201
Buried Alive with Ellen Zweig..207
A Little Chicken Soup..215
Comedy of Terrors..219
The Haunted Jaguar...231
Hallowed Ground..243
The Agony of Victory..247
Necessity is a Mother...261

THE LIFT FROM HELL
DUTIFUL TOOL OR DERANGED DEMON?

ORIGINALLY PUBLISHED IN
BRITISH CAR
OCTOBER, 1992

In the early

spring of 1974, my new wife Carol and I opened up a sports car shop on Chicago's soon-to-be-fashionable near north side. The fact that she went along with the idea and stuck by me through three financially disastrous years is a tribute to her gumption, loyalty, steadfastness, and lack of temperament. The fact that she's stuck with me ever since (through countless more hair-brained schemes and dumb adventures) is a source of constant amazement to everyone who knows us. Particularly her family, who could never quite figure why I felt compelled to quit a successful, family-owned packaging business the minute we got married so I could pursue my star-crossed destiny as a multimillionaire shop owner, racing legend and mechanical wizard. And I knew exactly how I was gonna make those millions, too, seeing as how I'd worked all the numbers out on the back of a cocktail napkin (several, in fact) and figured if I just had three perfect, pleasant, loyal, reliable and hard working mechanics plus an endless supply of rust-free, easy-to-fix foreign cars (which our shop would naturally repair in well under the specified flat-rate book time and never screw up so badly that their owners came after us with shotguns and/or blunt instruments) well, there was *no way* we could do anything but get filthy rich on the deal.

Perhaps it's not the absolute stupidest notion I've ever had, but it's certainly well up with the front runners....

In deference to my post-collegiate odyssey as a so-called flower child (actually a misnomer, as most of us smoked the leaves, seeds, sticks and stems as well) I christened the shop "Mellow Motors." Although in truth there was little mellow about the place from the very beginning, and even less as time went on. But wife Carol and I were filled with hope and enthusiasm the day we hung out our shingle in front of a large and venerable brickwork garage at 747 Wrightwood Street, just east of Halsted, which we'd rented from a gritty, Royko-esque Chicago character named Bruno, who once kindly invited me out into the alley so he could try parting my hair with a claw hammer.

Among the many exciting features of Bruno's ancient building (besides the walk-up toilet that threatened continually to fall through the floor and a gravel-filled cavern below housing the resident rat menagerie) was a fine and sturdy pre-Columbian example of that gotta-have-one necessity found in every bigtime professional car shop: a hydraulic lift. Now this particular lift was a real collectors' item with a fine patina of age (in fact, you'd get that patina all over yourself if you got anywhere near the thing) and the elderly rumpot next door swore it actually predated the internal combustion engine, and was used to hold up the rear ends of oversized horses during routine neuterings.

The lift in Bruno's garage rested on a single, massive centerpost that had to measure at least a yard in diameter, atop which were mounted four heavy, articulated arms that would form the letter "H" when perfectly aligned. Flopping over a worn-shiny brass lever on the wall (a relic from the *Lusitania* perhaps?) caused the thoroughly antique air compressor in the back corner to start clattering like a steam locomotive on square wheels, and soon, with much hissing, groaning, and ominous, deep-register bowel sounds, that huge cylinder would begin oozing slowly upwards—ascending as if from the pit of Hell itself—drooling grease and brackish water like that disgusting lizard creature in the movie *Alien....*

In a masterstroke of brilliant interior design, the lift in Bruno's garage was situated in a corner, barely three-and-a-half feet from the office wall. A constantly drizzling spigot on the wall ensured that the floor beneath our lift was always covered with a pudding-like melange of water, spilled oil and antifreeze, the lift's own personal excretions, several dozen pounds of used Oil-Dri, and a wide variety of tiny, irreplaceable, you-can't-find-them-anywhere-but-a dealership (*and* they're on back order!) shouldered bolts, woodruff keys, special washers and hermaphrodite fittings that were forever falling in the muck and, I believe to this day, getting sucked right through the blessed concrete to that place television preachers (at least those still out on bond) talk about incessantly on Sunday mornings.

I must admit I learned many hard and valuable mechanical lessons at the foot of that ancient lift. And, if some of them seem lighthearted and amusing today, it's only because laughter is, in the end, just the final, fitful blossoming of despair.

How well I recall Mellow Motors' first ever XKE clutch job! The bald fact is that I didn't know Jack Shit about changing a clutch on an E-type, but, *hey,* I ran a damn sports car shop, didn't I? It said so right there on my singularly embarrassing W2 form. I'd be damned if I was gonna let something as trifling as total ignorance get in my way. Why, I'd *personally* changed the clutch in my TR3 (several times, in fact) and one of our so-called "mechanics" had an uncle who used to walk by a Jaguar dealership *every day* on the way to work. Or at least he said he did.

Following a long discussion of possible tactics and strategy around the coffee machine (always the first major step at any car shop), we carefully peeled back the carpeting and interior hardware to get at the transmission tunnel. Only an XKE is a monocoque, see, so it don't have what you and Gomer and me would normally recognize as a transmission tunnel. Well, not a *removable* one, anyways. Hmmmm. The owner of the local British sports car slaughterhouse (a deservedly infamous garage called Excelsior Motors over on Damen Avenue in the heart of Chicago's taco and chili pepper belt) recommended I could save myself a lot of time and anguish by simply cutting the tunnel out with one of those high speed pneumatic finger removers, pulling the trans out the back TR3-fashion, replacing the offending clutch, and then tack-welding the tunnel back in place once everything was bolted together again. Nobody, he assured me, would be the wiser.

Somehow, that didn't exactly sound like the factory-recommended, shop manual procedure, and we eventually settled on a conservative, common sense, full-frontal assault. With much grunting, groaning, straining of muscles and severing of vital tendons, we removed the Jag's one-piece bonnet (which, I swear, is roughly the same size and weight as a Pratt & Whitney jet aircraft engine) undid every bolt and nut we could find, and proceeded to lift the entire engine/tans assembly (roughly the same size and weight as a Pratt & Whitney *piston* aircraft engine) out the top. Only it wouldn't. No matter how we jockeyed around with the jacks and the lift and the engine hoist and the rake of the car and the angle of the dangle, that sucker just flat *would not* clear the top tube of the front crossmember. It lacked a solid three-quarters of an inch. And that's *after* we pulled the damn water pump, oil pan, and crankshaft pulley! %*#@*!!! So we stood around in Stymie City for the next couple of hours, silently drinking coffee and smoking cigarettes and walking back over to our wedged-solid XKE clutch job every now and again to see if maybe the engine block had shrunk any.

In the end, I gave up and called service manager and legit mechanical guru Vince Woodfield over at the local Jag dealership, and he recommended we drop the whole shebang out the bottom (while warning us repeatedly *not* to let the ends of the torsion bars pop when we pulled the bolts out!) and that's exactly what we did. Let the torsion bars pop, I mean. But the hardest part was jockeying this massively jammed-up car/engine/trans assembly from where it was (imagine an alligator trying to swallow a diesel locomotive) to where we needed it so's we could complete the operation from the underside. Ultimately we resorted to spreading the front lift arms as wide as they would go, pushing that hapless E-type *waaay* forward on the lift (allowing access to everything on its soft underbelly clear back to the tailshaft) and then strapping the ass end of that car to the back of the lift with ratchet tie downs so it would just sorta *hang* there (albeit precariously) while we completed the rest of the operation.

And hopefully not fall on our heads!

Imagine the owner's surprise when he waltzed unexpectedly into the shop for a progress check and found his beloved Series One E-Type dangling off the business end of the Mellow Motors lift like it was giving birth to that same diesel locomotive mentioned above. Needless to say, he was not amused. And even less impressed with our methods. As was I, come to think of it. And you shoulda *seen* the damn plumber's wrench it took to twist those freaking torsion bars back into position. I swear, the handle on that sucker had to be three feet long! And we had to put yet another three or four feet of pipe on it to get the necessary leverage!

But the award for worst lift experience of all time is reserved for (fanfare and drum roll, please, typesetter): *The Sunday Afternoon of the Avalanched MG*. No question about it. See, back in those carefree, innocent and unfettered days of the middle-seventies (before the lawyers, do-gooders, and insurance companies got a stranglehold on this country's lower intestinal tract) we used to let employees, racing buddies, friends-of-the-shop, and people who bought us lots of drinks at the bar come in and work on their own personal cars on Sunday afternoons. It was a nice public relations gesture, you know? Especially since I could count on most of those dweebs to screw up their cars so badly they'd have to leave them in the shop for us to put right again—for *money!*—come Monday morning.

During the time in question, Mellow Motors' ever changing retinue of employees included a tall, thin, yet insidiously muscular fellow named Dale, who wore a wild, bushy, full-face beard and had the crazed eyes of a Viking warrior in the act of pillaging a Saxon village. He was a quiet sort, actually, but whenever you needed two pieces of metal violently separated from one another, Dale was your man. He also had (thanks to an insurance claim of perhaps dubious nature) the most incredible tool set you have ever seen on your life. I swear, Dale had at least one (or more!) of everything on the Snap-On catalog. Only problem was, Dale would spend literally hours in front of his shiny red, six-story tool cabinet, pondering exactly which precise combination of ratchet handle, extensions, knuckle-wobblers and six-point deepwell flex-sockets would be most appropriate for the job at hand.

Which is precisely why I sent Dale out on parts runs at every possible opportunity. He was good at getting the right stuff we needed, it kept him from not getting much of anything useful accomplished on whatever car he happened to be working on, and it allowed us free and unlimited use of his amazing tool set while he was gone. A good deal all around.

In any case, this one warm and pleasant late-summer Sunday afternoon, Dale had brought his brother-in-law's mustard-colored MGB over to our shop for a routine muffler job. Now this particular MGB was one of the unloved, late issue, fat-rubber-bumper models, and as such was bedeviled with a strange, crimped-end muffler system that I can only assume the factory assembled out of recycled fruit cocktail cans and was therefore guaranteed to blow out at least once a year. If not sooner. And the difficulty with the fat-bumper MGBs was that the damn exhaust pipe ran very nearly down the centerline (pardon me, *centreline*) of the car, which posed a bit if an access problem on and H-style lift like the resident piece at Mellow Motors. Our boy Dale solved this particular bother by purposely *mis*-aligning his brother-in-law's MG on the lift, allowing the entire exhaust system (along with 49.9% of the car's weight) to teeter alarmingly off to the left-hand side.

I remember being home that particular Sunday afternoon, resting my poor, bloodied knuckles around my fourth or fifth can of Old Style while watching our pre-Mike Ditka Chicago Bears getting pushed all over the field by, I believe, a local high school team. Then the phone rang. It was Dale, and I recall his exact opening words in perfect, crystalline detail: *"I don't think I broke my leg."*

Needless to say, that cheerful tidbit of news instantly wiped out the effect of three or more beers. *"You WHAT???!!!"*

It transpired that Dale had come upon a rather solidly rusted-up nut on the old exhaust system, and, after carefully selecting the appropriate drive-handle, multi-jointed extension combination, and deepwell six-point flex socket, Dale proceeded to tighten his jaw, plant his feet, and apply Significant Pressure as only he was able.

Which is about when his brother-in-law's MGB came hurtling out of the sky like an R.A.F. Spitfire (okay, an R.A.F. MG) riddled with anti-aircraft fire. I leave the fierceness, texture and decibel level of the accompanying noise to your imagination, but rest assured all three were of substantial magnitude. Fortunately, the car missed Dale by a whisker (or maybe less, since I recall a few stray beard hairs hanging off the undercarriage) as it crashed violently into the concrete floor beside the lift, driver's door downward. As if that weren't enough, Dale's brother-in-law's MG was now well and truly trapped; stuck *underneath* the lift (so there was no way it could go down) in the vertical axis and wedged in securely between the lift-post and the wall laterally. Not to mention that the windshield frame had neatly sheared off the business end of the water spigot, so a healthy (?) spray of our fine Chicago city water was thoroughly drenching the floor, the walls, and the MG's interior.

Such was the incredible, horrifying scene that greeted me as I walked in through the overhead door some ten minutes later. surveying the carnage, checking repeatedly to make sure Dale wasn't injured (all the while promising repeatedly to injure him myself) the two of us set about solving the puzzle of his brother-in-law's fountainlike MGB trapped beneath the Mellow Motors lift. It became painfully obvious that there was no finessing our way out of the situation, so we ordered two large pizzas and several cold sixpacks, called a few friends and employees, grabbed the odd passerby off the street, and *dragged* that sucker out (accompanied by terrible screeching, grinding, scraping, scuffing, steel-against-concrete noises) and, once clear, gave it a hefty *"one-two-three-NOW!"* shove and flopped it (*Ka-WHUMPFF!*) back over on its wheels.

Let me tell you, this was one very unhappy-looking MGB. The driver's side looked like it had been run over by a steamroller, the windshield was busted, two inches of water sloshed in the footwells, a brackish mixture of brake fluid, antifreeze and oil bathed the entire engine compartment, that fat, ugly and terribly expensive front bumper was badly scuffed (served it right!), the driver's side door handle was broken, every bit of glass on the car was either cracked or shattered, the radio antenna was sheared off, and countless assorted trim bits were suddenly due for replacement.

Oh, and it *still* had a bum muffler....

When you own a car repair facility, you are faced almost daily with legal and ethical questions regarding responsibility, liability, and culpability, and these concerns often form the very fabric and character of your business. Which is exactly what I had dead-center in my mind as Dale and I rolled his brother-in-law's newly scrunched MGB to a curbside space well down the block from Mellow Motors. "Dale," I told him in a warm, fatherly tone, "I want you to remember one simple thing."

"What's that?" he inquired earnestly.

I looked deep into his Viking-warrior-sacking-a-Saxon-village eyes, narrowed my own, and growled: *"Dale, this DID <u>NOT</u> happen in my shop!"*

THE NATURE OF BRAVERY
WHAT'S THE DIFFERENCE BETWEEN COURAGE AND FOOLHARDINESS?

ORIGINALLY PUBLISHED IN
Vintage Motorsport
MAY/JUNE 1994

This was originally going to be a funny column.

In fact, I drafted it up that way while I flew down to Florida for the first couple races of the season at Sebring and West Palm. And, strangely enough, it had the same exact title and concerned the same exact topic, and of course included my customary dosage of smart-alecky remarks and tongue-in-cheek bullshit. Only now I don't feel quite so funny, and perhaps it's time to rethink and rewrite some of the glib, devil-may-care phrases I inscribed on this screen just a dozen days ago.

An awful lot has happened since then.

On the drive up to Sebring—purely by accident—I saw the space shuttle launch from Cape Canaveral. Or, more accurately, I saw all these people pulled off the road and standing by the side of the highway, necks craned back and hands shielding their eyes as they stared and pointed towards the eastern sky. So I stopped and took a look myself. And there it was, streaking upwards into the flawless blue like a giant, orange-red comet of pure human inspiration. There was something all at once awesome, giddy, fearsome and profoundly honorable about this man-made projectile hurling itself into the void. Especially when you thought about the immense matrix of interdependent human thought and effort that put it up there; as if 10,000 individual voices were somehow sustaining an incredibly perfect chord. And yet I couldn't help focusing in on the few fragile souls sitting up there on the tip of that brilliant column of flame, plummeting upward, and wondering if their fingernails were digging into the seat rails the way mine do now and then on a steering wheel. How well were *they* smothering that spastic little demon of panic that lives inside all of us?

They had to be some brave, brave people, no question about it....

But then I met an astronaut at Moroso. A real one. A fit, funny, enthusiastic, down-to-earth (of all things!) and thoroughly self-effacing 41-year-old named Jim Bagian. Jim was on hand as guest and co-driver of well-known race insurance poobah John Gorsline, and eagerly awaiting his first-ever try in a racing car (if, indeed, your definition of "racing car" stretches far enough to cover a well-tweaked Mini). Twice in his life (1989, 1991), Jim has sat himself down and strapped himself in on top of a twenty story booster rocket and *waited*—his heart rate and respiration a matter of public record—waited for some faceless little men in lab coats to light the candle. "Jeez," I said respectfully, "you must be pretty damn brave to do a thing like *that!*"

Jim didn't especially think so. Far as he was concerned, he was just one more brick in the pyramid, and the fact that he was fortunate enough to sit way up there on the pointy end aimed up towards the heavens didn't make him any more vital, brave or important than anybody else on the team. What I interpreted as raw guts was really just a heartfelt confidence in the knowledge, wisdom, and good judgment of all the other bricks in the structure—that they would do *their* jobs with the same dedication and thoroughness he brought to his. And I immediately recognized the strong parallel to motorsports, in that both endeavors require a transcending, almost religious belief in man-made hardware and technology. Which, of course, means trusting—with your very *life!*—all the wonderful and unique characters who wield drafting pens, slide rules, welders and knock-off hammers long into the night. What I mistook for uncommon courage on Jim's part was, in reality, an even more uncommon faith in what human minds and hands and hearts can accomplish together.

At any rate, Jim spent the entire race weekend at Moroso with an enormous grin plastered across his face, and I must say that he did better than respectably well in John's well-prepped and much-traveled Mini. And if the image of a real, live NASA astronaut (who's twice been hurled into space on seven-odd million pounds of flaming rocket thrust!) charging out of the pits in a redlined Mini Cooper doesn't bring the faintest flicker of a smile to your face, you have no sense of irony.

When pressed, Astronaut Jim had some interesting observations about the differences between space flight and racecar driving. First off, he really appreciated the sense of hands-on *control* and Individual Responsibility you get in a racecar—things that have been generally absorbed out of the space program's technological nervous system (as Tom Wolfe so eloquently and entertainingly described in <u>*The Right Stuff*</u>). But, just as in astronauting, Jim didn't think you had to be uncommonly brave to drive racecars. On the other hand, it didn't hurt to have a bit of nerve when you needed it. And by "nerve," we mean that simple, rare, Right Stuff ability to remain cool, calm, composed, coordinated, and capable of sound judgment when things are happening very quickly and countless details require immediate and carefully measured attention (and when, all the while, that grim rat-bastard Mr. Pucker is trying to turn your break-fast into a bile-colored geyser and make your hands freeze up on the stick).

Consider fast, daunting stretches of pavement like The Kink at Elkhart Lake or The Diving Turn at Lime Rock or The Dip at Road Atlanta. Places like that require every racer to slide one of those precious little silver bullets of nerve into the chamber, flip off the safety, take careful aim, and squeeze off a round. It's hairy stuff. But there's a richly orchestrated sense of satisfaction in rising to such challenges, lap after lap, and especially in understanding that it's done with coolness and finesse rather than brass balls and flaming machismo. As my R.A.F. fighter pilot/racing driver character Tommy Edwards observes in _The Last Open Road,_ risk is often its own reward.

But sometimes—thankfully rarely—it all goes terribly wrong. Like it did for one horrible, indelible moment that same weekend at Moroso. There you are, accelerating out of Turn 6 onto the backstraight during afternoon practice on as fine, clear and sun-shiny a Friday afternoon as God ever created, and suddenly there's an explosion of dust and tires up ahead on the other side of the concrete retaining wall. A brutal, lead-pipe chunk of Allard racecar catapults spread eagle into the air, ricochets violently off a solid concrete light pole, and comes cartwheeling and somersaulting towards you along the knife-edge top of the barrier. You jam on the brakes and swerve off onto the grass as quickly as possible, pop the belts and scramble awkwardly out of the cockpit—_everything happening in desperate slow motion!_—and run frantically towards where the car has come to a steaming, twitching halt some twenty yards away, bent wheels still rotating.

But then you stop. Stop and stare at the twisted, teetering heap of metal and the unnatural, rag-doll slump of the helmeted figure behind the wheel. A man who was doing exactly what you were doing and enjoying exactly what you were enjoying only a few short heartbeats ago. But there is nothing you can do—_nothing!_—and helplessness swallows you like a sea of quicksand....

And of course it makes you think, in the deep, empty hollows of the night, about Risk and Value and What It All Means. But there are no answers. And then, less than a week later, you're at a surprise fiftieth birthday party for a good friend you never find time to see anymore, and some 41-year-old guy at the bar—same age as Astronaut Jim—suddenly goes electrified-rigid for an instant, then crumples to the floor like an accordion with the wind going out of it.

As people rush around madly to raise his head, call the medics and try their best at CPR, it's obvious to anyone who sees his face that this poor fellow will never grow another day older. And you discover that the shock, fear, outrage and helplessness take on the same sour taste and hollow form as they did in front of that grotesquely twisted Allard just a few days before.

I suppose the moral is that Death is waiting out there somewhere for all of us. Like that lean-faced, black-clad stranger you think you catch a glimpse of in your mirror sometimes, only to wheel around and find him gone. In the end, I suppose there are really only two ways out of this life—sick and slow or swift and sudden—and while we all make fine cocktail chatter about the painless grace of a Quick Exit, none of us are ever really ready to make the trip....

So you don't quit racing, even though you feel crushed and empty and cheated and saddened. After all, your rational self knows that the risks have not really changed and the odds have not varied one iota. You have merely been called upon to bear witness and feel some small share of the pain. No question you will find yourself ready to zip up your flameproofs, flip down the visor and accelerate through The Escape Hatch again the very next chance you get. After all, it's one of the only ways out of this world with a way back in at the opposite end. Just like a moonshot....

But don't confuse the desire—the *need*—to keep on racing with any sort of exceptional courage or bravery. Facing known and immediate risks for a finite fraction of time is perhaps nothing more than a busy, vibrant little place to hide from all the deadening certainties and uncertainties of everyday life. Real courage is going on and enduring and making fresh plans when the unthinkable and unspeakable stare back at you out of your dressing mirror every morning. Real courage is learning how to hammer those little silver bullets of momentary bravery into sheets so desperately thin and transparent that they stretch out wide enough to cover 60 seconds every minute and long enough to wrap around all 365 days of every year that's left. *Real* courage is keeping your heart, spirit and enthusiasm when every temptation is to turn into an angry vessel of bitterness and woe.

No, I don't suppose you have to be particularly brave to be a racing driver. But I must admit I've known a few who are. Like Sue Henning, who persevered valiantly against failing health and never allowed it to take away her smile, her enthusiasm or her plans for tomorrow. She sadly succumbed to cancer last winter after a long, hard-fought battle. But she remained an avid, eager and ever-improving vintage racer, a treasured friend, and hellacious good company throughout her final seasons. People like that are an object lesson in what *real* courage is all about. And, as surely as the sight of the space shuttle arcing ever upward on its pencil-thin column of flame, they are an inspiration.

THE PURLOINED ROLLS-ROYCE

A NEW YEAR'S EVE TO REMEMBER!

THIS STORY WAS REPORTED IN THE
CHICAGO SUN TIMES
ON JANUARY 15, 1978
IT HAS NOT BEEN PUBLISHED PREVIOUSLY

It was the cold, overcast Friday afternoon before New Year's Eve, and I was sitting at my sales desk at Loeber Motors in downtown Chicago, looking out past the gleaming display of fuel-injected Volkswagen Rabbits and Dashers and fuel-objected Alfa Romeo Alfettas and Spiders at the tombstone gray city canyon landscape of north Clark Street. It was around four o'clock in the afternoon, and the showroom was empty except for some loud, rich guy with a few too many cocktails under his belt giving one of the other salesmen a hard time in one of the glassed-in offices on the Mercedes floor. He was trying to buy a new 450SL for his wife or girlfriend at a solid $2800 under net dealer cost because some friend or business associate or golf buddy or elevator neighbor at the condominium—or maybe his dentist or lawyer—had told him *he* got one that cheap on account of he was such a shrewd negotiator. So the notion of paying anything more—especially with a couple stiff Manhattans floating around in his bloodstream—was patently unthinkable. And he wasn't much impressed when the salesman showed him the actual invoice on the car and explained as how the dealership couldn't stay in business very long if it sold cars for less than it paid for them. But the guy didn't believe him. Not one bit. Hell, *all* car salesmen lied. That's what they did for a living. And he wasn't about to put up with it. Not one bit. So he leaned in over the desk, dug in his heels, and started getting belligerent. But that was okay. That's what the glassed-in offices were for. To keep the ugly stuff from spilling out onto the showroom floor where some ordinary citizen might actually be trying to buy a car. The sad part was that this guy was going to use up the salesman's whole afternoon and on into the evening, even though they both knew this deal had NO SALE written all over it. Fact is, he probably never really wanted to buy the car in the first place. But at least now he could go back home to his wife or over to his side girlfriend's apartment and tell her about how he'd gone shopping for that glistening white 450SL with tan leather interior and matching, hand painted pinstripes that she wanted so badly, but "those bastards over at Loeber wouldn't give me a fair deal. They wanted both ears and the damn tail." And then he'd make sure to tell all his friends and business associates and golf buddies and elevator neighbors at the condominium—*and* his dentist and lawyer—not to do business with Loeber Motors on Clark Street on account of we were such a rotten, stinking, cheating, thieving, lying bunch of crooks.

But you get used to it.

Just like you get used to the long, empty hours when nothing much is going on and the cynical, streetwise, world-weary yet strangely optimistic and upbeat coffee-and-doughnut chatter from the other salesmen and the desperate, queasy feeling you'd get when the fifteenth of the month rolls around and you've got nothing at all on the sales board and the business cards of not a single likely prospect tucked into the leather binding of your desk calendar. Or the way people on the outside kind of look at you sideways when you tell them what you do for a living. Not to mention seeing a lot of those same people at their nasty, cheap, paranoid, lying and suspicious *worst* at least a few times every month—guaranteed—when they came in to shop for a car.

It's not a job for everybody.

Which is why hardly anybody winds up selling cars on purpose. Nobody goes to college to major in Retail Automobile Sales. And that's why it's mostly a place for young kids on the way up to get a baptism in street life and negotiating and a way station for occupationally displaced people from other deals, jobs, partnerships and marriages on their way to other, more promising, deals, jobs, partnerships and marriages. Or at least they think they are. But a lot of them get stuck there. You can make a decent buck if you wind up in a good store and know how to smile and hustle. But the burnout rate is high. There are a lot of pressures and distractions and after-hours temptations when you work that close to the street. And especially a street like north Clark Street, right around the corner from Chicago's infamous Rush Street nightclub district.

Time and again I'd see a salesman lose his way and start to slip, start to lose his edge and confidence. It could be booze or money or some waitress or hat-check girl on the side causing trouble at home or just a bad month that starts snowballing until you're so damn desperate and needy that you couldn't sell ice cubes in hell. Or sometimes it's too much success. Sometimes a guy gets on a roll where he's writing deals like he's got a magic pen. I remember seeing it happen to a busted-out commodities trader over on the Mercedes floor. All of a sudden, out of freaking nowhere, he's top man on the Benz board in the sales office because the market is too damn good and all his old commodity trading buddies are coming over to buy cars (in the company name, of course) before the year runs out and they've got to fork over a big chunk of whatever's left over to Uncle Sam. So he's making deals hand-over-fist and buying himself new clothes and fat cigars and twenty-five buck razor cuts at the barber shop and—again thanks to all of his old commodities trading buddies—powdering his nose eight or ten times a day in the dark little crap stall in the washroom just off the showroom floor. You can tell because his eyes look like shiny ball bearings and he has this dumb little sniffle that never seems to go away. Like most all sales personalities, he's got this illuminated notion—this *glow*—like it's all coming to him because of some special talent he's miraculously acquired or some special technique he's suddenly developed out of nowhere. Even if he can't quite put his finger on what it is. Worse yet (and, again, like most all sales personalities) he has this crazy, misguided idea that it's going to keep on happening. That it will *stay* this lush and easy and effortless forever. And of course that's when he stops working. That's when he forgets the simple, everyday mechanics of selling cars and taking care of customers that got him where he is. Which is why he's out of a job and out the door in another couple weeks.

It happened all the time.

But I loved it anyway. I loved it because I loved the cars we had to sell. It was a day short of 1978, and I honestly believed that our new, Bosch-injected VW Rabbit was the best damn small car you could buy. Really I did. And I sold the living hell out of them because of it. I also loved the style, charm, and quirky charisma of our Spica-injected Alfa Romeos—hell, I drove and raced one—even if they came off as troublesome and finicky to all the Fred Average/John Q. Public types who couldn't break the habit of pumping the damn gas pedal a few times to help it start in cold weather, thereby absolutely insuring that it never would. I knew Alfas weren't for everybody and so I sold them honestly. Warts and all. And I got a lot of nice referrals because of it.

In the other showroom we had Mercedes-Benz, and there was no doubt in my mind that they were genuinely the safest, smartest, best handling, best engineered, and best built luxury sedans you could buy. I'd talked my dad into a plain Jane, bottom-of-the-model-line Mercedes 280S many years before, and that was all he drove from then on. He only used them to trundle back and forth from the north side to downtown everyday and occasionally on weekend jaunts up to Ravinia Park or someplace with my mom, and really didn't care or understand much about what made them great cars. But he knew he enjoyed aiming through that famous 3-pointed gun sight on the hood and the way the understated composure of a Mercedes made doormen, car hikers, and people you were giving a lift to react when you pulled up to the curb. I, on the other hand, drove the living snot out of those cars every chance I got, and it was pretty damn amazing how fast and nimble that big, heavy chunk of a sedan could be on a country road or wailing around a freeway off ramp. Even if it *was* a little tough on the tire sidewalls....

Between the VW/Alfa and Mercedes showrooms was an enclosed sort of breeze-way that they'd turned into an elegant little foyer of a showroom with terra cotta tile on the floor, and that's where we always displayed the latest models from Rolls-Royce. And everybody's impressed—or at least as impressed as they ever could be by a blessed car salesman—when you casually explain as how you hawk Rollers for a living. Some of the magic apparently rubs off....

I have to admit I've never been much of a Rolls enthusiast. At least not since they quit building those elegant Silver Cloud editions from the late 1950s. And they screwed those up royally with that butt-ugly quad headlamp setup introduced on the series three versions in 1962. As for the Silver Shadows and long wheelbase Silver Wraith models we had on sale at Loeber, they didn't do much for me. In fact, I thought they were stuffy and ostentatious, had absolutely zero road feel through the steering and brakes, and handled like wallowing slop hogs. But of course *driving* was not what you bought a Rolls for, was it? No, a Rolls-Royce was a piece of social jewelry that you could leave parked in front of the Main Entrance damn near anywhere and get away with it. A guarantee that you would be noticed and marveled over and deferred to by parking garage attendants and *maiter d's*. A set of six-foot-plus elevator shoes that nobody but your tax accountant could see. And add in the rarified pleasure of motoring serenely down the road, nose ever so slightly in the air, all the while peering up the Spirit of Ecstasy's backside like you could maybe catch a glimpse of her icy silver ass.

Oh, the more expensive and exclusive Corniche coupes and ragtops were pretty keen sets of wheels (if outrageously priced—but that was the whole point, wasn't it?) only you never saw or sold very many. Only a few per year. And they commanded all kinds of legitimate attention. In fact, I remember one summer day this L.A. film producer guy pulled into the service drive in a creamy yellow Corniche convertible with an even creamier looking young thing in a patent leather miniskirt close by his side. He was your standard-issue L.A. film producer type; a short, fat Jewish guy with a well-tanned bald spot surrounded by a halo of greying, Brillo-pad hair, dark sunglasses surrounded by heavy black frames, and a couple Aztec- or maybe Inca-looking gold medallions clanking around on another cushion of greying, Brillo-pad hair where most people have a few shirt buttons. And buttoned, at that. But nobody except the service advisor paid much attention to him. Nope, all of our eyes were riveted on his passenger. Jesus, she was about the hottest, sexiest, most beautiful young girl any of us had ever seen. Even if she didn't really look old enough to buy herself a Harvey Wallbanger or a Skip-and-go-Naked. Not even on Rush Street. She had long, perfect legs and taut young breasts that sneered at gravity and this mane of silky blond hair down her back that rippled and cascaded whenever she laughed. And the way she moved. Like a cat stretching, you know? I guess this film producer guy was driving her cross-country from L.A. to New York in his fancy new Roller—probably banging her or getting himself a fresh blowjob at every damn Hilton and Holiday Inn along the way—when a fuse blew in the tape player just east of Moline so they had to stop in at the dealership to get it fixed. I mean, you'd never dream of trusting the high school dropout brake, shock and muffler expert at a streetcorner gas station in Moline with fixing your Rolls-Royce Corniche.

Even if he could.

And that was one of the neat things about working at an upscale imported car store on north Clark Street in Chicago. Sooner or later, the whole blessed world dropped in on you. Saints and sinners. Rich and poor. Famous and infamous. Drop-dead gorgeous to drop-dead disgusting. And oftentimes side-by-side. Like this fresh, hot young girl, trying to break into show biz by honking this fat film producer guy's horn all the way across country from L.A. to Manhattan. It just didn't seem right, you know? But that's what Rollses were all about, when you get right down to it.

To be honest, I always did a lot better with the Vee Dub and Alfa customers than I ever did with the Mercedes or Rolls-Royce types. Hell, I could talk *product* and *features* with the Alfa and VW prospects—really explain what the cars were about to them!—while most of your Mercedes and Rolls Royce shoppers seemed more interested in *deal* and *price.* They made it clear that they were busy, important, impatient, intelligent and well-informed people who already *knew* precisely what they were looking for, thank you very much. Even the really stupid ones.

But it was still a treat to work at a dealership like Loeber. We had a great selection of cars, a super location, and a diverse and endlessly fascinating clientele. Plus you could make good money if you were good at the game and hustled. Most car dealerships have an "up" system where all the salesmen (and ladies) wait around like ballplayers on the bench, waiting for their turn as each new prospective customer walks through the door. That's their "up." And it's too damn bad if it turns out to be some jerkoff mooch (dealership slang for somebody who wastes a salesman's time but has no real intention of buying a car) or LOF (for Lack Of Funds, ditto) who aren't really in the market. Too bad, Bub. Get yourself another cup of coffee and go back to the end of the line.

But not at Loeber. There was usually enough customer traffic walking in off north Clark Street that Loeber had an Open Floor. Which simply meant that he who grabbed, got. Oh, there were rules. You couldn't bull rush prospects as they came in off the street or "skate" (horn in on) another salesman's customer or "camp on" (try to get a share of) another salesman's deal. And "curbing" cars (making private deals with customers to sell cars that didn't come from the dealership or buying their trade-ins for a little more than the wholesale price the dealership offered) was an immediate firing offense. But everything else was pretty much up for grabs. And there were usually enough fresh new faces and repeat customers streaming into the showroom every day that everybody kept pretty busy.

The other neat thing about working there was that George Loeber—as well as his father before him—wanted to believe in the professionalism, ethics and honesty of the people they hired. Even though they wound up mistaken and sadly disappointed more times than either of them cared to remember. George turned out to be one of the really important people in my life, because he took the person inside me seriously even when I was full of know-it-all, post-adolescent bullshit. And he had a great and practical wisdom about the way things were and how most of them were destined to remain that way. George had seen and understood an awful lot about life, but he was always thoughtful, reserved, quick to question and slow to leap to conclusions. He wound up giving me a lot of very useful and accurate advice. But only when I asked for it.

Anyhow, a lot of car dealerships employ a "track" sales system where every customer is a mark and the salesman and the his evil, unseen sales manager play a sort of Good Cop/Bad routine once they get a prospect into the negotiating process. You know how it goes, where the salesman takes your offer across the showroom and into this ominous little office with closed venetian blinds on the windows to try and get his ogre of a sales manager to accept your deal. He's gone a long time, fighting hard for you (and he really *needs* this deal, because there's an important sales contest going on) but the truth is the two of them are down there having coffee together, letting you stew in your own juices and ponder how much you really *want* that new car. I mean, you'd already made the commitment to buy when you signed the offer and forked over a token deposit check. Now it's just a question of how much you're going to pay. And that's where the dealership feels it has home court advantage. You only buy a new car once every couple years, but they sell them every single day. So the whole idea is to drag the process out, wear the prospect down, fight for every available dollar, and make sure not to leave one red cent of potential gross profit on the table.

I had to go to a one-day school to learn a "track" system at the first place I sold cars, and I instantly despised it. It was sneaky, cynical, and thoroughly manipulative of both customer and, as it turned out, the salesman as well. Track stores simply didn't trust their salesmen to do the job they were hired for. But at Loeber, there was none of that crap. Sure, the sales manager had to approve your deals, and would occasionally tell you to hightail it the hell back to your desk and get more money—especially on a hot new model or one in short supply—but you were supposed to understand your job and have a feel for the market and furthermore be able to burrow a few feet into the psyche of the people sitting across from you and know what you could charge. Because every deal was different. There were cheap deals where the customer had read every damn consumer book on the newsstand, shopped at maybe five or six different dealerships, and fought you down to the last frigging nickel, and then there were "laydowns," who paid whatever you asked and were always fair game for add-ons like rustproofing and Polyglycoat and Scotchguarding and extended warranties. More challenging but equally rewarding were the "get-me-dones," who desperately wanted or needed a new car but were up to their assholes in debt already and barely able to pay the blessed interest on what they owed. They'd usually had a few credit problems somewhere along the way and didn't much care what they paid for a car or how astronomical the interest rate, just so long as you could get them on the road. You could make an awful lot of money selling cars to people who really couldn't afford them....

In spite of all of it, I enjoyed the hell out of selling cars at Loeber Motors on Clark Street. All you had to do was seize your opportunities with both hands, treat people as fairly as they deserved, and let the bad stuff roll off your back. In fact, that's precisely what I was thinking on the Friday evening before New Years' Eve as I looked out the showroom window at the beginnings of rush hour when this big, chauffeured Caddy limo pulled up to the curb and a tall, well dressed young black man got out of the back. I was out from behind my desk in a flash and positioned so I'd be just sort of casually strolling by when he waltzed through the door. I asked if I could be of any help.

He studied me for a moment, sizing me up. His face was unreadable, but I noticed something quietly intense going on behind his eyes. "My name is Charles Stevens," he told me like it should maybe mean something, "and I wondered if you have any used Rolls-Royces?" He looked like he was serious.

But you never know in the car business. Especially when it comes to something like a Rolls. You'd get "stroked" by mooches a thousand times for every genuine, ca$h money Rolls prospect who walks in off the street. Hey, a lot of guys just want to brag to their buddies or impress their dates with how they went shopping for a Roller. And you know going in that very few people have the bucks or mindset to do the deal. So you learn to look for things. You look at the clothes. You look at the shoes. You look at the watch. You look at the eyeglasses. You look at the haircut. You sniff the air and see if it smells like money. But you never assume. I've seen guys in $700 suits and $200 shoes who can't get a bank to finance them a cup of coffee, and I've seen guys in old, tattered coveralls who look like plumber's helpers drive out in a brand new Mercedes with no more down than their signature. So you never know.

In the end, you have to go with your gut.

My gut said this guy might be for real. He was wearing a nicely tailored gray business suit underneath a genuine suede topcoat with nicely understated fur trim at the cuffs and collar, expensive shoes, a genuine platinum watch, and Perry Ellis frames on his eyeglasses. Of course, there are other ways to get that kind of stuff besides paying over-the-counter retail. And then there was that limo parked outside. But the key thing was that he was soft spoken and reserved and didn't use a bunch of loud street slang like some preacher, pimp, drug hustler or ward politician who'd made a big score and was out to spend a couple Hefty bags full of twenties, fifties, and hundreds on a bad set of wheels. No, there was definitely something *different* about this guy.

So I took him out to the used car showroom, where we did indeed have a few used Rollers. And one caught his eye immediately. It was a 1971 Silver Shadow convertible—really the same car as the later Corniche ragtop except for a couple little chrome horn grilles underneath the headlamps—and this particular car had quite a story to go with it. It was silver with black guts and creamy white piping on the leather, and it really looked to be in topnotch condition. At least if you didn't know that the power steering pump was pissing fluid and the exhaust system was going bad and that the repair bill on those two little items would run as much as a new VW. Not to mention that it wasn't even our car. It was "on consignment" from this rich Jewish lawyer (strangely with the same last name as me, but pronounced differently) who had bought himself another Rolls but couldn't get together with the dealership (who knew all about the power steering pump and the exhaust system on account of they'd given him an estimate on the work) about what his trade should be worth. So the dealership offered to put his old Roller in their used car lineup "on consignment" to get it out of the deal and see if maybe anybody would be dumb enough to fork over the forty grand he seemed to think it was worth.

Now the deal on consignment cars was that the house got 10% of whatever the guy wanted for the car plus 100% of anything over that amount they realized, and so the silver Rolls had a fairly unrealistic $43,500 on the window sticker as an asking price. Hey, if there's one thing you learn in the car business, it's that you can *always* go down, but, once you're down, you can never go back up again. So you maybe pad a little something extra into the asking price—especially on an expensive used car—just so's you'll have something to give away once the negotiating starts in earnest.

Problem was, there hadn't been a lot of negotiating on this particular car because nobody seemed to want it. And particularly on the far side of 40 grand for a car, rare and beautiful as it was, that had a book value of maybe thirty-six and change. And that's *with* the steering pump and exhaust system fixed. And the time was rapidly approaching—the day after tomorrow, in fact—when that handsome silver Roller would suddenly be another year older and the sales manager would have to call Mr. Levy, his fine Rolls-Royce customer, and explain to him that it just wasn't working out and that he'd either have to come down seriously on the asking price or find someplace else to park his old car. At which point the rich lawyer most certainly would have become an *ex*-Satisfied Loeber Customer. So the dealership put a $1000 "spiff" on the car (a bonus to the salesman over and above his normal commission percentage for selling aging or hard-to-move merchandise) to see if they could somehow get rid of the damn thing.

And all of that was going through my mind as the well-dressed black guy carefully looked the car over. He was doing it from the outside first, walking around it several times and stopping to peer in at this or that before he ever asked about getting inside. "May I sit in it?" he said quietly.

"Sure. Help yourself."

So he climbs inside and I head over to the security lock box to get the keys and not incidentally leave him alone in the car for a little while. After all, you can't sell a $40,000-plus used Rolls by telling somebody how practical it is for picking up muddy Little Leaguers after practice or what great fuel mileage it gets or how well it handles on country roads or how safe it is in a head-on with a garbage truck or city bus. Nope, you gotta let the guy sit there, melting into that rich leather upholstery, staring right up the Spirit of Ecstasy's backside, and let the car work its magic on him.

Only this guy is hard to read. He's still got that same reserved, stone faced expression like he's not exactly sure what he wants to do next. "Can we go for a test drive?" he finally asks without looking at me.

"Sure," I tell him. "I'll go get a license plate." So I go back into the showroom and I see the Caddy limo is still sitting out there at the curb, engine idling against the cold while the driver, a pudgy, middle-aged white guy, smokes a Pall Mall with the window open and leafs through an afternoon edition of the *Sun Times*.

I go into the office to get a dealer plate and the sales manager wants to know what's up. "Is this guy for real?" he asks.

"I dunno. His name's Charles Stevens and he's hard to figure. But he came in the limo out there and the clothes and shoes check out."

"What's his story?"

I shake my head. "Haven't gotten that far yet. But he says he wants to go for a test drive. Whaddaya think?"

The sales manager cranes his head around the doorjamb to get a look at the Caddy limo idling outside. It's got livery plates on it, so he knows it's a rental. "What the hell," he finally shrugs. "Go for it."

So I take the black guy out on a test drive. Only by now it's well after five and the sky is black and traffic is nudging and halting and honking its way along Clark Street from one end to the other. I'm driving and giving the guy some lame pitch about Rolls history and mystique and apologizing about the cabbie who spurts out of nowhere and damn near takes our fender off and meanwhile I'm also trying to find out a little something about this guy. But the traffic is awful and it takes us maybe fifteen minutes to go three blocks. The cabbie who cut us off is just one car ahead of us. "Look," he says, "this is stupid. Why don't I come back tomorrow."

"Suits me."

So I swing around the block and head back to the dealership, and on the way we set a time for another test drive at ten the following morning. That would be Saturday. New Year's Eve. Back at the dealership he takes off in the Caddy limo and I go in to report to the sales manager. "He says he's coming back tomorrow morning for another test drive."

"Did you find out what he does?"

I shake my head.

"Hmmm. Did you ever talk price?"

I shake my head again.

The sales manager's lip curls. "Then he was probably just stroking you. Maybe he had some time to kill. You'll never see him again...."

Only who should show up at ten sharp the next morning but Charles Stevens, still wearing the same fine outfit only this time on foot. "I stayed downtown last night at a friend's apartment," he tells me to explain about the clothes. So I get the plate and we go out for another test drive. Again with me driving. It's Saturday morning, but, because it's New Year's Eve day, it feels more like a Sunday. It's a clear, cold day and there's hardly any traffic on the Outer Drive, and I've got Bach on the radio and I'm really laying it on thick about Rollers. But he's still as unreadable as the damn Sphinx and I don't know if I'm getting anywhere or not. So I decide to try asking him a few questions. We call it "qualifying" a customer, to see if he is indeed a live, bankable prospect for a genuinely expensive car. Charles Stevens tells me his father owns a string of grocery stores in predominantly black rural towns all across the south, but that they originally came from Chicago and still have a "nice, comfortable home" out southwest of the city. It's all plausible stuff, and he seems to fit the part. But it's also stuff that would be very hard to check out from some car dealership on north Clark Street in Chicago on New Year's Eve day.

I ask him if he wants to drive it, but he says no, not yet. So we head back to the dealership and pull inside the used car showroom and he gets out and walks around the car a few more times. Finally he pops the big one:

"How much is it?"

I'm not sure exactly where were going with this yet, so I do the stupid thing on purpose and point to the little $43,500 sticker on the lower right corner of the windshield. "There it is," I tell him.

He looks at the sticker for a half minute or so, drinking in its meaning. Then he looks back up at me. "But what can I buy it for?" he wants to know.

Well, he doesn't look or sound real sure of himself about the money part (and, surely, if this deal winds up going anywhere, the shrewd, penny-business father of his that owns all those grocery stores will get involved and the price will seek its proper market level) so I decide to hold my ground for the moment. Just to see what happens, you know? "I'm sorry, sir," I lie through my teeth, "but we *never* discount Rolls-Royce automobiles. Not even used ones."

Hell, it's always worth a try....

And then he about blasts me clear out of my socks when he nods imperceptibly and says: "All right, then. I'll take it."

Now let me explain what those words mean to me. It is the very last day of a very good year, and even so I am suddenly about to advance into a brand new tax bracket before the bells of midnight toll. As is the sales manager, who also gets a taste of the action on a sweet deal like this one.

So I go into one of the glassed-in offices to write up the deal. I mean, this is just too juicy to do out in the open at my desk, where word will quickly spread and other salesmen will start surreptitiously circling around like hyenas around a lion and its kill. When I'm done writing it up—one slightly used but still quite rare and handsome Rolls Royce Silver Shadow convertible at a gaudy $43,500 plus tax, title, license and document fee—I turn the paper around and slide it across the desk to him. It doesn't seem real, you know? But he looks it over and signs it "Charles Stevens," dates it, and pushes it back to me.

"And when do you want to pick it up?" I ask.

"As soon as possible." He says matter-of-factly. But then the other shoe drops. "Of course my father will want to come down and take a look at it. He's home today and not feeling very well."

"Sorry to hear it," I tell him while the wheels spin inside my head. I've got a signed deal, but that could easily go up in smoke if the old man puts the kibosh on things before the kid takes delivery. But it looks like the best I can do is get a signed deal contract and a deposit and hope that I can get the deal to hold up later. "What kind of deposit do you want to leave?" I ask him.

"What's customary?"

"Oh," I shrug while a few additional wheels start spinning, "I think a thousand dollars would do it."

Without a word he opens up his little leatherette portfolio, pulls out a checkbook, and starts writing.

"It's really a beautiful car," I tell him, but it's like he isn't listening. He tears off the check for $1000 and hands it over. He's got really nice handwriting. Almost like calligraphy. "Let me just take this over to the sales manager's office and get it approved."

So I go over to the manager's office and we barely get the door closed before we both start shaking hands and slapping each other on the back and dancing around the room in sort of a frenzied, artless version of an Irish Jig, ricocheting off the furniture and bouncing off the walls, all the while whooping and shouting in whispers so the guy can't hear us. After about five minutes of that, the manager initials the deal with vibrating fingers, we pull normal expressions down over our faces like window shades, and I head back over to rejoin my fine new customer Charles Stevens in the glassed-in office on the Mercedes floor. As I pass by one of the other salesmen's desk, he looks up and captures me with his eyes. "Home run ball?" he whispers enviously.

I look down on him, as I properly should, and whisper back, "Definitely. The only thing we don't know yet is whether it will stay fair."

I have to bite my lower lip a few times to get the smirk off my face before I go back into the office with Charles Stevens. "Listen," he says politely as soon as I enter, "I have an idea."

"What's that?"

"Can I use your phone?"

"Sure." I get him an outside line. And there, right in front of me, he puts in a call to his sick dad at home, tells him about the silver Rolls, and they banter back and forth for awhile before he finally hangs up. I try my best to eavesdrop, but he's talking very softly and I can't make out a lot of it. Geez, if I'd been over by the switchboard, I could've listened in on the whole thing. "As I mentioned," he says finally, "my father's home ill at our house in the suburbs. But I've talked to him and I'm quite sure he'll go along. We've both been very, umm, *fortunate* this year and it would only be right to celebrate somehow. And, after all, this *is* New Year's Eve."

"So?"

"So why don't we take the car out to him. Let him see it. If it's as I've told him, he'll give you a check for it on the spot. Paid in full…"

Something was starting to feel not quite right about this deal. This guy didn't actually expect us to fork over a Rolls- Royce Silver Shadow convertible—and especially somebody *else's* Rolls Royce Silver Shadow convertible—for a $45,000-plus personal check on a legal holiday, did he?

"…Then you leave me at home, bring the car and the check back to the dealership, and, when the check clears, I'll come by to pick it up."

Again, it didn't feel quite right. But only because it was too damn easy.

So I went and talked it over with the sales manager. And we both knew that, like a lot of other things in life, the longer a dream deal sits, the more it tends to go sour. No, *now* was the time. Strike while the iron is hot. Catch the old man when he's laid up sick and, better yet, on the cusp of a legal holiday when he can't call his banker or anybody else to find out what the car should really be worth. To be honest about it, both the sales manager and I had our greed glands in full secretion mode, our tongues were hanging out so far that we were tripping over them, and we were slipping around in the deep puddle of drool covering his office floor. "We gotta go for it," he panted help-lessly, and I was in full agreement. So he got the gas pump key and filled the Roller up while I went in to tell Charles Stevens it was a deal and to call his old man and tell him we were coming. Which he did.

We took off from the dealership sometime around 12:30—me at the wheel again with him in the passenger seat beside me (he explained that he really didn't want to drive it until he was properly familiar and fully insured)—and I followed his instructions out Interstate 55 southwest of the city to the Kingery Expressway. Along the way, we talked about all sorts of things. Or, rather, I did, just trying to keep the patter and energy of the deal going. But he didn't say much. Just short, polite answers to direct questions and not much more. He looked pretty sullen, actually. Especially for a guy whose dad was about to buy him a Rolls-Royce convertible for New Year's.

He had me take the exit ramp near the Argonne National Labs, where they chase atom particles around these huge underground tunnels in order to find out the nature of matter and either give mankind a supply of cheap, clean energy forever or fry this entire planet down to a burned-out cinder. It could go either way. Had I been thinking clearly, it might have occurred to me that not too many black families live out that way. Not even ones who operate a chain of successful grocery stores in rural black towns across the South....

We were out in the middle of nowhere, really, whooshing through this heavily wooded area with hardly any houses around, and it seemed particularly grim and desolate that afternoon, what with a colorless, overcast sky and patches of dirty gray snow scattered over the carpet of rotting leaves and the naked forests like bundles of dead, frozen sticks driven into the ground. It was graveyard quiet out there, and it was making me pretty uneasy. As was the fact that I'd been following his instructions about which way to go and where to turn, and he seemed a little hesitant sometimes about where he wanted to go. And then we pulled up to this one "T" intersection—again, out in the middle of freaking nowhere—and I suddenly realized we'd been through there a couple minutes before. My guts went all hollow and the hairs on the back of my neck stood on end like they were electrified, and that's when he pulled the gun.

It was just a little gun. Maybe a .22 or something and surely no bigger than what I'd seen high school swimming coaches use to start a race. And the guy didn't whip it out with a snarl or brandish it at me like some cowboy Hollywood gangster. No, he just kind of eased it up out of his pocket and held it like a tiny pet steel cobra on the armrest between us, pointed directly into my ribs.

He didn't say a word.

I'd never exactly had a gun pointed at me before, and, as often happens in strange and desperate situations, there was an aura of unreality about the whole thing. Like I was watching myself in a movie or something rather than actually being there in a used Rolls-Royce in the middle of nowhere staring down at the business end of a pistol held by someone who, to be perfectly honest, didn't look like he knew what he wanted to do next. And that was the scariest part. For a crazy moment, I had this stupid notion that I should try to save the car—I mean, it wasn't even ours, you know—and I got this dumb James Bond/Clint Eastwood idea that, since I was driving, I really had the upper hand. Hell, I was a decent amateur racing driver, and I could just floor it and speed up until we were going 90 or 100 or so and scare the crap out of him. He wouldn't dare shoot me at that speed because he'd surely be hurt or killed in the ensuing wreck. Then I'd tell him to throw the gun out the window. I actually got as far as giving the gas pedal a tiny, tentative nudge.

"Slow down," he said evenly, and moved his pet steel cobra a little closer so I could feel its nose against my side.

So much for that idea.

"Look," I told him, "if you want the car, take the car. Just let me out, okay? I got a wife and kids to take care of." That was actually a lie. To be sure, I had a wife. A great one, in fact. But we didn't have any kids yet. Still, we had plans to have kids someday, and I figured that counted.

"Just keep driving," he said, again without looking over.

Well, we kept driving around for maybe fifteen minutes or so, and the longer we went, the more uneasy I got about how he really didn't seem to know what he wanted to do next. I was pretty sure he'd wanted to pull the gun and take the car way back during the test drive on Lake Shore Drive earlier that morning. Or maybe even on Clark Street the night before. But he apparently couldn't get up the nerve. Why on earth come back to the dealership and go through the charade of calling his father and making a deal and getting more potential witnesses involved? And what was he planning to do with *me?* That, in fact, was the $64,000 question.

I had a second dumb, heroic notion about grabbing the door handle and just bailing out, but it seemed fraught with all sorts of potential ugly consequences. Including skull fractures, broken bones, and perhaps even the odd gunshot wound.

And, if I did bail out successfully and the Rolls subsequently crashed with nobody at the controls, wouldn't that put this guy in an even more desperate situation? It was sure to piss him off no matter how it came out.

"Listen," he said finally, "we're going to pull off into the woods up ahead here and I'm going to put you in the trunk."

"In the trunk?"

He nodded. "I'm not going to hurt you, but I'm going to take you out someplace where you don't know where you are and can't get to a phone."

Well, that sounded like a fair deal except for a couple key problems. Number one of which was that he didn't sound all that sure about it when he said he wasn't going to hurt me. I mean, if you've got nerve problems about it, it's probably a lot easier to turn your head and fire five or six rounds into some pleading, whimpering mound of clothing in a car trunk than to shoot somebody face to face. Not to mention that I knew this particular Rolls Royce had a bum exhaust system, so, even if he decided to do what he said he'd do and take me out into the hinterlands and dump me, I might not survive the ride. Even so, I didn't figure this was a particularly good time to inform him that I'd neglected to mention earlier as how his handsome, $43,500 Rolls Royce Silver Shadow convertible needed a new exhaust system. So there was nothing I could do but suck in a deep breath, grit my teeth and drive on by when he instructed me to pull up this lonely little dead end road into the forest preserve. "I told you to turn in there," he said angrily. You could see he was getting all nervous and agitated about how the situation was getting away from him.

"If I go up there you're going to shoot me," I heard myself saying.

"No, I won't!" he promised. But it didn't sound particularly convincing.

I could feel the whole thing coming to a head, and, although I hadn't the slightest idea what I could do, I knew as sure as that bullet would leave an ugly hole that I had to do something. And then kind providence provided an opportunity. We were coming up to a four-way stop out in the middle of nowhere, and here came some guy in a pickup truck up from our left and a family in a brand new Oldsmobile down from our right and a Ford wagon full of kids heading towards us from the other direction and, out of a driveway off to the side, a white Dodge van pulled up behind. Without even thinking about it, I eased off the brake and let the Rolls go right through the stop sign and yanked it to a halt crosswise in the middle of the intersection so nobody could move. The hand with the pet steel cobra in it came up off the armrest, but I turned right into his face and shouted, *"IF YOU'RE GOING TO SHOOT ME, YOU"RE GOING TO DO IT IN FRONT OF ALL THESE PEOPLE!"* and I bailed out of the car, scrambled to my feet, ran back to the Dodge van, and pounded violently on the driver's window. *"THIS GUY'S GOT A GUN!"* I hollered into the rolled-up glass.

Well, the guy in the van must have heard and comprehended, because he did an excellent interpretation of a jack-in-the-box jammed frantically into reverse as he dived down behind the van's dashboard. Meanwhile, my fine new customer "Charles Stevens" (which, come to think of it, was the name of a popular Chicago-area clothing retailer at the time) scrambled behind the wheel of the Rolls and squealed off, narrowly missing the front fender of the pickup on the way.

Turns out the guy in the van had a home remodeling business just a few hundred yards up the road behind us, and so he took me back there and opened up the shop so I could call the police. I swear, we had a police bulletin out about the black guy in the stolen silver Rolls-Royce convertible with Illinois dealer plate 1111 on the back no more than five minutes after he left the intersection. I mean, how much more conspicuous could you get?

So the local cops sent a patrolman over to pick me up and take me back to the little red brick station house to call the dealership and swear out a complaint. I've got to say that George Loeber and the sales manager took it really well, not giving a damn about the car and only wanting to make sure that I was okay. And of course I'd seen way too much cop stuff on TV and asked for a police artist so I could do a composite sketch to help them catch the guy. But the cop kind of blew me off. He didn't think finding a well-dressed young black guy in a silver Rolls ragtop with dealer plates on the back was going to be particularly difficult. And it didn't figure to be, either.

After the police stuff, the cop took me over to a nearby Mercedes dealership that we did a lot of dealer trades with to wait for one of the car hikers from Loeber to pick me up. And of course they meanwhile had to put in a call to the rich lawyer guy who owned the car and tell him what happened. "Really?" he said, the wheels instantly rotating in true lawyer fashion. "Okay. Just be sure to tell the insurance company it was worth forty grand."

It was well past closing by the time I got back to the showroom, but just about everybody on the sales staff had hung around to hear the story. "Jeez, weren't you *scared?*" one of them asked. But the fact is I wasn't. Or at least not like you'd think. While it was actually happening, it was almost as if I was in a movie or watching myself from the outside. It just didn't seem real, you know? And then, the next day—New Year's, remember?—I'm sitting quietly in front of my television set watching some old black-and-white *film noir* detective movie when I all of a sudden go all cold and queasy inside and start to tremble. And shake. And I can't seem to stop for a long, long time.

I guess it was some sort of delayed reaction.

Like I said a couple times already, you'd think a young black guy in anything as obvious as a silver Rolls convert would be pretty easy for the police to spot. Only it was New Year's Eve day, when there's generally a skeleton squad working out of many police departments on account of they need their maximum strength crew for the night shift. Especially between 11pm and 7 ayem, when many of the really good parties are keeping the neighbors up and spewing drunk drivers all over the highways. And maybe that's how "Charles Stevens" and his silver Rolls Royce slipped through the cracks and disappeared off the radar screen.

Come Monday afternoon at the dealership, I get a call from Art Petaque, who writes the police beat column for the Chicago Sun Times, and he's picked up the story off the State Police wire and wants to interview me about it. So I go to George Loeber and ask him what I should do and George tells me to just answer his questions and tell the truth. Which I do. Next day, there's a big headline and a three-paragraph blurb in his column titled *"Off He Went in their $40,000 Rolls."* It mentions how we gave the guy a free tank of gas, too.

And then the story gets even more interesting, as the Chicago police department doesn't know anything about the deal until they read the story in the paper and decide that the stolen Roller really belongs under their jurisdiction. So they send a squad car full of uniform cops around to get my side of the story. Well, when these razor sharp custodians of the public trust dig up as to how the car actually belongs—*not* to the dealership—but to some rich lawyer guy who really wants to get rid of it and has furthermore had a little trouble getting his price for it, and who, even further furthermore, just happens to have the same exact last name as the salesman it was supposedly heisted from (even though we're not related and it's pronounced differently) they quickly put two and two together and decide that they want me to take a lie detector test. Which I'm more than willing to do, actually. But George steps in and tells them to very kindly screw off. And George Loeber carries a lot of heavy clout around that particular part of Chicago. "I know him and he's telling the truth," George tells them flatly, "and that's good enough for me." Later on, after they've left, George takes me aside and explains as how voluntarily allowing the Chicago cops to give you a lie detector test when you don't absolutely have to is probably not a real good idea. Even if you've got nothing to hide. But then, George has known a *lot* of Chicago cops in his time....

In any case, the car never turns up and of course everybody at the dealership has a pet theory about where it's gone. Most of them involve a professional ring of car thieves (for whom this "Charles Stevens" character was most likely just a rookie point man) and that the Roller got re-sprayed and re-numbered or maybe even crated up inside an overseas shipping container bound for South America or Saudi Arabia or someplace else where it would command a decent price and no questions asked. Naturally the two insurance companies (the dealership's and the lawyer's own auto policy carrier) skirmished over who should be responsible for the loss, but eventually they worked it out, and the settlement must have been okay because the lawyer kept buying cars from us. And, as time passes the story fades until it's just something to get free cocktails on whenever I get a shot at a fresh set of ears.

But then one day, about six months later, I get a call from Art Petaque from the Chicago *Sun Times.* "You know they found your car?"

"My what?"

"Your car. The Rolls Royce that guy stole from you."

"Really?" I was pretty surprised, since we'd all decided it was a pro job and the Rolls was surely tooling around on another continent.

"Yeah," Art laughed. "And you won't believe the story."

Turns out that "Charles Stevens" was either a rank, rogue amateur or the deal he thought he had to dump the car went sour and he wound up stuck with it. Whatever happened, he started driving it to work on nice days. Can you believe it? He told his buddies and co-workers that some rich uncle of his down south had taken sick and had given him the Roller to use for awhile until he got better. And it looked like he maybe never would, poor guy.

But then "Charles Stevens" got in a little trouble with one of his bosses and got fired from his job. And I guess it must have seemed like a perfect time to maybe move and start a new life for himself. If he could just get a little bankroll together, you know? So he stopped by the local Jaguar dealership to try and trade the Roller (which by now was getting a little scuffed and tatty looking, making one hell of a racket though its burned-out exhaust system, and gulping and then spewing out full cans of power steering fluid every few miles) for a decent used Jag and a fistful of cash. Only the general manager at the dealership was also a part time deputy sheriff, and he remembered hearing the story about the stolen Rolls-Royce. So, while "Charles Stevens" was looking over a creamy green, low-mileage XJ-6, he called the cops. And they got him. But the most unbelievable and astounding part of the story, as it should, came right at the end. What do you think our buddy "Charles" had been doing for a living? And, remember, he was driving the damn Rolls to work now and then on nice, sunny days.

He was a corrections officer at an Indiana prison.

I kid you not.

Big Moments, Bad Moments

Some Thoughts about Things We'd Rather Not Think About....

AN EARLIER VERSION OF THIS "PLAY"
WAS PUBLISHED IN
VINTAGE MOTORSPORT
MAY/JUNE 1990

Crashes

are not a very happy subject. Sure, all racers like to while away their bar time playing the old "can you top this one," spinning wild tales of amazing close calls, narrow escapes, frenzied rotations, abrupt wall-flattenings, fiery explosions, and cataclysmic, somersaulting inversions that we have either witnessed, participated in, or provoked. But the fact is we all get a little pale and giddy-stupid inside when we actually happen to be there for a bad one.

Fortunately, modern safety equipment and trackside barriers have greatly reduced (but certainly not eliminated) the risk of injury when The Worst happens. Most usually, undesirable confrontations with the scenery and the laws of physics result in slightly to badly mangled racecars, devastated checking accounts, and severely bruised egos and psyches. Then we all gather around to offer support, sympathy, and fleeting celebrity status to the poor drool who's just turned his car into a free-form garden planter. But somewhere deep inside, most of us are thinking "that *moron.*" As if *we* would never have made the same dumb mistake. Hell no. *We,* after all, are in *control.*

SSssuuuuuurre we are.

Let me tell you how it happens.

From someone who's been there a few times....

It all starts with the busy little fellow who sits at the big rosewood desk behind your eyes. You know, that personal Chairman of the Board, C.E.O., C.O.O., and C.F.O. we all carry around in our heads. For the purpose of our story, let's call him Gene Schemer. Now Gene is a pretty successful sort of gent, what with a whole entire human being under his control, but he's also awfully busy. Especially when tax time rolls around or a receptive-looking female parks herself on the next barstool. And, like anybody else running a large and diverse corporate entity, he knows that good help is hard to find. And at no time is this more apparent than when the body he commands straps itself into a racecar. That's when the big intercom on his desk really starts buzzing.

Just listen:

GS: Yeah? Who is it?

INTERCOM VOICE: Excuse me, Sir. This is Prudence Program over in Limits and Measures. Anxiety's over here again, asking why we're doing this.

ANXIETY (simpering): I just wish you wouldn't do these things, Sir. You put us all at risk. I don't see why we can't take up badminton or philately or...

GS: Oh, *great!* How will I stand the excitement?

ANXIETY: Rosy Greer does needlepoint.

> *SOUND EFFECT OF MONSTER RACING ENGINE FIRING UP*
> *AND SETTLING DOWN TO AN IMPATIENT, CAMMY IDLE*

GS: Look, you twit, things are gonna start happening real fast around here, and the last thing I need is a jerk like you whimpering in my ear. Now *get the hell back to your post!*

ANXIETY (meekly): Yes sir.

GS: And you, Miss Program. Stay alert. We need you on call.

PP: Right, Sir.

> *ENGINE NOTE RISES AND THE WHOLE ROOM STARTS*
> *TO MOVE, LIKE A JET ROLLING DOWN A RUNWAY.*
> *G.S. PUNCHES ANOTHER BUTTON ON HIS INTERCOM.*

GS: Miss Niblits! Get me Ocular over in Sight and Sound.

MISS NIBLITS (in a tinny, efficient voice): I have that connection for you now, sir.

GS: Ocular? You in there?

OCULAR (very preoccupied, like an air-traffic controller at O'Hare): Yes, Mr. Schemer?

GS: I want you to keep an eye on that rev counter, dammit. You have any idea what that little slipup at Mid Ohio cost us?

OCULAR: That wasn't really my fault, Sir. Anxiety was up here leaning right over my shoulder, grinding his teeth.

GS: What the hell was Anxiety doing up in your department? He knows he's supposed to be down in Long Range Planning.

OCULAR: You know him, Sir. He pops up all over the place when things get dicey. And I can't stand the way he grinds his teeth...

GS (to himself): Sometimes I wonder who put that bastard on the payroll.

OCULAR: Excuse me, Sir [hollers into another microphone] Shift *NOW!*

ENGINE NOTE KEEPS RISING

OCULAR: Dammit, Nureyev, I said *SHIFT <u>NOW</u>!*

THE CAR LUNGES INTO TOP GEAR

Voice of NUREYEV, head of Motor Control, comes over the intercom: Hey, take it easy, Bro. We wuz only doin' 7300. Vito says this baby'll do seven-anna-half *easy.* No sweat.

GS: I heard that! Dammit, Nureyev, you know the redline's 7000!

NUREYEV: Oh – *heh-heh* – Hi, G.S. Didn't know you were on the line.

GS: I just *bet* you didn't. You better just watch your Goddam step or I'll put you in bean counting up in Ways and Means. That'll take the damn spring outta your step in a hurry!

NUREYEV (grumbling): Yes sir, G.S. Won't happen again.

OCULAR breaks in, somewhat agitated: Uh, we've got ourselves a little bit of a situation coming up here, Sir. There's a slower car ahead and it looks like we've either gotta ease off or dive under him at The Kink.

GS: Hmmmm? Whaddaya think?

OCULAR: I don't know, Sir. I'm just a lookout.

GS: How about you, Nureyev?

NUREYEV: You know me, Boss. I can do damn near anything. And Vito down in the Ballroom says it's a no-brainer.

Voice of PRUDENCE PROGRAM crackles out of the intercom: That's a negative, Sir. Very definitely a negative.

GS (thinks for a moment, rubbing his chin): So, Vito thinks we can make it, huh?

VITO'S gravelly voice snarls out of the speaker: Hey, no sweat, Big Guy.

PRUDENCE PROGRAM: Oh, *negative,* Sir. Very definitely negative. That Vito person in the Ballroom thinks with another organ besides his brain....

VITO (angry): Aah, up your giggy with a wah-wah brush, you dried-up old prune. No wonder we unplug you when we go out drinkin.'

OCULAR (very excited): Uh, we've definitely gotta have a decision here, Sir. I mean *right now!*

A high-pitched, sandpapery voice screeches desperately out of the intercom: Nureyev! Make Digit step on the brakes! We'll all be killed!

GS (angry): Who the hell is *that?*

Same voice, only faster and even higher-pitched: It's me, Sir. Anxiety. From Long Range Planning, remember?

GS (furious): YOU again! God-*dammit!* Get back to your fricking desk *THIS INSTANT!* You're supposed to be worrying about pork belly futures and this ache I get in my side and...

ANXIETY (whimpering): I worry about crashing, too, Sir. You know, big horrible crashes where your feet get smashed so hard your big toe winds up sticking out your bellybutton...

GS (beside himself): Listen to me, you little pipsqueak. If I had my way, you wouldn't even work here!

ANXIETY (voice even higher and faster): But there's so much to worry about, Sir. I'm working three shifts already and I could really use extra help.

OCULAR breaks in, alarmed: WE'VE GOT A PROBLEM! THE SLOW CAR IS MOVING OVER! HE DIDN'T SEE US! REPEAT: HE DIDN'T SEE US!

THE WHOLE ROOM TILTS AND SWERVES, FOLLOWED BY A SICKENING LURCH AS A WHEEL DROPS OFF THE PAVEMENT

GS: NUREYEV! WHAT THE HELL'S GOING ON?

ANXIETY (shrieking, voice cracking): OMIGOD!! WHAT'S HAPPENING??!!!

GS: GODDAM IT, GET OFF THIS FRIGGING LINE! NUREYEV!! HELLO??!!

NEW VOICE: Uh, no. This is Pucker, Sir. Down in Waste Disposal? We're getting a pretty nasty reading here on the Whoashit Meter.

GS: Dammit, Pucker, get off this line. I've gotta talk to Motor Control.

PUCKER: But Sir...

GS: I said *GET OFF THIS FRIGGING LINE.* No wonder you're stuck with a stinking, dead-end job like Waste Disposal.

Line goes dead. Then NUREYEV comes on, obviously VERY busy: Uh, You lookin' for me, Boss?

GS: Damn right I'm looking for you! What the hell's going on here?

ANOTHER MIGHTY LURCH AS A SECOND WHEEL SKATES INTO THE DIRT

NUREYEV (working desperately at the controls): Uh, the guy kinda moved over on us, Sir. Vito an' me didn't figure on that happening. But we'll be okay so long as we don't panic. We can ride it out.

PRUDENCE PROGRAM breaks in like a dive alarm: WE HAVE TWO IN THE DIRT, SIR! TWO IN THE DIRT!

GS: Goddam it, Nureyev! You and that hormone heap Vito are gonna wind up pumping sweat out of hair follicles if you don't get this mess straightened out. And I mean *NOW!* We're in big freaking *trouble* here.

SUDDENLY: A LONG, AGONIZED SHRIEK OF RUBBER
AND THE WHOLE ROOM BEGINS TO ROTATE WILDLY

GS: WHAT THE HELL HAPPENED???!!!!

NUREYEV (frantic): SOME IDIOT MASHED ON THE BRAKES! THE DAMN FRONT WHEELS ARE LOCKED! I CAN'T STEER!!!

PRUDENCE PROGRAM (panicking): LOSS OF CONTROL ALERT! LOSS OF CONTROL ALERT! ASSUME FETAL POSITIONS!

GS: WHO HIT THE BRAKES, DAMMIT?? I WANNA KNOW WHO HIT THE STINKING GODDAM BRAKES!! [nothing but a little static crackles over the intercom] *DAMMIT! MISS NIBLITS??*

MISS NIBLITS: Yes, Sir?

GS: GET ME DIGIT DOWN IN THE LOWER RIGHT QUADRANT!

MISS NIBLITS: Right away, sir.

DIGIT (voice quaking): Y-y-yes, sir?

GS: WHO THE HELL TOLD YOU TO HIT THE EFFING BRAKES?

DIGIT: It was Anxiety, Sir. He was running all up and down the nervous system yelling 'Crash Alert! Crash Alert!'

GS (weary and disgusted): Oh, good Lord. I *told* that ignoramus to get back to his desk. Miss Niblits, get Anxiety on the line. I don't care where the sonofabitch is, *FIND HIM!*

DIGIT (terrified): He said we're going to *crash,* Sir. Is it *true?*

GS SWIVELS BACK IN HIS LEATHER EXECUTIVE CHAIR AND PEERS
FURTIVELY OUT THE BIG PICTURE WINDOW. THE WHOLE WORLD
IS SPINNING AROUND LIKE AN OUT-OF-CONTROL AMUSEMENT
PARK RIDE SURROUNDED BY HEFTY CHUNKS OF CONCRETE
AND WHIRLING STRANDS OF ARMCO BARRIER

GS: I'll get back to you.

MISS NIBLITS: I have your party, Sir.

ANXIETY: Y-you wanted me, S-sir?

*GS OPENS HIS MOUTH TO SPEAK, BUT CAN'T FIND WORDS. HE SLUMPS BACK INTO
HIS CHAIR WITH A SIGH. THE SITUATION OUTSIDE IS COMPLETELY
BEYOND CONTROL, AND NOW IT'S JUST A MATTER OF WHAT, IF ANYTHING,
THEY'LL HIT. A STRANGE, STOIC SERENITY COMES OVER HIM...*

GS (very quietly): Tell me something, my friend. Who, exactly, gave you authority to apply the brakes?

ANXIETY: Uh, er, to tell you the truth, it was Pucker, Sir.

GS: He told you to lock the wheels so Nureyev couldn't steer? Pucker did that?

ANXIETY: Uh, well, er, not exactly, Sir. See, I just happened to be wandering past and I saw the Whoashit Meter, Sir. The needle was wrapped right off the dial. So naturally I thought...

GS (sighs heavily): Oh, never mind. Never mind. It doesn't really make any difference now. Why don't you just curl up in a fetal position like everybody else.

ANXIETY: Thank you, Sir.

*THE LINE GOES DEAD. GS PUTS HIS HEAD DOWN ON HIS DESK
AND COVERS IT WITH HIS ARMS. BUT THEN HE REACHES OUT
AND PRESSES THE INTERCOM BUTTON ONE LAST TIME.*

GS: Miss Niblits?

MISS NIBLITS: Yes, Sir?

GS: Hold my calls.

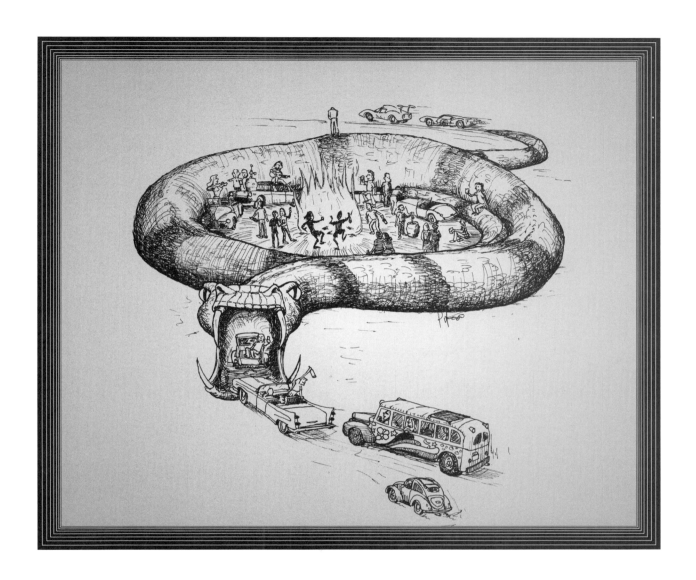

SURVIVING THE SNAKE PIT

IF THERE'S ONE THING SEBRING'S ALWAYS GOOD FOR,
IT'S MEMORIES....

ORIGINALLY PUBLISHED IN
VINTAGE MOTORSPORT
JULY/AUGUST 2000

The first World Championship sportscar race I ever attended was the Twelve Hours of Sebring in March of 1966, and, at the time, it was little more than a last-minute afterthought to a grueling spring break odyssey in Florida. But it turned out to be the highlight episode, as both the place and the race left an indelible impression. My buddy Dick Hummel and I had driven down from East Lansing, Michigan—straight through, natch—in his second-hand TR4, and our plan was to partake of the much-ballyhooed Spring Break partying and freeform anarchy in Fort Lauderdale. It took us less than 24 hours to decide that the aimless, seething, staggering, stumbling, sunburned, hung-over, beer-breathed crush of college kids (and mostly *male* college kids, at that) clogging the streets and beaches of Fort Lauderdale wasn't for us. So we pulled up stakes and headed south again, far as we could go, and wound up spending a scary and thoroughly memorable night in Key West playing poker with a strange collection of Elmore Leonard-style carnival sideshow characters we'd met in a strip club there. Come the crack of noon next morning, we awoke to find the sideshow characters had vanished, leaving us with their hotel bill! It was more than Dick and I had between us, but we managed to negotiate a deal with the unsmiling innkeeper that at least kept us out of jail.

With both time and money running low, we reckoned there wasn't much to do but turn around and head back to Michigan. At least we had some stories to tell. But then I picked up a morning paper off a park bench in Homestead and saw that the Twelve Hours of Sebring was running the very next day, and the raggedy road map we kept wedged between the seat and the transmission tunnel showed that Sebring was more or less right in our path. It took some mutual persuading and pooling of pocket change, but we figured if we watched our money carefully and took off early Sunday after the race was over (in other words, if one of us could sneak in and we ate nothing but Cheez-Whiz and whatever was left in the Fritos bags and Triscuit boxes piled up on the parcel shelf behind us on our drive back to East Lansing) we'd make it in plenty of time for Dick's Modern Lit class at 8 ayem on Monday morning. And as for the paper he had due on D.H. Lawrence, well, I'd drive and he could write it along the way. I could help, even. Not that I'd actually *read* any D.H. Lawrence, but even back then I had something of a reputation as a Major League bullshit artist. Just so long as no actual dates, places, events, chronologies, mathematical formulas, geometric equations, or knowledge of important historical facts and figures were involved....

And so we went to Sebring. We arrived late Friday night with the idea that it would be easier to sneak one of us in under the cover of darkness (it was) and then we could pitch our tent and get some much-needed shuteye before the race started at ten the next morning. But that was before we came face-to-face with the near riot going on in Green Park. 1966 was the year they opened the crossover bridge to Green Park, and, like crazed participants in some great, alcohol-fueled land rush, the party animals had swarmed over and planted their flag. This was *their* kind of territory: a perfectly isolated little island of turf and concrete surrounded on all sides by racetrack that, come tomorrow, would pound with speed and noise and horsepower until shrieking yellow eyes burned furious holes through the night. That was surely something worth celebrating. Without question, the *real* action all those hung-over fools in Fort Lauderdale were looking for was right here in Green Park. You could hear it in the music blasting over the car radios and feel it frothing and sizzling in the air around you and see it in the fearful, out-manned and out-gunned look on the faces of the cops.

The atmosphere was moist with possibilities.

It was the kind of night when *anything* could happen.

Come next morning with precious little sleep in between, I remember hanging on the fences through the strained, breathless silence before the start, then being battered by the explosion of noise and speed and color as the pack stampeded towards turn one. I'd never witnessed anything like it. We wandered along the edge of the track, watching from here and there as the Ford GT40s and Mk. IIs pounded the opposition like some sort of armored invasion from Dearborn. The stealthy-looking, appliance white Chaparrals stayed close for awhile, but dropped out early. The 330 P2 Ferraris sounded great but appeared overmatched. The big, thundering #10 Penske/Sunoco Corvette Grand Sport roadster of Thompson and Guldstrand looked great and ran in the top dozen before it, too, fell by the wayside. Conversely, the Porsche 906 Batmobiles sounded like chainsaws cutting up 55-gallon oil drums and I couldn't believe they could go on for 12 hours like that (but of course they could) and naturally Dick and I were rooting for the factory Triumph TR4s to beat the dreaded MGBs (they didn't) and for the beautiful, sexy, and melodious Alfa Tubolares to win their class (they did).

And then, out of nowhere, a white GT-40 shot off the road right in front of us, just a few hundred yards before the hairpin (Locked rear brakes? Broken halfshaft? Failed steering?), catapulted through the air, guillotined a telephone pole, and came hurtling down nose-first into the ground, bursting into flame on impact. In frozen terror we watched it burn furiously, each passing heartbeat leaving less and less doubt that the driver had to be dead. Neither of us had ever seen anybody killed before.

It was not the kind of thing you could snicker or swagger off.

Eventually they got the fire out and covered the charred remains with a tarp, but then some of the more adventurous idiots from Green Park swarmed over the fences to look for grisly souvenirs, and there was damn near a riot when the police tried to keep them back. It was pretty ugly, if you want the truth of it.

But the race went on, as they always seem to, and soon we became aware of the entertaining dice Dan Gurney and Ken Miles were having in two of the Ford Mk. IIs. Too entertaining, in fact, as that's the year Carroll Shelby waved a hammer at them from the pit wall to make them to knock it off. The cars droned on and on as a fat, orange-red sun oozed down into the horizon, and the night brought with it an eerie, other-worldly light show of tracer bullet headlamp beams and flashing tail lights and brake discs between them glowing the same orange-red as the setting sun as they swept on through the darkness. And then, almost shockingly, the noise stopped. The echo faded. The track went dark. It was over.

Turns out the leading Gurney/Grant Mk. II broke its engine (the camshaft, if memory serves) in the final moments and so the second-place Mk. II roadster of Miles/Ruby inherited the win. I think the only lap it led was the last one. Then poor Gurney got disqualified for pushing his car to the finish line, adding insult to injury. What a crushing disappointment that must have been, to have the win solidly in hand after twelve tough, hard hours of racing and God only knows how many hours, days, weeks and months of planning and preparation, and then to have it all go *SNAP!* in a single, cruel instant and crumble into worthless dust. But that was Sebring for you....

Meanwhile, the party was gearing up all over again in Green Park.

I've been back to Sebring many times since then—including a few tours on the participant side of the fences—but the first time is always The First Time, *n'est ce pas?* So this year it was a real treat when some of the guys from the live radio crew—the lot of them old, experienced hands at Sebring—took me back into that wild Friday night madness in Green Park. Drinks in hand, we climbed into the back of a pickup truck like it was an Adventureland ride at Disneyland and headed towards the infield. Inching along in heavy, horn-honking traffic, we passed the tacky carnival row of food vendors opposite the pits, where you can buy everything sweet, sour, spicy, sticky, or smothered in onions known to man. Off in the distance, you could hear shouts and laughter and the heavy throb of live music coming from Green Park. College kids had set up couches and sofas on top of vans and campers to watch and toast the passing parade, and neat vehicles or convertibles full of well-filled halter tops earned thunderous approval. There were cops directing traffic into Green Park, but there was none of the menace or confrontation I remembered from the sixties. In fact, the cops looked more like ushers than anything else. There was a band called F-Troop pounding out rock n' roll in a crush of grinning, wild-eyed college kids and grizzled (but just as grinning and wild-eyed) Sebring veterans, whooping and hollering and desperately urging on a clutch of hooch-lubricated, illegal substance-stimulated, and occasionally, ummmm, rather "extroverted" female dancers. Who, just like their adoring crowd, ranged from young, hard and luscious to your more worn down and leathery high-milage models.

Every year new meat comes flooding into Green Park—Lord only knows from where—and enough of it gets the bug and comes back again, year after year, to keep the party going. Oh, maybe guys like me and the radio crew are getting a little old for this sort of thing, but I have to admit I felt that same sizzling buzz of excitement I remembered from 1966.

It's nice to know there are still nights like that where anything can happen.

Even if nothing ever does....

First Times, Grizzled Gurus,
and Confessions of a Wild Man
You always remember the First Time....

DEVELOPED FROM A TWO-PART STORY
THAT ORIGINALLY APPEARED IN
BRITISH CAR
OCTOBER AND DECEMBER 1988

Every now

and then at big family gatherings (weddings, funerals, Groundhog Day, etc.) some far-flung relative or other will innocently ask: "So, howd'ja ever get started racin' those fancy sports cars, anyway?" This usually happens right after my wife has casually mentioned that we could have bought something really *nice*—Vermont, for example—with the money I have happily squandered on steel and grease. The individual in question undoubtedly wants no more than a few moments' polite conversation, but the poor fish better have a full drink and an empty bladder just to make it to where I take my first breath. The story goes something like this:

It all started back in junior high, while awkwardly traversing that rickety and uncertain bridge over hormone gap. Even then, I had a crude, embryonic interest in things that flashed past at high speed, rattling windowpanes and leaving a trail of eye-watering fumes in their wake. I indulged this fantasy the usual way, littering my bookshelves with copies of hot rod and custom car magazines and building flamed, pinstriped, and invariably glue-speckled plastic models of eye-gouge yellow Deuce Coupes, candy-apple red T Roadsters, sinister, black 40's Fords, and '57 Chevys so low to the ground that their fender skirts stuck to the wooden shelves. They had all of the latest street rod equipment, including teardrop spotlights at the corners of their windshields, lakes pipes running wickedly down their rocker panels, mag wheels or, maybe even better, Moon Discs, and errant fingerprints here and there in their hardly mirror finishes where I'd picked them up to admire them before the paint had fully dried.

I was at a dangerous, unstable, and thoroughly impressionable age, and my older brother Maury (old enough to *drive*, which rendered him a different species entirely) had this friend, Jay Porter, who really excelled when it came to impressing impressionable young persons like myself. Jay was simply *too cool*. He rode around town on a baby blue Vespa motor scooter and liked Jazz and wore Ray Ban aviator sunglasses (even at night!) and had this really cute girlfriend who would slip *her* arm around *him* whenever he put *his* arm around *her!*

Wow!

Now Jay, naturally enough, thought that hot rods were for street corner Neanderthals with hood boots and packs of Camels rolled up in their sleeves. He, on the other hand, had the innate class and *savoir faire* to be a Sports Car Enthusiast (pardon me, *afficionado*) and quickly introduced me to the thrilling, glamorous and romantic mystique of things like Monza, Maserati, MG, Stirling Moss, Mercedes-Benz, Luigi Musso, Morgans, Masten Gregory, the Mille Miglia, Aston Martin, Moretti, Monte Carlo, Molsheim, and the undulating, eight kilometer Mulsanne Straight at Le Mans. And those are just some of the M's....

I was quickly and totally enraptured, and started reading everything about it I could get my hands on: *Road and Track* and *Sports Car Illustrated* and the old, sepia and green tinted pages of *Sports Car Graphic.* To be honest, being nuts about European sports cars was about the only one of Jay Porter's dashing characteristics I could dare hope to emulate. Except for maybe wearing sunglasses at night.

I'm sure Jay never knew the effect he had on me. But, knowingly or not, he gave me that first heady and addictive taste for European-style road racing and exotic, two-seater sports cars from the far side of the Atlantic. And my passion grew quickly out of control, like *The Blob* in the movie of the same name, inhaling every available scrap of information and expanding in size until it was immense, obsessive, and possessed of an even more insatiable hunger. By the time I was old enough, I wanted to go sports car racing in the very worst way.

And that's exactly how I did it, too....

******

The year was 1970, and I was among the elective poor (those who spend all their money—most usually on things forgotten by dawn) who should *never* be confused with the non-elective poor (who have no money to spend). But there was this wonderful, magical *race*car, see—a clapped-out, road-grader-orange Triumph TR3—sitting on four flat tires on the furthest back corner of the local Saab/Lotus dealer's lot. My attraction was immediate and magnetic, seeing as how (at $600 *as was*) it looked like something I might could maybe possibly actually *afford.* Hell, I saw checks for more than a third of that (before taxes, anyway) every single Friday afternoon!

Summoning every pledge of honor and empty promise at my disposal, I managed to wheedle out a deal, putting down $200 in hard cash and signing a note for the balance. The particular document produced by the dealer was truly impressive, drawn as it was on heavy, parchment-type paper and chock-full of "therefores" and "whereases" and "parties of the first part" and "parties of the second part" and other, similarly obtuse and impenetrable legalese prose. It was called an "Iron-Clad Note," which in fact was spelled out right across the top in the kind of solemn Old English lettering you normally find in antique Bibles or chiseled into the headstones of well-to-do dead people.

As part of the agreement, a mechanic at the dealership had to stay late one evening to put in a new clutch so the thing would actually move as well as make loud, glorious noises, and I helped him out as best I could. Even after he asked me to leave. To be honest, at that point you could have put everything I knew about actual hands-on, nuts-and-bolts automobile mechanics into a very slim volume. A pamphlet, in fact. But I was eager as a Mouseketeer about learning *everything!* Which is probably why the poor mechanic kept sighing and rolling his eyes after each dumb question and looking at the clock to figure out how the hell soon he could be finished. And then there was the little matter of how I was going to get the damn thing off the property. In the end, we rigged up a makeshift towing arrangement using various modestly priced items from the J.C. Whitney catalogue and a few stout chunks of boilerplate and angle iron.

Rube Goldberg would have been proud.

So there I was, friends and neighbors, bursting with the pride and joy of ownership, rolling off the dealer's lot with my new Most-Treasured Possession in tow behind my trusty Volvo, "The Blue Swede." It was mine. *Mine! MINE! Ha-ha-ha-haa.* Why, I tooled down the street like the grand marshal of the Rose Bowl Parade, waving and nodding with happy condescension to anyone who gawked, stared, snickered, or blew their nose in my direction.

Although there *was* the minor little problem of just where, precisely, I was going to take this heap. My bachelor apartment (on one of the less fashionable streets of Chicago's fashionable Near North Side) was not a viable option, as it had no garage privileges. Or garage, for that matter. Or privileges, come to think of it. And, though leaving the TR3 parked on the street in this particular neighborhood would have done wonders for the power-to-weight ratio (in but a single night!), I though it might tow a bit awkwardly on cinder blocks.

At about this juncture, suddenly confronted by an idiot who didn't comprehend the practice of checking one's mirrors before changing lanes, I received my very first lesson in motor racing. It concerned the perils of flat-towing and proper tow-bar angles and why decent folks have honest-to-God trailers with honest-to-God trailer brakes on them. Turned out that if you stepped at all vigorously on the Volvo's middle pedal while flat-towing the racecar, TR3 would kind of stuff its nose up under the Blue Swede's rear bumper (see any male dog greeting his friends) and jack up the back end of the Volvo until you could see daylight under the rear tires. Really. I discovered it was best to have all eight wheels pointed in roughly the same direction when this happened....

Where were we? Ah, yes, looking for some place to put this glorious new treasure. Ultimately, storage and pre-race preparation of my new racecar (alright, my new *old* racecar) took place gypsy-fashion in an unending series of strange driveways and garages, usually with some friend's parents glaring out from behind the kitchen curtains. But I didn't mind. After all, they weren't *my* parents, right? Besides, there was work to be done. Lots of it. And so my dwindling cadre of friends and I spent many long, arduous hours huddled around that TR3, drinking record quantities of beer and discussing Important Things like which oil company stickers to put over the holes in the bodywork and whether to go with *white* numbers on *black* roundels or the more traditional and time honored black on white. Oh, and somebody gave me this genuine, el cheapo fiberglass racing seat which I actually installed *myself,* using a few chunks of stud grade 2X4 and some hardware store carriage bolts.

More on that later....

By now, you may be catching a whiff of the notion that I didn't know pig doots about racecar mechanics. Hah! That's what *you* think. Why, I had already *proven* (to my own satisfaction, anyway) that virtually any product of the Industrial Revolution—be it metric, SAE, or Whitworth—could be reduced to its tiniest component parts (if perhaps not actually *fixed)* by applying boundless enthusiasm, creative use of Anglo-Saxon invective, and a simple tool kit consisting of the rough-cast wrenches that came with a Zundapp Super Sabre motorcycle, an adjustable crescent wrench, a vise grip (my personal favorite, as any of the nuts and bolts I have worked on will readily attest), a large claw hammer, and three screwdrivers: a flat blade, a phillips, and a great, monstrous mutha that never touched a screw in its life but always saw *plenty* of heavy action.

My first big race weekend approached, and I made ready, putting my name on the car in carefully spaced stick-on letters and wearing my Nomex underwear around the apartment when no one else was there, just to, you know, get the *feel* of it. The particular event upcoming was a Midwestern Council of Sports Car Clubs Driver's School on Saturday and a race (assuming I passed through the school without killing anybody important) on Sunday. For those who may not be familiar with it, the Midwestern Council is a confederation of smaller sports car clubs in the Chicago-

Milwaukee-Madison area that began sanctioning low-pressure, low budget, high fun content schools and races back in 1959 as a kind of alternative to the local SCCA regions, which tended to be a little stuffy back then. Like you had to *know* somebody or *be* somebody to get in. Totally unlike today, when the SCCA actually has a bounty out on any warm body willing to cough up seventy bucks for dues. Go figure.

Anyhow, the Midwestern Council welcomed any and all from day one. *"Give us your tired, your poor,"* you know? And that, pretty much, is what the Council got. But even if it wasn't exactly the Social Register, the Council lacked not for spirit, competition, or camaraderie, and it set standards for Good Times and Good Value that still stand today. And I know that's true from personal experiences. Like this one:

I guess the first image that comes to mind about Driver's School was late Friday night—sometime after midnight, in fact—lying stretched out prone on the soaking wet pavement (it's raining, natch) of the Holiday Inn parking lot in South Beloit, Illinois. Why am I doing this? I'm doing this because a few hours earlier, before the requisite chalk talk and written test, the Midwestern Council Tech Worthies checked out my TR3 and discovered that my self-installed fiberglass racing seat had come a bit loose. In fact, it was anchored down no better than your grandmother's rocking chair. So now, armed with my trusty vise grips and adjustable crescent wrench and with rainwater draining into my ear, I am tightening up those carriage bolts with a vengeance. Naturally the adjustable crescent wrench is continually coming out of proper adjustment, slipping off the nut, and running my knuckles full tilt into all the jagged, sharp, hard and greasy metal bits that lurk beneath British sports cars for just such opportunities. But I am not deterred, as I reef foot-pound after foot-pound of grunting, sweating torque into those carriage bolts and clamp down without mercy on those 2x4s. Unfortunately, I am blissfully ignorant regarding the tensile strength and metalurgical properties of grade-zero Hardware Store fasteners and the fact that they react to massive inputs of torque by stretching. Like strands of shiny, cadmium-plated taffy.

Finally came the dawn, abuzz with promise and excitement. Alright, so maybe it *was* just a little cold and drizzly. But who cared? I'll tell you who cared. *I* cared! Because, for the first time in all recorded history, the damned Blue Swede wouldn't start! It ground and ground with nary a pop whilst all the other tow rigs, one by one, trundled out of the lot and headed for the racetrack. In the end I was alone, desperately turning the key and listening to that empty-chamber clicking noise you get when your battery has had quite enough of the ignition switch, thank you very much. Panic swelled up inside me like that disgusting reptilian thing that explodes out of the guy's chest in the movie *Alien*. And it was precisely here, gripped in a frozen cloud of panic, that I made my first Bold and Ridiculous move of the day. I unhitched the TR, flung my driving gear and toolbox behind the seat, hung the Blue Swede's license plate from the roll bar with coat hanger wire, and took off for the track—no lights, no horn, no turn signals, no windshield wipers (in fact, no windshield!), no registration, and that unmuffled Standard Triumph 4-banger bellowing triumphantly (what else?) into the sleepy early ayem stillness of South Beloit. I passed a State Patrol car along the way, and, believe it or not, he just kind of rolled his eyes and looked the other way. Poor guy probably didn't want to get writer's cramp.

I arrived at the track just in time to be extremely late and was assigned to my instructor, a happy, cherub-faced Midwestern Council lifer named Ross Fossbender, who, fortunately enough, knew a thing or two about TR3s. This proved invaluable, as he helped me identify and deal with a bewildering assortment of mechanical glitches, gremlins, meltdowns and malfunctions that started popping up like poison mushrooms out of a compost heap. In fact, that was one of the bright spots of the whole weekend, discovering that in racing (and especially in Midwestern Council-style racing) aid, assistance, empathy, and commiseration were always available in return for a little unseemly blubbering or gnashing of teeth.

As I recall, it was the brake lights that went first. No big problem. Then it was the brakes themselves. _BIG_ problem. Turns out the British have a habit of using genuine cow leather for the seals that keep thick, gooey, rear axle-type lubricants in their proper places and out of other places where they shouldn't ought to be. And, when the cow they came from gets old and antique enough, they tend to get a tad brittle and craggy. Which is why all that Castrol 90-weight was getting out of where it was supposed to be and into the rear brake drums in a big way, making the rear brakes alternately slip and grab (no big problem) and then slip on one side and grab on the other _(BIG_ problem). The phrase *"snaking into a corner"* took on an entirely new meaning!

Between sessions, Ross showed me how to clean the goop out of the drums and sand down the brake shoes, thus ensuring a few relatively drama-free laps before the car started going into its two-step tarantella again under heavy braking. And I was doing *lots* of heavy braking. You know, the kind where your jaw is clamped shut so tight your teeth start to crack. But that's pretty typical with rookie race drivers at their first-ever school. Hell, you're holding the wheel in a damn death grip, adrenaline is spurting out of your ears, the corners are rushing up at you like spring-loaded spooks on an amusement park ride, and it's all you can do to react in time to prevent disaster.

Calm, you are not.....

But I was managing to avoid a lot of that by spending so much of my time fixing the damn car rather than actually driving it. As I recall, it was the S.U. carburetors that betrayed me next, what with the chokes falling fully open (as they are wont to do in all but the very coldest weather, when you actually need them), causing the motor to run "a wee bit rich," as my ever-trusty, pamphlet-sized Official S.U. Tuning Manual described it. In this case, "a wee bit rich" meant that my engine was coughing, sputtering and strangling on its own juices while the car meanwhile trailed a massive, particle-laden cloud in its wake like an old fashioned, coal-fired locomotive. So Ross showed me how to wire up the chokes, and then it was, I believe, the exhaust coming adrift as I swept grandly through turn five in ragged emulation of a four-wheel drift. The pipe parted company with the car entirely, clattering across the pavement into swamp-muck oblivion, leaving the engine hellishly loud, my foot hellishly hot, and likely doing no good whatever for the life expectancy of the exhaust valves.

While all this was going on, I was simultaneously trying my best to figure out which way the track went, keeping my eyes peeled for other, equally overloaded and hyper-stimulated students, listening to Ross' calm, friendly advice, and coming to terms with what Triumph drivers euphemistically refer to as "handling." Now I have no idea who originally prepared this particular TR3 for motorized competition, but I can assure you he was no chassis engineer. In fact, I can assure you he was no engineer of any sort. Driving this car *at speed* could best be likened to two other, somewhat more obscure, sporting endeavors. The first is the one where those big, brawny, heavy-breathing Scottish fellows with beards and kilts and faces red as beets pick up great lengths of tree trunk and try to heave them farther than all the other big, brawny, heavy-breathing Scottish fellows with beards and kilts, etc. The other is the pastime you may have seen practiced by certain primitive, poor, but eminently practical South and Central American Indian tribes who tie 30-foot lengths of rope to their ankles and then dive—*head-freaking-first!*—off 36-foot wooden towers, thereby guaranteeing a *bona fide* Religious Experience at very low cost.

But I persevered, scaring myself silly while dodging between turn-in points, apexes, track-outs, and assorted additional mechanical disasters. The ugly truth is that my performance behind the wheel fell mostly into the "Animal Instinct" category, meaning that I possessed the innate knack for car control necessary to get myself out of most of the stupid jams I would never have gotten into if I had been using my brain rather than my rear end for basic navigation. I'm told it was entertaining to watch. From a distance. Ross summed it up rather succinctly after two laps in the passenger seat, directing me into the pits, removing himself from the car, and casually mentioning a well-known fact about TR3 racecars: "These things tip over, you know."

I didn't, actually.

As amazing as it sounds, the beer bust at the end of the day found a Novice Permit clutched in my quivering hands! The morrow would bring my first race! I could hardly believe it! So I covered up the TR3 for the night—convinced that my troubles were behind me—and Ross was kind enough to give me a lift back to the Holiday Inn, where I even managed to get The Blue Swede running again. Then it was off to enjoy the fruits (not to mention the malts and the hops) of my triple-threat victory over the demons of high speed, recalcitrant iron, and common sense.

******

Race Day arrived clear-skied, sunny and glorious. Yet I noticed a strange, queasy sensation in my stomach. My mouth tasted like it was full of cotton wads and sheet metal screws. My hands trembled around my morning cup of coffee. Yep, it was a hangover, all right. I can recognize the symptoms almost every time. But no matter! We're going *racing!*

Sure we are. Just as soon as we get the dead battery changed. And put some air in that left front tire. And fix the brand new drizzle of slick, greenish murk from the water pump. And how about the routine check that showed the front brake pads down to the backing plate metal? Naturally, I had nothing whatsoever in the way of spares. I mean, *who knew?* Most disconcerting of all, once actually underway, was the manner in which the shifter started dodging away from my hand like a drunk's beer. Saaaay, what the heck's going on here? But, before I could diagnose it any further, the distributor rotor broke, putting an end to my session.

Didn't have one of those, either.

But I was most curious about the shifter. My trusty crew (anyone seen walking by that answered to *"Hey, you!"*) and I set about removing the transmission tunnel, and soon the problem was obvious. You must understand that the entire engine/transmission unit of a Triumph TR3 is held in place at three specific points (not counting the ground strap and radiator hoses), and the aft-most of these is a stout, bonded rubber mount underneath the tailshaft of the transmission. But the one in my car was of such advanced age and infirmity that it had separated into two pieces, thereby allowing the whole shootin' match from cooling fan to U-joint to leap and flail violently about like the tail of an unlucky Stegosaurus being turned into supper by a Tyrannosaurus Rex.

My weekend of motoring glory was quickly dissolving into one of epic tragedy (albeit directed by Mel Brooks) but it was at that precise moment, when everything seemed blackest, that Mike Whelan appeared on the scene. I can't honestly say that he brightened things up appreciably. Mike was a mean-faced, wiry, taciturn old geezer who worked as a machinist, never had a kind word for anybody, and somehow managed to maintain a three- or four-day growth of stubble on his chin, no matter where or when you saw him. I always wondered how he did that, you know?

Anyhow, Mike had been knocking around the Council for years, most often at the wheel of a red TR3 with black, Jeep-center steel wheels and homemade Brooklands-style racing screens. It habitually wore Number 12, and it was hardly the trickest or the fastest thing around. I guess it would be fair to say that Mike Whelan and Colin Chapman were at opposite ends of the spectrum regarding design philosophy and racecar preparation. If there was ever a hard choice to be made between rock-solid sturdiness and light weight, Mike Whelan never paused to ponder. In fact, for racing cars, Mike's creations would have made pretty fair railroad bridges. On the other hand, Mike's cars were almost always still in one piece and chugging along under their own power when the checker came down. Which is a lot more than you can say for some of Colin Chapman's creations (although a few of Colin's cars *did* win some moderately important races in their day).

I didn't realize it that first time Mike walked over to where my makeshift crew and I were *chaining* (I kid you not!) the back end of the transmission down to the chassis crossmember, but he was destined to have a profound effect on my racing career. To be perfectly honest, I wasn't too impressed with him at first. I mean, he didn't *look* like a race car driver (I later found out that *nobody* who works on their own cars ever looks like the freshly pressed and perfectly coiffured guys you see in the cigarette ads) and his car didn't have any of the latest, trickest Go Faster stuff I'd seen and drooled over in all those catalogues. Besides, he was *The Competition.* Why, didn't this person realize (*grunt*) that I was gonna blow his freaking doors off (*gasp*) just as soon as I got this (*aarrghh*) damned tranny off my arm?

Mike came around many times as the day progressed, lending parts and advice and even some expert, hands-on assistance. And you had to give him top marks for keeping a straight face under the circumstances. Of course, Mike didn't smile all that often, anyway. He was a pretty tough character who didn't put a whole lot of stock in the goodness of human nature. And that attitude was based on a hefty backlog of personal experience. About the only time you'd ever see the corners of his mouth curl up in a gold-flecked smile was when something particularly evil or unfortunate happened to somebody who Had It Coming. And there were a whole bunch of people who fit into that category as far as Mike Whelan was concerned.

But even if he wasn't especially pleasant or cordial about it, Mike turned out to be one of the most knowledgeable and generous people I ever met. Not to mention the complete selection of necessary TR3 spares he always carried packed away in the back of his truck, as he had long ago learned those three basic and vital racing lessons:

Lesson 1: If you carry a spare for something, it is less likely to break.

Lesson 2: If you have no spare for something, and especially if there aren't any in the whole blessed country, and if, moreover, the factory hasn't made any in years, then that part is most certain to break into several jagged, unfixable pieces. On which you will cut yourself. Badly.

Lesson 3: If you plan to race a TR3 (or just about any British sports car), come prepared with an entire spare everything. Less frame.

In any case, Mike Whelan had it *all*, sorted out, organized, and packed neatly away in assorted coffee tins, segmented plastic tackle boxes, milk crates and corrugated cardboard cartons in the back of his truck. He quickly produced a new rotor for the distributor and a can of *BarsLeak* for the water pump drool and lent me a set of used brake pads and then helped triage and field dress the car out of his near endless supply of TR3 first aid kits.

Then came the time. My First Race. Thirty minutes that will remain seared indelibly into my memory until Bentleys are built by Volkswagen and Skodas and Wartburgs become sought-after classics. I motored my TR proudly up to the false grid, eager to show one and all what I could do. And I tried hard to emulate the other, more experienced drivers, who posed gallantly yet nonchalantly beside their gleaming steel steeds, pausing now and then to flick an imaginary speck of lint off a fender. Unfortunately, I discovered that you can't flick off greasy handprints.

"FIVE MINUTES!"

I leapt into the cockpit, yanked on my gloves, fumbled desperately at my helmet strap with glove-numbed fingers, and then entered into an epic *Beast from 20,000 Fathoms* wrestling match with my octopus of seatbelt and shoulder harness webbing. I might have been a bit excited.

"*TWO MINUTES!*"

I was winning my battle with the seat belts, slapping the latch smartly closed just as the grid marshal circled his hand overhead and shouted: "*WIND 'EM UP!*" I flipped the main and fuel pump switches *(clickclickclickclickclick)* and pressed the starter button. It responded with one of those ugly *Ka-thwinggg* noises that Lucas starters make when they're trying to break your heart. In desperation, I pressed it again. *Ka-ka-ka-thwingggg*. Shit. So I tried all the switches again in various orders and combinations, as if they were all somehow related in a grand and mysterious ritual that you had to get exactly right or the car wouldn't fire. Still no dice. As is typical of any racetrack, friendly, unknown hands appeared out of nowhere, pushing me forward, urging me on, and entreating me in strange, urgent voices:

"*Put it in gear!*"

The wheels locked up solid.

"*Not first! Try second!*"

Good idea.

"*Pop the clutch!*"

Thunka-thunka-thunka-thunka-thunka-thukk....

"*TURN ON THE IGNITION, DAMMIT!*"

Oh, yeah.

The engine burped, barked, coughed, and finally spluttered to life. I waved thanks over my shoulder and trundled onto the track, adrenaline spurting from every pore and orifice, and duly took the only space available at the very back end of the two-by-two queue behind the pace car. And then we were off on the warm-up lap. I twisted the steering wheel violently left-right-left-right, wrenching the car from side to side to heat up the tires (as I had seen all my heroes do on television) and doubtless sowing the seeds of fear and apprehension among my grid-mates. In fact, I think that's really why you really do it. But, in the process, it seems I also managed to get the damn seat loose again. More on that later....

GREEN FLAG!!!!

I hurled the TR *deeeeeep* into corner one, waiting until somewhat past the Last Plausible Moment before slamming indelicately on the brakes, slewing in towards the apex, barely (if at all) under control, while cutting a veritable swath through a legion of more experienced drivers who must have muttered to themselves, almost in unison, "Who is *this* asshole?" In a few short laps, I had charged, faked, ricocheted and intimidated my way up to fourth or fifth place, passing Mike's red number 12 TR in the process. A quick study of my driving must have convinced him that there was no point trying to beat me, as I was a lead-pipe cinch to beat myself.

Of course, *my* view of things was somewhat different (especially since I was mostly looking out the sides of the car instead of through the windscreen to see where I was going). Yes, I was sure as hell scary sideways most of the time, really tearing up the track (not to mention my equipment) on my way to certain glory. Only it was sometime around in here that I noticed myself kind of leaping and lurching and bouncing around in the cockpit like a wound-up pit bull on a very short leash. I made a mental note to do something significant about the mounting for my fancy fiberglass racing seat in the very near future.

Next on my rookie agenda was a quick lesson in the thermal properties of brake fluid. Hell, I was *racin,'* see, an' so I was usin' the middle pedal *hard!* Not wisely or well, perhaps. But *hard.* And, it seems, building up more fluid-boiling calories that the system could absorb. Imagine my surprise when I stood on the binders for corner seven and the pedal plummeted all the way to the floorboards with no noticeable effect. I take that back. There was a noticeable effect. Every orifice in my body slammed shut. So we were off into the tulies, my TR3 and I. And hardly for the last time. But the old girl wasn't painted earth-mover orange for nothing, and we rode it out with little more than a flash of embarrassment and some Nomex underwear now in need of laundering.

I crept back onto the circuit and was surprised to find a weak, spongy semblance of feel returning to the brake pedal. For the very first time, the Proctor of Prudence and the Specter of Dread Uncertainty made their voices heard over my internal clamor for speed and instant glory. I was beginning to believe that there might be a bit more to this racing business than grit, guts, and gushing adrenaline. And this is how we learn, friends and neighbors. You try to do something, and then, when you find yourself being sucked under and drowning in a frightening, terrifying situation that you never envisioned in your wildest dreams, you may pause to ask yourself, *"Why?"* If you manage to come up with an answer, you have probably learned something.

In any case, by this time I was uncertain exactly where I stood vis-à-vis my competition, but I was pretty secure in the notion that I was working my way aggressively toward the back of the field from whence I had come. And the goal became just to *get there*, you know? To finish the race and flash under the checkered flag in a blaze of personal, if unheralded, glory. And of course that's when the seat took a really bad lurch as I yanked the car into the double-apex, right-hand carousel at Turn Three and I guess my wrist must have hit the seatbelt/shoulder harness latch because the damn thing popped clear open. Oh, *swell.* In spite of what you must surely think by now, I am not totally ignorant, and at length I resigned myself to the fact that things had gotten a bit out of hand and that the only reasonable and intelligent thing to do was head for the pits and call it a day.

That's when the wheel came off.

And it didn't just *fall* off, either. Things fall off of racecars when you don't put them on good, and of all the things I knew how to put on racecars good, wheels were about the only one. Indeed, the part of the wheel *I* put on the car stayed right where it belonged, securely fastened to the hub with all four lug nuts properly torqued to official team specifications (two beads of sweat in the third crease of the forehead). No, it was the *rest* of the wheel, like some perforated steel doughnut with the center gnawed out out, parting company with the car. Found out later that hub centers tearing out of original equipment Standard-Triumph steel wheels is something of a congenital fault. Especially when the rims have been widened and fitted with high-grip racing tires.

And you laughed at Mike's Jeep-center wheels, didn't you?

But, to return to our hair-raising moment, I am just turning in towards the apex of corner seven (and, incidentally, flopping around in the car like a freshly caught mackerel) when the TR makes a sudden, sickening lurch in the general direction of Iowa and heads for the underbrush. I try twisting the wheel and hammering on the brakes, but the car no longer responds to my frantic efforts at the helm. That's because it is now sliding merrily along on three wheels and a scraping, spark-showering bit of frame. Yet I still found the steering wheel a great comfort (even though it no longer actually *steered* the car), as hanging onto it kept me from bouncing clear out of the cockpit as we bounded, leaped, and cavorted through the weeds until everything kind of slowed down and ground to a shuddering, laboring halt.

Suddenly it was very still, just as the hiss of steam and the snap of crisp metal and the tom-tom throb of blood pounding in my ears. And that's when this phantom wheel drops from the sky like an anvil and bounces off the hood right in front of my face *BAM!*, leaving a dent large enough for a diving board and a few poolside deck chairs. I was not amused.

In the end, after the wrecker deposited my crippled, unrollable, three-wheeled example of Fine British Craftsmanship beside the Blue Swede, it was Mike (natch) who came over lugging a spare wheel and a proper floor jack, cussing and muttering all the while about "Them #&@#!! stock Triumph wheel centers!" He was a World Class cusser and mutterer. Before the sun had set that day, he'd offered me space in his garage for a price that never even covered the beer I drank out of his refrigerator.

Mike Whelan was a hard guy to figure. He was an ex-Navy hard-hat diver who could weld a perfect bead under water and worked as machinist by trade. He was a good one, too. You should've seen the wheel spacers he made for me once, all neatly cut and bored and beveled and polished and radiused out of rough chunks of scrap aluminum. Wouldn't take anything for them, either. I remember Mike worked two jobs often as not, to feed his racing habit and a family with whom he seemed forever at war. He could be the meanest, orneriest, stubbornest SOB you ever met. But he was the one guy I could count on to *be there,* every late night in the garage and every gritty, sleepless dawn. He'd be working on my car instead of his own as likely as not, lending me parts, giving me advice I was too pig-headed and impetuous to follow, teaching me The Ropes. He had all those years of know-how and experience in his hip pocket (which means, more than anything, that he knew what *not* to do) and he was more than willing to share it. Which made him precisely what every eager, impatient, terminally enthusiastic but hopelessly ignorant young racer needs: a mentor, a tutor, a sponsor, a keeper and a friend. I'd have to say Mike Whelan loved racing as much as anybody I ever met in my life, even if it wasn't in his character to be particularly vocal or pleasant about it. And I guess maybe I forgot to tell him. I mean to actually say the words:

Thanks, Mike. Thanks a lot.

Brilliant Chrome and Bug Splat Radius
A Sideways Look at the world of Concours d'Elegance....

ORIGINALLY PUBLISHED IN
BRITISH CAR
AUGUST, 1993

Concours d'Elegance is a French phase that means "prettying up a car so much that it's too bloody nice to drive," and these days *Concours* displays have become sort of a resident ritual of many of our major vintage race weekends. They range from the majestic, manicured, white-glove-and-silver-tea-service coronation ceremony at Pebble Beach each year to the informal gathering of a few dozen old sportscars, musclecars, ponycars, big, chrome-slathered fifties convertibles, and even a niftily flamed Ford highboy roadster I saw lined up cheek-by-jowl on the front straight at Lime Rock a few autumns ago. The HSR's Walter Mitty Challenge at Road Atlanta normally has a pair of nicely-produced concours every April (street cars on Saturday, during quiet time on Sunday for the racers) and one of the prime organizers in the early days was my friend Maury Hatcher, whom I like in spite of the fact that he is a nit-picking, anal-retentive *concours* weasel mostly on account of he has a lovely and charming wife and didn't punch me square in the jaw the night I broke a condom filled with about eight gallons of water over his head in Pusser's Pub on Grand Bahama Island a few years back. But I had a good excuse in that I was on about my fourth or fifth Pusser's Painkiller, and besides it happened during the SVRA's blowout Bahamas Speed Week, so nobody much noticed. *Concours* gatherings on the closed-off streets of Elkhart Lake likewise became a major feature of Joe Marchetti's fantabulous CHR extravaganza at Road America each summer (and have continued, albeit without the same flair and sense of style, under the current administration) and the sights and sounds of the racecars firing up on the street behind Siebken's and roaring back to the racetrack with police escort late Friday evening is always one of the weekend's most indelible memories. Joe's show also set welcome standards for scoring by "French Rules," which have more to do with how far out of you socks a particular car knocks you rather than whether it has the correct radiator cap.

Although I confess to love these *concours* car parties dearly for all the handsome, sparkly-shiny lumps of base metal and unbridled imagination they bring together, they also sometimes fill me with a nagging sense of dread. That's because I'm occasionally honored/flattered/horrified & amazed to find myself selected as a judge. This makes no sense whatever to anyone who has seen the contents and byproducts of my own personal garage (most of which are best viewed with the doors down and lights off on the night of a new moon) but it seems my name has become more or less recognized these days—if not actually respected—in and around the vintage scene, and apparently the only requirements for a position as Official Vintage *Concours* Judge (aside from simply being asked) are as follows:

> *a)* You are perceived to Know Something (precisely *what* does not seem to be all that important)
>
> *b)* You like being fawned over, coddled, and brown-nosed by squinty-eyed, hardware-hungry *concours* entrants
>
> *c)* You are willing to drink free drinks and eat free meals
>
> *d)* You can manfully abstain from punching squarely in the nose a small but particularly virulent strain of *Concours* Weenies who are so bloody tight
> of sphincter that they couldn't shit toothpicks.

Mind you, I enjoy all the pomp, circumstance, hoohaw and fol-de-rol that goes along with *concours* judging (anyone who thinks the bloody *cars* are the center of attention has never been a judge!) but I must admit I find it hard to run my gaze across a field of marvelously presented and wildly diverse automobiles (many of which I would gladly kill for!) and then proceed to grade them like so many freshman term papers on the role of Southern narrow gauge railways in the outcome of the Civil War. It's like trying to issue some sort of quantified, numerical scores to the paintings and sculptures in an art museum—as if you could somehow compare Georges Seurat's grandly serene *"Sunday Afternoon on La Grande Jatte"* (surely a Bugatti Royale or dual cowl Packard Phaeton?) with Constantin Brancusi's soaring, effortless *"Bird in Space"* (no doubt one of Bertone's slippery B.A.T. aerodynamic studies for Alfa Romeo). Worse yet, a big part of the *concours* equation boils down to things like how clean and dust-free the work appears and how nice the frame or pedestal.

Pretty ridiculous, *n'est ce pas?*

Yet you'd be amazed at how many folks out there (see requirement #4 above) take this *concours d'elegance* stuff waaaay too seriously. As if there were some kind of Right Answers and Hard Criteria to go on in the *concours* biz, rather than the Whim Of The Day and behind-the-scenes politicking that *really* decide who takes Best In Show and who goes home with *bupkis.* By way of illustration, I recall an *awfully* nice pre-war Riley that lost out to a comparatively tatty Alvis at Elkhart Lake a few years back only because nobody liked the full-geek white sportcoat/matching Bermuda shorts/polka-dot silk ascot/curlycue pipe getup the Riley's owner was sporting (it turned out later that he was a really nice guy and it was all horoughly tongue-in-cheek, but we didn't know it at the time). Besides, nobody knew him, while the Alvis belonged to a well-liked sage, compatriot and elder statesman of the local sportycar fraternity.

My difficulties with the *Concours* Mentality escalate all the way up to critical mass whenever the subject turns to honest-to-goodness race cars, as nothing offends me near so much as a great old warrior that gets itself mummified and taxidermied into a "glass case job" for the parade and beauty show circuit, never again to turn a wheel in anger. This conflict between pure outward form and intended function (emphasis on the *fun* syllable) came into sharp focus at the CHR a few summers back, when an absolutely *gorgeous* Lotus Eleven LeMans (considerably more gorgeous, in fact, than anything Colin Chapman *ever* rolled out of his factory workshops!) was squared-off against my buddy John Muller's delightfully oddball Tojiero/Climax in the smallbore British sports/racer class. Now John's Tojiero is likewise perhaps a few shades finer than pure original (to say the least!) but he makes up for it by racing the bloody pee out of it every chance he gets. In fact, I co-drove an enduro with John in his Tojeiro the very next day, and I can assure you neither of us spared the rod one tiny bit. The Lotus, by contrast, was a Glass Case Job of the first order, locked away in a state of falsified perfection like a fairytale princess held captive in an ivory tower. Sad fate, that.

In any case, I was ultimately overruled by the other judges (who went with the Lotus, the Philistines!) but the experience prompted me to formulate the BS Levy Theory of Bug Splat Radius, which I offer up for the consideration of future *concours* judges, wherever they may gather. See, I reckon that if a car is *raced* (and preferably raced *hard*) that fact should have greater scoring value than any niggling oil drips, brake dust, stone chips, weepy fittings, or unsightly human residues on the driver's-side seat cushion. Hell, that last item should earn a quick 5-point bonus! My theory of Bug Splat Radius is likewise based on the scientifically proven proposition that, the faster a car is travelling, the larger the size of the Final Stain an insect of any given size and mass will leave on the coachwork (*Q: What's the last thing to go through a bug's mind when he hits your windshield? A: His asshole*). At any rate, I propose awarding an automatic one-point bonus for every verifiable millimeter of Bug Splat Radius on every actually raced *concours* entrant. And I further recommend measuring the long way if it's one of those stretched-out, comet-shaped "streamers."

I hope the above doesn't trigger any ugly hate mail from The Association Of *Concours* Weenies or those screwy, green and mean "Meat Is Murder" fanatics (but I guess even those folks consider insects a bit beyond the pale, God's creatures though they be). And, while we're on the subject, anybody who figures we can turn all this country's platter-bound livestock into happy, contented household pets has never been to a chicken ranch. Not hardly.

FROM BLACKPOOL TO BILOXI

BACK INTO HISTORY IN A 2500M

ORIGINALLY PUBLISHED IN
BRITISH CAR
JUNE/JULY, 1997

I was always attracted to TVRs because they were so patently outrageous, and the bug bit especially hard after I saw the latest 2500M models hidden away in a dimly lit corner of McCormick Place during the Chicago Auto Show one cold February evening in 1973. There were two of the hunchbacked little bottom feeders on display—one in a dazzling, eye-gouge yellow and the other a deep, rich metallic green—and directly behind them was a tantalizingly naked 2500M running chassis with its tubular steel backbone space frame and fabricated dual A-arms at all four corners and rack-and-pinion steering and cast aluminum wheels and, well, all the stuff I'd been told was right with the world (sports car-wise, anyway) in the pages of *ROAD & TRACK* magazine. And I guess I fell in love that night. More to the point, I was absolutely *convinced* that I could win myself an SCCA National Championship with one. Mind you, this grand notion was based on not one solitary scrap of hard empirical data, since about as far as I'd gotten in the world of motor sport was racing an assortment of ratty, el cheapo TR3s on the bush league Midwestern Council circuit, and while there was no question I could show the occasional turn of eye-bugging speed (well, *my* eyes were bugged, anyway) I had yet to assemble an automobile that would stay under me all the way to the checkered flag. Or sometimes even as far as the green one.

But no matter. After all, had I not seen my hero Bob Tullius in his Group 44 TR6 *almost* beat Bob Sharp's Datsun 240Z at the SCCA Runoffs at Road Atlanta, and surely (looking at the spec sheets, anyway) the Triumph-engined TVR with its wider track, fatter wheels, arguably better aerodynamics and ultra-sexy suspension would be absolutely *unbeatable*. Especially with a great undiscovered talent like myself at the wheel. All of which goes to show that I was more than a little pig-headed and naive at the time, and didn't really appreciate what Group 44 had done to that TR6 to make it so bloody fast (that particular car now belongs to my good friend Bill Warner, and, having driven it, may I say it bears the same resemblance to a standard-issue TR6 as Michelle Pfeiffer does to an empty dress) and all the time, testing, bags of gold, and hard-won knowledge and experience it takes to transform any production vehicle, no matter how exotic, into a viable track weapon. Plus Messrs. Tullius and Sharp had actually finished a few races in their time (and won a goodly share of them!) whereas my racing scrapbook was singularly devoid of press clippings and even the very best of my race weekend bar stories were about nickel-rocket flashes of brilliance and the depressing auto-mechanical premature ejaculations that inevitably followed. Not to mention that the TVR 2500M wasn't even homologated for competition by the SCCA, on account of something about they didn't build enough cars....

But of course I was going to change all that.

Right.

First step was to get myself a car, and, being in the throes of the usual Racer's Shortage of disposable income (but not nerve!) I waltzed into the nearest TVR dealership and boldly explained to the owner as how I was destined to win an important National Championship in a 2500M (if they would just give me a car, that is) and TVRs would subsequently sell like celebrity underwear. I must admit that the dealership's owner didn't know exactly what to make of me (no surprise there) and ultimately suggested I should go have a chat with the local TVR distributor, Bob Neal, who had a Pontiac/Volvo/British Leyland dealership in a somewhat unlikely location on far south Stony Island Avenue in Chicago. Turns out Bob was one of the first really successful black new car dealers in the country (not to mention one hell of a nice guy) and, to this day, I think Bob picked up the Midwest TVR distributorship for the same exact reason I wanted to race them. He thought they were pretty damn *neat!* Unfortunately, you don't get very far in the wholesale automobile business by handing out free samples (and especially to racers, who can be found in the *Great Encyclopedia of Life* under the heading *"Bottomless Pits")* but I guess he was impressed and/or bewildered enough by my sheer audacity and *chutzpah* that he wanted to put my boundless and reverberating enthusiasm for TVRs to work for him.

So we made a deal.

I was working for my father's manufacturers' rep business at the time—not long back from a free-form hippie odyssey "Out West" that included Boulder, Berkeley, and more neon-tinged dawns than I care to (or can!) remember—and my job included numerous sales trips throughout the Midwest and Southeast. Bob agreed to front up a 2500M demo for me to drive on those trips, with the idea that I would stop here and there along the way and try to convince established sports car agencies into signing on as TVR dealers. It really didn't take much in those days, just the wholesale price of two cars and $1500 worth of parts and—*presto!*—you were in the TVR business!

I thought it would be a laydown, you know?

So Bob handed me the keys to a deep maroon 2500M, and the first thing I did was hustle it over to my Mexican custom painter friend Danny Onate, who ran a little bump shop on the west side and specialized in putting luminous flame jobs, amazing murals, electrified feathers and psychedelic fish scales on drag cars, street rods, custom vans, and Harley fuel tanks. Danny was a *bona fide* genius with a spray gun who never wore a mask because he claimed the fumes made him "more creative," and spent several beers just eyeballing the shape and sculpturing of the TVR before he went to work. I told him I didn't want anything real radical (a mural of Elvis playing at Stonehenge or Lady Godiva mooning the Jaguar works in Coventry didn't seem quite appropriate) so he just highlighted here and there with a transparent candy-apple purple and added a sexy, asymmetrical gold racing stripe that went back from the NACA duct on the nose on the driver's side, over the top, across the back, and forward to the fender vent on the opposite side. When he was done, we pulled off the masking tape, stepped back a few paces, and agreed that it looked neat as hell. Fortunately Bob Neal thought so, too, since it would've gotten pretty damn uncomfortable if he hadn't.

I had a trip to take down to several textile plants in Georgia and Alabama and a Sunbeam alarm clock facility in Jackson, Mississippi, and, conveniently enough, the SCCA Runoffs were coming up at Road Atlanta around the same time. So this figured to be a sterling opportunity to slay all my dragons at once (I mean, hell, they were all lined up for me!) by opening a bunch of TVR dealerships on my way down through Kentucky and Tennessee and Georgia and everyplace else the Yankees laid waste to, followed by a stop at the Runoffs where I would promote the hell out of the car to its prime target audience and lobby the SCCA relentlessly about homologating the 2500M for production class competition. Oh, and I'd sell a shitload of plastic bags along the way in the process. As any fool can plainly see, I didn't have any serious deficiencies in the confidence or enthusiasm departments!

But I needed help, and to this end enlisted my good friend and stalwart companion Pat Fitzgerald, who filled in as a sort of *de facto* crew chief during much of my early racing career simply because he was just too good a sport to say "no." Pat's a successful architect today, and he was the perfect foil because he had a good eye and gifted hands and could actually *do* and *make* all the stuff that I could only talk about. In fact, between us we embodied the full yin and yang of self-expression, since I was always popping off crazy new schemes and improbable projects like a fire in a skyrocket factory, while Pat had the kind of soft-spoken, sure-handed, even-strain patience and persistence that produces perfect right angles and paint jobs without runs, drips, sags, or embalmed insect carcasses imbedded in the finish. I, on the other hand, tended to attack all hands-on mechanical and construction projects using the same general strategies made famous by Northern and Southern Civil War commanders Sherman and Pickett. And invariably with similar results.

Speaking of the Civil War, it hadn't even occurred to me that I was about to head south into, if not enemy, at least *foreign* territory. I really didn't know or understand much about the South back then, and, like a lot of inexperienced and misinformed Yankees, I wrongly assumed that, *a)* the War Between the States was over, and, *b)* that our side had won. But that's what happens if you grow up in a citified Northern megapolis like Chicago. You get to thinking that you come from the Center of the Universe. And of course that's ridiculous. I mean, everybody *knows* that the Center of the Universe is really in Manhattan.

Just ask a New Yorker....

But I digress. Back to the 2500M story. I made up some cheap but nifty TVR handout flyers and a bunch of pressure-sensitive stickers and campaign buttons ("TVR-*neat car!*") to use at Road Atlanta, and Pat built this magnificent, twelve-foot-high freestanding display to put up next to the car. It was terribly clever, what with pins and bolts and hinges so it would fold up to a very compact size. But not, of course, so compact that it would fit in a TVR 2500M. Only shoe boxes and ladies' handbags are that small. Fortunately, my old Triumph racer friend Mike Belfer and the rest of the yellow TR3 bunch from Milwaukee (who had been beating the stuffing out of me on the racetrack for years...mostly by dint of merely finishing) were also going to the Runoffs, and kindly agreed to stop off in Chicago on the way down and lash Pat's display to the roof of their truck and haul it down for me. Pat couldn't take more than an extended weekend off work, so it was agreed that I'd drive down solo, leaving a trail of furtive TVR and plastic bag pitches echoing in my wake, and then we'd rendezvous at the Atlanta airport and he'd ride back with me.

With everything set for the trip, I went on one last Sunday night date with the patient, wonderful and incredibly understanding young lady who would one day become my wife. Fact is, that maroon TVR demo with the asymmetrical gold racing stripe played a large part in our courtship. And her highly conservative father approved wholeheartedly, because he knew he didn't have a thing to worry about if we parked out at the end of some dark country road in a TVR 2500M! As far as he was concerned, that car was a chastity belt with mag wheels and a four-speed gearbox. But I got her home early that night, because I had to be off at the crack of dawn the next morning, barreling full steam for the Mason-Dixon line and one of the greatest sports car adventures of my life. Needless to say I was traveling light, seeing as how TVR 2500Ms don't have much in the way of what you or I might recognize as luggage space (although they compensate by making what little of it there is totally inaccessible).

The trip's first rude lesson was that the owners and sales managers of your average sports car dealership were not exactly waiting around on pins and needles for some frizzy-haired Jewish packaging salesman out of Chicago to burst in out of the blue and sign them up as TVR dealers. Not hardly. You'll recall the market was not exactly booming in those days, and the potential profit off a couple strange, bullfrog-profile English coupes built by some company in Blackpool that nobody'd ever heard of didn't balance off too well against the risks involved. Like fr'instance who, exactly, was backing up warranty claims, hmm? Most of these guys had experience with British Leyland (or, worse yet, Lotus) and so they were rather, shall we say, *sensitive* when it came to the topic of warranty claims.

The other hot news (literally) was that the TVR's interior was warmer by a dozen or more degrees than any car I could remember. Especially once I got down to the land of grits and red eye gravy. It wasn't till well past Chattanooga that I discovered the heater tap knob under the steering column, in defiance of all conventional wisdom, was hooked up to pull *out* for "OFF" and push *in* for "ON." Imagine that. I'd been running with the damn heater on full blast ever since I'd left Chicago!

I have to admit that I didn't exactly set the world on fire trying to open up TVR franchises for Bob Neal (although I think one guy I visited in Kentucky came on board later) but it was a heck of an experience anyway and some of the packaging prospects I called on were really impressed with the car. For sure they wouldn't forget me, and standing out from the crowd and being remembered are a big part of the game in the manufacturers' rep business. No matter what you're selling.

In any case, I met Pat at the Atlanta airport right on schedule, and, after an eye-opening (or occasionally eye-shutting, in Pat's case) drive out to the racetrack, we struggled through the usual SCCA red tape at registration and finally bullshitted our way into clearance to display the car up on a hill near the control tower. Which was a prime spot, since it's right on your way into or out of the paddock and adjacent to one of the best vantage points for spectating Road Atlanta's notorious bridge turn.

Next step was to hunt up the yellow TR3 guys and our display. And thence came the next rude shock. Seems a serious gust of wind came up and blew Pat's display clear off the top of Mike's truck. Before they even got out of Chicago! It happened on the notorious Dan Ryan Expressway that runs through Chicago's tough, poor and gritty South Side, and the *coup de grace* was duly administered by the somewhat inebriated driver of a rusted-out Buick, who must've thought he'd hit the mother and father of all Chicago potholes. Mike and his guys gathered up the remains as best they could and brought them, such as they were, the rest of the way down to Atlanta. It was an awful mess, but Pat figured how we could take a few pieces here and there and make a sort of TVR totem pole to put next to the car. That would just have to do.

In spite of everything, it was a fun weekend. The Runoffs always are. Our car attracted plenty of attention, and we literally peppered the grounds with posters and flyers and little oval stickers that read *"TVR: neat car!"* and *"TVR: only 500 cars per year!"* and *"TVR in C-Production"* and such. We even handed out printed garbage bags trumpeting *"Get rid of your trash, get a TVR!"* Why, you couldn't have missed us at the Runoffs at Road Atlanta that year if you were deaf, dumb, blind and dead.

As to how much good we actually did, it's hard to say. My conversations with anybody who would listen regarding homologating the 2500M met with a collective yawn of enthusiasm, and, as I recall, neither Bobs Tullius nor Sharp (or, in fact, any of the C-production entrants) seemed to be exactly quaking in their boots regarding the prospect of squaring off against a 2500M. And particularly one fielded by some unknown, ex-hippie blowhole from Chicago who couldn't even get a damn TR3 oxcart from green to checker without something major breaking or falling off the car.

Surely the best part was the trip back home with Pat. I had one more business stop to make at the Sunbeam alarm clock factory in Jackson, Mississippi, and the plant manager was an older gentleman known as "The Rev" because he served as a Baptist minister on Sunday mornings. The Rev really liked and respected my dad, and, although he and I couldn't have been more different in more different ways, we strangely hit it off. And then nothing would do but that Pat and I join his weekly church group luncheon. In fact, I wound up as sort of the feature attraction, since all the church elders wanted to hear firsthand about Berkeley and the hippies and what in tarnation was really going on out there. I tried to be honest and explain it the best I could, and, in the end, they nodded and shook my hand and thanked me quite genuinely for stopping by.

Then one of them, an elderly blind gentleman accompanied by an ancient seeing eye dog, took me aside and asked in a reassuring, fatherly tone, "Son, do you know what you did out there in California?"

I allowed as how I wasn't quite sure.

He patted me gently on the arm. "You climbed Fool's Hill, that's all."

The way he said it left no doubt that it was true.

"Sometimes," he continued gently, "God needs us to see the view from up there."

I sure hope so, because it seems I've climbed an awful lot of them over the years.

We left Jackson after lunch for a quick run down the scenic Natchez Trace Parkway, swooping through the historic Old South on a stretch of smooth, perfect blacktop that had never seen a frost heave or shuddered under the weight of an over-loaded cement truck. The parkway was mostly flat with one fast, gentle sweeper after another, just lazily arcing its way this way and that through the countryside, and I'll always remember it as one of the most beautiful drives I've ever taken. And the TVR loved it, cruising along at that supple, easy, soaring pace somewhere a bit past prudence but still pleasantly short of shuddering brakes and squealing tires. Every now and then we'd stop to check out historical markers along the way or visit the peacefully decaying graveyards of the old Confederacy and even more ancient Indian burial mounds that trace the history of this land all the way back before Jamestown.

It was pure Road Magic.

After a stroll through historic Natchez, we continued on up to Vicksburg and walked the hillocks and ravines where Union and Confederate boys stared at each other through gun sights, shoulder-to-shoulder with their comrades and eyeball-to-eyeball with the enemy lined up behind ridges barely fifty yards away. What a terrible, tragic war that was. And yet what noble deeds and bravery it inspired. It ultimately stuck this nation back together—not perfectly, not righteously, but at least whole—and the fact that no wars have been fought on our home soil ever since is one of the things that separates this country from the legions of less fortunate nations on this earth.

Road trips like that one from Jackson to Natchez to Vicksburg in the 2500M afford the benign distance from the needs and nuisances of everyday life to make those kinds of philosophical observations. They also put you in touch with the land and its history, and give you a feeling of inner kinship with people from all sorts of regions, religions, and walks of life. As I'd said from the very beginning, that TVR was a pretty neat sports car. It didn't do too poorly as a time machine, either....

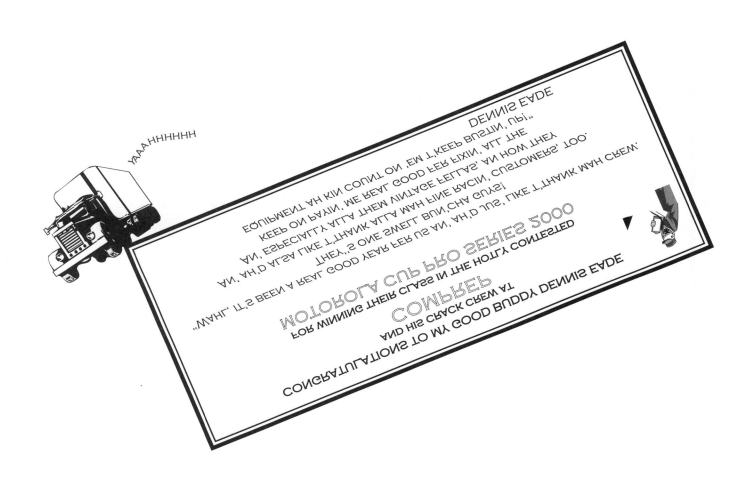

Elvis and Me
Fast Guys, Trick Parts, and Go-Faster Goodies

ORIGINALLY PUBLISHED IN
BRITISH CAR
JUNE 1991

I was but a young shirttail tad when I first realized that the One True Destiny of my life was to become

an internationally renowned Grand Prix megastar and endurance racing champion. Okay, so maybe I hadn't quite figured how my beat-up, six-hundred-dollar TR3 would lead me (by some mystical, predestined path) to Monaco, Monza and Le Mans. But I had *faith*. I was young. And innocent. And impressionable. And not a little stupid. Ah, youth, that bright springtime of springy muscle and brassy ignorance when great deeds still seem possible. And worth the freaking trouble.

To tell the truth, my original TR3 racecar was a bit of a heap (hey, what do you expect for 600 bucks?) but it had a rollbar, a gutted interior, a better motor than I knew, and a set of Goodyear R2s dating back to the signing of the Magna Carta by King John. Best of all, in spite of several embarrassingly obvious mechanical and cosmetical shortcomings, that TR was within what I laughingly referred to as "my racing budget." Actually, back in those days I didn't really have what you or I or anybody else could truly call "a racing budget," as my finances were governed instead by a sort of free-floating, fully elasticized Debt Ceiling governed only by the gross number of individuals and/or corporate financial entities to whom/which I could owe more money than I had to at any given time. If some demon-tweak doodad or high-performance whatsis put a shiny twinkle in my eye, hey, I *bought* it! And only resorted to cash when a guy wouldn't take my checks or credit cards anymore. This sort of activity is more-or-less S.O.P. among young, poor, under-employed (or occasionally unemployed) aspiring racers, and I'm proud to say our elected officials in Washington have seen the light and duly adopted those same, race-proven financial principles.

Believe it or not, I had no intimate knowledge of mechanics whatsoever when I bought/financed/finagled myself into that first raggedy TR3. My assumption was that sports car racing operated much as I'd observed in the popular Elvis Presley movies of the era. Not that I'd made a real study of those movies or anything, as mostly I'd caught only occasional glimpses of them whilst coming up for air from other, more pressing activities at the local Drive-in. But I had at least absorbed that, according to Elvis, racing cars worked something like this: you fired them up, put your foot down, and the best driver (who was also invariably the best singer and played the meanest lead guitar) eventually won the big race. Against insurmountable odds, natch. But the prize money was always enough to prevent the foreclosure on the Old Man's (played by either a bargain basement Mickey Rooney or Burgess Merideth imitation) garage where they worked on the car. And then of course he got the Big Factory Drive over in Europe and earned the hand of the large-boned girl with bouffant hair, succulent lips, heavy eye shadow and World Class yabboes.

By God, I could handle that.

What I didn't understand at the time was how the nuts-and-bolts reality of the machinery occasionally intruded on the story line. See, besides the Old Man, Elvis always had himself a super-handy pit crew that inevitably included a mechanical wizard sidekick (usually named 'Shorty,' 'Spike,' or 'Scotty') plus a bumbling, absent minded professor-type Pit Doofus ('Elmer') and, sometime during the movie, the three of them would put in there or four whole minutes in the garage, banging on the valve cover of Elvis' racecar with box-end wrenches. The large-boned girl with the bouffant hair was there, too, trying to help out (but of course she couldn't do much except stand around with her coveralls open about four buttons, on account of she was a *girl).* Yet, even so, she always managed to get at least one large and dramatic grease smudge across her cheek. Right under the eyeliner.

To my horror, I discovered that real life was quite a bit different. First off, I never managed to locate a mechanical whiz 'Shorty,' 'Spike,' or 'Scotty' to help me out. Or even an 'Elmer,' for that matter. Secondly, I learned that all you get by banging on your valve cover with a box-end wrench is a lumpy valve cover. And as to the large-boned girl mentioned above, none of the women I'd ever met were in anything even remotely resembling the same Silhouette Class as Elvis' ladies. And not one of them seemed enthused about Saturday nights spent hanging around a cold, dingy, back-alley garage until four in the morning, setting the wiring on fire or banging on the valve cover with a box end wrench. By the way, did you ever notice how the more Elvis ignored his leading ladies, the harder they chased after him? Somehow it worked precisely the opposite for me. To tell the truth, as little as I understood about car mechanics—and it was damn little, believe me—I knew even less about women....

Another thing I discovered was that the ratio of garage time to actual track time as depicted in the Elvis movies was grossly out of whack. I never did a scientific study about it or anything, but my guess is your average neophyte, incompetent, shadetree-variety toolbox bungler needs a minimum six to seven hours in the shop for every 60 seconds or so of track time. And that's assuming the idiot doesn't slow the process down by, say, knocking the car off its jackstands or setting his overalls on fire with a blowtorch. Or perhaps by making one of those silly little mechanical mistakes that mean you have to take everything apart (often for the umpty-hundredth time) because you've put the foofnik valve in backwards. Or left it out entirely. See, *there* it is. Over on the floor in the corner. Resting majestically under a used gasket box in a half-quart puddle of spilled gearlube.

But the toughest lesson of all had to do with the dirty little reality of how races are actually *won*. In defiance of every piece of racing fiction I'd ever read, seen on the screen, or listened to firsthand over a barstool, the hard fact was—and is—that most races are won by superior equipment rather than gallant driving. Honest. Oh, sometimes a really *great* driver in a reasonably good car can beat a middling average driver in a somewhat better car. And for sure lousy drivers can find ways to lose in almost *any*thing. But *nobody* wins races in a truly lousy car. Not even Stroker Ace. In fact, it was well before halftime on my first-ever race weekend that I discovered the horrid, Orwellian truth of things: not all TR3s (or MGBs, Sprites, Spitfires, or whatever) are created equal. Some turned out to be *lots* more equal than others....

Which caused me to abandon my search for an appropriately large-boned pit tootsie (complete with Max Factor cheek smudge) and turn my full attention to the classic and inevitable rookie racer's snipe hunt: ferreting out the jealously guarded speed secrets of...*The Fast Guys*.

Anyone with eyes could see the differences between genuine Fast Guy racecars and my own. Fast Guy cars were invariably low, slick, swift and sanitary, whereas *my* TR3 looked like one of those plastic car models seven-year-olds build, complete with gluebobs, fingerprint smudges, and dangling chrome trim. Plus, the Fast Guys all had the latest, super-trick tuned exhaust headers and spun aluminum velocity stacks and God knows what-all going on inside their engines. For sure, Fast Guy motors produced a piercing, razor-sharp howl that was all lean meat, while my poor engine sounded more like the putt-putt Massey Ferguson tractor mill from which it rightfully descended. But, *hey*, all I needed to close the gap was some of those real, Fast Guy racing parts! Then maybe I could be (dare I even think it?) a Fast Guy myself!

It was all so bloody simple....

And so, dear reader, I steeled my loins (which can get awfully cold in the wintertime), abandoned any remaining semblance of fiscal responsibility, and descended into the bewildering, labyrinth nether world of Trick Parts and Go-Faster Goodies. As if by magic, I acquired literally dozens of poorly printed, highly priced catalogs chock-full of things I just *had* to have. My credit cards began to heave and pulsate in my billfold, as if possessed by a life and will of their own. Indeed, what I originally perceived as no more than the purchase a few alloy trinkets became the entrance to a churning, never-ending, downward technological spiral that ground up innocence (and any available cash balances) like cheap hamburger meat.

Abandon hope, all ye that enter here....

But of course you never find that out until later. See, the way it works is this: no matter *where* you race or *what* you race, there is always somebody who has established himself as The Fast Guy for your particular marque and model. So you start hanging around him, you know, like maybe some of that Fast Guy magic will rub off. But it never, ever does. That's because Fast Guys are always too cool. In fact, it's one of the basic Fast Guy rules.

Fr'example, a genuine Fast Guy never gives a simple, direct answer to a simple, direct question. Not *ever*. Like, say you mosey over after a race during which the Fast Guy has lapped you maybe five or six times as if your racecar is dragging a freaking twelve-foot Yule log behind it on a forty-foot length of anchor chain. So you ease up beside him and nonchalantly inquire: *"Hey, what kinda brake pads you runnin' on thet thing anyway?"* or *"Hey, what'cha doin' fer tire pressures front n'back, huh?"* or maybe *"Hey, howcum you blow by me like I'm dragging a twelve-foot Yule log on a forty-foot length of anchor chain?"*

Invariably, the Fast Guy just smiles, winks, and says something thoroughly inscrutable like *"piston domes."*

"Piston domes?"

"Hell, yes. You *got* to have the pop-up piston domes to get higher compression and the proper flame front propagation."

"Flame front? Propa*what?*"

"Absolutely. Gotta have the right flame front."

"Whaa?? You *do???*"

"Surrrre," he answers like you maybe should've learned it in grade school.

Naturally, the Fast Guy just *happens* to have a spare set of pop-up, domed pistons back home in his garage. Which he will happily sell you–used–for about what you earn in a week. By the way, the reason he has an extra set lying around is because he's already switched to a new flat-top piston setup on *his* engine, so he can use a new, top-secret, high-lift/mega-overlap cam that produces more horsepower than you could *ever* get with pop-up pistons. But of course you don't know that, and the Fast Guy isn't about to tell you. So you cough up the cash (unless he's still taking your checks) and then spend forty or fifty carefree garage hours—generally between midnight and six ayem—putting in your new (used) set of high-domed, pop-up pistons. Or trick new scatter-pattern cam. Or lightweight aluminum flywheel. Or whatever.

Thing is, once you get everything installed and buttoned back together (a process which inevitably puts your banker on a first-name basis with the guy who runs your local machine shop) you discover that, besides making you motor run a hell of a lot stronger, the new pistons (or cam, or head, or whatever) often make it run a bunch *shorter* as well. Yessir, no more than two laps into your new engine's first practice session there commences a mighty clattering sound wrapped in a foul-smelling, impenetrable curtain of smoke and steam. *Whoops.* You instinctively switch off (talk about closing the barn after the horse has left!) and pull silently to the side, feeling a great void in the general area of your wallet. She's done blowed, by crackey! *Shit!*

Later on, the Fast Guy comes around to offer his condolences and cluck over the jagged, fist-sized hole in the side of your engine block. He shakes his head slowly from side to side and whispers *"crank balancer."*

"Crank balancer?"

"Hell, yeah. Y'just *gotta* have the crank balancer. Makes all the difference in the world..." And, naturally enough, he just *happens* to have an extra one back home in his garage. Which is when it slowly begins to dawn that rookies like you are situated at the very bottom of the trick parts food chain, like some giant, dim-witted, prehistoric species of hardware-sucking carp. And you yearn to escape. To get out. To get ahead. To get *even*. To become (drum roll, please)...a real, live Fast Guy yourself!

All it takes is more than you'll ever have....

SPACE AVAILABLE

YOUR MESSAGE HERE

(CHEAP)

DREAMS ON THE CHOPPING BLOCK

WHERE CA$H IS KING!

BASED ON A "PURE BS" COLUMN IN
VINTAGE MOTORSPORT
MARCH/APRIL 1997

I'd never

been to the famous classic car auction at Auburn, Indiana before, but my wife and I figured it might be a swell opportunity to introduce my novel to a new group of Likely Prospects that we probably wouldn't run into at your average vintage race. And it turned out to be a pretty good idea, as we sold quite a few books–even though it seemed like I had to lather up a pretty hefty sales pitch for each and every one.

"You got enny Packards in thet book?" a thick, pasty faced guy in Sears coveralls wanted to know.

"Sure do," I beamed furtively. "Cadillacs, too…"

He peered at me kind of sideways from beneath a Marine-issue crewcut. *"Hmpf,"* he allowed cautiously, *"do tell…."* He picked the book up but didn't open it. Like he was checking its weight, you know? After a long moment of consideration, he set it back down—still unopened—apparently having decided it didn't weigh enough to be worth twenty-five bucks. Hell, you could buy a good used starter for that much at Auburn if you shopped hard.

"…and I got Fords and Chevys and Plymouths and even Henry Js," I called after him as he meandered over towards where the guy in the next booth was giving a spiel about his *"revolutionary new miracle ONCE IN A LIFETIME CAR WAX that is absolutely guaranteed to bring your car to a sparkling, dazzling shine that will last until the Second Coming of Christ with but a single, easy home application. It also cures bad breath, eliminates perspiration odor, flattens abs, fixes even the foulest foot fungus, and reverses the aging process as well, my friends. All this and more for the UNBELIEVABLE, ONCE-IN-A-LIFETIME INTRODUCTORY AUBURN SHOW SPECIAL PRICE OF $19.99!"*

I had to admit, at 25 bucks even, my book—which doesn't even have any blessed *pictures* in it—didn't look like much of a bargain by comparison….

And that's a huge part of deal at Auburn: BARGAINS! The important thing is not so much what you buy, but *how much you paid for it!* Sure, there were acres upon acres of truly fascinating machines, including representative examples of damn near every four-wheeled wet dream known to man, laid out cheek-by-jowl in the surrounding tents or lined up fenderline-to-fenderline on the huge asphalt slab of a parking lot. They were all there, from stately, elegant, coachbuilt Rollses and Duesenbergs to garish, whale-tail Panteras and Countachs and Porsche Turbos with all their brazen aerodynamic laundry hanging out in the breeze. There were dozens of to-die-for, drive-in queen '57 Chevys with continental kits and pastel pink 2-seater T-Birds with creamy off-white upholstery. And all around them swarms of recent-model (can you say gray market? I thought you could!) Benzes and Bimmers and Ferrari 308s and more damn Vipers and Corvettes than you would ever be able to choose from. There were hordes of chuffing, fat-tired, '60s-era musclecars, and here and there you came across flamboyant, pearlescent-flamed highboy street rods right next to handsome old brass-lamp Reos and Mercers. At Auburn, you'll probably see every kind of car that ever made your head swivel on Main Street.

And every one of them on sale to the highest bidder.

Assuming it clears reserve, that is.

Which brings us to a few things you need to know about classic and "special interest" car auctions. Like sometimes a car is not really there so much to *sell* as to *establish its value.* Owners who want to "test the market" or satisfy their bankers (along with motorhead husbands trying to keep the little missus from consulting a divorce attorney—"honest, Honey, I'm *trying* to sell it!") will run a car over the blocks with a purposely high reserve. Just to show it off a little and see what happens, you know? And you've got to beware of the sharks. There's a famous old game of musical chairs where a bunch of traders and their agents will buy and sell a particular car (or type of car) back and forth to one another over a series of auctions, bidding it up and kiting the price a little higher each time. And then, one fine day, a new voice pipes up. Some poor fish who has been watching the market diligently and thinks he knows what these things are worth. The bidding is hectic, and maybe he goes even a little higher than he should, but, hey, this is a *hot* item, right? And then, a little ways down the road, he maybe brings it to another auction, rolls it over the block, and is surprised and shocked at the lack of interest. Except for what he's paying on the note, that is....

So you have to be a little careful.

Although Auburn is mostly an American car show, there were some great old British sports cars, too, and the one that caught my eye was surely the nicest, finest, neatest, cleanest, most perfectly immaculate Series 1½ Jaguar E-type convertible I've ever seen in my life. It was done up in a shimmering lipstick red, and there were even mirrors spread out on the ground so you could see how the undercarriage was all painted and polished and more exquisitely detailed than any Jag E-Type that ever rolled off the assembly line in Coventry.

"When did you finish the restoration?" I asked one of the guys clustered around it with chamois and paste wax.

"Two days ago," he told me, and you could see the pent-up weariness and strain clouding his eyes. "It took us six years."

"Your car?" I asked.

He nodded.

"Are you really here to sell it?" I whispered knowingly. "Or are you just testing the waters to see what it might be worth?"

"No," he said with a deep sigh of resignation. "We're gonna sell it. My wife said if I don't, I shouldn't bother coming home."

"Jeez. That's too bad."

The guy shrugged like it was No Big Deal, but the hound dog look on his face made you wonder.

"Did'ja at least get to drive it a little? You know, take it for a blast out on the highway or down a twisty road someplace?"

He shook his head.

"Not even over to a hamburger stand to show off?"

"Nope," he answered with a curious lack of emotion. "To tell you the truth, I really didn't want to."

"You didn't? Why's that?"

"Because then the juices'd start flowing again and I'd want to keep it."

Like any car guy who's ever had an Unfulfilled Dream Project parked over an antique oil stain in the garage, I certainly understood how that worked. Unfulfilled or not, it's still a dream, and dreams get harder and harder to come by as you get older. It was kind of a sad story, really. "So," I finally asked, "how'd you come up with a reserve price on something like this?"

The owner shrugged. "I just took what I've got in it and divided by half."

I certainly understood how *that* worked, too...

So I made a point of sneaking away from my book-hawking duties on Saturday afternoon (by that time my spiel was down to *"A ONCE-IN-A-LIFETIME SHOW SPECIAL PRICE OF $22.95 and guaranteed to teach you HOW TO FIX ANY PART OF ANY CAR with no more than THE CONTENTS OF AN AVERAGE LADY'S HANDBAG!")* just to watch that gorgeous E-type roll over the block.

And it was amazing how the climate changed once you peeled out of the sunlight and ventured into that dark, crowded cavern of a building. It was actually an old tobacco drying barn that they'd bought someplace down South and shipped up to Auburn, and it looked a lot like the World's Biggest Barn. It was dark and huge and noisy inside, and the high energy Kruse teams were essentially running two shows back to back in the middle of the floor, each with its own bidders, gawkers and hangers-on. The incessant babble from the auctioneers and all the helpers, car pimps, plants, and shills out working the crowd made for a truly frenetic scene. As the cars rolled eagerly onto the turntables, one after another, they came to rest in a blazing pool of violet-tinged stage light that made them glisten and sparkle like one of Elvis' sequin suits.

But as soon as the bidding started in earnest, you realized the cars were just momentary ornaments hung on the *real* reason everybody was there. The money. When a deal really got moving, the air sparked and crackled with an electricity you could *feel*, like a high-stakes craps table when somebody's really on a roll. If the bidding was wild and competitive enough and the final figure astounding, there'd be approving murmurs and applause afterwards for the big winner. It was kind of creepy in a way. Like what they were really buying had something to do with status and respect....

And as soon as one car rolled out of the floodlights—before you could even stop to think about it—another one took its place and the auctioneer started up full blast without skipping a beat: *"PRACTICALLY BRAND SPANKING NEW. FULL CUSTOM TRIM. ONCE OWNED BY THE DALAI LAMA HIMSELF...,"* and, if it was a genuinely good one, the old electricity started to spark and crackle all over again. It's something every diehard Car Nut needs to witness and marvel over at least once in his life.

But *caveat emptor*, eh?

Better yet, just leave the old wallet and checkbook at home. You really don't belong in this business if you've got an honest weakness for the metal. Just ask the poor fish who took a fraction of what he had in it for the nicest damn Series 1½ Jaguar E-Type ragtop I'll ever see.

OF REPAIR AND REPLACE

WHAT THE SHOP MANUALS DON'T TELL YOU....

SLIGHTLY REVISED VERSION OF A
STORY ORIGINALLY PUBLISHED IN
AutoWeek
MAY 21, 1984

Today's

subject is endangered species. And, more specifically, Automobile Mechanics. The casual observer, noticing large flocks of them congregating in the drearier back-parts of car dealerships and individual, rogue examples prowling around the service bays of street-corner gas stations, may mistakenly believe that the breed is flourishing. Unfortunately, most of these creatures are not true Automobile Mechanics at all, but rather a bastardized modern hybrid known as Parts Exchangers. The difference between the two is enormous, even though they share similar plumage and habitats. If you need clarification, grab a thick edition of Webster's, flip to the R's, and look up the definition of two familiar words: "Repair" and "Replace."

They're not the same, are they?

But the two varieties are easily identified, even though they look quite identical due to the protective coloration both absorb from the viscera of internal combustion equipment and dust of rusty mufflers they encounter as their workday progresses. Pale complexions are also common, the result of standing or lying perpetually in the shadow of whatever happens to be up on the lift or supported on jackstands above them. And their hands are a dead giveaway. Observe what appears to be heavy eyeliner under the fingernails (not to mention those that are either split, smashed, purplish black from contact or completely missing). Cuts, slits, abrasions, burns, gashes and contusions of the thumb and knuckles are also common. In fact, mechanics' hands generally look like they've been picking up running eggbeaters by the business end.

But true Auto Mechanics are DMMs (Doctors of Moving Metal) and share all the talents required by doctors of other, more complex machines of flesh, bone and sinew. There is never a problem confusing DMMs with actual medical doctors, however, as the latter have summer homes and softer, more delicate hands, unmarked except for tiny dimples from handling errant golf balls on Wednesday afternoons. But, just like the medical doctor, the DMM achieves the pinnacle of his craft by mastering three areas of study: Diagnosis, Tools, and Operational Strategy.

I myself once aspired to be a DMM. I even quit a promising white-collar family business to pursue the trade in one of the more catastrophically ill-advised but nonetheless enriching career moves of my entire life. I made a mistake common to the very lowest of the Mechanic species (the loathsome Shadetree variety) by surmising that a love of the infernal combustion machine combined with boundless enthusiasm and a little brute strength was a reasonable substitute for actual knowledge, skill and experience. During this period, I also had the opportunity to hire (and fire) a series of purported mechanics and came to the first small, nagging inkling of my realization that the real McCoy are rare indeed.

I'm not a mechanic by trade anymore (and both I and the sick automobiles I encounter are much the better for it) but I still dabble in the socket-box from time to time, and years of hard, evil lessons have left me a passable amateur wrench-wielder. But I'm no DMM, and I'll be the first to admit it. A real one will spot my work and instantly turn a whiter shade of pale. Take my electrical connections—*please!*—which generally look like tent-caterpillar cocoons of black electrical tape festering on a wire. Or observe the ugly, uneven chips in the blades of ruined screwdrivers that have been pressed into service as impromptu chisels and the telltale marks of vise-grip teeth on assorted, rounded-off nuts and bolt heads. Plus real DMMs never look like they've been bobbing for apples in a tub of gearlube. And the true mechanics who have helped me out with my racecars over the years recognize immediately that I'm not one of them. In fact, they often call me by the name of another trade entirely.

You know, the one that cuts up meat for a living.

But back to DMMs and the way they pursue their craft. The first step, as mentioned above, is Diagnosis. This is the thing that really separates them from Parts Exchangers. The latter will just keep throwing new parts at every problem until either *a)* the problem is cured, *b)* the parts counterman runs out of parts, or, *c)* the vehicle's owner is forced into bankruptcy. Whichever comes first. Conversely, a true *maestro* DMM has the diagnostic expertise to actually figure out what's gone wrong before ever reaching for the ratchet handle. Still, their methods are as varied as those employed in the world of medicine. Some use an empirical, rational, pure-logic Western approach, while others are mystical, faith-healer types who lay their hands on the sickness in the metal or simply feel it through cosmic intuition. And, just as in the medical field, either path is correct if it winds up curing the blessed problem.

Which brings us to another interesting difference between medical doctors and DMMs. If a flesh-and-bone doctor screws up a diagnosis royally and the patient drops dead, he still sends his bill to Medicare or the insurance company or the family of the deceased. Oh, he may get hit with a lawsuit big enough to finance a Formula One team for the balance of the decade, but his profession has developed ways to protect him from that eventuality (incidentally supporting the bulk of two other professions, malpractice lawyers and insurance underwriters, in the process). But when an Auto Mechanic screws up, he usually ends up putting whatever he messed up right again. Often on his own time and at his own expense.

To bring the concept of diagnosis into practical focus, let me tell you a true story from the days of my callow youth. I was an undergrad at Michigan State University back in the days of peace signs, love beads, strange new chemical compounds, marches on Washington and *"KILL, BUBBA, KILL!"* and, as a heavily infected sports car and motorsports junkie, I became friendly with the owner/salesman/front man/shop foreman of the tiny local Volvo dealer, one Bruce Stratton. I was studying filmmaking and graduate-level screwing off, and Bruce was sort of the black sheep of a well-to-do family who simply liked to fool around with cars. Bruce was also an amateur racer of some repute, and he had bought an honest-to-goodness, ex-works, 289 Shelby Cobra race car with which to amuse himself. We met one day when I'd stopped by to leave a circular trail of saliva tracks around the Cobra on his showroom floor.

Bruce had a mechanic—a *real* mechanic—working for him whose name escapes me now, but he was short and tough and bulky as a fireplug, wore his hair in a Navy-cut flattop, and had an X-rated tattoo on his sewer-pipe-diameter forearm. I remember he used to race a pretty red '57 Chevy hobby-stocker at the local quarter-mile oval, just for laughs. There was another partner in the Volvo business, a guy who wasn't around all the time on account of he had to take care of this and that at his family's furniture business. His name was R.J. Hull, and he built and raced an F Prod Volvo P1800 that he flat-towed to the tracks on its rain tires with the racing slicks piled up inside. R.J. was about as nice and easygoing a guy as you'd ever want to meet. Oh, maybe there was something a little, well, *dangerous* about the way he'd smile and stare off through brick walls. Or how his eyes would narrow down and the way he'd set his jaw when he strapped his helmet on and climbed behind the wheel of his racecar. R.J. won himself the SCCA National Championship in that P1800. Twice. You can look it up if you want.

But we were talking about diagnostic skills, weren't we?

Well, I wound up buying Bruce's wife's Volvo122S after I blew up the second or third engine in my ancient VW convertible. For those of you who may not be familiar with the 122S, it was a really neat car. While the PV444 and PV544 models that came before had the dated look of slightly shrunken '40 Fords, the 122S was much more modern and up-to-date. It looked like a slightly shrunken '52 Plymouth. But it was nice to drive, comfortable on long trips, handled amazingly well, and the shifter was certainly better than a Mack, Diamond Reo or White. Unfortunately, it was a terrible color: Dull Battleship Gray, inside and out. But it was hell for sturdy, and, as students never have any money left (as opposed to poor people, who never have any money, period), sturdiness was a resounding virtue.

One day, several months into my ownership of the 122S, it started to make a noise like a washing machine full of sour balls on the spin cycle. I lifted the hood and listened intently. I went and got a big screwdriver and placed one end (the handle, thank God) into my ear and probed various places on the engine with the other end, emulating a diagnostic trick I had seen real mechanics use. I discovered that there are a lot of little guys with tiny ball-peen hammers wailing away and tossing buckets of steel marbles bearings around inside a running engine. So I called on the collective automotive genius of my Russian History class:

"Sounds like a rod knock to me."

"Naw, it's a lifter."

"Pull one spark plug wire at a time and listen."

"YYEEEOOOOWWWW!!!"

That last one was me.

I finally motored on down to Bruce's place, looking for a little free advice (the only kind I could afford). I was trying to figure out how to explain tactfully that I was, umm, somewhat financially embarrassed and therefore unable to assume the role of actual *customer*, but that I just wanted to, ahh, kind of find out, err, what the problem might be and how I, ahem, might be able to repair same by myself. I no sooner pulled in the garage door and switched off than Bruce's mechanic bellowed: "$#(':)%?@ timing gear's ready to fall right out of that %$#:@*$ thing."

So much for Diagnosis.

The next skill of the DMM is knowledge of Tools. When my wife and I had our shop, I observed mechanics with great and varied assortments of tools. I recall we had one, a short, pencil-thin Appalachian type with bulging thyroid eyes, slicked-back hillbilly hair, and a protruding Adam's apple, who showed up for his first day, fresh out of trade school, carrying every tool he owned in what appeared to be a lunch box. Conversely, we had another fellow—a tall, muscular Viking type with a passion for fast cars—who, thanks to an insurance claim of perhaps dubious validity, owned at least one of everything in the entire Snap-On catalog. And neither one of them could change a damn spark plug without cracking the insulator or stripping the threads. Or both.

The third skill of the *true* Auto Mechanic is Operational Strategy, i.e., Now That I Know What's Wrong, and I Have The Tools To Fix It, just how do I go about Getting It Did? The truth is that there is no substitute for experience. For example: I think that performing a clutch job on an XK-E is just about the most difficult thing a man can do besides striking a match on a wet cake of soap. That's because I've agonized through a couple of them without benefit of an experienced hand beside mine, and I'm thoroughly convinced that this particular series of Jaguars were put together to stay together. Sealed, like bank vaults. First you try going in through the transmission tunnel like most other British cars. Only there isn't any, on account of it's part of the welded-up monocoque. So then you try hauling the motor and trans out the top with the bonnet removed. Strike two. The thing doesn't clear by two inches or more without some major hacksaw surgery to the upper front crossmember. How about taking the head off and dropping the whole gargantuan, locomotive-sized mess out the bottom? To do an effing *clutch* job? Now some smart-aleck Jag mechanic is going to write in and describe, in condescending detail, how easy it is to R&R a clutch on an E-Type. And furthermore how he does two a day, one before morning tea and one after, and then takes the afternoon off. Bah! Where was he when I needed him?

See what I mean about experience?

Remember the bad timing gear on my 122S? Well, Bruce and his mechanic were getting ready to close up shop and step down the street for a few rounds of pool and a couple of cold ones. I gave them my very best basset-hound eyes, and they reluctantly agreed to let me work on the Volvo while they worked on other, more important things. The mechanic pointed into the engine compartment and rattled off the directions: *"Pull that @#*$%! and then those #%@$^!! bolts out and watch that the %$#:@! &^%*$*@!! doesn't %$@&$#!!!"* He was a man of few and amazingly versatile words.

They disappeared into the gathering night and I began, carefully following his colorful directions. Lo and behold, in less than four or five multiples of the flat-rate time for the entire job, I actually had the timing cover off and the culprit gear exposed. And it was easy to appreciate the source of the noise. The Volvo timing gear features a steel inner ring keyed onto the camshaft and a steel outer ring meshing into the other timing gear. For reasons I have never fathomed, the canny Swedes elected to fill the space between those two metal rings with some sort of beeswax-colored plastic. What was happening on my particular car (and on most all Volvos of this design sooner or later) was a sort of mutual tissue-rejection between the metal and the plastic. Bruce had left me a brand new set of gears and a gasket, and his mechanic even showed me three times how to line up the timing marks so that the valves and pistons wouldn't try to park in the same stall when I turned the motor over.

So I took off the timing gear nuts. Hey, this was going to be a snap. All I had to do was take the old gears off and put the new ones on and, *voila,* I'd be finished. So I pulled on the old timing gear. It wouldn't budge. So I pulled on it again. Harder. But it refused to move. So I got two screwdrivers and tried to pry it off. After which I got another, somewhat larger pair of screwdrivers to replace the ones I'd bent. Then I got a hammer and tapped on it. Then I tried prying and tapping together. Then tapping and prying. I tapped. I pried. I levered. I yanked. I pulled. I cursed. I sweated. I swore. And I made no impression whatsoever on the timing gear, which, to all outward appearances, was about as ready to fall out as a dangling baby tooth before I even started.

I was exhausted and thoroughly humiliated by the time Bruce and his mechanic ricocheted back into the garage, obviously well on their way to a squinty and painful noon breakfast the following morning. "You still here?" the mechanic boomed, punctuating with a beer belch of sufficient magnitude to shake dust from the rafters.

"Uhh, I'm having a little trouble..." I offered meekly.

"You work like a #$%&@!! Old woman!" he bellowed, rummaging around on the tool bench. He came back with a crowbar better than a yard long, a piece of heavy pipe another yard long, and a short-handled sledge that must have run six or seven pounds. He jammed the end of the crowbar deep behind the gear, slid the pipe over it to multiply the leverage a few thousandfold, and gave the gear a mighty wallop with the sledge. I swear, it sounded like a manhole cover hitting the pavement after a six-story drop.

The timing gear popped off like a damn bottle cap.

Because that's the crowning, secret skill of a true, master mechanic. Knowing how much of a hell of a *whop!* you can give it to bust it loose.

Only without breaking it....

ROLLING YOUR OWN

*OR: HOW TO IMPRESS A NEW WIFE
WITH YOUR MOTORSPORTS HOBBY!*

ORIGINALLY PUBLISHED IN
BRITISH CAR
DECEMBER, 1993

I'm sure

a proper anthropological study would show that amateur racing types, while publicly poo-poohing the danger aspect of the sport, stand ready at the drop of a bar tab to relate to anyone within earshot all the wide-eyed close calls and hilarious near-misses they have endured, enjoyed, and moreover escaped. Ask a simple, rube question like "So, you ever had an *accident?*" and, in less time than it takes to blow the foam off your beer, you'll have every would-be Michael Schumacher in the joint playing *Can You Top This?* with hackle raising stories of their own Brilliant Avoidances, Blind Luck, and Bent Remains....

The fact is that trying to make an automobile go as fast as it can (even if said automobile is a bone-stock Bugeye) can be a truly fraught and perilous endeavor. And especially so when carried out in the company of other likewise hardheaded credit and/or insurance risks hell-bent on beating you to the checker. In spite of that, our little end of motorsport has developed a pretty decent safety record over the years, mostly due to intelligent car prep and driver licensing requirements, tireless support from our corner workers and other volunteer officials, and moreover plenty of room to screw up and lots of soft stuff to run into at most modern racetracks. As I tell the worried wives of my VSCDA driving school students (or husbands, as the case may often be these days): "Hey, if you like to drive fast, the safest place to do it—by far!—is on a racetrack, where you have everything working in your favor."

And that's precisely what I was telling my brand new wife Carol one early May morning back in 1974. I had just stumbled in from the tiny one-car garage behind our equally tiny one-room apartment, where I had been spending the greater majority of my dusk-to-dawn hours ever since our honeymoon (hours, I might add, that are most usually reserved for post-nuptial bliss amongst your average rank-and-file newlyweds). But I had a perfect excuse, on account of I was just putting the finishing touches on my new, ultra-killer TR3 racecar which just absolutely *had* to be on the track that coming Sunday or...well...er...or I might not get that surprise early-ayem phone call from Ron Dennis or Roger Penske come Monday morning.

Let me set the scene. Carol and I were married on Valentine's Day, 1974 (also incidentally her birthday, cleverly finessing me out of two major Important Dates To Remember—not to mention presents to buy!—every year since) and I had somehow convinced her that what we really needed to do was quit our jobs, borrow seed money from every relative too embarrassed to say "no," and open ourselves a foreign car repair shop on Chicago's up-and-coming near north side. In truth, it was a hair-brained and half-baked scheme (not to mention poorly executed) and I can best sum up that shamefully self-indulgent period of my life by admitting that I used most of the money not specifically earmarked for lease, light, and phone service deposits on a big, blowout Grand Opening Party. To which I naturally invited all my great racing friends and hardly anybody else. It was one hell of a prayer meeting, all right, what with a rented copy of the movie *Grand Prix* playing over and over and over again on a similarly rented screen and plenty of beer and munchies for fuel and lots of strange and interesting sportycars parked all over the place (some of which, available garage space being what it is in downtown Chicago, threatening to remain as long-term residents afterwards). Finally, towards the end of the evening, we culminated the festivities with a noisy, smoky, and dizzyingly fume-laden indoor wheelie contest aboard Bruce Smerch's well-used—and badly in need of a ring job—Yamaha 250 ring-ding. What a swell Grand Opening bash! Only these friends of mine, it should be noted, did mostly all their own mechanical work, and, like virtually all bush-league racers everywhere, were inevitably flat deadass broke from the last beer of the race weekend Sunday evening to the following payday. As any sharp marketing consultant would gladly point out (for a price, anyway), they did not amount to a particularly "viable" or "promising" customer base.

But that's why I loved them, because we had so much in common. We were all slaves of the same drug and infected with the same debilitating need, and if there's any addiction more consuming, devastating or relentless in the human experience, I've yet to come across it. Not even in my hippie days. So it didn't take long before I was broke, too (especially after that big sendoff party) and coming to the horrid realization that good, employable sportycar mechanics were as rare as championship-winning baseball teams and unsullied virgins in our particular section of Chicago. Worse yet, I was B.R. (Between Racecars) then, seeing as how I'd parted out my old killer TR3 shortly before we got engaged (the one with the WWI camouflage paint job to hide all the lumps and the tiny, matching biplane rear wing mounted on the rear deck) in a futile attempt to go Formula Ford racing and make some sort of name for myself.

Besides "Mud," I mean.

So my racing prospects looked bleak indeed. I had no car, no money, and Carol and I were treading furiously in ever-deeper financial water at Mellow Motors. And that's when my personal racing mentor Mike Whelan stepped in. Now Mike was a tough old bird, a grizzled, mean-faced veteran machinist with the general look and demeanor of the guy who pulls the switch on Death Row. But he loved racing and TR3s, and helped a lot more people than me learn the ropes and what this sport is all about. Even if he wasn't particularly pleasant about it along the way. Anyhow, Mike had this old, used-up, worn-out, spare TR3 racecar sitting in the garage beside his own, and he surprised the hell out of me one day when he asked, with just the faintest hint of a twinkle in his eye, if I'd like to chauffeur it for the season.

Now you have to understand that this particular TR3 looked just a tad rough and raggedy, what with umpty-dozen racing seasons in Lord only knows how many different hands under its lap belts before it got put out to pasture. But I had to admit it was the right sort of car. Back then I was blindly, even foolishly loyal to Triumphs, mostly because my first street sports car had been a TR3A (at the tender and impressionable age of sixteen) and yet another example became my first-ever racecar about a dozen years later. Based on this backlog of solid empirical data, I'd convinced myself (with the aid of proper stimulants) that a TR3 was unquestionably *the* Ultimate Weapon for E-Production class racing. And it's precisely this sort of blind, witless allegiance that causes most of your major world wars.

So I took Mike up on his offer. I mean, what did I have to lose? Besides, there was a natural yin-and-yang synergy to our partnership. I fancied myself something of a budding chassis expert (there not being any hard evidence as yet to the contrary) while Mike was cocksure he could build as wicked a race engine as the next guy if only somebody—hell, *any*body—felt like shelling out the money for parts. Within a six pack we had cemented an unholy alliance whereby we would each toss in a little cash (and/or press our credit card limits) and Mike would build us a proper Stage-Umpteen race motor while I concentrated on crafting the trickest, best-handling TR3 chassis in all of Christendom. No question we would be serious contenders for the championship.

In fact, it went without saying.

But we said it a lot anyway....

And so we set to work.

The first race of the Midwestern Council season came. And went. And of course Mike and I were just spectators hanging on the damn fence, seeing as how my super-duper chassis was still scattered all over my garage floor in assorted milk crates and cardboard boxes, while Mike's killer motor was meanwhile scattered all over the whole damn continent, being massaged by assorted Proven Triumph Wizards who never _once_ kept a delivery promise. As a machinist himself, perhaps Mike should have expected that. In any case, I had the chassis more-or-less done and ready for painting a couple weeks later, and I well recall the warm spring night my friends Bob DeStefano and Pat Fitzgerald dropped by to help out with the spray job. We had to keep the doors shut so neither my landlord, neighbors, or the police could see what we were up to (can you say _Fire Hazard?)_ which ensured that every single molecule of lacquer vapor stayed right in there with us. In fact, the beer was really an unnecessary extra, and, by the time we were done, virtually everything in that garage had been painted. Including my landlord's pet cat. But he looked absolutely stunning, since I'd picked a tasteful, creamy, ivory-hued off-white with deep, rich, metallic brown accents. The car came out pretty nice, too (in spite of the fumes!) winding up with the same handsome visual impact as an extremely large saddle shoe.

My wife nicknamed the TR3 "Spats."

But Mike's killer engine still wasn't finished, so we decided to plug in an old $30 junkyard motor he had lying around his garage for our first race. Just to see how every-thing else worked, you know? And it worked pretty damn good, if I do say so myself. Sure, we were down on power (pathetically down on power would be more like it) but the car handled fine and nothing major fell off. At least until the engine blew, that is. Turns out we didn't have a baffled oil pan on that particular motor, and you could actually hear the old lump running dry at the pickup all the way around the Turn 3/3A carousel. But I was embroiled in a swell scrap with a blue-and-yellow Porsche bathtub for maybe fifth place and not paying too much attention. Besides, Mike had told me to just _"run her 'till she blows."_ Which she did. In comprehensive fashion. On maybe the third or fourth lap. _BANG! Clatterclatterclatterclatter._ But, hey, it was only thirty bucks, right? Of course, that's if you don't count the entry fee or the cheap hotel room or the gas money or the wear and tear on the...well, now you know why broken-down racing bums should _never_ keep accurate books.

You really don't want to know....

That particular race was ultimately won by the mustard-colored Porsche Speedster of my friend Bob Hindman, but not until he withstood a mighty attack from the handsome, well driven, but woefully under-powered and under-financed Saab Sonnet V4 of my good Irish buddy Tommy Fennel. It was a late-edition Sonnet painted deep royal blue with a white shamrock on the nose for luck, and Tommy could run damn near dead even with Bob's Porsche around our home circuit at Blackhawk Farms. You'd have to say Bob's Porsche was perhaps a little more car than the Saab and that Bob also enjoyed a slight edge as far as race savvy and experience. But Tommy was a typically crazy-brave Irishman who wheeled the bloody pee out of that car every time he got in it, and that can be a great equalizer as long as the old cashola holds out. The bottom line is that Tommy gave Bob all he could handle—and then some!—and no question Mike and my goal was to prove that a TR3 could run heads-up with those guys. And maybe even *beat* 'em, too!

As if the rest of the world gave two shits, you know?

Come two weeks later, Mike had gathered in all his pieces and bolted together one snappy-looking TR3 race motor, and I'd spent the time putting proper numbers and graphics and assorted doodads and finishing touches on our car. Like I spelled out "MELLOW MOTORS" beneath the grille and "JUST MARRIED" across the spare tire cover in back, both in hopes that my new spouse would consider this a cooperative venture rather than the lunatic obsession of a reappearing stranger who was now soiling her linens and sucking her checking account dry on a weekly basis.

We all rode out to Blackhawk together with "Spats" hitched on Mike's trailer behind us, and I'd have to say we were feeling pretty optimistic about our chances. Fact is, we were downright smug. Or at least Mike and I were. To tell the truth, Carol looked a little of tired and nervous. But I guess that's to be expected, seeing as how this was her first race since we were married and she wasn't exactly used to getting up at 4 ayem on a Sunday morning so she could take a shower and put her makeup on and go over to the shop to meet Mike and load up the car and tow off into the fading darkness about the time the paper boy usually comes around so her idiot husband can make his blessed 8 ayem drivers' meeting at Blackhawk. If you're a racer and your wife or girl-friend is reading this right now, that sound you hear is the gnashing of her teeth. Better go out and buy her some nice flowers or something. Soon....

Just on account, you know?

But back to the racetrack. From the minute we put our new car on the circuit, we were on-the-pace *competitive*. Better than competitive, even, as we either took pole or outside front row in qualifying (I can't remember for sure, but ask me a couple years from now and it will most certainly be the pole). And came The Race, with me in our spanking fresh, ivory-and brown TR3 with "JUST MARRIED" spelled out across the back squared off against Bob Hindman's wicked little mustard-colored Porsche, the both of us weaving menacingly back and forth on the pace lap in order to heat up the tires and intimidate the living hell out of each other. And what a race we had! From the drop of the green flag, Bob and I ran doorhandle-to-doorhandle and snoot-to-boot, passing and re-passing a couple times every lap. And, all the while, Tommy Fennel's deep blue Sonnet filled our mirrors to overflowing, lurking and feinting and dodging for a way to get by. I couldn't believe it!

And that, of course, is when the damn throttle linkage fell off. Just like that. And there was nothing I could do but idle sadly around to the pits while Bob and Tommy disappeared towards corner one, still beating the bloody hell out of each other with joyous abandon. *Shit!* I clambered out and Mike came over and popped the hood and of course it didn't take long at all to locate the @#!!*&#?! swivel end that had dropped off the damn linkage arm (as they are wont to do) because some dumb asshole who'd had it apart about a dozen times to adjust the linkage (hint: it wasn't Mike) forgot to replace the stinking cotter pin the last time he put it back together. So Mike went back to his toolbox and got another tiny cotter pin and fixed it, and then looked up to discover—lo and behold—that the race wasn't over yet. We looked at each other, and Mike suggested I should maybe go back out and at least get a finish out of the deal (instead of a DNF) since even a few points might come in handy when we hit the stretch run for the championship at the end of the season. Besides, it was a way to salvage some small scrap of honor (if not actual glory) for our proud, new machine.

So I climb back in, do up the belts, and head back out into the fray. Only whom should I spy in my Raydot mirrors while exiting pit lane? Why, Bob and Tommy, of course, coming up fast down the pit straight and still obviously going at it hammer and tongs for the lead. By all rights I *should* have pulled meekly aside and waited for them to streak past so as not to spoil their race. But, hey, I had about fifty yards or so on them, a decent head of steam up, and by God I was not about to let any damn E-Production Porsche Speedster or Saab Sonnet get around our new killer TR3 racecar without at least *earning* it. So I set my jaw, put my foot down, and drove that car to the absolute limit of my ability.

Or maybe just a little beyond....

See, there's this gentle dogleg left around Station 2 at Blackhawk, and back in those days (not having yet met up with the Kink at Road America, the Diving Turn at Lime Rock, the fast, bumpy downhill carousel into The Boot at Watkins Glen, or the hair-raising, high speed Dip at Road Atlanta) I considered it a pretty damn intimidating stretch of asphalt. In a 2-litre production car on the tires of the period, it was just *barely* flat out, and you had to calmly but decisively "thread the needle" if you wanted to make it without lifting. I'd gotten to where I could do it without too much grimacing or seat cushion dimpling, but in truth it still made my hands strangle up just a tad on the steering wheel every trip through. And, naturally enough, that's where all hell broke loose. To this very day, I couldn't tell you if:

> *a)* I hit a patch of oil
>
> *b)* Something broke on the car
>
> *c)* My thread missed the eyelet of the needle entirely.

All I know is that suddenly the back end shot out from under me and I found myself skittering along a precarious 45-degree angle to the track's natural trajectory. I instinctively grabbed for a fistful of opposite lock, but all that accomplished was to make the car snap around the other way. Viciously. And, in less time than it takes to tell, I was well on my way to learning that age-old racer's theorem: *"if it snakes three times and you haven't caught it, you may as well put your head down...."*

Which I did.

The trackside scenery scythed towards me in a great sideways rush (imagine a fastball's view of an oncoming bat!) and then something hooked a rut underneath and everything started tumbling. And cartwheeling. And tumbling some more. Sky and ground/sky and ground/sky and ground flickered around me like an old time movie on a bum projector, and then all of a sudden everything slammed to a frightening halt that was deep and hollow and pitch-freaking-black inside. My brain was still racing at warp speed—bracing itself for the next series of impacts!—but I gradually came to realize that everything had gone all quiet and my nostrils were filling with the loamy scent of rye grass and upended clods of farm country turf and...and freaking *gasoline!*

OH, SHIT!

I unhooked my belts in frantic slow motion, terrified that I was about to become some ghastly sort of Castrol-basted barbecue (and kosher, no less!) but just then a squadron of strangely upside-down, white-clad corner worker legs came scurrying up from all directions, banded together in a single mighty heave, and created an impromptu escape hatch just large enough for me to scramble through into the welcome daylight. I was *free*! Even more important, I was 100 percent OK (although I must admit our "championship" TR3 looked a bit the worse for wear) thanks to the comer workers, safety equipment, runoff room, etc. mentioned at the top of this story.

A moment later Bob Hindman and Tommy Fennel surprised the heck out of me by pulling right off the track and stopping to see if I was all right (or perhaps to check if any loose change had fallen out of my pockets while the TR3 was flipping and somersaulting its way across the landscape). Geez, I thought to myself, that's awful damn sporting of them, abandoning their race just to see how I was....

Except of course they weren't. Seems they'd taken the checkered flag just about the time yrs. trly. was pulling out of pit lane! The race was freaking *OVER!* And there I was, running like a damn madman, trying like hell to get away from two guys who weren't even *racing* anymore....

All of which made me feel pretty damn stupid.

As you can well imagine.

In fact, that's precisely what I was thinking as they loaded me into the ambulance for a perfunctory trip to the trackside medical center. The safety crew takes you there after any serious wreck, even if you feel perfectly fine. Just to see if your blood pressure is somewhere on the charts and that your eyeballs are still pointing in approximately the same direction. And naturally the meat wagon passed directly in front of my lovely new wife as it headed into the paddock, and about all I could do was flash her a sheepish wave and a prize-winning Village Idiot grin.

Looking back, I was still pretty green at this racing stuff when Carol and I were first married, and finding your feet and learning the ropes inevitably takes a little time and seasoning. Or, as some wise sage or other once put it, "Doing things *right* comes from experience, and experience almost always comes from doing them *wrong.*"

So you'd think I'd have the hang of it by now, what with all the time I've put in and all the patently stupid and occasionally cataclysmic mistakes I've made along the way. And yet I still manage to surprise myself every now and again with some brand new and totally revolutionary approach to screwing up. But if you think it's taken *me* a long time to catch on, you should really take a long, hard look at my wife. After all, it's nearly thirtysomething racing seasons later and we're still together....

God bless her for it, too!

Body and Soul

Is "Real" a Relative Term?

ORIGINALLY PUBLISHED IN
VINTAGE MOTORSPORT
MAY/JUNE 1993

"Daddy

what's a *real* car?" That's what my precocious 12-year-old was asking me as we strolled through the paddock at the 1991 edition of the Chicago Historic Races at Road America. Seems he'd just overheard a discussion wherein several self-styled automotive experts (his father included) passed off one hot-looking Italian sports/racer as "not a *real* car" while giving a respectful nod of approval to another that—at least to his innocent eyes—appeared relatively equivalent.

"Well, my boy, " I said, giving it a couple good "harrumphs" like Nigel Bruce as Dr. Watson opposite Basil Rathbone's thoroughly definitive Sherlock Holmes in those great old black-and-white movies. "Let me explain it to you. A *real* car is, well, ahh, err, sorta...." And, in hardly any time at all, the emperor had no clothes.

For, hidden inside that simple, straightforward 12-year-old's question was the Gordian Knot of our beloved hobby-cum-sport-cum-business. While all motorsports addicts lust after certain specific marques, models, and even particular chassis numbers, it should be obvious that no racecar was ever built to be immortal. In fact, precisely the opposite. Goals in a race shop seldom extend much past next weekend at Monaco or maybe next year at Le Mans, and just about every vehicle rolling out the overhead doors represents a down-to-the-wire, last-minute, back-to-back all-nighter compromise between what *wants* to be done, what *needs* to be done and what *can* be done with the time and resources available. And from the moment a new racecar fires up in anger for its first test run, it is committed to a single, simply-understood Suicide Mission: *Beat the opposition to the finish line.* Period. Full stop.

Surely the best of them blaze across the motorsports horizon like skyrockets, enjoying a few brief moments of glory before arcing into their downward spiral and fizzling out (while the lads burning the midnight oil back home work on *new* rockets that will hopefully shoot a bit higher and farther and burn a shade or two brighter). In the meantime, the old nails are bored, stroked, cammed, carbed, lightened, lowered and generally drilled through like Swiss cheese in a desperate effort to keep pace with the opposition. Then, as soon as the new lot are ready, the old stalwarts are rendered off to privateers, unceremoniously cast aside on the scrapheap of mid-grid and worse, trickling down ever-poorer from presentable to raggedy to fulltime junk as the real world spirals away from them like a spinning top....

And then they're generally forgotten; packed away in dark, cobwebbed corners of forgotten sheds and garages like prom flowers pressed between the leaves of never-opened high school yearbooks. They possess no real value until some person appears (check your mirror) who aches to possess them. Someone who cares and remembers (and, moreover, has the ready cash!) and is fortunate enough to find their decrepit remains hidden under dirty tarps and packed away in dozens of ancient coffee tins and greasy cardboard boxes.

Then life begins again.

The car is re-invented all over again—as if for the very first time!—and, after three or four multiples of the money and hours originally estimated, the new owner can finally lean back against a perfectly pounded and riveted aluminum fender and run his trembling hands up and down the chrome plated velocity stacks, muttering "it's mine...*mine...MINE...HAHAHAHAHAHAHAHA!"* as if owning the damn metal somehow imbues him with a share of the glory as well.

Call it *Collector's Syndrome.* And it's generally not pretty.

Ah, but racing cars differ from other popular families, classes and phylum of collectibles in several important ways. First, unlike paintings, postage stamps or pre-Columbian pot fragments, racecars must be *used* to be properly *appreciated,* rather than *appreciated* to be properly *used.* Second, while other artworks and artifacts exist as finite objects, racecars usually represent an ongoing mechanical *process,* wherein bits and pieces are constantly being worn out, replaced, broken, repaired, modified, deleted and/or regenerated to keep the damn thing running competitively. Or, later in its career, just running. As a result, the configuration and presentation of any particular vehicle can be arbitrarily frozen at a particular historical instant—like a snapshot—but there is often no such thing as a "definitive version."

Complicating matters further is the fact that the worth (and, subsequently, *market value*) of any vintage racecar inevitably reflects two totally separate yet forever-entangled perceptions. *Body* and *Soul,* if you will. The "body" (i.e., the nuts-and-bolts reality of the piece) is easy enough to comprehend: An assemblage of cast, forged, hammered and hewn bits of alloy that somehow transformed the builder's creativity, resources and sense of craftsmanship into a realized whole with a singular seat-of-the-pants character and, hopefully, race-winning speed and stamina.

But the "soul" of a racecar is ever so much harder to define. Perhaps it's the way a certain make, model or specific chassis number serves as a *vessel for history and imagination.* This elusive and amorphous aura exists entirely separately from (and, in fact, transcends) the base metal and finite spatial reality of the piece, and often serves as the real "substance" of the asking price. Since this phenomenon of a racecar's "soul" is very much in the eye of the beholder, experienced traders always advise *caveat emptor* in regard to the used-and-abused racecar business. For, while experts may agree that Judy Garland wore three pairs of magic slippers during the filming of "The Wizard of Oz" (or was it four?) there is no shortage of low pumps, Elmer's Glue-All and ruby-red sequins on the open market (not to mention crafty leather beaters who'll do you a much nicer job of it than the prop boys at MGM ever did).

While an educated eye can readily ascertain the relative *accuracy* of a particular chassis, engine, intake manifold, body contour or castellated fastener, *authenticity* is a far thornier and more abstract sort of proposition. Take, for instance, the case of the lucky English gent who got his hands on the recognizable remains of a Ferrari 246 Dino Formula 1 car (the type that took Mike Hawthorn to the 1958 World Driving Championship by a single point over the brilliant but unlucky Stirling Moss and the last proper front-engined design to ever win a Grand Prix). While contemplating a total ground-up restoration, this chap had a swell idea. "Say, as long as I have to make *one* of everything on the bloody car, why not make *two*?" And so he did. The result was a perfect, bookend pair of Ferrari 246 Dino Grand Prix *monopostos* that were pretty much nut-for-nut and bolt-for-bolt identical. Yet he started with but one car and, naturally enough, but one legit chassis number. As you can imagine, the Guardians of Public Outrage on the U.K. vintage scene had a great old English Flap about it. And the English are truly World Class when it comes to that sort of thing. In fact, I believe they told him at one point that he could race the "real" car, but not "the other one." Problem was, nobody could tell the difference!

Or howzabout the infamous "James Dean Lotus," an engineless hodgepodge of Lotus 8, 9 and 10 components that the star-crossed actor/racer intended to campaign with a robust Offenhauser four-banger stuffed under the hood. At the time, the wily and resourceful Colin Chapman was probably only too happy to see so much redundant scrap rolling out of his shop on a single set of wheels. Meanwhile, at the other end of the transaction, young Dean was tragically killed in his Porsche 550 Spyder (ironically in a highway accident on his way to the races) before he ever so much as saw, let alone sat in, his new Lotus. The car was eventually sold off and raced for several years by John Timanus and others with a variety of engines, but, in truth, the car's real life history never came close to equaling the mist of Hollywood special-effects mystique swirling around James Dean's unfulfilled dreams. In any case, following 30-odd years of wandering and an incredibly convoluted scenario, rag-and-bone remnantes of this particular vehicle came to roost in the garages of two equally ardent U.K.-based Lotus *aficionados*. And, just like those amazing flatworms you studied in high school biology class, these bits miraculously regenerated themselves into–you guessed it!–two complete "James Dean" Loti. Okay, panelists*: Who had the REAL "James Dean" Lotus*? Well, of course, nobody there could figure it out either, and we had another fine old English Flap (the Brits do it better than anyone, don't they?), and this time it came complete with nasty letters, threatened lawsuits and all that sort of thing.

My, my, my.

I suppose one can understand all the above hoo-hah as it applies to truly rare and unique automobiles of which only a handful were produced (often complicated by the fact that neither Colin, Ettore, Enzo or others I could mention were particularly circumspect when it came to record keeping), but things get harder to fathom when considering more mundane machinery. For example, conventional wisdom holds that Colin Chapman built right around 132 of his wonderful Lotus 23 and 23B models, of which it is whispered a miraculous 150 or so survive to this day. Isn't that remarkable? Actually, it's not too hard to understand, since 23s are historically significant, lovely to look at, absolutely marvelous to drive and not too difficult to replicate. Or, as one well respected Lotus wrench unabashedly explained, "I can build you a brand-new 23 from scratch *cheaper* and *better* than I can 'restore' a used-up example that needs everything." But is such a creation a *real* car? "Certainly not!" I hear you shriek, beating your little fists on the kitchen table.

Ah, but who is to say?

It gets even worse in the more modern "Historic" race groups, where a lot of the favored iron springs from genuinely common automotive gene pools. Take the case of the one-man-band owner/wrench/racer who always wanted to campaign a Trans-Am Series-spec Camaro. Unlike early Loti and Grand Prix Ferraris, used Camaro remains are relatively easy to come by, and certainly the knowledge and hardware to prepare such a car is available to anybody willing to expend the time, research, elbow grease and hard cash. All of which this fellow was willing to do. Up to a point. Problem was, certain Powers-That-Be insisted that he start with a "real" Trans-Am chassis (meaning any piece-of-dogmeat garbage wagon that ever lined up *anywhere* on an official Trans-Am grid—even if it ran dead effing last and driven by some guy from West Bumjump,

Idaho, that nobody ever heard of before or since). Turns out the best deal he could find was the rusted-out hulk of a club racer that ran at the back end of the pack in one or two Trans Ams (before retiring in a cloud of smoke, anyway) and campaigned extensively on the amateur circuit until it was pretty much Regional Maintenanced to death. Yet the asking price was damn near half our hero's budget, on account of it was a "real" car. So instead he did what a lot of Trans-Am teams did back in ze olt dayz. He hunted down a decent, rust-free street chassis, cleaned it up, gutted it out, put in a period-correct roll structure, followed the factory books and blueprints to the letter, and *built* himself as accurate a Trans-Am privateer Camaro as you could find anywhere. Only it wasn't a "real" car, of course. Which still might have worked if he'd kept his mouth shut, but the poor guy was honest (and naïve) enough to tell everybody the truth about what he'd done. You should have heard the blessed uproar over how anyone would dare to show up with such a flagrant "cheater."

After all, his Camaro had no "soul."

But then consider the case of one of the nicer Yenko Stingers to appear on the vintage scene. I happened to notice its entire original (and thoroughly rotted-out!) Corvair unibody resting against the back wall of the shop from whence it came. And rightly so, too, since the poor old heap had been bent, banged, pranged, rusted-through and comprehensively used up over the years, and neither I nor the restorers saw a damn thing wrong with installing a stronger, cleaner, straighter and infinitely safer shell. But when you go and replace a complete unibody, what happens to the "real" car? And how different is this Corvair from the Camaro mentioned above, except that the Camaro's owner doesn't have a useless pile of junk with a torched-out hole where the "authentic" chassis number used to be cluttering up his garage?

And what about the so-called "replicars" we drool over in the magazines but can't quite figure out what we'd do with if we actually owned them? Should they, too, have a place under the vintage racing umbrella? Are they somehow less authentic than running dry sumps, roller rockers, Carillo rods, aluminum flywheels, Tilton throwout bearings and double-pumper Holleys on supposedly '50s-era V-8s? Or upgrading drum brakes to discs, or solid discs to vented discs? The answer perhaps has more to do with practicality and plain old human speed greed than anything to do with aesthetics or suitability for on-track enjoyment.

In an effort to help resolve all this confusion (fat chance!), may I humbly (ditto) set forth a few suggested definitions to put us all, as they say, on the same page:

Real Cars: Regardless of how many times they have been bent, broken, crashed, crushed, blown up, shattered or burned to the ground, or likewise how often they have been rebuilt, modified, reconfigured, cobbled, cut-up, discarded, picked over or packed away in cardboard boxes in three separate garages, or even considering how they may have been recently reassembled *in toto* from entirely new parts to a far higher standard than they were ever built in the first place, *Real Cars* are hereby defined as vehicles which have occupied the same continuous and recognizable hole in the atmosphere since they were originally thrown together at the last minute by the constructor of record (at least as agreed to by a majority of the people at the bar on any given evening).

Imitations: Cars done *in the style of* other, more valuable and authentic cars. As the popular cliché relates, "imitation is the sincerest form of flattery," and wouldn't you just love to see our vintage paddocks bristling with C- and D-Type Jaguars, pontoon-fendered Testa Rossas, Lotus Elevens, Porsche 550 Spyders and 289 Cobras? Sure you would! As long as they were faithful to the size, shape, general specifications and overall performance envelope of the originals, and also so long as they were properly identified as what they are. Creating rules to cover all the potential controversies could be a real hornet's nest, as some "replicars" are very true to the originals (like certain British C- and D-Type copies) and others, though far from historically accurate, do manage to capture much of the original car's flavor and character (Westfield Eleven, Ferrari V-12 rebodies, Beck 550 Spyders and the better "Cobras"). On the other hand, nobody wants to see a VeeDub floorpan with an ersatz fiberglass body parading around like it's an MG TD (or—horrors!—a Type 35 Bugatti). May I suggest the Law of Solomon (each case of eligibility and group classification evaluated according to its particular merits) might work better than the Law of Hammurabi (everything written down in a codified set of rules–complete with ambiguities, obtuse definitions and the inevitable loopholes). Far as I can see, the central question should always be:

Does it *look* like a duck?

Does it *waddle* like a duck?

Does it *quack* like a duck? If so, perhaps it deserves an opportunity to *fly* like a duck as well–just so long as it's properly labeled as an imitation and never tries to pass itself off as the real thing—either on the racetrack or when the stacks of money and pink slips are changing hands.

Bitsa: A car whipped up from original factory spares mysteriously discovered after selling prices escalated through the ceiling. Now exactly where all these brand-spanking-new old parts come from is beyond me, and those of you who spend five hours in the can every month thumbing through the tissue-thin pages of *Hemmings Motor News* are familiar with the notation "N.O.S." which, near as I can figure, must stand for "Not Overly Suspicious" or "Nearly Original Stuff" or "Natural Ontogeny Specious" or somesuch. In any case, most "unraced spares" and "flatworm cars" (see James Dean Lotus story above) involve bitsas. Or at least bits of bitsas.

Forgery: An imitation or bitsa somebody tries to pass off as a real car.

Fake: A forgery your friend bought.

Car With a Clouded History: A forgery you bought.

Obviously, the legal, historical, ethical, emotional, moral and especially monetary implications of the above can become terribly confusing, and perhaps it would be in the best interests of all concerned to recognize that there is a difference between what a car is (or is not) on the racetrack ("body") and what it is (or is not) as it rolls across the auction block ("body" *and* "soul"). As to my 12-year-old's original question about what makes a "real" car, I ultimately threw my hands skyward and echoed the sentiments of equally frustrated Supreme Court Justice Potter Stewart, who tried desperately to pin down a workable definition of obscenity in 1964. "I can't tell you exactly what it is," hizzoner finally admitted, "but I sure as hell know it when I see it."

DISCLAIMER

The above piece includes many paddock rumors, third-hand stories and other hearsay evidence related in such a manner as to indicate that they might, in fact, be facts. The author, however, makes no claims as to their accuracy, authenticity or legitimacy (even though I heard a lot of them personally from totally unimpeachable sources whom I can't quite seem to recall at the moment on account of it was getting real late and maybe I'd had a few too many). Anyhow, they're great yarns, and some of them might even actually be true. Besides, I only repeat them in order to illustrate my point, whatever it may be.

WANTED: FREE RIDES IN FINE, SPORTED PROVENANCE SPORTS CARS, SPORTS/RACERS. CASE SHEER OF PRIME CONCERN. FAST, A SMALL NIFTINESS AND GT PROTOTYPES AND OF THAT CONSIDERATION AND WELL-PREPARED EXAMPLES OF FAMOUS CLASSIC SHAMELESS BLOODY, BLUE-BLOODED GOBSMACKING COOLNESS CARS. AUTHENTICITY AND RIDE MOOCH BS LEVY IN SPREAD A LITTLE PRINTER'S INK AROUND AND JUST MAYBE, IN WHICH PROVENANCE AND OF COURSE THEY DON'T HAVE ANY. I CAN SPREAD A LITTLE PROVIDE SOME, FOR CARE OF THE AUTHENTICITY YOU CRAVE(!). CONTACT WEBSITE AT WWW.LASTOPENROAD.COM! FORMULA CARS. UNLESS OF EXAMPLES OF FAMOUS CLASSIC WILL SUFFICE (AND AUTHENTICITY AND

THE ECSTASY OF THE AGONY

LIVING WITH A TR3 WAS DIVINE TORTURE....

ORIGINALLY PUBLISHED IN SLIGHTLY SHORTER FORM IN
AutoWeek
JANUARY 23, 1984

The evolution of the British sports

car has always been one of life's great mysteries. How did this tiny island nation famous for practicality, civility and inclement weather ever manage to produce vehicles so impractical, uncivil, and featuring weather protection no better than a leaky canvas tent? But build them they did, and during the late '50s and early '60s, Americans were buying every last one they could ship across the Atlantic. There were the MGs, Jaguars, Healeys and Sunbeams, and then the one that captured the hearts and minds of tens of thousands of Americans as an affordable distillation of what a true British sports car ought to be: the Triumph TR3.

It could hardly be called a handsome or beautiful car. Rather, it had a jaunty, Churchillian Bulldog friendly-toughness about it. And if it lacked style and glamour, it fairly oozed character. In fact, a typical TR3 would often leave drippings of character wherever it was parked.

Mechanically, the TR3 followed the classic British sports car recipe. First, find a heavy, lump-of-iron pushrod motor from either a mail truck, commercial vehicle, or piece of earth-moving equipment. In the TR3's case, the source was a Massey-Ferguson tractor. Really. Then transform said lump into a real Sports Car motor by fitting a pair of S.U. carburetors and a throaty exhaust. Blend in a four-speed gearbox with optional Laycock de Normanville electric overdrive for highway cruising and a steep rear end ratio for jackrabbit starts. Then bolt said components into a heavy-yet-willowy ladder-type frame (running the frame rails *under* the back axle), affix suspension components from a nondescript family sedan (sorry, saloon), add in front disc brakes, optional wire wheels, gutty two-place bodywork and frost with Lucas electrics to ensure that the owner stays home in inclement weather. It's easy to see how Stonehenge and the TR3 sprang from the same cultural gene pool.

But the totality of the TR3 was always something more than the sum of its rather pedestrian parts. If it wasn't particularly fast in an absolute sense (although performance was respectable), the combination of a narrow track, choppy ride, skinny Dunlop Road Speed tires, a rear axle that had a mind of its own, and a torquey engine with a

WWI fighter plane exhaust note gave a great impression of speed at even moderate velocities. And that's what the TR3 was all about: it was a four-alarm ball to drive on a sunny afternoon. You could roar through the countryside with the wind belting you in the kidneys over those wonderful cut-down doors with the world's biggest and most flexible steering wheel vibrating in your hands, the stubby shift lever close-at-hand, the pedals begging to be heel-and-toed, and easily imagine you were a real boy racer.

Because of the humble and industrial strength nature of its components, the TR3 was a pretty rugged piece. Although this ruggedness should not ever be confused with reliability. Indeed, while major internal fractures were rare even in the hands of Mittyesque world champions like myself, the TR3 could build up a National Debt's-worth of nickel-and-dime problems. Better pens than mine have vilified the late 1950's and early 1960's products of Lucas, the Prince of Darkness. Suffice to say that a three-inch deep puddle or heavy morning dew could bring your TR3 to a silent halt just as surely as a stone wall. But that was just part of the fun, since popping the distributor cap and giving the innards a good wipe was usually enough to get you going again. And what a fine, primeval sense of accomplishment when you got the fire lit again. Likewise, the handsome S.U. carburetors were a tinkerer's delight. An afternoon spent balancing a brace of S.U.s amounted to an existential experience on a par with building an ornate sandcastle directly in the path of the incoming tide.

When I was 14 or so, my older brother and I tried desperately to finesse my dad into a real, two-seater sports car. Because he came out of the Impala convertible ethic of motoring, the path of least resistance and easiest sell was a Chevy Corvette. Not that I thought all that much of Corvettes. Hell, I'd read all the popular Europhile sportycar magazines (remember, I didn't have my license yet) and had come to the unsubstantiated but thoroughly committed conclusion that Corvettes were crude, two-seater trucks posing as genuine, *pur sang* sports cars. But my dad got one anyway. And it was pretty neat, too. Only it got stolen and stripped by the Midnight Auto boys (a fate that befell an amazingly large percentage of Chicago's Corvette population in those days). So he got another one. And *that* one got stolen and stripped. In fact, it disappeared the very night before I got my driver's license. No lie. And I would like to thank that particular thief, wherever he may be, for very likely saving my life. Had I the awesome V8 power, less than awesome handling, and less than less than awesome brakes of a Corvette at my disposal at the tender-yet-immortal age of sixteen, I would probably not be typing these words today. In fact, I would be little more than a few old scrapes in the pavement and a long-dried stain on the edge of some forgotten country road....

In any case, the insurance company gave my dad the long playing edition of the head shaking act regarding any more Corvettes, and what I really wanted him to get was an XK-150S Jaguar. But my dad knew a few people who owned Jags, and he was smart enough to figure that, if he could barely afford to *buy* a Jaguar, there was no way in hell that he could afford to *keep* one. So I tried to steer him towards other sports cars with genuine roll-up windows. Like the Sunbeam Alpine and Alfa Spider. But we were over at the local sports car dealership one day and this bright red TR3 caught his fancy with its jaunty-friendly grin and bargain-basement cost of admission.

Fact is, I think that car *winked* at him, you know?

Well, I couldn't have been more surprised. Or happier. And I'll never forget the day we picked it up from the dealership. It was early January, bitter cold, and there were about eight inches of fresh snow on the ground so that all plows were mustered. My brother drove us over in my mom's toasty-warm Pontiac and there it was, waiting for us, all gleaming red and freshly washed and beginning to ice over.

Now you have to understand that my dad was about the size of your average professional wrestler (albeit with chest and waist measurements reversed) and I watched in bemused horror as he bullied and stuffed and grunted his way behind the wheel. But he finally managed it, closed the door, and then peered disapprovingly at the considerable gap between the side curtain and the top, through which fresh snowflakes were filtering into his ear. But he sighed, twisted the ignition key, and hit that fighter-plane starter button with the choke full-out. *Contact!* The willing tractor 4-banger spluttered to life and settled down to a lumpy, cold-blooded idle.

And so we were off. I remember my dad didn't speak the entire way home. He was preoccupied by the way the TR3 chopped and skipped and hopped from one snow-rut to the next like some demented carnival ride. And how the heater, even on full blast, felt like an asthmatic hamster wheezing on his ankle. And why, when it was snowing *outside,* it was also snowing *inside.* By the time we pulled into our driveway, I knew I was home free. He *hated* that car. But we were going to keep it.

I loved that car. At a time in life when identity and crisis of same are equal importance with the nature of Ultimate truth and a date to the pep rally, that TR3 proved to be a motherlode of bolt-on panache. I started wearing stringback driving gloves and imported, wrap-around Barrafuldi sunglasses with interchangeable lenses. Strange new British phrases crept into my speech. In short, I became insufferable. But that's because driving the TR3 had convinced me that I was destined to be the greatest Grand Prix driver who ever lived. Either that or the first Jewish Pope. But the net result was that I was a highway menace every time I climbed behind the wheel.

I remember, the very first weekend we had the car, I got my hands on a big screwdriver and took off the windshield. In the middle of effing winter, mind you. And then I drove over to see my friend Al Lewis to show him how cool it looked. My friend Al was smitten by sports cars as severely as I was, and, also like myself, he has never grown out of it. Anyhow, it was one of those sunny winter days when the snow is still spanking-white but the roads are mostly clear, cold concrete. Naturally nothing would do but that we go for a little spin and savor the delights of crisp air, twisty roads, and possible frostbite. And a favorite twisty road was not very far away, as Al's folks lived right close by the Sheridan Road ravines, which have been offering guilty pleasure to Chicagoland sportycar and café racer types for decades.

So we dove into the ravines at full tilt. And whom should we spy coming the opposite way but two other fools in an MG TD—also ripping along with its top down and windshield flat—and, naturally, nothing would do but that we gave chase. An informal contest of speed ensued. And that's when I hit that waiting patch of ice and got my first serious lesson in elbow-flailing tank-slappers and the inevitable ensuing crunch. I was crushed. As was the left rear fender of my dad's new TR3. But I also learned one of the great and wonderful things about Triumph sports cars. They're easy to fix. Why, the metal from which TR3 rear fenders are made is almost identical in weight and malleability to you average beer can. Grasping the fender from the bottom with both hands and giving a forlorn tug was all I needed to do to repair the damage.

My dad was never the wiser.

Surely the joys of winter motoring *sans* top and windshield faded quickly, but my love of the car grew and grew. Except for one thing. While a TR3 was a wonderful tool for helping to *secure* a date, it was a bloody awful place to actually take one. What I'm referring to, of course, is the completely natural cascade of adolescent hormones that accounts for several shelves-worth of blemish creams and lotions at you local drugstore. In short, while the TR3 was great to drive, it was an unmitigated disaster when it came to parking. Perhaps, had I been more wiry and athletic, or attracted to girls of less bountiful proportions, it might have been different....

I recall one particular female acquaintance who seemed quite likely to introduce me to the wonders of procreation mechanics, yet a place to consummate our nefarious ends eluded us. Attempts within the confines of the TR3 were fraught with discomfort and the possibility of permanent injury. Finally, in the spring, I developed a plan. We would take Sheridan Road to Gilson Park in Wilmette, which fronted on Lake Michigan and was famous among the local high school and college populations for the fascinating submarine races featured just a few hundred yards offshore almost every evening. The way I had it figured, we'd begin in the car, and, when body temperatures had risen sufficiently, I'd pluck out the old Army blanket I'd secreted away behind the seats, escort her to the beach, and we could have our way with one another. Unfortunately, the evening selected was smack-dab in the middle of the smelt run, and our secluded spot was overrun with hip-booted smelt fishermen and blazing bright Coleman lanterns. Buckets full of flopping little silvery fish are not exactly conducive to romance....

But, that one drawback aside, the TR3 was a wondrous conveyance. The gearbox was one of those great English four-speeds that wear in like new harness leather, getting smoother and more supple with use. The sound of air rushing through the wire-mesh filters and into the yawning, pot-metal throats of the twin S.U.s was exhilarating. The ability to reach down over those marvelous cut-down doors and literally *touch* the pavement with your fingertips was captivating. And the smell of raw gasoline after every bloody fill-up was, well, nauseating.

Always good for a chuckle in a sudden squall was the TR3's convertible top. You didn't so much "pull up" a TR3 top as erect it. Like a tent. In fact, its combination of spidery metal framework and wholly separate vinyl covering, bedeviled as it was with all manner of recalcitrant snaps, obviously sprang from a Druid mentality conditioned to shelter made from fresh-cut saplings and scraped animal skins. Not to mention that the operation could only be done from the outside of the vehicle, and while it took less time than courtship or an engine overhaul, it was a lengthy process whose difficulty was always directly proportional to the severity of the weather. It seemed that, regardless of the D.P.M. (drops per minute) or D.P.S.F. (drops per square foot) or even S.O.D. (size of drops), assembling the top and affixing the side curtains always took exactly long enough to saturate as many layers of clothing as one might be wearing at the time. Rain also brought out the virtues of the TR3's wipers, which moved with the grace of an epileptic chicken in mid-fit and seemed more likely to frighten the raindrops away than sweep them from the windscreen.

Windscreen. Ah, yes. And bonnet. And dashpot. And scuttle. Along with any genuine English sports car, you receive a genuine English owners' manual, and you learn, as George Bernard Shaw once noted, that *"the English and the Americans are two peoples separated by a common language."* Which is perhaps why I wanted so desperately to get to know that TR3 intimately. To mingle my flesh with its metal and thus intertwine its heritage with mine. So I decided to change the oil. Reasonable first move, right? Following the directions in the manual, I unscrewed the long bolt running up through the filter canister from underneath (using a suitable spanner, of course!) and cautiously withdrew it. See, according to an English car manual, you don't simply take things off your car. You *withdraw* them.

But, even with the long bolt withdrawn, the canister remained steadfastly in its original position. So I gave a light tug. No effect. So I tugged a bit harder. It didn't budge. At which point I resorted to tapping with an appropriate tool (i.e.: anything suitably heavy that falls to hand under the car). Still nothing. So I moved the drain pan in order to get my eyes underneath and maybe see why the damn thing wouldn't come loose. I must say that the Castrol 40-weight seemed to keep the swelling down.

Even so, I loved that car. Warts and all. Every cut knuckle, every blown fuse, every flirtation with the laws of physics and poorly placed telephone poles only brought us closer together. In the end, when my father finally tired of trips downtown that reminded him of a personal interview with Torquemada, the TR3 was traded in on something else. I don't know what happened to it afterward. In fact, I really can't explain what happened to Triumphs in general. Or MGs, or Healeys, for that matter. Because an even greater mystery than their origin is the strange disappearance of the little English two-seaters. Like the dinosaurs, these simple, great, yet pea-brained vehicles suddenly and quickly vanished from an American retail landscape where they had flourished for so many years. Surely, there were reasons. The stodgy, old school management of their factories combined with an out-of-control labor force demanding a larger and larger slice of an ever-diminishing economic pie. Competition from the very countries that were hurling bombs and rockets at the British and ourselves just twenty-five years before. And, of course, our own government, which somehow got itself into the automotive engineering business, sounding the death knell forever for simple, enjoyable cars that could be diagnosed, taken apart and fixed by your average shade-tree mechanic equipped with ordinary hand tools. But, whatever the reasons, those crude, wonderful, stone battle-ax cars that were such a joy to wield in anger fell through the cracks of history, even in the face of continuing consumer demand.

I think I'll have one again someday, fixed up really fine. But not too fine. To be authentic, a TR3 needs at least one little scrape or dent and either a leaky needle and seat in one carburetor or an ominous glow from the generator light at low revs. And, of course, one broken tail-light lens, which always took the place of rear bumpers on a

TR3. Yes, I'll have one again, and when neighbors ask me, I'll explain as how what great investments old British sports cars are, and how I'm just keeping it safe and dry there in the garage, hanging on to it for posterity and waiting for the day some teenage Cyberspace Millionaire in need of a lobotomy offers me my weight in precious metals for it. But, if there happens to be a nice, sunny afternoon along the way, with a fine warm breeze through the maple trees and the sun mounted in the sky so if you squint your eyes just so you can see age 16 again:

Ignition switch *on.*

Pull choke two notches.

Press starter button fully home.

Contact!

And then we'll be off again, that TR3 and I, in a WWI fighter plane attack on secluded country lanes, scattering farm animals, chasing the past....

136

THE CAR THAT NEVER WAS

MY FIFTEEN MINUTES OF SHAME....

ORIGINALLY PUBLISHED IN SHORTER FORM IN

BRITISH CAR

APRIL/MAY 1998

Late pop

artist/glitterati guru Andy Warhol once opined that "everybody is famous for fifteen minutes," and, like a lot of our cherished twentieth century soundbytes, the quote became a key part of our cultural mythology regardless of its relationship to truth or real life. Then again, what sort of wisdom do you expect from a guy who leaped into the limelight from the top of an oversized Campbell's soup can? But, in the end, you're either find yourself one of the chosen few frozen in the high beams of the public eye or just another rank-and-file tosser out on the cold, darkened side of the TV screen, sunken a half-foot down into an overstuffed La-Z-Boy with a Miller Lite in your hand, your jaw hanging open, and potato chip crumbs dribbling down your shirt.

But maybe there's some truth to Andy Warhol's notion after all, since I recall my wife Carol and I floated ever-so-briefly through the glare of the media spotlight back when we ran Mellow Motors, our gallant but perpetually struggling foreign car repair [sic] business on Chicago's soon-to-be-trendy near north side.

It happened like this....

Regular readers will recall that I have long harbored a festering infatuation with TVRs, and Mellow Motors wound up handling a solid 80 or 90 percent of the TVR service business in and around the Chicagoland area as a result. Or, in other words, about a half dozen cars. I was also under the misguided delusion that, if I could just get my hands on a stray TVR 2500M to build into a racecar, I would take both myself and my fancied marque to undreamed heights of fame and fortune. Or undreamed by anybody but me, anyway. Nevermind that I only had a few short seasons under my belt in a series of poverty case TR3s that never ran more than a few fitful laps before something new (or not so new, come to think of it) bent, broke, burned, busted, blew up, or belched smoke and fire. Nevermind also that I, personally, was the self-styled toolbox pixie and drafting table charlatan who had turned those TR3s into the borderline lethal nickel rockets they had become. Nevermind as well that, in spite of my own bull-headed cock-suredness, I possessed neither the accumulated skills, racecraft experience, or likely raw talent to drive even the Best Car By Far to victory against genuine top level competition. And nevermind finally that the Sports Car Club of America didn't even recognize the 2500M model as a legit production class racer on account of something about the factory in Blackpool never built enough cars to satisfy the rulebook. To me, those were just trifling minor details (facts though they were) and I wasn't about to let them darken my dreams, stay my purpose, or rain on my parade.

No, sir!

But the first little problem was getting hold of a TVR donor car, seeing as how times were tough at Mellow Motors and even the faithful moths in our cash register drawer had fluttered away to avoid the threat of starvation. But enter stage left (through the overhead service door, natch) a streety, Runyonesque Chicago character whom we shall call Nick The Greek because, *a)* his name may actually have been "Nick," *b)* he may actually have been Greek, and, *c)* the statute of limitations may not have run out on some of the things he allegedly may or may not have done. Nick was one of those tough, gritty, well-connected types who do their business on the street and on the fly and always seem to have many important deals cooking and an awful lot of phone calls to make and return. Nick was a good guy to know because he understood how Things Get Done in a city like Chicago, where "cops" and "robbers" often turn out to be flip sides of the selfsame coin. People such as Nick made good friends and scary enemies, and it was important to understand that they valued loyalty and silence far above honesty and righteousness in their dealings with others.

As you may have sussed already, Nick also liked nifty sports cars, and owned (or at least he and the bank owned) a two-year-old, metallic blue 2500M. But, as yet another creature of the mean streets of Chicago, that TVR was aged well beyond its years and had certainly seen better days already. Between Nick's Cab Driver On A Mission driving style and our city's hard winters, humungous potholes and the brutal perils of overnight parking, that TVR had been beaten, banged and scuffed until it carried itself with the general grace of a one-holer outhouse with the door dangling open on a single, rusty hinge. That car needed serious help. But, as any crooked alderman from Chicago's justly infamous First Ward will gladly inform tell you, serious help costs serious money. In fact, the more serious the help required, the more zeroes you generally need to place on the left side of the decimal point. Why, even the crappy, half-assed, baling wire and spit variety we dished out at Mellow Motors could get expensive. And, what with car payments still owing and none of his pending street deals currently coming to a boil, it's entirely possible that my buddy Nick was looking for a back way out of the situation. And finding the back way out is always an important street smarts skill in any of your major metropolitan cities....

Naturally I'd told Nick all about my racing aspirations—about how I'd plaster both TVR's name and my own across the sky like streaking comets if I only had the chance—and I knew better than to ask questions when Nick offered me his car to prepare and race. Just like that. And it didn't even surprise me that he didn't want any credit or his name on the car or anything in the way of compensation for this grand and generous gesture. But I understood. After all, guys in Nick's social strata tend to be a little shy of publicity. And when they do get their pictures in the paper, they're generally holding a hat or coat or subpoena or something in front of their faces.

In any case, I had my 2500M, and I figured it was none of my business if Nick's act of largess slipped his mind a few days later when he called his insurance company and told them about the sorry looking TVR that was no longer parked in front of his apartment. After all, we were busily stripping that sucker down to the bare frame. Which is no big deal with a 2500M so long as you know where all the various bolts and brackets are that hold the body on and have about eight stout bodies on hand to lift it off. Neither of which applied in our case, so it turned into one of those heroic, life-or-death, push-pull struggles reminiscent of that famous Greek (or was it Roman?) statue where a bunch of well-physiqued Olympian God and Goddess types are all twisted up with this fifty-foot long Hollywood Special Effects sea serpent that appears (at least at the moment of the sculpting, anyway) to have the decidedly upper hand.

But we persevered, cursed and grunted mightily, and finally got the blasted thing apart with much sweating, screaming, bloodying of knuckles and bruising of shins. And the results of our labors reaffirmed that the independently sprung TVR 2500M chassis was indeed a thing of beauty. We also discovered that the handsome, fiberglass bodyshell was a damn sight heavier than any of us anticipated. And we knew that with absolute certainty, since every man Jack of us got our toes or fingers caught under the damn thing at one time or another during the evening.

As I saw it, the TVR project broke down into four distinct sub-categories:

> Engine and driveline
>
> Chassis, steering, and brakes
>
> Body and paint
>
> Ways and Means (i.e.: somehow weaseling my way into things like

hot camshafts, oil coolers, tube headers, custom wheels, and a set of Goodyear racing slicks that weren't exactly in our thoroughly non-existent original budget).

I duly appointed myself group leader and project engineer and for each of the above-mentioned categories (I mean, who else would do it?) except that my wife, Carol, had her heart set on building the engine. Honest she did. You may not believe this, but I somehow managed to marry a lovely, charming, bright, funny, intelligent, cultured, feminine, caring and thoroughly refined young woman, who, for reasons that will forever escape damn near everyone who knows us, has elected to stick by me through a veritable gauntlet run of hard knocks, rude awakenings and outrageous fortune.

Most of it self-inflicted.

God bless her.

Anyhow, Carol figured as long as we'd quit two decent white collar jobs to go into this goofy sports car business, she at least ought to know how an engine goes together. And, seeing as how she is by nature a far neater, cleaner, more patient and better organized person than myself, it seemed likely she could do at least as good a job as I ever could. And probably better. Besides, with me looking gently over her shoulder and screaming directly into her ear every time she placed a socket on a capscrew, what could possibly go wrong?

My plan was simple. We'd build the car, run it for the balance of the season with the flexible and easygoing Midwest Council of Sports Car Clubs, create a groundswell of interest in TVR 2500Ms wrapped up in a veritable whirlwind of publicity and goodwill, somehow get the car accepted by the SCCA as a C-Production racecar, go on to win my birthright National Championship the following season (while Mellow Motors simultaneously raked in mountains of cash restoring fine British sports cars for the above mentioned Andy Warhol and the rest of the Beautiful People) and I think the whole scenario ended with Carol and I building a stunning seaside villa on the same lush, private Caribbean island where Elvis, Colin Chapman, and D.B. Cooper moved when they decided to get the heck out of the limelight and enjoy themselves a little....

Where was I?

Oh, yes. The TVR project. But before we go any further, I need to introduce the last major character in the story. Enter stage right (through the overhead service door in the passenger seat of a tow truck with a sadly neglected Jaguar 3.8S sedan dangling from the business end of the hook) another streety, Runyonesque big city player by the name of Johnny R. Now Johnny R. was a true Jamaican—by temperament, nationality, accent, and preference in smoking materials (remember this was the 70's, when disco was *king!*)—but he had his oft-bloodshot eyes focused, albeit not too steadily, on a stateside media career. Fact is, Johnny R. was pretty well known around the local network TV scene (although in what capacity I leave to your imagination) but, like a lot of folks tiptoeing around the shadowy edges of fame and fortune, he didn't have two nickels to rub together (unless they were nickel bags, that is) to fix his car.

After I'd written up a 3-page repair order on the Jag and closed up shop, Johnny R. and I headed down the street to the Burwood Tap, where, over a few too many beers, I spilled my guts about my rare and wonderful TVR race car and how my wife was building the motor and how we were gonna set the whole damn world on its ear (or maybe on fire, I can't remember which) when we unveiled it at Blackhawk Farms Raceway in a few weeks' time. Well, Johnny R. knew an open wound of financial opportunity when he saw one, and casually mentioned as how he knew practically *everybody* in the local news media. Why, it would be child's play to set up a TV news feature on my wife and I and our wonderful little shop at Mellow Motors and our rare and exciting, one-of-a-kind TVR race car. If I would just sort of let him *owe* me for all the spit and baling wire needed to make his decrepit old Jag streetworthy again, that is....

In fact, borderline streetworthy would do.

Who could resist a sparkling deal like that?

And that, dear friends, is the tantalizing and thoroughly worthless allure of fame in its purest distilled form: notoriety. It comes without compensation, commitment, career opportunity or staying power, and amounts to little more than an Alka-Seltzer fizz of skyrocket dust glittering across the evening sky. Right around 6 o'clock news time. After which it fades to nothing like the echo of a belch.

Like I said, who could resist it?

So I fixed up Johnny R.'s Jag enough to be more or less ambulatory, and, like all slap-dash, down-and-dirty, emergency-field-dressing resuscitation jobs on clapped out beaters, it turned out to be a monumental task. In fact, Johnny R.'s Jag reminded me of those First Aid meets our Boy Scout troop used to enter back when I was a wee lad. They were held in the local high school gymnasium, and each patrol would be given its own little square of wooden floor space surrounded by dozens of other patrols on their own little square of floor, and the lot of you would be standing at fidgety attention while they brought over a few Cub Scouts with red dots stuck here and there on their singularly lint-attracting dark blue uniforms. Each dot served to identify where various imaginary bumps, bruises, burns, broken bones, venous or arterial bleeding, bear maulings, skull fractures, crushed ribs, venomous snake or insect bites and breathing stoppages might be. Then they'd read a scenario that went something like this:

A young hiker was climbing a high tension pole in a thunderstorm when it was struck by lightning. The jolt knocked him completely unconscious, stopped his breathing, and he fell 50 feet to the ground, lacerating his back on the climbing spikes all the way down and receiving a compound fracture of his left arm and both legs along with four deep, sucking puncture wounds in the chest, third degree burns, and a pit viper bite on the inner thigh when he landed face down on a pitchfork stuck in a burning bale of hay that a cottonmouth water moccasin was resting on in a puddle of polluted water.

It was hard to know where to start, you know?

Meanwhile, the TVR was progressing somewhat better. Or so it seemed. I'd somehow managed to hassle together most of the parts we needed to finish it (you don't want to know how) and Carol had done an exemplary job of checking all the clearances, degreeing in the cam, and properly torquing all the rod bolts and such on the motor. And it looked pretty spiffy there on the engine stand with its gold painted block and black crinkle-finish valve cover and chromed tube headers sprouting off the side. Sure, it was in a pretty mild state of tune, what with those wheezy Stromberg carbs and a weak, ¾ grind cam, but I figured the TVR would be so damn nimble that we really wouldn't *need* monstrous power. In that regard, we'd stripped absolutely everything that would come loose off the body, and even made this nifty plexiglass rear window that lopped off a good twenty pounds all by itself. By God, this thing was gonna be *light!*

But I did my best work (or so I thought, anyway) on the chassis. I put in all solid bushings and shortened the springs to lower it (more on that later) and actually paid hard cash for a set of Koni racing shocks and a Corvette aluminum radiator for which I personally fabricated a set of nearly symmetrical (at least if you squinted hard) mounting brackets that almost fit under the hood. A quick trip to the local British Car boneyard (Excelsior Motors on Ashland Avenue, which was essentially a grim slaughterhouse for derelict TRs, MGs, Jags, and Healeys) produced appropriate front and rear swaybars of the precise diameters I'd settled on after much scientific deliberation and about six shots of Cuervo Gold with beer chasers. I bought DS11 brake pads and some low-rider slot mags of the proper dimensions and bolt pattern (both oddball, of course) and my old TR3 mentor/master machinist Mike Whelan made me a set of exquisite wheel spacers for both ends of the car. I must admit that chassis looked pretty damn cool, sitting there all squat and defiant on its fat new racing slicks. Why, it was near as wide as it was long. Then we dropped the body on—just for an initial trial fitting, you understand—and spent the entire rest of the night *oohing* and *aahing* and toasting one another about what a Mean Mutha of a racecar that TVR was gonna be. *Yeah!*

As fate would have it, my grandfather-in-law ran a big, ultra heavy duty welding and fabricating shop on the south side that built railroad bridges and smelting ovens and such, and they'd already done a few after-hours freebies for me on some of my old TR3 racecars. In fact, their type of work was ideal training for TR3s! So I spent a day down there putting the rollbar in while one of the guys welded up the spider gears in the diff on account of no way could I afford a genuine limited slip. And then I discovered that I couldn't get the damn diff back *in* on account of the way I'd designed the effing rollbar. Imagine a late, late night, a lot of unpaid overtime, and plenty of colorful language. Much of it aimed in my direction....

Meanwhile, I'd seen to it that my Jamaican buddy Johnny R. was once again prowling the streets and alleyways of Chicago in his ill-running, knock-kneed and loose jointed 3.8 Jaguar sedan, and he had indeed come through with the promised ***MEDIA CONNECTION*** with the local TV newspeople. Sure enough, a young Bryant (or was it Greg?) Gumbel and a small film crew showed up the Wednesday afternoon after I'd brought the car back from the welding shop. So, with cameras rolling, I went on at serious length about road racing and TVRs and how my lovely, charming, etc. etc. wife had built the engine and how we were gonna KICK ASS AND TAKE NAMES out at Blackhawk Farms Raceway that coming weekend. Yes indeed. And I must admit they seemed pretty interested in what we were doing. Although young Mr. Gumbel appeared somewhat skeptical that we were actually going to get it done in time, since, to his untrained eye, that 2500M race car looked like nothing more than an eclectic pile of mismatched junk on four shiny new wheels. But I assured him we'd be there, and he likewise assured me that the camera crew would be there, too, in order to capture our hoped-for moment of glory for posterity.

No sooner had the TV crew left the shop than I found myself looking at that half-finished race car project with a brand new set of eyes. Young Mr. Gumbel's eyes, in fact. Like him, I was wondering just how in hell I expected to get the engine and tranny installed, all the plumbing and wiring done, do the interior, mount the nose, paint the body, install that nifty rear window, take care of all the odds n' ends hardware, fire it up, tune it, bleed the brakes, and do a quick-and-dirty alignment so all the wheels would be pointing in approximately the same direction when we got it on the track.

All in two days.

Well, the first thing we discovered was that, despite the use of highly accurate measuring instruments (my thumb and fingers, mostly) the intake manifold failed to clear the forward roll bar brace by a scant but solid 3/8ths of an inch. Much heating, beating, sawing, prying, sweating, cursing, gnashing of teeth, and wailing upon with the largest sledge in the shop later, we arrived at a more reasonably tailored fit. Sort of. Then things went swimmingly for several hours until we had it all thrown together for painting, and it was at this juncture that I stepped back for a once-over and realized that the rocker panels of my hopefully low-slung new race car were a good 12" off the floor. It gave the TVR a strange, Crazed-Bullfrog-In-Mid-Leap sort of stance. What I'd somehow failed to account for (among countless other things, truth be known) was that all the shaving and discarding of parts and lopping off of coils I'd done had, by the rules of inverse proportion, made the car that much lighter yet the springs that much stiffer. So now the car was sitting *way* too high. Summoning all the engineering and organizational skills that made me fit to work overtime on a shitbox like Johnny R.'s clapped-out Jag for no money, I put the TVR up on jackstands, ripped out the springs, and went to work with a hacksaw while my bleary-eyed crew started spray painting the fiberglass a deep, lustrous metallic brown.

By the time the second coat of lacquer dried sufficiently to not show fingerprints from more than thirty feet away, I was underneath re-installing the springs, which were by now down to something like half their original length. Give or take a half coil. Only now I'd gone maybe a bit too far the other way, seeing as how the car—and especially the sump—was sitting *real* low. Like so low a mouse running for cover underneath that car would've cracked his skull wide open. But no problem, since, as any chassis engineer will gladly tell you, a coil spring is just one long torsion bar coiled up into loops, and the shorter you make that bar—like fr'instance by cutting off about half of those loops—the stiffer it becomes. So I didn't have to worry about bottoming out, seeing as how you could've dropped a hippopotamus on any freaking corner of that car and not deflected it more than a scant few thousandths of an inch. If that. As an old TR3 racer, I figured that to be a good thing, since most TR racers generally tend to think there's no such thing as being too stiff.

I understand Healey and MG racer types tend to drink a lot, too....

In any case, it was back together, and now it was just a matter of readjusting the 12 degrees of negative camber and half-inch of toe we'd somehow developed at both ends of the car, pop riveting the rear window in place, installing the dash and seat, running the wires and cables, hooking up the plumbing and instruments, firing it up, tuning the motor, bleeding the brakes, loading it on the trailer, picking up my racing gear at home, driving out to Blackhawk, clearing tech, putting numbers on the sides, and heading out for first practice. Which, if memory serves, was due to start in about 90 minutes. But I'd actually made it out to Blackhawk in 90 minutes once.

In an E-Type.

Doing triple digits all the way.

OK, so we weren't gonna make first practice. So what? After all, we'd been up about 3 days straight, and I really figured I needed a shower and a shave since *HOLY COW, EVERYBODY!! WE'RE GONNA BE ON TEEVEE!!!* In any case, following the usual last minute catastrophes *("MY GOD! THE EFFING CAR IS TOO WIDE FOR THE EFFING TRAILER"* was my personal favorite) we were eventually on our way, buzzed to the very redline with excitement, adrenaline, and far too much caffeine, heading towards an ominous gray horizon and our promised date with fame and destiny. Sure enough, the TV crew was waiting in the paddock for us. Huddled under a tarp, in fact, since—what else?—it had started to rain. Not a heavy rain, mind you, just one of those mean, cold, incessant drizzles that leave the grass wet and the pavement thoroughly soaked.

And I didn't have any rain tires.

Have you ever tried to drive on slicks in the rain?

All I can say is: *"don't."*

Especially in a car that's sprung stiffer than a roller skate.

The kindly stewards of the Midwest Council let me out during another group's qualifying session just to get the feel of the car, and I think I can sum it up by stating that it was bloody awful. At least for half a lap, anyway, until I hit a small rise in the pavement in the middle of corner five (it felt like I'd run over a damn sewer pipe!) and went spinning merrily off into the weeds. But that was okay, since we'd stripped the entire windshield wiper assembly out during our Fanatical Lightening Campaign and hadn't bothered to bring it along in case it rained. And why continue around when you can't see where the heck you're going?

And so, dear friends, our great moment of Televised Glory amounted to starting dead last and plummeting rapidly rearwards from there, driving on slicks in the rain in a car with no windshield wipers and a chassis set up so damn stiff that every minor pavement ripple became, in effect, a launching pad. It was all I could do to keep from spinning again, and I think the leaders must've lapped me a half dozen times or more. And of course it was all being captured on tape for the six o'clock news, too. Afterwards they pointed the camera at me one last time and I gave some sort of lame speech about how "our car just needs a little sorting, see" and vowed that "we'll be back." But it may have been a little hard to understand on account of I'd been up about 90 or 100 hours straight and my mouth was all sore and bent out of shape from biting off way more than I could chew.

And that, dear friends, is what the Channel 5 news crew reduced to about ten or twelve seconds of my wife looking marvelous, adventurous, funny, cheerful, loyal and refined (as always) and me looking like perhaps the single biggest boob in television news history. But our families (as families do) told us it was wonderful and we both looked great. And they, to the best of my knowledge, were about the only people who paid any attention at all to our little eye-blink blur on the five o'clock local news. We didn't even make the big shows at six and ten. Thank goodness.

There's a little more to the story, as I deluded myself that maybe the suspension wasn't really too stiff (if the track had only been *dry,* right?) and I decided, a la Tim Allen, that what we really needed was *MORE POWER!* So I ignored the softer springs and skinnier swaybars and proper chassis settings that I really should have been thinking about and tore into that wonderfully smooth, torquey and cool-running motor Carol had put together to turn it into a real killer. Yeah, *that* was the ticket! So I milled a bunch more off the head, swapped some other Triumph stuff for what was purported to be an insanely radical cam, replaced the Strombergs with a pair of fat, two-inch S.U.s, and, possessed by a brilliant flash of gestalt engineering, removed that heavy, ugly, cast iron balancer from the nose of the crankshaft and replaced it with a light-weight aluminum hardware store pulley in order to reduce the rotating mass.

As you can see, what I didn't know about applied suspension dynamics was easily surpassed by what I didn't understand about engine balance and harmonics. When we headed out to Blackhawk for the TVR's second outing (arriving at the last minute as usual and starting once again from the back of the pack) the agony of defeat dropped by for an encore before the race even started. I recall I was trundling out of the last corner at the end of the pace lap, one steely eye focused on the starter's stand, waiting for the slightest flinch, and the other glued nervously to a temperature gauge that was already well into the red zone. In cunning anticipation of the flag, I dropped back a few car lengths and floored it. And that would be when that long and thoroughly unbalanced crankshaft cracked like Lash LaRue's trademark whip and threw a connecting rod clear through the side of the block. Before the green flag ever waved....

And that was about the end of it, really. Not only was I hung well over the edge financially, but it was slowing beginning to dawn on me that I was in *waaaaay* over my head. Eventually, I don't recall exactly how, I wound up selling the oil soaked, legally suspect and comprehensively blowed-up remains of that car to some guy down south who was planning to make an autocrosser out of it. I remember the money was almost enough to pay half the bills I'd run up in my frantic, mad dash sprint to finish the car so I could win the big race and get famous on TV and become one of Andy Warhol's Beautiful People and eventually buy that seaside villa down in the islands that Carol and I so richly deserved so we could get away from all the hoopla, headaches and heartaches of fame. Instead, I'd damn near ruined us. But at least I'd come to realize that I didn't know so much—in fact, not much of anything!—when it came to all the fancy racecar stuff I'd imagined myself so bloody wise and expert about.

And that, in the end, is where real knowledge begins....

A PALETTE FOR SPEED

SELECTED WORKS OF FAVORITE AUTOMOTIVE ARTISTS

PENDLETON CARRINGTON

GALLERIES

Potside Patrons

Advertisers

Age & Treachery Racing
Skip Barber Racing School & Race Series
Dave Bean Engineering
Bond Corp/Crystal Tack Cloth
British Car
Lee Chapman Racing
Chateau Dekon
Classic Impressions
Continental Auto Sports
Cope Machinery Company
Joe Curto the Carburetor Man
Donovan Motorcar Service
Driving Impressions
Grassroots Motorsports
Andy Greene Vintage Race Cars
GT Classics/Caterham 7
Historic Sports Car Racing, Ltd.
Marcovicci-Wenz Engineering
Midwestern Council of Sport Car Clubs

Monoposto Racing/Formula 70
Moss Motors, Ltd.
Munchwerkes
Jay Nadelson/Investors' Capital L.L.C.
Jim Nichols
Ragtops & Roadsters
The Rosedale Barbeque
The Seneca Lodge
Siebkens Resort
Sportscar Vintage Racing Association
The Tacrea House
Victory Lane
Vintage Sportscar Drivers Association
Vintage Motorsport
Vintage Racing Services, Inc.
Virginia International Raceway
Bob Woodman Tires
WordSpeed
Zapata Racing

Sponsors

A Little O.F.F. Racing
(Ross Bremer & Karen Perrin)
Nino Barlini
Chip Bond
Gino Borghesa
Bobby Brown
Phil & Jolene Brown
Nick & Nora Charles
Lynne & Big Eff'n Al Cole
Dan Cotter
Veronica DeGuenther
Michael Delaney
Walter & Kieth Denahan
Kevin Doyle
Bob & Linda Feighner
Bruce & John A. Fernie
A Special Friend

Les Gonda
Charles Hersch
Ian Keith James
The Lucurell Family
Bill Lyman
Don & Helen Muñoz
Ken & Vicki Searles
Jeff Snook
Erich Stahler
Mike Stott
Glen & Betty Stuffers
Jon Targett
Tom Treutlein
Duck & Sue Waddle
Jack & Jackie Webster
John & Lisa Weinberger
Bob Woodward

GASOLINE FUELS OUR IMAGINATIONS
WITH IMAGES OF SPEED, DISTANCE, FREEDOM,
CHALLENGE, DANGER, SOLITUDE AND ESCAPE

THESE ARE SOME OF MY FAVORITES

Burt Levy

Roger Blanchard

contact the artist at 610 967-4682 • blanchard@enter.net

C- Type Jaguar
watercolor
image size 11" x 15 1/2"
signed/numbered edition of 100 prints

British Greenery (MG)
watercolor
image size 14" x 21"
signed/numbered edition of 300 prints

Alfredo De la Maria

available from Classic Impressions Automotive Art 1.800.488.7742
or online at www.racingpilot.com

Taking Over The Town
image size 24" x 32"
limited edition of 500 prints

Trois Heures du Pau
image size 24" x 34"
limited edition of 100 prints

Tom Fritz

contact the artist at 805 499.1630

Ogle That
original oil on canvas
image size 24" x 36"
depiction of a '27 roadster on the dry lake

Of Dust and Fury
original oil on panel
image size 20" x 40"
depiction of a '32 roadster at speed on the lakes

Robert E. Gillespie

contact the artist at 315 536-7185 • www.glenspeed.com

Cunninghams at Stone Bridge, 1952
acrylic on canvas
image size 24" x 30"
275 signed and numbered lithographs on
archival paper, image size 15" x 20"

Carrera Panamericana, 1952
acrylic on canvas
image size 24" x 30"
100 signed and numbered lithographs on
archival paper, co-signed by Burt Levy
image size 16" x 20"

Tom Hale

contact the artist at 248 476.9529

Duesenberg & Rose
original acrylic painting
image size 42" x 64"
limited edition 12" x 16" print available

Packard & Rose
original acrylic painting
image size 42" x 72"
limited edition 12" x 16" print available

Jay Koka

contact the artist at 519 343-4040 • www.jaykokastudio.com

Young Girls in the Canyon
acrylic on canvas
image size 36" x 48"

Paul Nesse, *bronzes*

contact the artist at 651 430-0460

1954 Le Mans-winning
Ferrari 375 Plus
Bronze, edition of 18

Monaco GP-winning
Bugatti Type 35B
Bronze, *Edition of 24*

Mark Maholm, *bronzes*

contact the artist at 330 896-9013 • communityzero.com/markmaholm

Lorenzo Bandini in the
1967 Ferrari 312
Detailed Bronze

Dan Gurney's
1967 F1 Eagle
Detailed Bronze

John Napier Hill

contact the artist at 708 246-2905

85/100 JNH

Ayrton Senna: F/1 Grand Prix Champion, 1988. McLaren Honda MP4/4

Senna
pencil drawing
image size 13" x 15"

Sandra Leitzinger

contact the artist at 814 466-7355

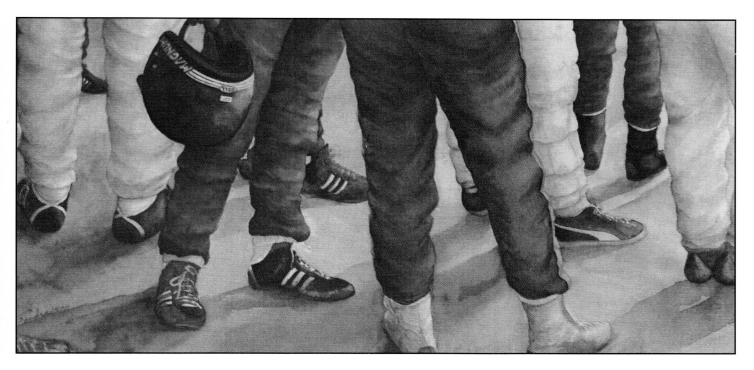

Drivers Meeting
watercolor
image size 15 3/4" x 27 1/2"

Randy Owens

contact the artist at 410 956.0144 • www.randyowens-originals.com

Monaco Ferrari 1 & 2
original painting

Porsches at LeMans
*original serigraph made from
hand-cut stencils and
handprinted by the artist*

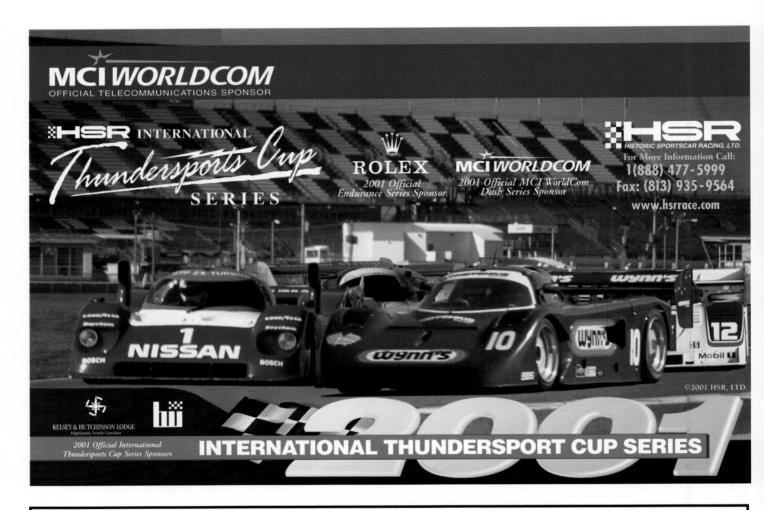

The early days—with hair, no less!—BS in one of his "plague of TR3s" at a Midwestern Council of Sports Car Clubs race at Blackhawk Farms in 1972. The Council continues to run a full schedule of low key, high fun content club races, time trials and drivers' schools for both current and vintage machinery, with track events at Blackhawk Farms, Road America, GingerMan and Grattan every season. Consult the Midwestern Council website for further information.

Final chapter in the Killer TR3 saga?
Note: Burt was waaay ahead of the curve on the whole vintage thing!

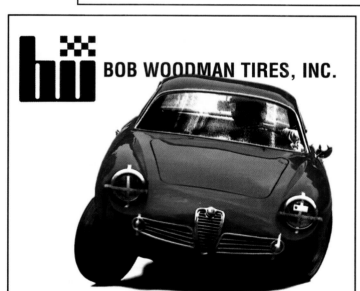

"The Car that Never Was" in the only race it ever finished. Or started, for that matter.... Pat Ryder photo.

Burt at Mid-Ohio in 1986 driving the Alfa Romeo AUSCA Spider he built and campaigned on the vintage circuit with sponsorship help from famous Chicagoland restaurateur and enthusiast Joe Marchetti. The car scored 13 class wins in 15 races during the 1986-1987 seasons. Sidell Tilghman photo.

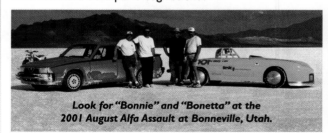

Burt in Joe Marchetti's Ferrari 250LM during the Chicago Historic Races Enduro at Road America in July, 1987. The experience became the topic of his very first "Pure BS" column for Vintage Motorsport! Art Eastman Photo.

BS in David Whiteside's 1959 Lotus 17 at Lime Rock Park, Connecticut, 1993. David and Burt teamed up to win the HSR's Rolex Vintage Endurance Championship with it in 1993 and again in 1994.

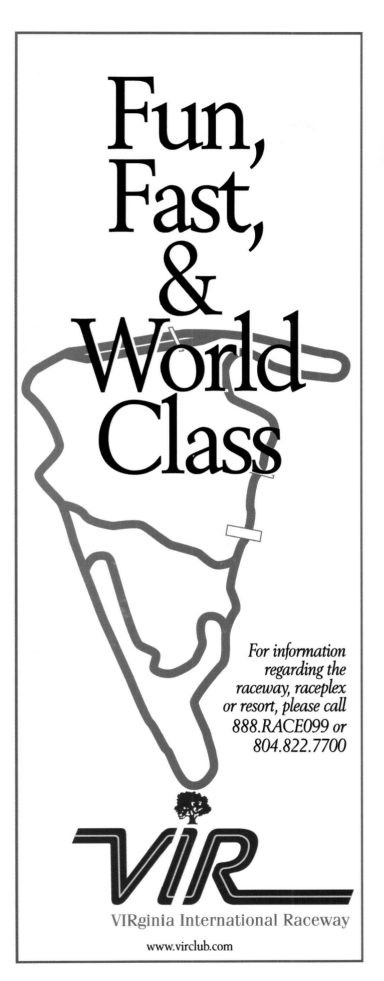

Old and new. BS in the "new" Cunningham C4R he shook down at Watkins Glen, NY, in September, 1997, and owner/longtime friend Al Lewis in the "old" Chevron B-36 he and Burt drove to victory in the International Challenge Enduro at Road America in July of the same year. Bob Harrington photos.

BS testing the original Jim Hall Chaparral at Shannonville, Canada, 1997. The car had just undergone a 10-year restoration by his friend and longtime Rolex Challenge nemisis Jack Boxstrom. Bob Harrington photo.

Left: Burt co-driving Charlie Kolb's Chevron B-8 at Gingerman, Michigan, 1998.

Above: Co-driving frequent ride-mooch victim John Targett's MGB at Summit Point, W. Va. This came out a bit better than "Comedy of Terrors," as John and Burt scored a class win.

Burt dives Al Lewis' Chevron under
Lowell Blossom's Lola at Road America
ALL BOB HARRINGTON PHOTOS THIS PAGE
Burt co-driving Lowell Blossom's Chevron B-19
at Watkins Glen.

Rain and Shine! In Alex Quattlebaum's
Elva Spyder at the Grand Bahama Vintage
Grand Prix and sloshing to a class win at Road
Atlanta in the Pinto from Hell!

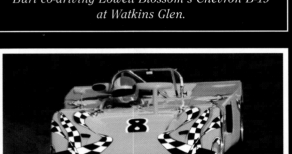

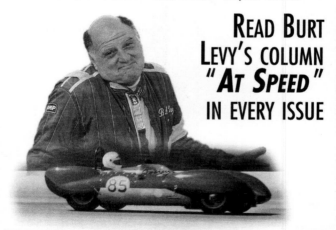

DEATH OF THE DIP

*"PROGRESS" MARKS THE END OF ONE OF
THE GREATEST THRILLS IN AMERICAN RACING*

EXPANDED FROM A ROAD ATLANTA RACE REPORT IN THE
MONOPOSTO REGISTER NEWSLETTER
MAY, 1998

I'll never

forget my first trip to Road Atlanta. It was 1973, and I was on hand as a fourth-string hanger-on and backup beer runner for a local Chicago racer who'd managed to qualify for the SCCA Runoffs in an ex-BRE Datsun 510 Trans Am car. Things being how they are for fourth string hangers-on, I never got any actual laps around the track the entire week. But I sure walked every inch of it on the picnic basket and beer cooler side of the fences, and I must admit I was gobsmacked by the way it swooped and arced and climbed and plunged through the kudzu-draped pine trees and orange-red Georgia clay. The Road Atlanta esses—perhaps the most photographed bit of asphalt this side of the Laguna Seca Corkscrew—descends from turns 3 to 5 like a huge, supple blacksnake slithering down a hill, and, in one of the first magazine stories I ever wrote (for *Alfa Owner* in January of 1983) I christened the gut-hollowing drop from the blind, over-the-top Bridge Turn at 11 to the difficult, flattening out sweeper through turn 12 *"The Asphalt Waterfall."* It was pretty damn dramatic, and surely the signature feature of the old Road Atlanta. Plus, back in those days, the pit entrance peeled off to driver's left up at the top, and it was an awesome place to watch ballsy guys like the late Jim Fitzgerald come blasting over the crest all hung out to dry, drift well into pit lane, and keep the gas pedal mashed to the throttle stops as they plummeted down the waterfall into that terribly difficult and unforgiving needle-thread of a final corner. It was one *hell* of a racetrack, and I made up my mind right then that someday, somehow, I was going to find a way to race there myself.

It took every bit of 10 years to make it happen, mostly spent flogging around our local bush league Midwestern Council of Sports Car Clubs circuit in a succession of under-funded, nickel rocket TR3s. But I ultimately got the funding together—or the credit limits, anyway—to do a season of National racing in a showroom stock Alfa of admirable speed (if questionable legality) and qualified for those same SCCA Runoffs at Road Atlanta myself. I'll never forget the buzz of anticipation as we took that long tow down to Road Atlanta for my first ever crack at the circuit. And well I remember the wide-eyed look staring back at me from the rear view mirror as I pulled in after my first practice session on Monday morning. Up in the Midwest, we've got mostly flat tracks like Blackhawk Farms and Brainerd and Indianapolis Raceway Park, and the hilly ones we do have, like Grattan and Mid-Ohio, weren't anywhere near as fast as this place. Sure, you could get up a pretty impressive head of steam at Road America, but most of the corners there are simple, late apex 90s taken in 2nd or 3rd gears and separated from each other by long straighaways.

Road Atlanta was something else entirely....

First of all, you were *flying!* Once you got your courage up, those beautiful esses were a flat-out, downhill slalom schuss that you entered blind, took in 4th gear, and left little margin for error. And however fast your car could go, it would reach that speed down that looong Road Atlanta backstretch. Then you'd blast over the blind, flat-out crest at Turn 9, plunge into the infamous and intimidating Road Atlanta Dip, and it would go even faster. Plus you'd feel it go all up on tiptoes over the top and it would take you several laps—every blessed time you went there!—to get up the stones to keep your foot planted as you plummeted down into The Dip. Your head knew that the car would stabilize when the track went through the bottom of the gully and swooped uphill again on the far side, but there were other parts of your anatomy that weren't so easy to convince. And the fun was hardly over, since now you were hurtling towards yet another blind crest under an overpass bridge that looked for all the world like a garage door opened into outer space. The bridge turn at Station 11 was always the visual trademark of Road Atlanta, and it was a gut check of a corner that required nerve, calm, confidence, and finesse in about equal measure. It was one of those places where you were either wise enough to leave a little margin for error or, sooner or later, you went for one hell of a nasty ride....

The fascinating thing was how the White Knuckle Zone at Road Atlanta moved around depending on what type of car you were driving. In a smallbore machine, the hardest part was Turn 12 at the bottom of the hill. You knew if you came charging out from under the bridge and lined it up just so, you could take that final sweeper flat. Maybe. And if the faster guys were doing it, you had to try it, too. But it was the sort of place that tempted you to turn in early—exactly like the kink at Road America and for exactly the same reasons—and I remember a onetime business partner at Road Atlanta track telling me that the Turn 12 guardrail was the most impacted stretch of Armco in American racing. I had no reason to doubt him.

But in a really *fast* car, the scariest part moved back to Station 9, where you crested the hill at over 170 (sometimes *well* over) and the steering went all queasy light in your hands. A few Can Am cars—including Mark Donohue's Porsche and Denny Hulme's McLaren—caught air under the nose and flipped over backwards there in spectacular fashion. I know I've driven their predecessor, my Canadian friend Jack Boxstrom's brutish and aerodynamically medieval Sadler/Chevy, over that crest at something around 150, and was only too happy to say the hell with lap times and give it a *big* confidence lift. Then the redoubtable Brian Redman tried it in the same car, kept it floored over the top, and returned to the pits with eyes the size of fried eggs. "I turned the wheel and it didn't feel like it was connected to *anything!*" he mumbled through suitably clenched teeth. But that's what made it great. And the very best thing about Road Atlanta—beyond all the speed and elevation changes and places that made your hands tighten up on the wheel—was the way the whole thing flowed together in a sensual, meaningful rhythm. It was a magnificent place to drive, full of what Derek Bell calls "mighty corners," and it tested you for style, grace and composure as well as sheer, raw guts every single lap.

But it's gone now, sacrificed on the divergent altars of speed, sanity, and safety. Typically, it went in stages, like the corpse of some great warrior being consumed by a swarm of teeming, bureaucratic carrion. First they widened the whole track, turning the esses from a flat-out, needle thread *schuss* into a place where you could be a little sloppy and still get away with it. Then they changed the ill-conceived but thoroughly spectacular pit entrance, widening the downhill slope from 11 to 12 and effectively diluting much of the challenge under the bridge. It also changed the angle of attack on 12, thereby saving a lot of expensive Armco but eliminating a lot of the pucker factor as well. And now, finally, The Dip is no more. It's been bulldozed, filled in, and replaced by one of those fiddly little flick-flick chicanes that create additional overtaking opportunities for the pros but fail to inspire either awe or respect on either side of the fences.

New owner Dan Panoz is spending a hell of a lot of money on Road Atlanta—God bless him!—and I'll be first in line to buy a ticket to see the CART or F1 guys run there. And surely what was thrilling, daunting and demanding in a club racer at 140 or so would be genuinely lethal in a CART or F1 machine at something like 100 more. Why, they'd come crashing down on the bump stops like blessed pile drivers when they hit the bottom of that dip at something around 230. Plus, at that speed, there's simply not enough runoff available to make it a risk worth taking. And I accept that.

But I miss the old Road Atlanta. Miss the way the mean old girl made my guts go hollow and hands cinch up on the wheel. Sure, she was a car eater and made you pay for your mistakes. But, in return, she gave you one hell of a damn ride. Like so many of the world's truly great circuits, the speed, safety, liability and spectator concerns of modern racing have forced the powers-that-be to take the *cojones* out of it. Oh, it's still a neat place to drive and race, and the swoop and scenery of it are still some of the best anywhere. But, like a lot of things as you get older, it sure as hell doesn't measure up to the memories....

GOING FOR THE GOLDEN JUGULAR
SWIMMING WITH THE SHARKS OF THE RETAIL CAR BUSINESS

UPDATED FROM A STORY ORIGINALLY PUBLISHED IN
AutoWeek
MARCH 5, 1984

How many

professional car salesmen do you know? I mean really *professional* car salesmen, not the warm bodies you find lurking around dealer showrooms, watching the eyes of their latest hot prospects like a fisherman watches a bobber. I mean professionals you'd take your car questions to just as you'd take your medical questions to your doctor or legal hassles to your lawyer. There aren't many around, are there? Why, back in 1982, when the great engine of American commerce was sputtering along on three cylinders and belching out thick, black clouds of unemployment, the major metropolitan papers *always* carried ads for car salesmen. Do you know anybody who went to college or grad school to learn how to be a car salesman? In fact, if you asked the entire high school graduating class of your home state what line of work they aspired to, would one single person answer: "Car salesman"?

It seems very wrong that people of this occupation, the front-line, in-the-trenches retail representatives of the largest and arguably most important non-government industry in the world, should have a social standing somewhere between convicted embezzlers and accused child molesters. But, unfortunately, the lingering odor surrounding much of the car retailing business has been self-produced.

Think back to the original idea of the retail automobile dealership. Fledgling manufacturers in the horseless carriage era sought representatives in each city, town and hamlet to present their products to John Q. Public and, if lucky enough to close the deal, provide reliable service and a ready supply of replacement parts so that one satisfied customer might lead to others.

As the industry and the country grew together, dealers for various makes appeared in every rural village and urban neighborhood. In fact, the concept of a handy local dealership and service depot became the cornerstone of traditional retailing for auto manufacturers everywhere.

Through World War II, dealers struggled and failed by the score with no new cars to sell and precious little gas to fuel those already on the road. America, along with the auto industry, lost the last of its innocence and acquired much of its strength through the ordeal. Then, after the armistice, a jubilant, robust, and increasingly prosperous population sought the mobility and delicious extravagance of new wheels. The dealers reacted like starving men at a sumptuous buffet. They gorged themselves. No price was too high, no tactic too low. They had control of supply, and demand was overwhelming and irresistible. And, in those days before the government stepped in and stopped it, there was no such thing as a "window sticker" price. The general rule of thumb was "whatever the market will bear," and fortunes were made.

So were habits.

The worst of these, and a practice which will probably last as long as the industry, is the concept of the car "deal" itself. Think what would happen if you walked up to the check-out counter at your local grocery with a four-pound roast selling at $4.98 a pound and a six-pack of designer beer for $6.49:

(Sound of cash register ringing.)

"That'll be $26.41 plus $1.98 tax for a total of $28.39, sir."

That's when you give the checker your toughest, steely-eyed stare. "Tellya what," you snarl through defiantly clenched teeth, "I'll give ya twenty bucks for the beef and you throw in the suds and tax."

Try it the next time you go shopping.

But the retail car business is different. The window sticker on a new car includes a profit for the dealer, usually between 7 and 15 percent, depending on the model. But out of this gross profit, he must pay for his place of business, his clerical help, his salesmen's commissions, and a monthly percentage to the banks, brokers and finance companies who actually own the cars until they are sold. It is only after all these costs are deducted that the dealer arrives at his net profit.

So why should it seem odd that, given half a chance, the dealer (and his representative, the salesman) will go for the golden jugular. Especially when a large percentage of the population walks into a car dealership sure that they are about to be ripped off and therefore carrying a Gibraltar-sized chip on their collective shoulder. It's gotten to where it's not so much about *product* anymore, but about *The Deal*. And making *price* the single most important thing in what should really be a handy, neighborhood, service-oriented distribution business has created a monster:

The Volume Dealer.

In this age of mobility, the consumer has a selection of many dealerships in any given locale, and the ability (if so inclined) to play one against the other. Which means that the guy who does things the cheapest, pays his people the least, the guy without enough parts and service facilities to take care of all the cars he sells, the guy way out in the boondocks where lease rates and property taxes are less and therefore, obviously, furthest away from the original idea of a neighborhood dealership and service depot, is the guy selling the most cars for the least money and whoring up the market for everybody else.

You've seen him on TV:

"Hey, this is honest Herb Harlot here, begging you shamelessly to drive on out to Herb's Freeway Motors, the volume dealer. We're located just 50 minutes too far out of your way to be of any use when it comes to servicing your car, and our salespeople don't know an air bag from an enema bag. But, by God, they understand *price*, and they just eat and breathe *cheap*. So come on out and take a look at 60 acres of new cars. And forget about sticker price. Forget wholesale. We'll do whatever it takes, because we've just *got* to keep moving new cars in big volume, before our bankers figure out if we're making any money or going broke. Remember, at Honest Herb's we're not interested in net profit. At Herb's it's gross, gross, *gross...*"

What's *really* gross is that, on a new car purchase financed over three to five years as is common today, a $250 difference in "the deal" amounts to less than ten bucks a month difference in the payment. It's not even coffee money. At least not at Starbuck's, anyway....

But it seems old John Q. is out to get back at the car retailing business for gouging him and his friends, neighbors and relatives every chance it's ever had, even though his search for the cheapest, rock-bottomest, most profitless deal that he can wheedle out of that same industry doesn't strike him as reciprocal gouging. Not at all.

And that's why the *profession* of retail car sales barely exists. Because John Q. thinks the industry is incapable of producing honest, well-meaning, well-informed, and motivated individuals. And the industry, to a great degree, is only too happy to return the favor and treat Mr. Public like a con-game mark.

I already mentioned that this is all wrong, didn't I?

Because it doesn't have to be this way. And it isn't. Not everywhere. I've worked in several dealerships, and I've seen all the bad stuff: Manipulative "Sales System" courses where you leave your ethics at the door along with your hat and coat. I've also seen quality dealerships with quality personnel that conduct themselves with fairness, honesty and integrity. But the quality personnel is always the hard part.

Remember what I said about nobody aspiring to be a professional automobile salesman? Even the people I rate as top professionals generally came out of other fields. They got involved in small, entrepreneurial businesses that somehow went belly-up or sold some other product or service or just happened to grow up around the car sales businesses. Almost without exception, they are occupationally displaced people.

And even the good ones suffer from the special occupational hazards of car retailing. They get the unwelcome opportunity to see human beings at their absolute worst at least a few times every month. Guaranteed. They ride, like all salesman, on the current of a financial sea that may turn dangerously turbulent, or, worse yet, deadly calm at any time. The hours are tough and long and the boredom level is always directly proportional to the lack of self-motivation. Sloth can be a problem. So can smoking, drinking and all the other popular social drugs. Burnout is common. And, for those who work that way, so is the self-poisoning of the soul that afflicts those who deal deceitfully and condescendingly with others.

But, for the best of them, working in those few quality dealerships where the goal is to do the job as it should be done, there are rich rewards. They can earn a better-than-decent living. Customers they have taken good care of, not just at the time of sale, but to whom they have become reliable car consultants for every possible automotive question or transportation trauma, refer their friends and neighbors. They can build a respectable clientele. And be respectable in the bargain. True car sales professionals are a unique and interesting breed: quick thinking, personable, knowledgeable, and inevitably cynical from the dealings they've had with the darker side of human nature. Yet, in order to succeed, they must remain possessed by an irresistible optimism.

It can be a fine and decent way to make a living. Surely, there's plenty of room in any industry for people willing to become true *professionals*. Just as surely, there will be more and more room in John Q.'s mindset for dealerships oriented toward quality, honesty, and service as opposed to price first, last, and always. Why, car dealers and sales professionals might someday be considered equal to doctors or even lawyers.

That is a step up, isn't it?

A GREED FOR SPEED

Or: How I Caused The Most Expensive Wreck The Skip Barber Race Series Had Ever Seen !

THIS STORY HAS NEVER BEEN PUBLISHED BEFORE.
AFTER YOU READ IT, YOU'LL KNOW WHY....

It's no secret that the whole idea behind all this writing stuff is to drive other people's racecars. After my mechanic rolled my beloved Alfa in drivers' school in the spring of 1984 (with me as his instructor, make of it what you will) I took a side job I had previously turned down as a local stringer for *On Track* magazine covering the IMSA and SCCA Trans Am pro races here in the Midwest. Hey, it was a way to stay involved in the sport, if only on the fringes. And that eventually led to more stories for more magazines and, finally, my first vintage race and my first major ride mooch in a Ferrari 250 Short Wheelbase Berlinetta (always one of my favorite Ferraris, and perhaps the last genuine dual-purpose car from any major manufacturer) at the Walter Mitty Challenge at Road Atlanta. It was thanks to famous Chicago restaurateur and Ferrari trader Joe Marchetti, who, for reasons I will never fully understand but forever be thankful for, became sort of a patron and trusted me with some incredibly important machinery. I wrote a feature about the experience for *AutoWeek,* got a nice check in the mail and a bit of recognition, and instantly realized I was on to something. With nothing more than a free-form combination of brass, bullshit, and good fortune, I'd managed to score a drive in a car that was worth significantly more than my house. And you could throw in my neighbor's house, too.

This led to a sort of self-styled career as perhaps the sport's premiere journalist ride mooch, and it is frankly astounding how many famous and fabulous cars I've gotten to drive—and race!—under the thoroughly transparent pretext of "writing magazine stories about them." The list includes everything from prewar Bugattis and Austin Seven specials to LeMans-winning Ferraris and Ford GT-40s to modern IMSA proto- types and NASCAR stock cars to gen-yew-wine Formula 1 Grand Prix *monopostos* to just about every kind of rank-and-file MG, Alfa, TR, Healey, Lotus, Porsche, Jaguar, Lister, Lola, Cooper, Viper, Corvette and what have you that you can imagine.

Hey, it's a tough job, but *somebody's* gotta do it!

There's a secret, though. Inside the very best of them—and they can be Sprites just as easily as Shelby Cobras—the first thing that vanishes is the car. It does what you ask it to so well that you forget all about it. Then it's just you and the racetrack. And that's the *real* magic, holding the wheel in your hands and flowing the car into the delicious, enveloping suction of the road ahead. There's nothing else like it. And so much the better if there's some guy up ahead you're trying to hunt down or someone you fear (but also trust!) stalking you from behind. Then the game is truly afoot! And I think the thing that makes racing so different from anything else is that it requires both the right and left sides of the brain in equal measure—a unique, fine, and delicate balance between instantaneous gut reaction/primal animal instinct and the plotting, planning, scheming and reasoning qualities that somehow set man apart from other creatures.

You could say I'm an addict.

And you'd be right.

But the hard part—always—is finding new suckers, sponsors, story angles and sales pitches to keep my next fix coming. And by far the most shameless one I ever dreamed up was the "Arrive and Drive" feature idea I sold to *SportsCar* magazine. See, back in *ze olt dayz,* everybody had to start out by buying a car, some driving gear, and a tow rig, heading off to driving school, doing everything wrong at least twice, and spending at least two years (and easily three times as much as the original investment!) learning all the stuff you really should have known before you started. Think of it as the classically Gestalt "sink-or-swim" school of racing, where every lesson is learned the hard way and every trick new part you buy is damn near obsolete by the time you get it out of the box.

Fortunately, this modern age of manufactured ease, TV remotes and vibro-massaging La-Z-Boys has presented us with an appropriate alternative. Called "Arrive-and-Drive," these are deals where you rent or lease your racing fix by the season or weekend and everything is taken care of: car, crew, spares, repairs, sandwiches, cold drinks, encouragement, and advice. All you need to bring is your helmet, gloves and racing suit (and sometimes even those are provided) plus the optional dewy, doe-eyed and overly well-developed Significant Other to make saliva flow all up and down pit lane.

There are lots of different Arrive-and-Drive situations on the market these days, and they range from available seats in [often under-funded] "pro" cars to rent-a-rides in various amateur series to first-timer drivers' school deals from established concerns like Bob Bondurant, Skip Barber, Jim Russell, Derek Daley, et al. The point is that all these people had Arrive-and-Drive race rides to peddle, and that I love to race. So why not do a magazine story about it to promote and publicize what they're offering and, not incidentally, get to drive in a bunch more free races. Hey, it sounded like a win-win proposition to me (unless I won, of course, in which case it would instantly escalate into a win-win-win proposition….).

Well, this particular scam turned out to be a genuine masterstroke as far as ride mooching was concerned. I got to drive several different kinds of cars in some really competitive races—all with full, professional crews on hand to take care of things, cold drinks in the cooler, and every bit of it absolutely gratis!—and all I had to do was show up on the first day of practice with my helmet in hand and, hopefully, bring the damn thing home in one piece. Then, afterwards, I'd type up a little thumbnail profile of each drive, rating it on grins (how much fun it was), green (how much it would cost if you were just an ordinary, check-writing duffer rather than a shameless journalist ride mooch), and glory (what it could do for you if you harbored dreams of a hoped-for pro career). It was a pretty sweet deal.

One of the rides I dearly wanted to score was in the Skip Barber Formula Ford (now Formula Dodge) race series. I've always been a big fan of professional driving schools (sure wish they'd been around when I got started!) as I think you can compress what would take you a season or more to learn by the old sink-or-swim method into a few pleasant—if incredibly hectic!—Arrive-and-Drive weekends. I have friends who are instructors at many of those schools, and I rate and recommend them all very highly. But Skip's program was unique in that it was, I believe, the first to offer an in-house racing series for customers who wanted to go a step further and actually *race,* but didn't necessarily want the hassle and waiting around or need the spectator crowds and tin cup glory of running with established sanctioning bodies like the SCCA, IMSA, or any of a dozen smaller local clubs.

The concept was pretty simple. You go through Skip's school program or prove suitable previous experience elsewhere, do a few lapping (practice) days to demonstrate that you're reasonably heads-up in an open-wheeled racecar and know enough to keep the machine out of the shrubbery, and then sign up for a race weekend at Lime Rock, Sebring, Moroso, Mid-Ohio, Road America, or any of a half-dozen other tracks all across the country. Then book your reservations, pack your gear, and show up. That's it. And what a strangely peaceful feeling it is to arrive—as I did—at a track like Road America on an early summer Saturday morning and find the vast, green hillsides and huge paddock virtually empty. Silent. Serene. Beautiful. It was actually a little eerie.

Soon other Skippy people begin to arrive and gather around the racecars lined up adjacent to the short pit chute between "Haybale" (the tight, 1st-gear final corner) and Turn One (a 2nd-gear right-hander that is actually the lefthand Turn Five of the full circuit run in the opposite direction) on the Skip Barber "short course" at Road

America. To tell the truth, once I grew accustomed to it, I liked the short course even better than the big, 4-mile monster everybody raves about. The Skippy version eliminates the two lengthy "library sections" up the long, long pit straight and the other endless straightaway between Stations Three and Five, but keeps in tact the fast, blind, climbing and diving bends and swoops through Turn Six, Hurry Downs, the Carousel, Canada Corner, and, of course, the infamous Kink at station eleven. Now The Kink is one of what the great champion Derek Bell always calls "Mighty Corners," and it's more than just a suck-'em-up/hold-your-breath proposition, as carrying a lot of speed through The Kink is fundamental to a good lap time and absolutely essential if you plan on getting a run on the guy ahead of you heading into Canada Corner. Which is really the only legit passing opportunity in the Skippy cars on the "short course" at Road America. Unless the fellow up ahead is either a rank newcomer, not very good, or makes a huge mistake someplace.

Let me tell you what it's like from inside a Skippy racecar. Heading into the tight, 2nd-gear left-hander at Station Eight, you brake late and hard and run down through the gearbox on a downhill slope that flattens at the bottom and "catches" the car a little just before you turn in. It's a textbook late-apex 90—on the power early, and maybe even a little trail braking if you've had your Wheaties—and then powering up through 2nd and 3rd down a short straightaway that seems to gently disappear off to the right up ahead. As you get closer, you see it's more of a blind crest, and there's a worker station in the shade of a grand old Oak Tree on your right, complete with a wrecker and ambulance at the ready to give you some sense of what's coming. Just past the worker station—still accelerating hard in 3rd—the road begins curving and falling away endlessly to the right as you short-shift up into 4th. It's very fast and dramatic as you come swooping down the carousel, balancing the car with tiny, gentle strokes of steering or feathering the throttle a little to trim the car out (although I'm sure the really *fast* guys just keep it planted and ride it out). It's amazing how long the carousel is—it seems to go on for*ever*—and, in a Skippy car, you have to resist the temptation to swing it to the inside early and hug the security of the curbing if you want a quick exit. Thanks to the Safety Police there's a big, ugly gravel trap off to your left these days, but back when I drove the Skippy cars there a dense, handsome forest came right up to the edge of the track with a two-tier wall of hay bales in front of it—right at the edge of the blessed pavement!—apparently to protect the trees. It was daunting, but incredibly beautiful and natural. But there's really no time to appreciate it as you come slicing down this corner that seems to go on and on and on. Finally, up out of the corner of your eye, you see this raised bit of yellow curbing with black tire marks all over it down where the road flattens out, and that's when you gently commit the car in to clip that final apex—foot still to the floor—and drift out onto a short, narrow straightaway running through the bottom of a valley. If you've done everything just right in a Skippy car, you're upshifting into 5th at something slightly over the magic ton....

Up ahead lies one of the most daunting, dramatic and dangerous corners in North American racing. And possibly the world. Oh, if you laid The Kink out in the middle of an open field someplace I suppose it wouldn't be too bad. After all, it's just a simple little bend to the right taken at ultra high speed. But optics and the old penalty factor make The Kink at Road America something to reckon with. From inside the race-car, it looks like the road disappears sharply to the right around a steep cliff wall. And, straight ahead, all you can see is a dense, shadowy forest with a skinny strip of blue Armco barrier in front of it, just a scant few feet beyond the edge of the pavement. Or at least that's the way it used to be. These days, the forest has been mowed back a ways and the Armco on both sides has been replaced by some really ugly—and thoroughly intimidating!—concrete walls. But I think it was maybe even scarier before, because now it seems less blind and claustrophobic. Although the mean black streaks and Heavy Impact smudges on the concrete are not exactly confidence boosters. In any case, you head into The Kink really flying, and you have to fight off three nasty self-preservation impulses every lap if you want to do it right. The first is to lift or brake. I mean, it *looks* like a blessed 3rd gear corner as you come running up on it flat-out in fifth. The second (and more dangerous) is to turn in too early. Hey, it's a natural reac-tion. There's this really threatening-looking forest staring you squarely in the eyeballs and your gut reaction is to try and steer away from it. And I mean *now!* In fact, it's typical to see drivers new to Road America turning in earlier and earlier the faster they go. Which is, simply put, a recipe for certain disaster somewhere down the line.

In fact, there's a great story about how Paul Newman was having that exact turn-in problem when he raced at Road America in the Trans Am days, driving a Nissan Turbo along with his friend and teammate (and my friend as well, God rest his soul) Jim Fitzgerald. According to legend, Fitzy snuck out on the circuit late at night with a spray can of white paint and made a secret little turn-in mark on the far lefthand side of the pavement heading into The Kink. I think he put another one at the blind right-hand entry to Hurry Downs as well. Now I don't know if that story is actually true, but

I *do* know that those two marks were still there when I drove the Skippy cars at Road America. At least if you knew where to look for them. And knowing where they were and using them for a sort of crutch amounted to a huge advantage at a mighty corner like The Kink. It at least took a little of the terror out of it.

Especially if you were going fast.

Fact is, no matter how many times I've driven at Road America, I have to work myself up to taking The Kink as fast as I comfortably can every race weekend and even every session. It's that intimidating. And, all the while, I know the really *fast* guys are going through it even quicker! They're just a little calmer and more comfortable in the car, a little more graceful under pressure, have a fear threshold that's a little further away, and have far bigger *babalones* than I do....

Oh, and then there's that third Bad Thing that can happen in The Kink. The one that almost always writes off a car. You come flying up to it, somehow resist the temptation to back off, make that good, smooth, thread-the-needle turn-in, feel the tires starting to skate, get a bit panicky—hey, you're really *travelling* here!—and react by lifting off the gas. At which point, if you understand the least little thing about vehicle dynamics, the weight shifts gently towards the nose, the rear unloads ever so slightly, and, in the purely technical terms of physics, all hell breaks loose. The general trajectory of your typical Kink Incident sees the car slice across and dip two—or even four!—wheels into the dirt off to driver's left at the exit. But a lot of times the situation is still salvageable if you can just remember to stay calm, keep the car straight, bleed off a little speed, and wait for the track to come back to you as it bends gently left again a short way up the road. But, more likely, you're just a wee bit too excited and get the car cocked all catty-wumpus trying to horse it back onto the pavement or maybe leap into Full Panic Mode and slam on the bakes (so now you can't steer, either) and wind up ricocheting back across the track, impacting the inside Armco (or, these days, concrete) and scattering big chunks of racecar all up and down the road for the next several hundred yards. This particular scenario has played out so many times at Road America that it's referred to by drivers and corner workers as "getting *Kinked*," and that's usually the way the racecar looks afterward. If you're lucky. The Skippy guys have seen it more times than they care to remember, and it almost always uses up a racecar.

Speaking of the Skippy racecars, they're really pretty good, in spite of seeing a lot of heavy combat service and being constantly either maintained or repaired. They're essentially "ruggedized" Formula Fords (er, Dodges) built with three separate cockpit sizes (plus adjustments) so that they can accommodate anyone from an F1 pipsqueak to a burly Harley guy, and the chassis are about state of the art for the Nursery Formula genre. No question they're a lot more Genuine Racecar than tarted-up rental go-kart. Not to mention that they're Serious Fast, so you've got to treat them with respect. But the best part is that the Skippy guys work overtime to not only keep them running, but to keep them as equal as possible as well. Now this is a lot tougher than it sounds, since no two racecars (or engines!) ever work or feel exactly the same. Even if they're built side-by-side at the same time by the same hands and out of the same parts bins. Don't ask me why, but it's true. And any experienced racer will tell you the same thing. So the Skippy instructors test the cars before every series weekend, and by tweaking one here or hobbling another there (usually by stuffing an extra disc in the muffler to trim off a few unwanted horsepower) try to get them all within a half-second window at that particular track under those particular conditions.

You can't ask for much more than that.

And then you've got the seasoned wisdom of the Skippy race weekend format, which is designed to give everybody their paid-for track time and race heats while also providing sufficient income at reasonable enough rates that the whole thing makes sense as a business. So all the drivers get divvied up into four groups of maybe 10 or 12 each (and, if you run the whole series for the points championship, you'll wind up running head-to-head against everybody a few times) and, as one group gets into the cars and the second group suits up and gets ready, the third and fourth groups are out on the corners with the Skippy observer/instructors. There are regular corner workers, too (most often earning trade-'em-up points for Skippy Series seat time) but I've always felt that being on a corner station is a great exercise for would-be racing drivers. You can see who's quick and why, and also the pivotal difference between actual *racing* and merely knowing how to go fast. Not to mention the contrast between deft touch and scrambling desperation that separates those who actually know how it's done from those who are simply hanging on for dear life.

After the checker, group one decompresses a bit before heading out to the corners, group two gets into the cars, group three comes in and starts to suit up and get ready, and group four remains out on the corner stations. And all the while there's input, instruction, and inspiration available from the Skippy guys while the Skippy wrenches gas up and check over the cars between sessions. Meanwhile all the drivers who just came in swap stories, tall tales and outright lies about either what they just did or what they're about to do next time they get a shot. This sort of rotation goes on all day, both days, and each participant gets two practice sessions and a points race on Saturday plus a 3-lap warmup and a points race on Sunday.

It's a hell of a lot of fun.

Not to mention a lot of fun for the money.

And pretty damn competitive up at the sharp end of the grid!

Skippy series entrants run the gamut from young kids with maybe the dream of a Racing Future glinting in their eyes to middle aged, successful business and professional folks who just want to give it a try to Skippy wrenches and workers who've piled up enough hours for a weekend race seat to older, highly experienced drivers who love to race but can't afford the time or hassle of running in "regular" racing series. Or who simply love the competitive challenge of *knowing* that all the cars are as equal as they can be, and that—at least in this tiny little corner of the racing world—it all comes down to breaks, strategy and genuine driving skill. Period. So the groups sort themselves out pretty quickly on a race weekend, with the fast guys establishing themselves at the front, a strung-out gaggle of duffers in the middle, and the inevitable tail-end Charlies groping around at the back. But they have a good time, too, since it's probably their first-ever race weekend and they're doing, by and large, the most exciting and involving thing they've ever done in their lives.

In any case it's a hell of a format, and I applaud Skip Barber and his people (and most especially longtime Skippy general manager Carl Lopez, who has written *the* textbook for learning how to race—*Going Faster!*—which I recommend wholeheartedly) as they provide a complete, soup-to-nuts encounter with the racing experience along with a much needed alternative to conventional amateur racing. Plus they've evolved a higher, more advanced and expensive rung on the ladder with their entry-level pro series—again in identical cars prepared by the Skippy staff—to provide young, well-funded talent a clear path towards a professional racing career. Skip and his people can be really proud of what they've done, because they've built an entire motorsports subculture (referred to by many of the Skip Barber insiders as "Skippy World") based on fun, fundamentals, and fair-and-square racing.

So how did I get in?

Well, I had a little help from circumstances. See, in the world of racing, Ride Mooch Journalists are about as welcome as tax auditors. And, believe me, tax auditors are not very welcome. That's because not too many Ride Mooch Journalists can pee a hole in the snow when it comes to actually driving a damn racecar (although they invariably think they can) and, as a group, they enjoy a sadly well-earned reputation for going slowly, brutalizing equipment, and leaving a trail of bent and/or blown-up racing cars scattered along the guardrails. And then waltzing away to their keyboards without so much as a by your leave. This may be because (and I speak from the inside here) the journalistic profession has more than its share of arrogant, carping, mean-spirited, ego possessed wannabe freeloaders who generally hold the rest of the world up to impossible standards that they could never hope to measure up to themselves.

But that's another story....

In any case, I wanted to include the Skippy race series in my arrive-and-drive story because, well, I wanted to go *racing!* There, I've said it. God, it made me feel clean. And I was fortunate to find myself probing into the situation during a sensitive cusp in the previously fine relations between Skippy World and the SCCA. And there were reasons. For many years, Skip Barber Race Series events had been run under the SCCA sanctioning umbrella as "restricted regionals," and this made sense because SCCA members represented a fat part of the Skippy World target market and the club had a lot of experience, clout and expertise to offer when it came to putting on race events. But there was the usual mound of SCCA paperwork and legalistic red tape involved (just read the Court of Appeals section in *SportsCar* every month and you'll get the idea—not to mention a few good laughs!) plus the perception in certain quarters that Skippy World was actually in competition with and even undermining the SCCA's own amateur racing program.

Then along came the rival "pro" International Motor Sports Association (IMSA) founded by respected ex-SCCA president John Bishop, and the folks at Skippy World decided to run their own new "pro" spec series under the IMSA banner. Which didn't sit real well with a few major players in the SCCA hierarchy, as there was a definite sense of betrayal regarding IMSA's impact on the SCCA's own "pro" series and an openly adversarial attitude between the two groups. And I choose to put "pro" in quotes because I always figured that if the prize money ain't enough to cover bringing the blessed car to the track and buying brake pads and beer for the weekend, it's not really "pro" racing at all. Nope, it's just plain old amateur racing with a few more spectators in the stands (maybe) and a nifty tax dodge thrown in. But I digress....

In any case, Skippy World was one of many groups and individuals caught in the venomous crossfire between the SCCA and IMSA. In fact, the SCCA house magazine, *SportsCar,* wouldn't accept advertising from the new Barber Pro Series, even though they continued to run (and happily accept payment for) large display ads for the rest of the Skippy World programs. Go figure. Fortunately for me, the smoldering embers of this confrontation were still giving off a little heat when I initially mentioned the Skip Barber Ford Series as part of my article pitch to the editors of *SportsCar* (which, as mentioned above, is the SCCA's in-house organ and remains forever faithful to the organization's party line—sometimes to a fault). But it had been a long time and things had mellowed out and changed a bit, so that after I did some industrial strength selling and schmoozing about how the Skippy Series really *belonged* in the story, I finally got the go ahead. And the Skippy people seemed genuinely happy to have me (although a tad nervous that I might do the usual Ride Mooch Journalist thing and wrap up a few cars) because they dearly wanted their old Favored Trading Partner status back with the SCCA along with improved visibility to the rank-and-file SCCA membership.

So it looked like a good deal for everybody.

Especially me, since I'd get to *race!*

******

So that's how I found myself up at Road America for the first race of the Midwestern Skip Barber Series season, and, if I do say so myself, I did passably well for a guy who really didn't have much seat time in open wheelers (although I had raced the long course at Road America many times, and, what with all the fast, blind corners, knowing what's coming up around the next bend is a pretty big deal). Plus the grid comes down to Saturday qualifying times at that first race of the season, while finishing position Saturday sets Sunday's grid and series points totals take over at subsequent events throughout the season. Even though it was almost twenty years ago, I remember that weekend vividly. As, come to think of it, I remember every particularly good or bad racing weekend that I've ever had. And most of them, when you get right down to it, are either one or the other....

I guess I was lucky in that I wound up in a reasonably "soft" group—at least compared to some of the others—and managed I think fourth quick on Saturday's grid. Which I parlayed (mostly thanks to mistakes by other drivers, who were perhaps a bit too juiced up on this first race weekend of the season and kindly goofed or spun themselves out of contention) into a solid if distant second behind a nice young man named Tony Stefanelli. Now Tony turned out to be a pretty neat guy. He was smart and quick and thoughtful and analytical and just starting out on what he hoped would be the path to a genuine pro career (which it was, sort of, as he drove in the pro S2000 series in my friend Marty Ryba's Lola for a few seasons and might have gone even further if the money and breaks had been there when he needed them). Although I didn't realize or wouldn't admit it at the time (hey, I had an ego to feed and care for!) Tony was, at the very heart of things, simply a better driver than I. That's one of those obvious truths that only come to you later in life. Like after you get a little distance, wisdom and perspective (which generally come handsomely gift wrapped with bifocal glasses and a giant, economy-sized bottle of Maalox).

But I was still pretty damn ecstatic about second place (remember, Journalist Ride Mooches were mostly supposed to go slow and wreck things) and I really had a buzz on when we suited up to do it all over again on Sunday. Only this time, I found myself on the decidedly undesirable outside line at the start, tried to compensate by anticipating and getting a jump at the flag, misjudged it totally, and lifted off just as everybody else in Wisconsin was slamming the throttle down so hard the cables stretched. In a heartbeat I found myself fast-shuffled back to fifth or so, and, in ostensibly equal cars, it was going to take an awful lot of doing to try and pick them off one at a time and climb back up to where I figured I belonged. But, as so often happens in racing, the fates intervened. Seems the guy running second behind Tony (one of the Skippy wrenches, as I recall) got a little optimistic through the climbing, slightly off-camber right that's Turn One on the Skippy short course, dropped two in the dirt and snapped into a spin right in front of the rest of us. The two guys ahead of me shot apart like a trick billiard shot—one off in the grass to the left, one off in the grass to the right—revealing the thoroughly horrifying sight of this yellow and red Skippy Ford stalled about three-quarters backward and squarely in my gunsights. I slammed on the brakes, smoke poured off the tires, and it looked like there was no doubt I was going to collect him. But some little well-conditioned synapse in my brain—or it happened so fast, maybe it didn't even go through my brain at all?—pulled my foot off the brake at the last possible instant so I could steer the car hard right and jink around him. I honestly couldn't believe I'd missed him! And, judging by the pulsating bulge of his eyes behind his racing visor, neither could he!

There was even better news up ahead, as one of the other guys had spun on the grass and the other one got into a big tank-slapper and all of a sudden I was in second again and actually pulling away. Meanwhile Tony had checked out of town and the schlamozzle (to use one of David Hobbs' favorite expressions) on the exit of turn one had broken me away from my pursuers. So I drove a lonely, thankful race to a lucky second place and finished up the weekend feeling pretty damn good about myself.

And, need I mention, dying to come back!

I mean, I'd had more fun, more track time, and better wheel-to-wheel competition with less hassle, heartache, waiting around, blood blisters, burns and abrasions than I'd ever experienced running my own cars. Plus the people were really nice, varied and interesting and, unlike a "normal" race weekend, everything wrapped up reasonably early on Sunday so's you could get home at a decent hour and not have to unload the damn racecar and put the damn gear away at three or four ayem and subsequently finding yourself dragging into work the following morning like one of the titular heroes from George Romero's classically gruesome horror thriller *Night of the Living Dead.*

This was too good to stop.

So I put the old schmooze machine in high and called Skip Barber's "general manager in charge of a bewildering barrage of details" Carl Lopez and explained as how what the series really needed was a professional quality newsletter full of race reports and personality profiles—hey, everybody likes to see their name in print!—and that, furthermore, I knew just the guy who could do it. If they'd just let me swap out the newsletter work out for seat time, that is....

Well, I don't know if it was the phase of the moon or the fact that I was still working on that story for *SportsCar* or sheer amazement that I had gone reasonably well and not wrecked anything, but damn if they didn't invite me back for a lapping day at Mid-Ohio and another race weekend at Road America! Although I must admit the Mid-Ohio deal was a bit sobering. Oh, it was fun all right, but, on a track I thought I knew reasonably well, I was a good two seconds off the day's pacesetter and apparently not carrying enough speed through the "momentum" sections that really make the difference at Mid-Ohio. To be brutally honest with myself about it, while Mid-Ohio is far slower than Road America, it's a very technical track that requires a lot of flow and finesse, while you can get around Road America pretty well with a fistful of late-apex point-and-squirt and three brave pills per lap.

In spite of the ego downsizing I'd experienced at Mid-Ohio (hey, maybe it was the car, right?) I was pretty excited to be heading back up to Road America and reasonably confident I could do well there again. In fact, I was secretly thinking I could maybe even *win* one of these things (if I got in against the right people and got a few breaks, anyway) and how absolutely magnificent that would look on my résumé. Driving up to Elkhart, I caught myself daydreaming about the headline on the story I myself might have to write (under some bogus *nom de plume,* of course, since, although it's always a great thrill getting praise from the press, it's considered extremely bad journalistic form to get caught doing the praising oneself...):

"Guest Writer WINS! Beats Series Regulars!"

It was a pretty intoxicating notion. And damn if I didn't almost pull it off that very afternoon. As did three other guys. Because four of us broke away from the field in a pack; drafting, dicing, passing and re-passing like the four of us were fastened together with bungee cords. And we kept it up for the entire race distance. I've got to rate it as one of the most thrilling and exciting races I've ever enjoyed. Positions shuffled every single lap and nobody could manage to break away or hold an advantage because the four cars running together created such a prodigious draft down the curving, high speed chute between The Kink and Canada Corner that if you were second, third, or fourth in line, about halfway down that straightaway—flashing under this magnificently tunnel-like cathedral of trees with the engine straining and the whole car kind of vibrating with the speed—all of a sudden the pea-shooter exhaust pipe in front of you would start to get bigger. And bigger. And bigger. Like it was the business end of a damn vacuum cleaner, you know? And all you had to do was let that suction pull you in, inch by inch, foot by foot—the tach showing a good 200 rpm more than you could ever manage on your own—and then all you had to do was jink out of line at just the right moment and let the momentum carry you wailing by. There was nothing the other guy could do. And then, next lap, he'd do the same right back to you.

It was a pretty damn spectacular race (or at least that's what it felt like from where I was sitting!) as each of the four of us had our turns at the head of the pack, hanging onto the back, and stuck in the middle, and naturally it all came down to who was in front on the final lap. And so all the while, each of us was thinking and scheming and feinting and jockeying to be in what we figured to be exactly the right position when Crunch Time rolled around. The one thing we all knew is that the guy on the point coming out of The Kink was most likely *not* going to still be in front come the checker. My best guess was that the place you really wanted to be was in second, but it didn't work out and I wound up in third as we swooped down the Carousel in tight formation. I reckoned I might still have a shot as we swept through The Kink. But the guy in front of me jinked out of the draft maybe a hair too soon, lost his momentum about halfway by, and now I had cars side-by-side in front of me, a pretty decent head of steam, and no place to go. Shit. And while I'm sitting there in an advanced state of indecision, trying to figure out which one of these Bozos I should follow, all of a sudden the fourth place guy pulls alongside me and now the bunch of us look like a speeded-up pace lap as we head into Canada Corner for the very last time.

Well, I think it's a credit to all of us that nobody banged into anybody else (believe me, it was tempting!) and the bottom line is I got squeezed out fair and square and came home bringing up the rear in fourth at the flag. Damn. Even so, it was still one of the best freaking races I'd ever been in. And it was nice knowing, at least in this particular group, that I could run heads-up with the guys at the front. So that night I told my wife and son (who were staying at Siebken's and had spent Saturday swimming and taking that long, lovely hike around Elkhart Lake) that they really ought to come to the track on Sunday because I thought I might do pretty well. And, since there really isn't much in the way of a crowd on a Skippy weekend (except for the other drivers families and friends, anyway) I wanted someone on hand to bear witness. Just in case I ever needed any backup, you know?

Did I mention that the first race I brought my wife to after we were married was the time I rolled Mike Whelan's TR3?

But I figured things were looking rosy. And they got even rosier when one of the guys running "my" car in another group spun it gently into the guardrail and wrote off a corner, rendering it *hors de combat* for the rest of the weekend. So they brought out one of the spare cars the Skippy guys always have on hand at a series weekend—a handsome dark blue car, I remember it distinctly—and the really interesting thing about this particular piece of machinery was that it had a brand new engine that had just been installed the night before after somebody had gotten a bit extravagant with the rev counter and planted the telltale somewheres around the middle of the water temperature gauge. Even more intriguing was the fact that it was fresh out of the rebuild shop, didn't have a mile on it, and had furthermore never been "equalized" with the engines in the other cars.

Hmmmm.

And I knew from my first practice lap—in fact, from my first uphill blast from Turn One to the lefthander under the bridge at the top—that I had what the late, great Mark Donohue habitually referred to as "an unfair advantage." Maybe it only amounted to a few measly horsepower, but, when you're talking barely 100 horsepower all told, that adds up to a serious, Major League load of whupass. In fact, the difference in grunt was so large and obvious that I was already working on my victory speech before we'd even finished the damn warmup.

Hey, this race was *mine!*

Or mine to lose, anyway....

I was gridded up third based on series points, and, come the green, I powered right by the second place guy going up the hill between one and two. Which, very honestly, should never, *ever* happen unless the other guy makes a thorough mess of the preceding corner. Oh, you can feint to the inside if you like—just to get the other guy nervous—but the fact is that unless you've got some huge power advantage on the other guy, it ain't gonna work. Only this time it did. Hell, I'd never managed to get that kind of an edge even with the cleverest and best concealed cheating I could come up with back when I was running my own cars....

So we stream through Hurry Downs and I know the one guy still ahead of me is just so much dead meat (even if *he* doesn't know it yet) and all I have to do is wait for that favorite drafting spot between The Kink and Canada Corner, wail on by, and motor gently (just to make it look legit, you know?) off into the sunset, leaving those in my slipstream to mutter obscenities into their balaclavas.

Truth is, I was already drinking the champagne....

So we brake and snick down to 2nd for the tight left hander at 8, power out on the short straight to the top of The Carousel, and I almost have a notion to pull out and try him there. But there really isn't room—it's just not a long enough stretch—and so we swoop down through the Carousel with me about a car length behind (and, to be honest, I'm being a bit sloppy and cavalier with the car because I've got, you know, such a *huge* advantage) and, as we run out at the bottom, upshifting into top, I'm thinking about my wife and son, sitting with the other friends and families on the steep, shady hillside overlooking Canada Corner, and how it's going to look when *I'm* the one on the point—and pulling away!—when the pack comes snaking into view.

This is just too damn good.

And meanwhile that Big Grunt motor of mine is pulling me closer and closer to the guy ahead of me as we approach the turn-in for The Kink. In fact, he's coming at me as dramatically as he did the previous day in the heaviest of the full suction draft two-thirds of the way down the straightaway. And it's not until we've sucked it up, tightened our jaws, and started that gentle but decisive arc into The Kink that I realize I'm going to be up his damn gearbox before we get all the way through the corner.

I'm going *that* much faster!

At which point I lift....

Just a tiny bit....

But it's enough.

I feel the car go all light and uncertain under me and my guts instantly turn as hollow and scary as an abandoned mineshaft. The left side tires kiss the dirt and kick up a few clouds of dust, but I'm still going pretty straight and the other car is still right there in front of me. And, at that exact moment, a large and unquestionably Neanderthal lobe on my brain decides that we're really not so bad off and maybe we can still pass this guy before Canada Corner and continue on to win the race. And that would be the same part of my brain that impatiently decided to horse the car back onto the black part rather than waiting for the pavement to come back to me.

At which point, as anyone familiar with The Kink will instantly imagine, all hell broke loose. The lip on the pavement kicked the back end sideways and spit the car across the track, where it speared into the guardrail at about a 45 degree angle *(IMPACT!)* bounced off *(airborne?)* and went spinning merrily down the Armco *(IMPACT! IMPACT! IMPACT!)* in a chunky shower of dust, dirt, fiberglass, wheels, and assorted Skippy Ford car parts, finally coming to rest *(WHUMP!)* nose-first into the guardrail another hundred yards down the road with yours truly still hunkered down behind the wheel in Full Combat Race Driver mode, not exactly realizing yet what had taken place.

It takes a few moments to sink in....

But eventually, as the fresh dust swirls around you and a splatter of dirt from your backwash patters across the shredded fiberglass in front of you and you notice an all-too-familiar wheel wobbling drunkenly across the roadway, you begin to understand. It's all in agonizing slow motion and terribly quiet, and it seems to take forever to slowly rotate your head—heavy, like a tank turret—and catch the curious sight of your own exhaust pipe sticking out of the guardrail a ways up the track, vibrating like a tuning fork. Then you rotate your head forward again as steam begins to rise from the ruptured radiator and see the mess in front of you as if for the very first time. The right front wheel is flattened on two sides and bent up at an unnatural angle—like a broken chicken leg—and the other one missing completely. There are fragments of shattered blue fiberglass and disemboweled racecar guts strewn all across the track and down the guardrail. And that's when two things slowly begin to glimmer in your mind. The first is sort of a prayer. And not the prayer you might expect, the: *"Geez, thank God I'm OK! Oh, thank You! Thank You!"* but rather the kind you might expect from a man adrift in a leaky lifeboat or trapped inside a burning airplane. It's one of those Deals With God prayers, you know, which are inevitably about what a swell, upstanding, God fearing, church going, charity giving sort of person you'll be if you can just hit the old Rewind Button on reality and make like this never happened.

But, as always, the answer is silence.

And then you start gingerly checking yourself over, hoping, in some sick way, that you're injured. Not *badly* injured, mind you, but just enough to be whisked away in an ambulance and taken into town. That way you won't have to face anybody....

Turns out I was okay except for a slightly jammed finger that must've got caught in the steering wheel (which says a lot about the safety of the Skip Barber cars) and the longer I sat there, the more the ugly reality of it seeped in—like a cold November rain through light summer clothing. I recall how extraordinarily quiet and still everything seemed. And now there was nothing to do but take a long, deep breath, sigh, and climb on out of what remained of the cockpit. Damn.

Only what I didn't realize at the time—remember, everything goes into slow motion during a wreck—was that the last two guys hadn't come around yet. They were a couple of middle-aged first-timers, friends who'd more or less dared each other into trying the Skippy World experience and who were having the time of their lives running wheel-to-wheel with each other at the back of the pack. They were *racing,* dammit (albeit far adrift of everybody else) and the terrified yet self-satisfied grins on their faces all weekend long left no doubt that they were having the time of their lives.

Except for when they rounded The Kink, nose-to-tail at maybe 100 or so, and discovered about three hundred pounds of dirt and assorted racecar parts scattered thither and yon across the roadway. Whether they didn't see the yellow flags or if they were so far behind that the flags were down because the corner workers were already on their way over to me is open to question, but, for whatever reason, they were not prepared in the least for the scene that greeted them.

I, meanwhile, was about halfway out of the remains of my car, feeling thick and groggy and wondering what the heck old glib Mr. Schmooze, the Journalist Racecar Mooch, was going to be able to come up with to say. Which is about when the first of the backmarkers beheld the wreck in all its grotesque glory, slammed on the brakes (so now he couldn't steer, of course!) took a tire flat-spotting slide down the middle of the roadway, glanced off the back of my wreck *("What the hell was THAT??!!")* chucking me over the side and face shield-first into the grass. He then proceeded back across the track, brakes still in full seizure mode, and neatly collected the other poor fish on his way into the guardrail on the opposite side. Just that quickly, three of Skippy World's fine single-seater racecars were reduced to scrap. I'm led to believe it was some sort of new record for sheer tonnage destroyed in a single incident.

To be honest, the shame and self-loathing were the worst of the aftermath. Oh, yeah. And the money. Sure, I was on a gratis/freebie/right-this-way, Mr. Ride Mooch Journalist deal that weekend. But the only shred of dignity I could salvage was by holding my Visa card up in trembling hands and offering to pay the same $2500 deductible that any other Skippy racer would have had to pay for a first incident. And believe me, that amounts to one hell of a deal. I mean, where else can you total out three complete race-cars for twenty-five hundred bucks? *Fuggedaboudit!*

I have to say all the Skippy people were really nice about the whole thing. Supportive, too. They've been around and seen this kind of mess before, and were quick to remind me that human beings make mistakes, and, in a racing environment, you usually wind up paying for them. And thankfully only the machinery got hurt and nobody was injured. Just think how much worse that would have been. But none of that seemed to help much with the shame and self-loathing. In fact, it hangs around for a long, long time. But eventually you get over it (or maybe figure out how to bury it someplace) because you've got to live with yourself, and it's ever so much easier if you genuinely like the guy staring back from the mirror. Besides, experiences like that add depth to your character. They make for great bar stories, too. But I bet not a month goes by that I don't rerun the opening lap of that Sunday morning Skippy race at Road America on the inside of my eyelids. I can see it all like it happened just yesterday.

Hell, that was my race to *win!*

If I'd only been a little patient, you know?

The Percy Wordsworth Dovetonsils memorial

Poetry Pages

Stop that snickering!

In the Eye of the Storm

There is a peace in speed
I could never find in stillness.
A solitude so pure,
rich and satisfying
that it saves me from the future
and protects me from the past.
Inside that secret center
-that teeming, streaming vortex-
there is only now...
now...
now...
grabbed onto with both hands
and cradled like a baby.

Alley Reelings

Alleycat winking one-eyed whisker at me
old shoe coughed out soggy lacing
broken flash bottle strewn
...like stars!

After the Checker

Winning is the grand, giddy, glittering sea of smiles
that comes and fades so quickly
after the good part is over.
It soon dissolves,
the echo of a fanfare,
the hollow black emptiness
where a skyrocket crackled across the sky,
a few tiny lines of agate type
in the day before yesterday's newspaper.

By then the bug is alive again
the want
the need
the hunger to hurl headlong
through that tiny, blinking opening
in the headstone granite of time,
chasing after the future together
like we can catch it by the tail!

The Slow Way Out

You can't fool that question
with a long cigarette ash
balancing act....

Bad Apples

Eve's apple
that bonked Sir Issac Newton
—smack!—
into the twentieth century
is the rotten one in every bunch.
But I don't mind
having eaten her apple
(so much)
when I'm eating
her pie.

For Someone Special

A fully orchestrated moan?
For what?
If you take pride in your sand castles,
the tide will make an empty fool of you.

Written for the Chicago Historic Races Program, 1996

They start as dreams
forged of steel and sweat
tempered in blood
to shine for brief moments
—crackling hot!—
in a shower of victory wine
(or leave their twisted pieces
among shattered kilometer stones)
then fade away...

...'till loving hands
pluck those memories
from dim, forgotten places,
making them whole,
to become dreams
once again.

Clockworks

It's broken, see
and that's why it isn't
winding them off anymore.
But you can still hear it—
screaming no-ticking black!

<u>Screwed but not Kissed</u>

The Difference Between Elegance and Opulence is that You Can't Buy Class....

THIS STORY WAS PREVIOUSLY PRINTED IN MUCH SHORTER
AND YET FAR MORE OBTUSE FORM IN THE
*SMALL CLAIMS COURT RECORDS OF
SHEBOYGAN COUNTY, WISCONSIN,*
WHERE IT WAS KNOWN SIMPLY AS
CASE # 00SC0034

Now while I've got your attention, let me drag my soapbox out and climb aboard for a few nasty words about the big—no, make that *enormous!*—and beautiful new Osthoff Resort in Elkhart Lake, Wisconsin. I mean, what's the point of being a writer if you can't air your dirty linen in public? I have to admit I was initially opposed to ("appalled by" might be a more appropriate phrase) the building of the "new" Osthoff. Sure, there was a lot of legitimate history there, dating back to the days when there were just the clean, white clapboard faces of Siebken's and Schwartz's resorts keeping a lazy eye on one another across the shady, lefthand bend on Lake Street where MGs, Jaguars, Ferraris and Cunninghams thundered past, clipping straw off the haybales, during the famous street races of the early 1950's. And just down the street was The Osthoff Hotel, also in matching white clapboard with contrasting green shutters so the three of them made a perfect set. The Osthoff was considered pretty much the snooty crown jewel of the whole bunch and, as accurately recounted in *The Last Open Road,* served as Official Headquarters for the SCCA when the races were in town.

Mind you that the resort hotels in Elkhart Lake go back long before the races, first as quiet, comfortable lakeside places for the famous Beer Barons of Milwaukee and the Cattle Barons of Chicago to send their families up from the sweltering city summers. Then, during the roaring twenties, as notorious, wide-open gambling spots where the streets were lined every weekend with shiny Packards and Duesenbergs and maids were up early at the starch pots, ironing fresh, white shirts for the guests and linen napkins and tablecloths for the evening's tables. But the repeal of prohibition, the depression, and a war that made The War to End All Wars look like an exhibition game cut the heart and spirit out of Elkhart Lake. The town fell on hard times, and the races were heartily embraced by the local innkeepers, businessmen, chamber-of-commerce types and bartenders as a great way to rejuvenate tourism. Which they did.

But, following an errant MG's brush against the spectator-lined snow fencing in front of The Osthoff in 1952 (injury tally: a few bumps and bruises and one broken leg) and the genuinely sickening accident at the south end of Franklin Street in Watkins Glen a few weeks later, when Freddy Wacker's Allard sideswiped the crowd, mowed down a handful of spectators, and killed a 7-year old boy (covered in a grisly two-page photo spread in *Life* magazine) the Wisconsin state legislature shut down the street races in Elkhart Lake. Only the locals had developed a taste for the excitement and the welcome flood of tourists and income the races brought to town, and it was only a few more years before the magnificent permanent racetrack at Road America was completed. And what a facility it was! And still is today....

Siebken's and Schwartz's continued, and the town as a whole managed to retain much of its original charm and simplicity (albeit with a bit of rust and peeled paint showing here and there and the lingering odor of mildew in some of the accommodations) but The Osthoff went through a fallow period and was eventually resurrected as a summer theatre camp, Camp Harand, for the children of artsy/craftsy Midwestern families who believed in that sort of thing. In fact, there was always a lot of wonderfully smalltime showbiz going on in Elkhart Lake, and my family and I always enjoyed the sometimes amazing, occasionally amateurish, but always enthusiastic Broadway Revues put on by the young wait and housekeeping staff/aspiring show people at Schwartz's. These shows continued through several sets of owners, even after Schwartz's was made over and re-christened "Barefoot Bay" in the first of Elkhart Lake's unwelcome moves into the modern, brand-name present.

Meanwhile Camp Harand closed down, and you could look through gaps in the weary wooden fence around the property and see finger-carved initials and small, eager handprints that generations of giggling young actors, singers and hoofers had left in wet concrete in front of fireplaces that no longer existed inside of buildings that no longer stood at the end of each summer. I always thought I heard the echo of small, happy ghosts rustling through the leaves whenever I walked by and, like the rest of Elkhart Lake—even with a dash of sadness thrown in—it was a uniquely warm and peaceful place to be.

So I was a bit concerned when I heard that a local Big Cheese (in fact, about the Biggest Cheese in the area) had bought the property and was planning to build a handsome, opulent and immense "new" Osthoff that, at least to my mind, threatened to dwarf everything in town and steamroller that old time sense of serenity and simplicity that my family and I had come to love about Elkhart Lake. Worse yet, their plans called for closing a section of Lake Street—*Closing part of the original street circuit? Unthinkable!*—and rerouting it around the backside of the property. I followed intently the protracted and ultimately futile civic battle between the ragtag local Save Lake Street coalition and the Big Cheese who wanted to build the place. Disney could've made one helluva movie out of it. You know, quaint, quirky, little-guy townspeople band together to take on Big Corporate Interests in order to save their sweet, home-spun way of life. Only this time the wrong side won. But I guess contradicting the truth never stopped Hollywood before. And what a property! Imagine a bunch of oddball-yet-lovable small town characters led by maybe a divorced, recovering alcoholic loser of a Public Defender trying to redeem himself and put his life back together by taking on the case. We could maybe even make him a gay, blind, paraplegic war vet Black or Hispanic guy and kill several Hollywood birds with one Sly Stone. Unless DeNiro or Dustin Hoffman are interested, that is....

But that's another story.

The point is that the new Osthoff eventually and inevitably got the rubber stamp of approval from the local city fathers and they built the blessed thing, and, to be fair, a great effort was put forth to fit it into the style and context of the rest of the town. Only it was so bloody *big!* My wife and son and I always walk the charming little path around Elkhart Lake every morning when we're in town, and, upon seeing The Osthoff for the first time from the opposite shoreline, it struck us all like some huge, over-stuffed love seat that's simply too big for the room. And I mean *waaay* too big. "It looks like a part of Disney World," my young son observed. And indeed it did. Not that there's anything wrong with Disney World. Goofy forbid. But a monumental structure like The Osthoff did sort of overpower the small town quaintness and old time sense of the past we'd all come to cherish about Elkhart Lake.

Hey, that's progress.

But time passed, the landscaping came in, some of the ugly BRAND NEW sheen faded into the scenery, and we all got used to it. Fact is, it's a pretty swell place. And certainly a hell of a lot plusher than anything else in town. So I finally broke down and forked over a whole bunch more than I usually do so my family and I could stay there in July of 1999, when *Montezuma's Ferrari* was unleashed on a largely unsuspecting public during the blowout Brian Redman International Challenge vintage weekend at Road America. And I must admit it was pretty damn nice. Or it *was* nice, anyway, until they lost my effing decals.

Let me explain. As part of the hoopla and folderol involved in launching a new Buddy Palumbo novel, we always have some logo-emblazoned decals and doodads to sell, give away with copies, and generally help promote the experience. In fact, our decals have been without question our very best advertising tool. Is there one on *your* racecar or favorite street machine? There should be. In any case, it should come as no surprise to anyone who knows me that everything came down to the Last Freaking Moment and my suppliers had to overnight two big cartons to me in care of The Osthoff. One contained cloisonné pins, earrings, tie tacs etc. featuring Art Eastman's marvelous "prancing chili peppers" logo that may eventually get us sued by Ferrari (which came via FedEx) and one containing logo decals, which was sent UP Red. A whole *bunch* of decals, in fact. Like 10,000 of them. Value? Oh, say, $2110.64 at net cost. Or one carton weighing forty-four pounds, as UPS described it when they faxed up the proof of delivery. Which we needed, on account of the good people at The Osthoff's front desk had somehow *signed* for both shipments, but could only come up with the carton of cloisonné jewelry when I arrived to pick them up.

Hmmm.

To be honest, things were really going too well to get upset about it. I mean, the new books were selling like proverbial hotcakes and we were raking money in left, right, and center. Thank goodness. Not to mention that the manager of The Osthoff, whom we will call Lola (seeing as how that's her name) seemed genuinely concerned about our mutual (or what I *thought* to be our mutual) problem and assured me that the missing decals would surely reappear. Only they didn't. In fact, we even stayed on a few extra days to wind down after the weekend (although I always have difficulty sleeping when I'm paying three figures per night for the privilege—call it a hereditary quirk) but the decals had apparently vanished into thin air....

No problem. They could be replaced.

My 2110 bucks, however (not to mention the freebie decals I would be mailing out after the fact and the money we doubtless would have made selling them) was a different matter. "Oh, not to worry," Lola from The Osthoff assured me. "We'll file an insurance claim." Which, in fact, she did.

Including the domino effect collateral damages mentioned above, the bottom line on the letter Lola sent to the insurance company came to $3560 (although from the outset I was willing to settle for the out-of-pocket $2110.64 replacement cost, but, as an experienced ex-used car salesman, I knew that, once a figure is mentioned, it will likely go down, but it will never, *ever* go back up again). To be honest, I was a little reluctant to settle my bill at the end of our stay with the decal money still floating out there in limbo, but again Lola told me: "Don't worry. Everything will be taken care of." Well, as a writer, I suppose I should know better than to trust anybody who would end a sentence with a preposition. Or maybe I'd misinterpreted. Maybe it was that old Chicago First Ward Alderman interpretation of "Everything will be taken care of," in which either some genuinely embarrassing State's Evidence or a key witness or two conveniently vanish into oblivion....

But I didn't know that at the time—hey, I'm a trusting sort of guy—so I paid the bill (and it was more than the blessed decals, believe me!), went happily back home to the suburbs of Chicago, and, when the time came some 30 days later, duly paid my vendor for the missing decals (Think Fast Ink check number 1831, dated 9-1-99) as they had been produced in good faith—albeit at the last possible moment—and shipped as directed to The Osthoff and signed for by the fine folks at their front desk. After which, well, who the hell knows what happened to them? I only know *I* never saw them. But not to worry. I had Lola's word that "Everything would be taken care of."

I now bring you an edited, condensed, Hollywood Time Passage montage of the weeks and months that followed. First we have a few phone calls back and forth between Lola and myself. Helpful, encouraging calls. The claim was progressing. Then the calls became more, umm, "cordial." It appears I'm becoming a bit of a nuisance. Finally, after about five weeks, I ask her for the insurance claim number and call them myself. The eager and cheerful young lady at the other end of the line looks up the paperwork and cheerily informs me: "Oh, by the language of the policy, our [the insurance company's] liability is limited to ten dollars."

Imagine the look on my face. It will help if you either suck on a very sour lemon or chew on the tail of a kipper snack that has been left out for several days. Either will do. As you can further imagine, my fingers were a veritable blur on the keypad as I dialed Lola up at The Osthoff to register my surprise, concern, and the early symptoms of what would eventually become thorough, flaming indignation. "Oh, *no!*" Lola gushed supportively into the receiver. "That can't *possibly* be right."

And of course it couldn't.

Or could it?

See, there are these three quaint, musty old statutes dating back to the days of plank roads and witch burnings buried in the pages of the Wisconsin Innkeepers' Law, and one of them (254.82, to be exact) states very clearly that, in cases of fire or theft, the innkeeper's liability is limited to, and I quote, "$200 for each trunk and its contents, $75 for each valise and its contents, and $10 for each box, bundle, or package and its contents, so placed under the care of the hotelkeeper." Or, as the late, great Mike Royko would have put it in my beloved, hometown Chicago-ese: "Hey, here's a sawbuck, kid. Now *scram!*"

We now embark on Round Two of our long-running Phone Call Montage. Only now I'm having trouble getting through. Seems Lola is generally either "unavailable" or "in a meeting" or "showing a property" or hiding under a desk someplace whenever I call. And all of a sudden she's not particularly good about phoning me back, either. So I invoice them for the loss. That doesn't work. They ignore it. So I have my friend, some-time teammate, and favorite southern-fried shyster lawyer David Whiteside send one of those nasty, threatening, shyster lawyer-type letters ("don't make me open up a can of whupass here, lady") demanding satisfaction. I also send reams of faxes, which, over time, evolve in tone from thoughtful essays on reason, fairness, and good business ethics to threats of legal action and questions of ancestry. At last I get Lola on the phone again—some three months after the fact—and it seems like we're finally getting down to serious negotiations. I tell her I'll gladly settle for my out-of-pocket $2110.64 cost. She checks with her boss (the above-mentioned Big Cheese) and calls back. The most they can go is $1000 in cash (geez, things must be awful tough in the luxury resort hotel business up in Sheboygan County!) but would I take the rest in lodging?

Sure I would! A nice room like the one we'd had in July would be great. And I'm not picky. Any race weekend we're up there would be fine.

Back to the Big Cheese, then back to me. It was starting to feel like one of those "track store" car dealerships where your friendly salesman (the good guy) keeps run-ning back and forth to his manager (the Spawn of Hell, who is busy pulling the legs off live chickens in his office under the back stairs) to get The Deal approved. Reply from the Spawn of Hell: *"Not on a race weekend. We're always booked solid. You'll have to make it some other time."*

Visualize me biting clear through the tail of that week-old kipper snack. It seemed thoroughly astounding to me that the same fine, respectable folks who readily admitted they'd managed to lose my $2110.64 worth of decals due to their own negli-gence and/or incompetence (take your pick—and remember, this is a high-line, high profile sort of property that surely spends more than that on blessed *flower arrange-ments* every weekend!) could:

> *a)* Be so cheap
>
> *b)* Be so unethical

c) Not only dictate *how* they would be willing to "take care of everything," but stipulate *when* as well.

d) Treat a customer so shabbily—especially when said customer had written two books (both, strangely enough, on sale right there in The Osthoff gift shop!) and many magazine articles mentioning, praising and recommending both Elkhart Lake in general and The Osthoff in particular.

As I ruminated over the above, I found myself elevated to a clear, cleansing purity of anger, frustration, seething outrage, and flaming indignation. So I called a lawyer. A few of them, in fact....

And the gist of it all was that, because of the quaint old statute mentioned above ("Here's a sawbuck, kid. Now *scram!"*) I was most likely screwed. Besides which, what self-respecting lawyer would want to take on the Biggest Cheese in town for a lousy 2100 bucks. Or, as one of them put it: "If you'd slipped on the stairs and broke your back or spilled hot coffee in you lap and scalded the family jewels, we might really *have* something. But two measly grand worth of decals? *Fuggeddaboudit!"*

But I was raised with a firm belief in the fairness, equity, and nobility of our legal system (we're pretty damn naïve in my family, if you want the truth of it) so I ponied up 76 bucks cash American and, following a few false starts trying to "jailhouse lawyer" my way through Wisconsin's typically (and I think purposely) impenetrable legal system, successfully filed a Small Claims action (case number 00SC000034) in the Sheboygan County courthouse on January 7th, some five months and countless blood pressure points after the original incident.

Upon receipt of the summons cordially inviting her to join me at a pre-trial conference on February 28th, my friend Lola responded with not one, not two, but *three* letters. Plus a phone mail message. The first, dated January 13th (but received on the 20th) informed me, in language at once terse and grammatically impenetrable, that the insurance company had suddenly and dramatically changed their mind. I quote in full and verbatim: *"Upon submittal of your claim, to the insurance company has awarded $500.00 against the claim made for your missing property."* Enclosed was a check from The Osthoff (their check #19323 dated 1/13/00) in the amount of $500. Except that I received another, somewhat longer and more confusing letter from The Osthoff—dated Jan. 20th and certified, no less—the very same day. In it, Lola apologized once more for my loss and informed me rather redundantly that, and again I quote verbatim: *"The insurance company has responded with a payment of $500, the maximum amount allowed under the language of the policy"* and that *"we are willing to issue you a check for $500."* Would that be the check I already had? It went on to advise: *"We feel this offer is more than generous, as State Statute 254.82 on page 10 of the Wisconsin Lodging Laws limits the innkeeper's liability to $10 for this type of property."*

Or, in other words: "Here's your five hunnert bucks, kid. Now *scram!*"

Except then I checked my phone mail, and here was yet another message from Lola (I'm not really surprised she didn't want to speak to me in person) telling me not to cash the check, because they'd stopped payment. Confused? I sure was. And then I received letter number three (dated Jan. 21 and likewise certified) confirming the phone message about disregarding the first letter and the check, advising me that The Osthoff's response to my Small Claims action was on the way, and apologizing, and again I quote, *"for any inconvenience this may have caused you."*

Honestly, I've never gotten so many mixed signals from anybody since Mary Lou Gundersen in the fifth grade. Not that it made much difference, since I'd already decided pretty much where, precisely, The Osthoff and their insurance company could put their "generous" offer.

What followed was a protracted trip through the conference rooms, corridors, solemn courtrooms, and blind alleyways an innocent prole with a legitimate beef travels trying to make his way through (not to mention sense of) the incomprehensible maze we call our legal system. It entailed three separate midwinter journeys up to the Sheboygan County courthouse, including one at 4:30 ayem on a black, frozen, sub-zero morning to make an 8:30 hearing that it turned out I really didn't have to attend on account of Lola and The Osthoff had already filed a written response but neglected to send me a copy in time to abort the trip! And that would be the same morning that I waited and waited in court only to find that my case wasn't even on the docket and also the same morning I called fellow scribe Tom Waller of the Sheboygan Press and invited him out for coffee so I could explain, in simple laymen's terms, how much I wanted to walk into the lobby of The Osthoff carrying a bucket of fresh moose puke and pour it all over their fine front desk.

Tom had written a nice piece about me when I'd been the lunchtime speaker at the local Kiwanis Club meeting (the same exact weekend we'd stayed at The Osthoff, launched the new book, and come up short one box of decals, in fact) and he was quick to grasp the Quixotic aspects of my story. Not to mention the juicy Local Scandal angle, as Lola's boss is indeed a Big Cheese in those parts. So he wrote a few column inches about it in the local paper and you would not believe how offended and outraged Lola and The Osthoff got. I had some damn nerve going public.

Meanwhile, I girded myself for battle in court. I even sent in the required $89 fee for a jury trial. Only there wasn't going to be any of the hoped-for Perry Mason stuff on account of the judge had looked over all the paperwork and sent out a letter advising that he was going to issue a summary judgement based on that quaint old ten-dollar statute mentioned above (translation: "Here's yer sawbuck, kid. Now *scram!*"). It looked like I was sunk. But then, at the eleventh hour, while re-reading the bloody Wisconsin Innkeeper's statutes for the umpty-hundreth time, it suddenly occurred to me that neither of the two conditions mentioned in old 254.82 ("fire" and "theft") actually applied in this case. And one of the other statutes (254.81, dealing, strangely enough, with hotel-keeper's liability for baggage delivered over for safekeeping) had no specified loss limit. So I wrote a letter to the judge, overnighted it to the court, and showed up at the appointed time with my jaw set, cold fire in my eyes, and reams of receipts and paper-work under both arms—ready to do battle at the bar.

Only I didn't get to. The judge ran his eyes over everything—some of it perhaps for the first time—pushed his glasses back up his nose, and invoked a summary judge-ment based on a *third* statute (254.80 to be exact, which neither I, The Osthoff, the insurance company, or any of the lawyers I'd consulted had ever mentioned or thought applied) and awarded me the maximum allowable compensation under the law.

That would be three hundred bucks.

Plus court costs.

"B-but, your honor," I sputtered respectfully, my voice venturing into octave ranges it hasn't seen since before unfolding my very first Playmate of the Month, "I haven't even presented my case yet!" I spread my hands imploringly over the four or five pounds of paperwork I had piled in front of me in neat, relentless little stacks.

The judge frowned down from the bench like he was looking through the wrong end of a pair of binoculars, trying to figure out where that awful, grating, squeaking, sputtering noise was coming from. "I've already ruled," he said flatly, his lips curled down in an expression of monumental boredom and annoyance.

"B-but your honor," I squeaked even higher, "can't I *appeal?*"

Boredom and annoyance quickly blossomed into genuine disdain as he wearily explained as how, sure, I could appeal (fat lot of good it would do me) and now could you please gather up all your neat little stacks of paper and kindly disappear. And don't let the courtroom door hit you in the ass on the way out.

So The Osthoff duly forked over a check for $472.25, which, considering their "generous" original offer of *"Five hunnert bucks kid. Now SCRAM!"* means I worked extremely hard and made three separate early ayem trips up to the Sheboygan County courthouse in order to arrive at an impressive, additional, bonus net loss of $27.75!

Am I a great lawyer or what?

And, no, I never did appeal. It's just not worth it. Too much time and effort and frustration for way too little gain. Besides, I figured out a better way. I decided to put the story in my new anthology. That would be the book you're reading right this minute. I mean, it's a pretty entertaining yarn, isn't it?

And that's how I'll get my money back.

Besides, people out there need to know how bad a Big Cheese from Wisconsin can really smell....

GOING FOURTH

SOMETIMES A LITTLE FREE-FORM MEANDERING
HELPS US REALIZE WHERE WE ARE....

THIS STORY WAS EXPANDED FROM A FEW PARAGRAPHS
IN THE MID-OHIO RACE REPORT FOR THE
MONOPOSTO REGISTER NEWSLETTER
AUGUST, 1998

It had been a pretty decent weekend at Mid Ohio. The new car ran well, I had a great dice (albeit well down towards the back end of the field) with somebody I trusted and enjoyed sharing a beer with afterwards, and I was fortunate to stay with the car's owner and his wife in their quaint old country farmhouse directly across from the backside of the racetrack, where we could hear the echo of the racecars warming up while we drank coffee around an old wooden table in the kitchen every morning and made plans for the day ahead. It was the Sunday before the Fourth of July—hot and thick and muggy as it often is when summer settles in over our mid-American farm belt—and the night before a thunderstorm of truly biblical proportions rolled in over the cornfields, putting on a display of celestial power and threatening grandeur I will never forget. I watched the whole show nuzzled deep inside a feather comforter in a comfortably creaky old bed at the top of the stairs, and it was magic to feel the hot, sticky calm of the night go nervously on alert as the weather front advanced across the rolling acres of corn. You could hear the crack and rumble of the thunder growing louder and and feel the wind picking up and then the first heavy splatter of fat raindrops against the windowsill. And then it came in torrents, thrashing down through wicked gusts of wind that bent trees back and beat like an angry mob against the shutters. It was right on top of us, each blinding, blue-white flash of lightning accompanied by a simultaneous and shattering blast of thunder that froze the world and the blood in your veins. It was the kind of night that fills you with a murderous sense of awe and a queasy awareness of your own sniveling mortality. And it was nice to be there at the top of the stairs, burrowed inside that feather comforter in a comfortably creaky old farmhouse that had withstood a thousand such storms and would doubtless withstand a thousand more. From long before I was born until long after all I knew were gone, if you stopped to think about it. There was a strange, floating sensation of security in that.

The storm passed on as the sky faintly lightened, and it drizzled on and off through the morning as we had our coffee and toast, headed over to the racetrack, and went through the usual mountain of problems getting everything in synch between me and the car. But the weather ultimately cleared up fine and things came right when it counted and I wound up winning the tight, back-and-forth battle at the rear of the pack mentioned above. Amazingly, it turned out to be good for a second place finish in a poorly subscribed class, and everybody seemed pretty satisfied with that. I know I was.

Afterwards we watched a few more races, packed up our gear, said our long good-byes, and trundled out the paddock heading off in our separate directions. Normally I would've made straight for the Interstate to pound my way home at the usual sleepy/wary 10 to 12-over with one eye peeled in the mirror for cops, but this particular late Sunday afternoon I didn't have far to go or any special rush to get there. There was a business appointment in Indianapolis the following morning, and using the usual major arteries made no sense because I would have to go south to Columbus, then west on I-70 and back north again to Indianapolis. So I decided to take country back roads, navigating mostly by the late afternoon sun, heading west into it until I found myself on too dull or busy a road, then turning south on the next likely looking lane and putting the sun over my right shoulder until I found a tempting opportunity to head towards it again. Sure, it took me more than twice as long to get there, but it was a lot more interesting than droning down the interstate just so I could pound a few with the traveling salesmen in the bar at the Holiday Inn or watch another who-knows-how-many hours of television before nodding off to sleep.

It turned out to be a richly rewarding drive. Without planning any of it, I stumbled across sections of the old Owl Creek Trail that the settlers once traveled. And the site of the Cherokee Relay Station, where creaking, dusty stagecoaches stopped to pick up and drop off passengers, let the others stretch their legs, and hitched up new teams of horses. Further on I stopped at a historical marker that was no more than a small, brass plaque hidden away in the foliage by the side of the road. It marked the sad, lonely gravesite of three poor soldiers who were laid to rest there on a frigid and long forgotten December 20th during the war of 1812. History tells us they were just as likely to have died of disease or exposure as in a hail of enemy gunfire.

I went through a bunch of peaceful little farm towns that still look much as they did before the first TV antenna sunk its talons into a brick farmhouse chimney and the cold glow of the tube began replacing the fireplace as the source of spiritual heat in American homes. The Fourth of July was barely a week away, and so there was fresh red-white-and-blue bunting draped over the stone monuments and war memorials in the town squares, protected by antique brass cannons worn shiny by generations of tiny hands. But you could tell the American flags hanging at ease in the still air were part of the everyday scenery in these towns. And they were everywhere. In front of schools and county buildings, farms and feed stores, churches and manufacturing plants, and suspended on angled poles from front porches that smelled of fruit pies, bicycle grease, overstuffed chairs and baseball gloves. You got the feeling most of them were there every day. And came in every night....

By sheer chance, I wound up passing the birthplace and childhood homes of both Wilbur Wright and President Warren G. Harding. And then, deep in the quiet Ohio farmland, I passed two Amish families in horse drawn buggies coming home from a long Sunday in church. With their straw hats, aprons and bonnets, they had the gentle, soft-focus look of a Monet or Renoir in the early evening light, and they waved hello as I went past. As if they understood perfectly what a normally hell-bent stranger from the big city was doing, prowling through the quiet serenity of their landscape towards the end of the Lord's day.

I crossed the Ohio/Indiana border through the town of Fort Recovery, where, somewhat surrealistically, a local ensemble called the Ohio Valley British Brass Band was giving a smashing evening concert performance in front of a reconstructed an old fort outpost from the early 1800s. Families from both states had gathered on blankets and lawn chairs to watch and listen, and I bought a sandwich and had a nice little picnic for myself while the band worked its way smartly through parade ground standards like *The William Tell Overture,* a few Sousa marches, and Von Suppe's famous *Light Cavalry.* They did a nice job of it, too. Heading out of town after the concert, I saw some fool kid on a bike with his cap turned around backwards almost get creamed by a pickup truck while doing a "look ma, no hands!" to impress a likely local dolly. Young men everywhere do stuff like that when they're dangling over the cusp of puberty. And I couldn't really blame him...she was *cute!* But the driver of the pickup had to lock up all four to avoid hitting him, and so he called the kid over and gave him a proper chewing out. Only without using all the trendy cusswords we're so used to hearing on the streets of New York, Los Angeles, and Chicago. Or on the movie channel of your choice, for that matter. And the kid took it, too, nodding and hanging his head and answering "Yessir. I know it was. Yessir." at the appropriate intervals. Most places I come from, the kid would've launched a middle finger skyward, spit out a couple taunting *"F.U.s,"* and pedaled off into a nearby alley. Laughing.

The point is that there's still a lot of the America of Norman Rockwell and Norman Vincent Peale out there. By sheer acreage, it's still by a thousand times the biggest part of the country. And there's a lot more than Andy, Opie and Aunt Bea out there—real people with real lives, jobs, joys, dreams, dramas, friends, families, heartaches and happiness—but a lot of us tend to miss it (or *dis*miss it, take your pick) when it flashes by as a blur of same-old scenery on the Interstate. No, you've got to take the byways and back roads every now and then and get a good look at the America that feeds us, frees us, and supplies most of the toys, tools and table fare of our culture. It's a wonderful and deeply reassuring experience, and I recommend it highly.

BURIED ALIVE WITH ELLEN ZWEIG
A HARSH LOOK AT THE COLD REALITIES OF WINTER RALLYING

ORIGINALLY PUBLISHED IN
BRITISH CAR
FEBRUARY, 1992

I discovered a lot of exciting new things when I was sixteen. Like fr'instance my high school chemistry class was taught in a strange, foreign language that had nothing whatever to do with English. And girls (who had seemed such a bloody *nuisance* just a few years before) suddenly developed wondrous new topography and appeal. I also discovered that my father's TR3 would only enter our driveway *so fast* before winding up in Mrs. Walton's peonies. As you can imagine, that led me to seek other, more covert places to test the adhesive properties of Dunlop's finest and my own budding skills as a future World Champion.

Which, in a roundabout way, is how I got into Rallying.

As practiced by experts, TSD rallying is a rather dry and tedious exercise wherein one follows clearly written and numbered instructions leading you up, down, and all around these lovely, serpentine country backroads at ridiculously reasonable, proper, and precise average speeds such as 38.654 miles-per-hour. Indeed, I observed that crack rallye teams were almost always controlled by the navigator *(never* the driver) whose job it was to bark out the operative route commands whilst simultaneously calculating arrival times and average speeds via pre-microchip devices such as Heuer chronographs, manually operated Stevens and Curta rallye calculators, and maybe a Halda Speedpilot if they were *really* serious. The idea, obviously, was to stay precisely on course and exactly on time at all times, so that when you rounded a bend or crested a hill and found yourself confronted by a hidden checkpoint, you would be right on the dot in the mileage and milliseconds department. This was known as "zeroing" a checkpoint, and the team capable of accomplishing this thoroughly anal-retentive feat most often and effectively usually wound up with the first place mugs. Not to mention a little something to pour in them....

Although never much good for collecting hardware for the mantlepiece back home, my interpretation of the sport was *ever* so much more entertaining. The "Levy Method" of rallying involved getting seriously lost at every possible opportunity, and then driving like bloody hell to get back on schedule. And getting lost was easy, as the tiny, hard-to-see route signs favored by most rallyemasters tend to blur a bit at 80 or so. Plus I was forever bedeviled with inexperienced, greenhorn rookie navigators who didn't really know what they were doing. I mean, who would ride with me twice?

So I was ceaselessly on the lookout for someone—*any*one—willing to sit on the passenger side of my dad's TR3, buried in a clutter of maps, instruction sheets, scratch paper, clipboards, stopwatches, and a well-thumbed copy of *Lary Ried's Rallye Tables*, all the while hanging desperately onto the little metal grab rail over the glove box while I demonstrated everything I *thought* I'd learned about High Performance Driving in the few short months since I'd earned my license. On, I'm ashamed and embarrassed to admit, my third and final try. I should also mention that navigating a TR3 required quite a bit of yelling, as Triumphs put up a thoroughly hellacious clatter at full chat. So good lungs were a real plus when it came to rallye navigators. Especially female-type rallye navigators. And one such creature was a poor, hapless blind date of mine named Ellen Zweig (nickname "Zwiggy") who only agreed to go because she recognized the obvious advantages of First Blind Dates held during daylight hours.

Did I mention it was the dead of winter? In fact, the adorable pet name of this particular rallye was *"S'no Safari"* (get it?) and the weatherman co-operated by depositing many thousand cubic yards of the stuff all across the Midwest during the preceding weeks. Ah, but Rallye Sunday dawned bright and sunny (if a tad below zero temperature-wise) and off we sped, laughing and chattering (well, our teeth were chattering, anyway) whilst light-heartedly scraping patches of ice off the inside of the TR3's windshield. Those familiar with the breed need no reminder that the so-called "weather protection" on a TR3 amounts to little more than a few brittle sticks and ragged scraps of animal skin of the sort favored by the marque's Druid ancestors, while the so-called "heater" in a TR3 generates BTUs equal in strength and area affected to the average domestic automobile's cigarette lighter. But, as I mentioned, at least it was sunny....

As we rolled merrily along, heading for the shopping center parking lot where the rallye was scheduled to begin, I took pains to explain the subtle nuances of stop-watches, average speeds, advanced logarithmic calculations and all the Sneaky Stuff rallyemasters tend to pull in order to send pea-brained, neophyte rallyists down rutted, Farmer Brown sideroads with axle-deep muck holes at the end. Zwiggy interrupted from time to time to ask a question, request a clarification, or recall some article of warm clothing she'd inadvertently left at home.

We stopped at a gas station for a tankful of high test (which always made the interior reek something horrid 'til the first couple gallons burned off) and then joined the rest of the rallye faithful gathered at the windward corner of a desolate shopping center parking lot. I couldn't help noticing that all the experienced hands had left their rorty little sports cars at home (where they rightly belonged in such weather) and were ensconced in big, fat, comfortable and thoroughly un-sportscarlike Ford, Chevrolet, and Plymouth sedans with big, fat, and equally comfortable and un-sportscarlike heaters and defrosters. "It sure is *cold* in here," Zwiggy observed. No fool she!

"It'll warm up once we get going," I lied.

"I smell gasoline," she continued.

"You do? *Really?*" I lied some more.

"And there's ice on the floor over here. A sheet of actual *ice!*"

Well, cold or not, Zwiggy turned out to be a pretty decent navigator. In fact, we made the first half-dozen checkpoints without getting lost one single time. We even zeroed a hidden checkpoint. Amazing! Plus the brilliant sunshine had pushed the ambient temperature all the way up to damn near zero. The downside was having to putter along these wonderfully swoopy and challenging country backroads at 38.654 mph, but I reckon that's the price of success in the bigtime TSD rallying game.

But then fate stepped in. Another rallye team in a brand-spanking-new, Honduras Maroon, fuel-injected Corvette flew right past a key intersection and attempted a quick U-turn to get back on course. Unfortunately, what appeared to be a level, snow-covered verge on the edge of the road was, in truth, an enormous ditch filled with several hundred cubic tons of fresh, powdery white snow. The Corvette swung wide, sunk in, teetered drunkenly off balance for a moment—clawing helplessly for traction—then slipped slowly out of sight like the Andrea Doria going down.

Needless to say, Zwiggy and I went over for a closer look. We found the Corvette lying on its side in the ditch in full profile position, the driver's-side door almost equal to ground level. "Need any help?" We inquired of the perplexed-looking young Corvette driver at our feet.

"Naw," he scoffed grandly, flashing me one of those musclebound Corvette-guy smiles. "This baby's got *Positraction.*" Which he proceeded to prove without question by gunning the engine, feathering the clutch, and digging two short, deep, and perfectly equal horizontal ruts in the wall of snow beneath him. Clouds of blue smoke billowed from the ditch as all the oil drained to the low side bank of the big, chuffing V8 before the whole shebang shut down in a grim, shuddering death-rattle of hydraulic lock. "Say," the Corvette guy finally admitted, "maybe we *could* use a little hand."

So the big-shouldered Corvette driver and his highly pneumatic Corvette-guy girlfriend (Corvettes always seem to attract, umm, *ample* women) clambered out of their hole in the ground and piled into what is laughingly referred to as "the back seat" of a

Triumph TR3. Imagine stuffing a pair of water buffaloes into a steamer trunk. But at least it warmed things up a bit with all that living, breathing Corvette meat crammed inside our poor little Triumph.

It took about ten minutes to locate an open gas station, where we left Corvette Charlie and his bosomy girlfriend to negotiate the going market rate for re-floating a sunken Corvette. And a brand new, top-of-the-line, fuel injected and Positraction-equipped example at that. No question the enterprising local with the tow truck concession appreciated an Open Wound of Economic Opportunity when he saw one. But Zwiggy and I were gone. Off to chase the rallye route once again. _Behind at last!_

Well, I drove masterfully (natch!), winding every gear to the redline, braking at the Last Possible Instant, and, if the desperate little dents Zwiggy's fingernails were leaving in the little metal grab bar in front of the passenger seat were any indication, she was impressed as well. On unknown stretches of road, I resorted to "The Levy Rule of Twice" to estimate proper cornering speeds. Simply put, if the Illinois Highway Department put up a sign advertising that a particular curve or ess bend could be safely taken at 40mph by somebody's elderly grandmother in a '58 DeSoto Adventurer with balding, under-inflated tires and bad shocks, I figured it was safe to assume that a budding World Championship talent in a fine example of the British sports car builder's art could reasonably be expected to negotiate that same curve or ess bend at roughly twice that speed.

And it worked pretty well, too.

Only you could get in some really deep doo-doo if, like, say, one of those turn signs happened to be missing. Like fr'instance if it'd been knocked down by an errant snowplow or something.

I bet you know what's coming....

Yes, friends and neighbors, Zwiggy and I crested a small rise at something approaching the magic 'ton,' only to discover a sharp lefthand turn dead ahead totally unannounced by the Illinois Highway Department. Oh, _shit!_ Not to mention that it was off in the cold, deep shade of a massive, two-story snow bank that had been gently melting in the sun all day. So the pavement was covered with a sheet of glare ice.

Double "Oh, _shit!_"

No way were we gonna make it.

Summoning all the technical and intuitive driving skills I'd amassed in three full months of actual, behind-the-wheel experience, I slammed desperately on the brake pedal, shut my eyes, prayed it would end quickly, and braced for impact. The TR fish-tailed wildly left-right-left-right (they don't steer very well with the brakes locked, do they?) plowed straight into the snow bank *(KA-WHUMPFFF!)* and everything went black.

But I knew I wasn't dead, because I could hear Zwiggy screaming at me. *"YOU @#"*#%&!@! IDIOT!!!"* she shrieked, sounding more than a trifle upset. *"WHERE THE FREAKING HELL ARE WE??!!"*

Where indeed? All around us was nothing but bitter cold and pitiless dark. Hell, we were *inside* the damn snow bank! Trapped! Surrounded! Buried alive like the hapless victims in some morbid Edgar Allen Poe story. I tried opening my door, but it wouldn't budge a solitary millimeter.

"Try your door," I advised Zwiggy calmly.

Grunting sounds. Followed by: *"It won't open, you stupid bastard."*

"Push harder," I suggested.

Louder grunting sounds. *"I'm pushing as hard as I CAN, you #@!*#*)%! moron. You think I LIKE it in here?"* Then she started muttering under her breath, which always seems to be a bad sign when it comes to blind dates, regular dates, steady dates, and even fiancees and spouses.

I had to *do* something, you know? So I slid the side curtain back on my side and began gingerly digging my hand upwards through the pitch-black wall of snow, searching for the row of little pull-up fasteners that hold a TR3's top to the windshield frame. With fingers numb as frozen toads, I burrowed along mole-fashion, unsnapping them one-by-one. And then, suddenly...*voila!* We were bathed in sunlight! Not to mention about 800 pounds of fresh, wet snow.

Free at last! Free at last! Great God almighty, we're...Say, wait a minute here. Sure, *we're* free. But our faithful TR was stil! buried well up over the waterline in crash-compacted snow. I looked over at the mound of lovely slush that was my date, scanned the dead-empty winter landscape around us, and realized we were smack-dab in the middle of Nowhere Special, Illinois, with both sun and ambient temperature about to drop over the horizon like a tin duck in a shooting gallery.

I'll spare you the grisly details of our extended forced march to the nearest farm-house (emphasis on the "far" portion of the word) except to say that my blind date Zwiggy never uttered a single word and studiously avoided my eyes lest she spit in them. We eventually managed to borrow a shovel from a local farmer who knew better than to be out in such weather and then trudged grimly back through the gathering evening gloom to dig the car out. By the time we finally arrived at the rallye's endpoint, the winners were rinsing the victory beer out their first-place mugs and heading for the door. To complete the disaster, the thermometer took a further 20-degree nosedive during our drive home which I still recall as the coldest, darkest, and most deathly silent ride ever taken by two people in a Triumph TR3. Well, deathly silent except for the sad, plaintive cry of the TR3's heater fan, which tends to whirl around in a state of ineffectual, frenzied anguish like a cheap food processor full of paper clips.

Believe it or not, blind date Zwiggy and I spent the next several days in bed. Only not together. Not hardly We were both laid up with the worst cases of sneezing, sniffling, eye-watering damn-near pneumonia you have ever seen in your life.

Fact is, I don't recall that she ever went out with me again.

BURT'S TWICE-COOKED CHICKEN
HEY, A LITTLE CHICKEN SOUP IS ALWAYS GOOD FOR WHAT AILS YOU!

This recipe is based, in part, on an ancient Chinese method for cooking chicken in hot water, but with an extra twist that puts the meat through a second, high temperature cooking cycle in the oven. This process renders off much of the layer of fat underneath the skin, makes the skin crispy, delicious, and arguably more healthy (or at least less unhealthy!) and leaves the meat underneath the skin terrifically moist and with a very unique flavor. It also leaves behind a wonderful soup that you can put away for wintry nights or whenever you have a bad cold. Like my mom always said, *"it's good for what ails you!"*

INGREDIENTS

One fairly large frying chicken w/giblets

Three or four fat carrots, sliced.

Two or three healthy stalks of celery, sliced.

One largish Spanish onion, peeled, cut into small wedges and separated. Save outer skin!

One huge or two medium turnips, peeled and cut into odd, irregularly shaped geometric cubes about ½ inch per side.

One medium parsnip, ditto.

A scant ¼ cup of finely chopped fresh parsley and thinly sliced green onions (scallions) in a roughly 50/50 mix.

A few cloves of fresh garlic.

A tablespoon or so of Olive oil.

A teaspoon or so of peanut oil (optional).

¼ of a fresh lemon

A healthy splash of Dry Vermouth.

Kosher (sea) salt to taste and/or two or three chicken bullion cubes.

Pepper to taste.

THE PROCESS

Start out by putting a medium pot (say 4-6 quarts) and a backup teakettle of water on to boil. You'll need them later. When the water in the pot boils, add a little- say ½ to 1 teaspoon-of Kosher salt (unless you've fallen under the spell of the Dietary Thought Police, that is, and believe that salt is second only to crack cocaine in the evil little granules department). You can also use two or three chicken bullion cubes in place of some or all of the salt for a richer flavor. Then add about a quarter of our sliced-up carrot, celery, turnip, and parsnip veggies. Also add all of the onion's papery outer skin (yep, throw it right in there!). Bring to a boil, then lower heat to simmer.

In a second, larger pot, heat up a couple tablespoons of oil (I usually use 2/3rds good olive oil mixed with 1/3 peanut oil, but it probably doesn't make any difference) and gently fry up two smashed & chopped cloves of garlic to flavor the oil, then remove. If my chicken came with a proper big glob of fat on the skin flap around the cavity, I'll remove it, chop it up, and toss it in the oil to render down and add even a little more flavor (we'll be skimming it off later). Then I'll take another quarter of my carved-up Spanish onion and sauté it over medium heat until translucent. By the way, you can use just about any kind of onion here, but each will yield a different flavor. If you like things on the sweet side like I do, stick to the Spanish or Vidalia types.

While the onions are cooking, wash that nicely sized whole frying chicken inside and out. I prefer frying rather than roasting or stewing chickens for this recipe because they tend to be less fatty. Pat dry. Then turn up the heat under the cooking pot, push the onions aside to make space for the chicken in the middle, and set it in the pot to put a quick sear of heat on the skin (a minute or less on each side) and make sure to turn the chicken so you get the top, bottom, and both sides. And use your hands, for gosh sakes! Nobody's looking. If your chicken came with a neck and giblets inside, you can throw those in as well and stir everything around a bit to keep it from burning. At this point, add a nice, healthy splash of dry vermouth. Makes a wonderful smell, doesn't it? As a final touch, squeeze the juice of ¼ of a medium fresh lemon into the pot.

Now pour the simmering veggie stock from the other pot (complete with all the veggies!) over the chicken, and add hot water from the teakettle as necessary until the chicken is thoroughly submerged. If you like, you can even toss the squeezed lemon wedge in since you can't eat it and the pot's probably closer than the trash can. Keep the heat under the pot on Maximum Scorch and drink a good, healthy shot of the vermouth. It doesn't taste very good by itself, does it? When the stock in the pot comes to a boil again, turn the heat down to medium low and let it sit at a gentle, rolling boil for about three minutes or so and then TURN OFF THE HEAT AND COVER THE POT TIGHTLY! No kidding. But you're going to need heat elsewhere later on, so turn the oven up to the redline (say about 475-500 or so) to get it ready.

The chicken has to sit there in the dark and stew for about 30 minutes, and this is a good time to make a salad or slice up the rest of the veggies you'll be putting in the soup (the ones you already put in will be strained out because they'd be way too mushy and tasteless by now). I generally use ½ Spanish onion to 3 fat carrots and 3 ditto stalks of celery to one large or two medium turnips and a single, scrawny parsnip. You gotta keep an eye on those parsnips, on account of they're really loud and pushy on the old taste buds and tend to overpower all the other flavors if you give them half a chance. I'll also chop up my mixture of fresh parsley and a couple thinly sliced green onions (scallions) to put in the soup later as a finishing touch. Now is also a good time to take a slug of decent scotch or pop a nice cold beer (Pilsner Urquell has always been one of my favorites) to get the taste of that damn vermouth out of your mouth.

After the chicken has been doing the backstroke in the hot water for about a half-hour, remove it carefully and set in a big bowl or Pyrex dish to cool a bit. To keep from mussing the skin, try putting a slotted spoon or a plumber's wrench or something down into the bird's cavity in order to lift it out of the water. Now clean up the floor and the top of the stove, you slob.

Have another slug of scotch

While the bird is cooling, strain the stock through cheesecloth laid inside a colander and set aside to cool for another fifteen minutes or so (if it's wintertime, set it outside, but covered so the raccoons don't get at it) and then carefully skim the fat off. Do it over the sink, since it can get pretty messy after a vermouth and two scotches. Put the skimmed stock back on the stove, toss in the remaining veggies, bring to a nice, rolling boil for ten minutes, add the parsley/scallion mix, and lower to simmer and cook until the carrots and turnips are just getting tender. Add salt & pepper to taste, and dilute a little with hot water if necessary. Then you can add the noodles, rice, or matzo balls of your choice. I'm partial to using one of the commercially available matzo ball mixes, but I add some of the chopped parsley/scallion mix and a little beer or seltzer to make them light and fluffy, then adjust the consistency (Horrors! Sacrilege!) with seasoned Italian bread crumbs. Hey, what do you expect from a lousy Jew married to a wonderful Italian? You can also skip the noodle/rice/matzo ball part and just put it up in the freezer. Where you will most likely forget all about it and ultimately wind up throwing it away eight or nine years from now when you find it hiding out behind a box of freezer-burned Chicken Kiev portions and a two-year-old Christmas ham.

But back to the chicken, eh? Now that the oven is nice and hot and your chicken has cooled enough that you can handle it without excessive juggling or making those stupid *"woob-woob-woob-woob"* noises like Curly from the Three Stooges, we are ready for the grand finale. Put a raised wire rack over a roasting pan with a half-inch or so of hot water underneath (or you can use some of the soup stock and even throw the strained glop from the cheesecloth in if you like a really *big* mess). Then cut up the chicken and lay it out on the rack. You can halve it, quarter it, or split and butterfly it like a Muslim bending down to pray, but you definitely want as much of the skin side up as possible. Then simply pop it in the super-hot oven, pop another beer for yourself, and remember to keep an eye on it so's you don't mummify the poor thing or set it afire. When the skin turns a nice, even, crispy-looking golden brown, it's ready to take out, cool for a minute or two, and serve.

You'll find this recipe also makes for great cold leftover chicken (get the picnic basket!) and you can fool around with the basic, twice-cooked process all sorts of different ways. Such as:

Skip the veggies completely (except maybe a little sweet onion) and put a couple tea bags in the water with the lemon (chamomile is probably my favorite) before pouring it over the chicken.

Skip the lemon and add a little hot stuff *("BAM!")* like cayenne or a gutted & chopped jalepeno or a few squirts of pineapple hot sauce to the water.

Cook a few strips of bacon on a rack in the oven until crisp and crumble into the finished soup.

Order out from The Colonel and let somebody else do the work!

COMEDY OF TERRORS
IN THE END, WINNING IS SIMPLY A STATE OF MIND....

ORIGINALLY PUBLISHED IN
BRITISH CAR
OCTOBER/NOVEMBER 1998

I think

the easiest way to evaluate how you really feel about people is to measure the time you spend with them. In that regard, I usually find myself wandering over by John Targett's modest bivouac every weekend we wind up in the same paddock together. Sure, I could just as easily venture over by the Big Rig boys, where my sketchy credentials as motoring scribe, all purpose ego fluffer, and potential booster of resale values is usually good for a few mugs of suds and maybe even a drive or two. But I'm drawn to people who got the itch the same way I did and are destined to scratch it the same exact way—One Man Band fashion—prepping the car, packing the rig, towing all night, unloading the rig, meeting your friends, scrambling to make first practice, fixing what broke or wore out, qualifying the car, fixing what else broke or wore out, racing the car, savoring the moment through an amber glass or two, saying goodbyes, packing the rig, towing back home, unloading the rig, and then phoning in early Monday to order another load of pricey replacement parts to fix the other stuff that broke or wore out during the race. It's sort of a holy crusade, really, full of long distances, strange lands, wild adventures, weird and wonderful characters, great challenges, evil setbacks, endless windmills to tilt at, and those rare friendships and moments of gleaming accomplishment that make it all worthwhile.

I'm unashamedly partial to the Don Quixote types who do it all themselves, and especially when they're genuinely nice people and even more especially when they have a bit of talent. In my estimation, John Targett gets top marks on the entire lot. He's an expatriate Brit out of Ohio who campaigns an authentic period copy (originally built in 1963, I think) of the factory MGBs that raced at Sebring and Le Mans. It's got all the pukka light alloy body panels (painted proper BRG, of course!) and runs with a full windshield and white fiberglass hardtop, knockoff wire wheels, sexy plexiglass headlamp covers, and a grapefruit-section Monza fliptop fuel filler that's mostly decoration these days, as the fuel cell is in the trunk. John knows he's giving up some poundage and aero to the quicker sprint-spec Bs around, but he likes running the car "as it was" and makes up a lot of the difference on driving. In spite of his gentle, courteous, and ever bemused manner in the paddock, John drives with great skill, finesse, quickness and determination, and I rank him highly by any standard. But John doesn't evidence any desire to move up in class to 200mph GT Prototypes or razor-reflex formula cars.

He loves racing his MGB.

Always has.

And he's got no higher aspirations than to do right by it.

I suppose in the greater scheme of things that might not amount to much, but, to the MG faithful, it's something rather special. And even more so when you look at the gauntlet John has run to pursue this motorized Holy Grail. I cannot recall many race weekends when John hasn't had more than his share of mechanical disasters, gremlins to deal with, and bum luck to endure. Yet, in spite of all the problems, frustrations, and Sad Sack setbacks, John inevitably enjoys his race weekends and grins his way through it regardless of thankless effort applied or cruel lessons learned. Take a few years back at Watkins Glen, when, in typically gracious manner, John offered a share of the 2-hour Paine Webber enduro to a longtime friend and fellow racer of the Porsche persuasion (make of it what you will) who proceeded to make a minor judgmental miscalculation *(oh SHIT!)* and rolled the bloody car. To the extent that not a single straight panel remained. Now most of us—myself included—would've found ourselves internally deadlocked over whether to clench our frenzied fingers around the fellow's throat or billfold first. But not John. He looked briefly disappointed, sighed, shrugged his shoulders—*what can you do?*—and gave it all a wan little smile.

After all, he'd handed him the keys....

In any case, I was highly flattered when John offered me a share of the driving at the SVRA's "Badger 200" Enduro for pre-1973 production cars at Road America. After all, when one of the Big Rig guys offers you a drive—even in a car worth a small king's ransom (by the way, what *is* the market in small kings these days?)—it's no earth-shaking deal because they've usually got other toys to play with and the wherewithal to fix it should something go awry. So it's a risk they can afford to take. But, for a guy like John, trusting someone with his beloved MGB puts his whole racing lifestyle on the line. If the car gets wrecked, rolled, burnt, bent, busted, blown up, or otherwise rent asunder, it will put a jagged hole through the heart of his racing budget and keep him away from the sport he loves until he can afford to put things right again.

But the temptation was more than I could resist. Especially since it was a beautiful summer weekend and Road America is one of my very favorite circuits. Not to mention that I'd never enjoyed any firsthand race experience with an MGB before (unless you call watching a pair of indecently quick black and silver examples streak off into the distance from the cockpit of my battered TR3 back when I first started racing with the Midwest Council of Sports Car Clubs). On the other hand, 200 miles of heavy flogging sounded like a mighty long haul for some of the creaky, craggy old vintage iron on the entry list. Not to mention some of the creaky, craggy old vintage drivers who planned on nudging them along. But John's car had shown a good turn of speed over the years (between the aforementioned mechanical gremlins and the odd poltergeist visitation, anyway) and I thought, should luck be with us, we might do reasonably well. Especially since all the big gun Corvettes, Mustangs, and Camaros figured to be out of brakes by half distance.

Road America is *hard* on brakes.

Still, I was a little concerned about the fact that John's MG had been sort of a Disaster Magnet over the years, and the trend continued when John ventured out for first practice and promptly had the hood (er, "bonnet") catch pop open on his very first lap. At speed. Now this really shouldn't have been a problem, since John has wisely fitted his car with a leather hood strap (like the factory cars) to guard against just such contingencies. Unfortunately, the aerodynamics of the situation proved entirely too much for the puny little pop rivets holding the bloody strap in place, and before you could say *"KA-WHAP!"* the hood slapped back over the windshield like an enormous effing rat trap, rendering John instantaneously blind for all practical purposes. It is a measure of John's skill and kinship with the fates that he brought the car back other- wise unscathed (although the MG's alloy hood had assumed the approximate profile of a caved-in barn roof after a record snow). Oh, well.

My good friend and SVRA tech maven Jack Woehrle (who has raced on the Sattiday Night Stock Car circuit and therefore has magic hands when it comes to impromptu bodywork!) helped us bend it back to a reasonable shape over a couple of jackstands and a stack of Mini Cooper rain tires, but it was not exactly what you could call a *concours*-quality restoration. Not hardly. At my suggestion, John drilled a few new holes in the now lumpy hood and added a couple hood pins—just to make sure, you know?—and the overall effect was to give John's once-lovely B the unmistakable look of a severely beaten middleweight the morning after the big fight.

Then there was the little matter of the engine. In attendance Friday afternoon was our mutual friend and my old (I dare not say how old) Midwest Council E-Production nemesis Dick Leuning. Remember those indecently quick black-and-silver MGBs my ratty TR3 was chasing a few paragraphs and countless moons ago? Well, Dick built them both and drove one of them, and he's been successfully campaigning

MGBs out of his respected *MGs Limited* shop in Milwaukee ever since. Simply put, what he doesn't know about B-series MG race cars isn't worth knowing, and he's supplied a lot of the hard parts and savvy that make John's car (and several other quick MGBs) go so well. Anyhow, Dick gave John the following advice regarding Sunday's 200-mile enduro: "As your engine builder, I encourage you to do it. Hell, I can always use more business. But, as your friend, I don't think you should. You've got a pretty wild motor in there with 13-to-1 compression and a really hot cam. The thing doesn't even start pulling until five grand, and you've got to be shifting it a little past seven if you don't want to be sweeping up the pieces. An all-out sprint motor like that one's not meant to be flogged for 2 ½ hours without letup. And you really don't have the right gear for this track, so you'll either have to lug it or stretch it coming out of the corners. Neither of which will do it much good. Plus it's used a half quart of oil already in just two thirty minute practice sessions. To be perfectly honest, I wouldn't trust it to go the distance. For sure I wouldn't risk it if it was my car."

You had to admire Dick for his candor—a lot of tuners would simply say "run her 'til she blows" and laugh all the way to the bank—and so I told John that maybe running the Badger 200 in his snaggle-hooded B wasn't such a good idea after all. Especially after two tentative practice laps Friday afternoon showed Dick was spot-on about the gearing. Coming out of three critical corners, I had to either shift in mid-drift (never highly recommended), wind it well past 7000, or stick it in 3rd and have the engine fall flat on its nose. The tightish 4:55 rear also forced us to use that goofy Laycock de Normanville overdrive so beloved by British sports car designers three times each lap, and, at least in my experience, the o/d is a dodgy proposition at best under racing conditions. Especially over a 200 mile distance. "Listen," I advised John, looking him squarely in the pupils, "Dick doesn't think the motor will last, and he should know. If the damn thing blows, it's gonna screw up half your season, and I really don't want to feel responsible."

John looked back at me, reason and adventure wrestling in his eyes.

"Think it over," I continued. "I know I wouldn't run it if it was *my* car. Really I wouldn't." Well, that was most probably a lie, but I was a better man for telling it. But in John's eyes, it looked like adventure had reason in a submission hold.

The Badger 200 was slated for nine ayem Sunday morning, and, to be perfectly honest, I reckoned we were out of it. But then I ran into John late Saturday afternoon and, sure enough, adventure had won out. "I'm going to run it either way," he said with admirable if misguided conviction, "and I'd love to have you share it with me."

"What if the motor blows while I'm in the car?"

"Well, then I guess it's my problem, isn't it?"

"And you're *sure* you want to do this?"

"Absolutely."

So we shook on it.

Hell, why not?

Seeing as how there was a warmup at 8:20 Sunday morning and seeing as how we had new tires and brake pads to bed in and furthermore seeing as how I only had two laps in the bloody car, the plan was for me to show up bright and early to take it out for a little pre-race familiarization. So I pedaled over from Elkhart at 7:30 while my family soundly slept (cheeky bastards!) and John, crew chief Tony Elliott, and the rest of John's enthusiastic if marginally experienced and thoroughly disorganized entourage (Bill, Marty, Dick, Ron, Brandon, Moe, Larry, and Curly) showed up shortly thereafter to ready the machine. And we were in trouble right off when we discovered one of John's freshly bought-and-mounted race tires had lost 14 pounds of air overnight. So we took it off and one of the guys toted it over to the tire vendor to have it put right. Only nobody was there, since it seems the tire busting crew had surfed through Siebken's bar the previous evening on a veritable tidal wave of tap beer and Jagermeister shooters, and even those who were borderline ambulatory come sunup weren't feeling all that right.

So we put on the spare and checked the fluids and I got my suit on and climbed behind the wheel, and that's when we hit Serious Snag #2 on a day when it was only fitting to number them in order to keep them properly organized. Seems the car wouldn't start. Or, more properly, it wouldn't run once it started. Being the insanely quick studies we are, it only took the eight of us fifteen minutes to agree that the gas in the fuel tank (or was it the fuel in the gas tank?) was not making it through John's brand-new-as-of-yesterday fuel pump and on to the carburetors as originally intended by the engineering lads back in Abingdon-on-Thames. Hmmm. So somebody dashed off for yet another new fuel pump (and of course the fuel pump place wasn't open yet, either) and by this time the warmup was over and race time was fast approaching and the tire guys still hadn't shown up and the crews who were on top of what they were doing already had their fuel jugs, spares, tools, jacks, and other assorted paraphernalia neatly lined up along the pit wall and were bringing their cars to grid. We, on the other hand, were thrashing about like fresh-caught flounders in the bottom of a wooden boat, knowing only that, if the universe were to suddenly and benignly turn upside down and cause the boat to sink, everything would be all right again.

But chaos inevitably engenders activity and desperation is a great motivator, and, believe it or not, John and Tony and the guys somehow got everything screwed back together—at the last possible instant, natch!—even if we worried that the engine wouldn't last or ditto the old balding spare on the LR (the tire guys *still* hadn't shown!) or that John's puny little battery would no way restart the car four or five times and still provide enough juice to go the distance. No question it would be a triumph of major proportions (that would be a Vitesse or a Mayflower, wouldn't it?) if we somehow, some way made it to the finish.

THOUGHTFUL DIGRESSION: There are no laurels, loving cups, fat wads of prize money or moments of illuminated glory in the world of vintage racing. It's just for fun, really. But it's *serious* fun, doing something that requires nerve, grace, skill, patience, and experience—not to mention a bit of luck!—to do well. And, of all the forms of motor sport, none tests ourselves and our beloved 4-wheeled toys—not to mention our relationship with the fates and furies—like endurance racing. It goes far beyond who can drive fastest or who owns the best car, and the classic old fable about the tortoise and the hare comes to mind often. Best of all, it's a true team effort, in that no one person on a team can win it for you, but *anybody* on a team can lose it for you. In the end, endurance races are generally not won by the winners, but lost by the losers. Still, you tend to feel like a winner every time you so much as finish one of these things. It gives you a special little glow of accomplishment, you know? As if you've been weighed on the great fish scale of life and judged a keeper. Better yet, it's a glow with an afterglow and an after-afterglow built right in.

And now, back to out regularly scheduled programming....

So we make it to the grid in the nick of time and John starts the race with the tired old spare on the LR (don't ask about the tire guys, OK?) and, as the cars take the green in a historically accurate but thoroughly ridiculous standing start—boy, do I wish I'd had the concession on Corvette clutches that day!—crew chief Tony Elliott turns to me, eyes bubbling with excitement like soup coming to a boil. "Well," he says expectantly, "we're on the dance floor."

And indeed we were.

To tell the truth, I honestly didn't believe I'd ever get in the car. What with all the problems and glitches and mad, slapdash scurrying around, I'd fallen victim to a wave of negative vibrations and really didn't think we'd make it to the first pitstop. Let alone the checkered flag. But then John starts reeling off a series of strong, consistent laps—some even a mite *too* strong for a 200 mile contest!—and, all of a sudden, I find myself sucked into an unthinkably optimistic notion that we might not only *finish* this stupid race, but—dare I say it?—figure respectably in the results as well. After all, a lot of the faster cars were *not* gonna be around come the checker.

Of course, it's precisely when you start believing that sort of thing that the racing gods reach their collective thumbs down out of the heavens and squash your infantile sense of optimism like a bug on a windowsill. If you're very quiet, you can even hear them snickering about it from behind a convenient cloud formation.

Which is why I shouldn't have been much surprised when John was late coming 'round some 20-odd minutes into the contest. Like half a minute late. Oh-oh. As visions of blown motors and crunched bodywork danced in our heads, the MG suddenly appeared, limping up pit lane with a flat LR tire. *Shit!* Naturally it was a complete Chinese Fire Drill as John bailed out, we replaced the offending tire with a freshly bought-and-mounted spare, filled up the gas (why not?), and sent him back out to complete his stint behind the wheel. The rules for this race specified three mandatory 5-minute pit stops, and I was thoroughly amazed to discover that our first stop—bum tire and all!—had only taken 5 minutes and 38 seconds. Not bad at all! And that, of course, is when John came limping up pit lane again with yet *another* flat LR! We checked every-where for sharp edges or rubbing, but the inescapable conclusion was that, while the fine young men at the tire concession might have known how to put tubes in tires and install those tires and tubes on wire wheels, they hadn't quite got the bit about keeping air *inside* those tubes and tires down quite yet. Then again, they'd had a pretty rough night of it at Siebken's. John was gently upset about it—*hey, what can you do?*—but I'm happy to report that crew chief Tony Elliott went properly berserk.

And well he should, since we were now out of spares and had to send Tony back to *a)* chew the tire guy a new asshole and *b)* then beg sheepishly for him to perhaps pretty please in a hurry remount and balance one of the two tires he'd changed for us the previous day. Only this time keeping the majority of the air *in* the tire, thank you very much. By the time all the running and screaming and barreling headlong through the paddock and banging of knockoffs and gnashing of teeth and was over, we'd spent about nine more minutes in the pits.

"Look," I told John, "this pretty much puts us out of it. You want to just pack it in and save the car for your sprint race later this afternoon?"

"No." John answered in a dangerously even tone. "I want to finish this thing." His gaze had the same brave, unwavering certainty as those proud and famous Texas volunteers who defended the Alamo against Santa Ana. And we all know how *that* particular story turned out, don't we?

But then things seemed to settle down a bit (and about effing time!) as our boy John went out and did a splendid and solid 40 minutes without further incident. *Hallelujah!* I meanwhile gave him pit signals and watched my sunburn get redder—the weather was utterly fabulous!—and, soon enough, it was time to put on my flameproofs and signal John to come in. But he was really into his rhythm and missed the signal the first time around, and now we'd screwed up again because the rules said you got penalized if any one driver went more than 40 minutes between pitstops. Don't ask me why. But he made it in next lap and we managed to refuel without setting the car afire and, as I climbed in and fumbled with the belts, John advised me that the overdrive was acting up but otherwise things were fine. At five minutes on the dot I motored back onto a strangely vacant track (we were hardly the only team to suffer the slings and arrows of misfortune that day!) and proceeded to reel off what I fervently hope will be remembered as a series of decent and workmanlike laps.

Until….

Until the brakes started to feel a little funny. Sometimes the pedal was up and sometimes it was low and the usual ploy of giving it a pump or two helped sometimes and didn't seem to do much of anything others. And for sure the infamous Laycock de Normanville overdrive had developed a severe case of pre-menstrual cramps and was engaging and disengaging whenever it bloody well felt like it. The good news was that the motor none of us thought would go the distance was pulling sweet, smooth and strong, showing plenty of oil pressure, and running thumbs-up perfect on both oil and water temperatures.

How about that?

And that's about when the brake pedal went clear to the floor heading down into the 2nd gear left-hander at Station Five at something approaching two miles a minute. Need I mention that my eyes grew large as DeSoto hubcaps even as every other orifice on by body slammed down to *f*22 and beyond? That my grip on the wheel could've turned coal to diamonds? That my backside inhaled the greater majority of the driver's seat upholstery? It is only thanks to a large runoff area and discovering a tiny smidgen of brake left waaay down at the bottom (after *furious* pumping!) that we made it through the corner. Turns out a seal had ruptured on one of the rear wheel cylinders. Oh, well...

I will not burden you with the numerous negative side effects of doing Road America without brakes, but I cannot honestly recommend the experience except as fodder for bar stories or to impress silly young women with overly developed breasts. In any case, the rest of the lap was spent driving like one of those little old ladies who can't see much beyond the steering wheel, and, for a nanosecond or two, I considered simply soldiering on as best I could to the finish. I mean, there couldn't be many laps left and an awful lot of cars were already strewn along the sides of the road or sitting silently in the pits (hell, I hadn't even *seen* another ambulatory race car for at least six laps!) so we might actually be doing fairly well in spite of all our mishaps and disasters. But then I inhaled half the seat cushion again heading into Canada Corner and decided that, if I was going to try for the finish this thing without brakes (or with *almost* no brakes, since there was still that tiny little smidgen way down at the bottom of the pedal travel after a dozen or so pumps) I sure as heck wanted John make the call.

And that's about when the corner marshals showed me the meatball flag to inform me that something was wrong with my car. Fact is, I was mightily impressed that they could appreciate my lack of brakes from the sidelines. *Geez,* I thought, *those guys are good!* Only they weren't meatballing me for the brakes. No, sir. Seems we had yet another—is anyone counting?—tire going down. Only this time on the *right* rear!

Well, I trundled on in and naturally the pit stewards wandered up and looked the car over—*Yup, tire goin' down. No two ways about it!*—and, while John replaced it (racking up yet another penalty on account of I was still in the car and the rules clearly stipulated that you can't work on *any*thing while the driver is in the car) I explained as how we had maybe $1/16^{th}$ to $1/32^{nd}$ of the brakes left and that he was really going to need his upholstery cleaned after the race. And that would be *after* we'd surgically removed most of it from my lower intestine.

About then somebody hollered that the lead car was on its second-to-last lap, so I gingerly ventured back on the circuit to do one *very* slow lap and duly pass under the checkered flag to a great tumult of waving and shouting and clapping of hands from the scant handful of misguided early morning drunks up in the grandstands.

As you can imagine, it took quite awhile for the officials to sort out timing and scoring and all the various penalties. Of which we had a bunch. While we were fairly certain that we'd completed 42 laps (which would've brought us home 7th overall and

First in Class in a field mostly consisting of limping stragglers, borderline deceased and walking wounded) the powers that be penalized us ruthlessly for our many blatant and unrepentant transgressions, affronts to humanity, and crimes against nature. We were handslapped 2 laps for a short pitstop (even though we'd already done our three required 5-minute jobs and then some when the tires went flat) and then we were horeswhipped a whopping, Death Penalty *18 laps* (can you believe it?) because John went one lousy lap past the 40 minute limit when he missed my "in" signal. All of which dropped us down to dead freaking last among the actual finishers.

Funny part is, we still won our class.

By 20 laps!

Seems the only other cars entered dropped out on the very first lap!

Go figure.

Why, there may even be a nice little First Place cup, plaque, or bowling trophy involved, which I will duly place among the other treasured dust collectors on the shelf, mantlepiece, windowsill, or commode lid of my choice. And, as sure as old Lucas starter motors make distressing noises, the day will come when we'll have my wife's relatives over for dinner and some cousin or uncle who knows diddlysquat about racing (and could care less) will look at that gleaming, plated bauble on its neatly veneered base, rub his chin, and politely remark, "First place, huh? That's pretty impressive."

"Yep, sure is." I'll tell him, swirling my third or fourth Tanqueray and Tonic around in its glass. "One of the best damn races I ever drove. Proud as hell of it. We finished dead last."

Then he'll look at me all funny and quietly ease away, convinced that racing vintage sports cars is even dumber than he thought and that I'm even nuttier than he ever imagined. Which was plenty already.

But, hey, it *was* a great race. We battled. We fought. We sweated. We struggled. We scratched. We clawed. We persevered. We lost. We laughed. And then we won. Most important, we *survived!* And, like I said awhile back, just finishing one of these things makes you feel like you've been weighed on the great fish scale of life and judged a keeper. That in itself is worth more than any cheap wooden plaque or plated tin cup.

Although those are nice, too....

THE HAUNTED JAGUAR

COULD THERE BE A GHOST IN THE MACHINE?

THIS STORY ORIGINALLY APPEARED IN
BRITISH CAR
AUGUST, 1995

Call me

a kneejerk reactionary, but I'm afraid I harbor a smarmy, rose-colored fondness for the days before cars had modules, sensors, Pieziolectric anti-knock crystals, and all the other cyber-electric microchip gizmos that have taken mechanicing out from under the shadetree—*forever!*—and changed a real Frontier Man's occupation into something more suited to computer wonks. Of course, it's simply advancing age and lack of understanding that makes me so contrary. After all, today's cars are almost disgustingly good. In spite of all the incessant wailing from the rabid consumerist faction (who seem to be on some sort of unholy witch hunt for anybody who ever tried to actually *do* or *build* anything in this world) we are currently enjoying a true renaissance of value, style, mechanical competence, drivability and reliability from every manufacturer who hopes to survive in today's competitive world market. But, like a figure so perfectly rendered it casts no shadows, the resulting generation of autos also tend to be a little dull. There's not a lot of personality to be found in seamless perfection. In fact, when you get right down to it, character in an automobile is mostly made up of endearing quirks and flaws.

This brave but colorless new world makes a lot of us yearn for the crude and occasionally ill-tempered cars of our adolescence. Many of them were wild, impetuous, devious and and unpredictable characters, but drivers of those automobiles (and British Sports Cars most especially) understood that there was a sense of responsibility and risk built into their ownership. But they were risks and responsibilities happily accepted in return for the enjoyment, adventure, and bolt-on personal panache that came as part of the bargain. In fact, the secret, unspoken essence of the British Sports Car magic and mystique was that they turned every 'round-the-block errand and cross-country trip into a truly sporting proposition. After all, you might not make it....

Plus there was always a sort of cloak-and-dagger mystery about finding out why your Jag wouldn't start or what caused your TR3 to stagger to a halt and refuse to run anymore. If you were sharp enough and savvy enough, that's when you'd don your coveralls and Sherlock Holmes deerstalker hat and try to puzzle your way through it. You always began with the two usual suspects (Sparks and Fuel, in that order) and carefully started at the plugs and then the jets and worked your way backwards through those two systems until you located the culprit:

It was Colonel Mustard in the Distributor Cap with the Cracked Rotor!

It was Miss Scarlet in the Float Chamber with the leaking Needle and Seat!

It was Professor Plum in the S.U. fuel pump with, well, an S.U. fuel pump!

But the whole idea is that you could usually find the fly in the ointment if you had your wits about you, searching back piece-by-piece from symptom to cause to source. And, when you were finished diagnosing the problem, you could most likely fix it (or at the very least jerry-rig it enough to get home) with little more than the contents of a young lady's handbag.

Those days are gone forever, and now we have engine compartments full of Nerd Circuits and Magic Crystals and all this other mega-tech Star Trek stuff that doesn't even have effing screwdriver slots so's you can open 'er up and have a little looksee inside. So, while the automobile industry has given us some incredibly great cars, they've taken away our *access* to them. All we know how to do anymore is stick the key in the ignition switch and twist it to the right. They've got us right where they want us!

"Open the pod door, Hal...."

Far as I can tell, it all really started back in the middle 1970s, when LSW (Long Suffering Wife) Carol and I operated our little hole-in-the-wall foreign car shop on Chicago's soon-to-be-trendy near north side. It was called "Mellow Motors" in deference to my recently completed hippie days, but, frankly speaking, there was very little mellow about the motors that sputtered, surged, coughed, and death-rattled their way through our overhead service door. Most of them were from that sad mechanical generation between the first fitful attempts at pollution control and the eventual development of today's accurate, well-engineered, and generally bulletproof engine management systems. Smog plumbing of the day, particularly on carbureted British sportscars, was made up of heavy, seize-prone rotary air pumps and fat rubber hoses and rusty tin canisters and little "don't touch me" stamped metal covers over all the favorite carburetor adjustments every self-respecting British Car mechanic loved to fiddle with. Whether he knew what he was doing or not. But we *had* to fiddle, because we'd driven enough MGs and Spridgets and Triumphs over the years to know that they should run cleaner, pull stronger, and feel one hell of a lot peppier than this sorry lot. Worse yet, a lot of those heaps had already been 'fixed' by other know-it-all idiots who had no idea what they were doing any more than we did. Which is why you were likely as not to find air pumps removed and the attendant hoses and plumbing blocked off with bolts or plugged with old condensers. Rather than fixing the problem, it often made things worse, and the resulting engines tended to wheeze and cough and hack like the sad, old men who hang around the lion house at the Lincoln Park Zoo in wintertime.

To be fair, the Brits were not alone in this, as the early Bosch electronic fuel injection as found on those unloved Type III VW Fastbacks and Squarebacks was a genuine spaghetti-wire nightmare (and they were all the same blessed beige color, too!) while the SPICA mechanical injection featured on Alfa Romeos of the period had its own congenital problems with cold starting and plug fouling (especially if some idiot gas station wrench who didn't know what he was doing had messed with it!) and both systems were regularly and rather rudely referred to as "Fuel Objection" by our staff of less-than-charitable mechanics.

But it brought a lot of work in, and that helped pay the bills. Well, some of them, anyway. And surely the evolution of today's seamlessly smooth, responsive, reliable and Environmentally Correct powerplants had to wait for the development of microchip engine management systems and black box electronics. All of which were totally foreign to the sensibilities of our particular Foreign Car Shop (how can you find Colonel Mustard inside a sealed vault?) and therefore regarded with steely-eyed doses of doubt, mistrust, and suspicion when they began to appear. I mean, the only black box *I* understood at all was a Lucas voltage regulator, and I knew enough about those damn things to replace one every chance I got.

Let me tell you a story about my first-ever Black Box experience:

We had this one regular customer with a pretty decent MGB GT (I'll call him Mr. X, for reasons that will shortly become obvious) who had recently come into a bit of money thanks to a tidy little import business he ran on the side. Use your imagination. In any case, he decided to reward himself for his enterprise and entrepreneurial skills by buying a very nice, clean, and recently out-of-warranty XKE coupe. It was one of the generally unloved 2+2 versions (which will hold two full size human beings in front and a couple of headless, legless torsos in back) and was powered by an early version of Jaguar's monstrous-yet-magnificent V-12. Now Mr. X *loved* that Jag, and had its deep maroon paint washed and waxed at frequent intervals and never allowed its off-white leather interior to become despoiled with old McDonald's wrappers, empty soda cans, wads of used Kleenex, discolored pennies, or ossified French fries like a lot of our regular customers. Not to mention virtually all of our employees.

I recall it was late July, just when the first truly oppressive wave of midsummer heat descended on our fair city, and around 8:45 one morning I got a frantic call from Mr. X. Seems he was calling from a phone booth adjacent to the North Avenue exit of Chicago's beautiful (but jampacked at that hour) Lake Shore Drive. And the reason he was in that phone booth was because his beautiful maroon Jag had come to a sudden and silent halt—as if the very breath of life had gone out of it!—whilst negotiating the bumper-to-bumper rush hour crawl over the North Avenue bridge. After which it stubbornly refused to refire. So Mr. X had to get out of his svelte, gleaming E-Type and beg the assistance of a carload of low-to-minimum wage-types in a badly abused and thoroughly asymmetrical Chevy Nova to get his Jag over to the sidelines. Whereupon he walked down to the public phone booth at the North Avenue beach and called for help. Not all Jags had car phones back in 1975. In fact, nobody did. And people paid a hell of a lot more attention to their driving then, too....

Like any grease monkey worth his salt, I tried to diagnose the problem over the phone, but this is akin to attempting brain surgery over the phone, and the best you can do is ask a bunch of questions that generally slide right past (or shoot clear over the head of) your average, inexperienced, non-gearhead mechanical duffer. Just listen:

"Did it have any juice? I mean, would the starter spin?"

"Uh, yeah, sure. I *guess* so...."

"But was it *engaging?*"

"I dunno. Like I told you, it wouldn't start."

"But did it *try* to start?"

"Uh, yeah, sure, I *guess* so...."

Conversations such as this inevitably wind up being an irritant to both parties involved, and occasionally give rise to that old repair shop standard: "Well, why don't you back it up to the phone so I can fix it for you?" But there was no call for that since Mr. X's E-Type was a good quarter-mile away, sitting sadly but proudly by the side of the road while a rush hour crush of Fords and Plymouths and Chevy Impalas grumbled by, sniggering at the silent Jaguar as only the lower classes can.

"Well," I finally said, "why don't I call our towing service and have it picked up? Put the key under the floormat and you can either take a cab or my tow truck guy will give you a lift to work when he gets there."

Imagine my surprise when my towing guy got there about an hour later (a near record in rush hour) only to find no Jaguar and no Mr. X and furthermore nobody willing to pay him for a steamy, uncomfortable ride through the dregs of rush hour traffic in an ancient GMC tow truck with no air conditioning. Most guys I know in the towing business do it to make a living, and charity jobs on phantom Jaguars just do not put a lot of pork, beans or rice on the table.

All sorts of ugly scenarios raced through my head. Perhaps the police had towed Mr. X's E-Type off to the pound, where tabby-sized sewer rats were already gnawing their way into that lovely, off-white leather upholstery. Or, worse yet, perhaps they'd discovered evidence of Mr. X's clandestine import business somewhere in the car and so now both he *and* his lovely Jaguar were guests of the city. Whatever happened, I figured to have some kind of supporting-cast guilt and/or liability in the deal, and I was already starting to wonder how much the tab would be.

And then the phone rang.

It was Mr. X, of course. And he sounded absolutely radiant. "Hey, guess what?" he crooned into the receiver. "I went back to put the key under the mat, and I figured, hey, what the hell, why not give it one more try? So I put the key in and she fired right up and purred like a kitten all the way in to work. Never skipped a beat."

"Gee, that's great," I told him without much in the way of enthusiasm. I was busy wondering how I could keep our towing guy from caressing Mr. X's skull with a tire iron if he ever got wind of it. "Listen," I told him, "maybe you oughta bring it in anyway. Just for a quick looksee, you know?"

"Yeah, I guess so," he agreed halfheartedly. "But I'm tellin' you, she never ran so good. Maybe I'll stop over tomorrow if I can find the time...."

And that was the end of it. At least until about 5:45 that same evening, anyway. I was just packing up after an exceedingly sweaty, greasy, and occasionally downright bloody clutch job on a TVR 2500M and looking forward to a large can of hand cleaner and an even larger cold beer (several, in fact) when the phone rang. It was Mr. X again, and—would you believe it?—he was calling from that *exact* same phone booth at the North Avenue beach near Lake Shore Drive. "It did it *again!*" he half-growled/half-whimpered, "and at the same damn place! Only this time I was going northbound instead of southbound."

Of course this made no sense, as any experienced mechanical whiz knows that a general proximity to any particular location or geographic feature of the Chicago city landscape shouldn't really have an effect on the flow of fuel and sparks to an automobile engine. Even a Coventry-built Jaguar V-12. So I tried my best to interrogate Mr. X and discover any clues, traces, hints or symptoms that might help me arrive at a truly empirical and scientific diagnosis. So I asked him "What happened?"

"Jeez, I dunno. I was creeping along in rush hour traffic and everything was running just fine—hell, the damn air conditioner was even working pretty good—and then, all of a sudden, it was like somebody just pulled the plug...."

"Pulled the plug?"

"Yeah. It just cut out on me. Quit dead. At least this time I was in the righthand lane so's I could coast it over to the side."

"Did it make any strange noises?"

"Naw, it just quit running, that's all."

"Hmmm. Did'ja *smell* anything funny?" Far as I'm concerned, the old schnozola is one of Mom Nature's very best diagnostic tools when it comes to sniffing out odd and mysterious car problems.

"Nah. Seemed like always to me."

"Hmmmm. Was it overheating?"

"Well, it was, you know, sorta *warm*..." Well, that went without saying. I mean, we're talking about a Jaguar V-12 on a hot July day in bumper-to-bumper rush hour traffic with the air conditioning going full blast.

"What did the gauge say?"

"The *gauge?*"

"Yeah. The water temperature gauge."

"Is that one of those little dials over the radio?"

I bit my lip to keep from saying anything rude. "Yes," I finally admitted, "it's one of those little dials over the radio. You're supposed to look at it every now and then. Like when you're changing stations...."

"But listen," Mr. X countered, "it wasn't, you know, like *boiling* or *steaming* or anything. I just got to the North Avenue overpass and—*wham!*—she stopped running. Just like that. And she wouldn't fire up again, either."

"Maybe you oughta try a different way home?" I advised, only half joking. "Listen, why don't you give it about fifteen minutes and try again. You're not that far away, so if it starts, drive right on over. I'll be here for another hour or so anyway."

"And what if it *doesn't* start?"

And that's when I gave Mr. X the phone number of my towing service. I was damned if I was gonna call them again for a maroon XKE 2+2 V-12 coupe stranded by the North Avenue overpass on Lake Shore Drive during rush hour. Not twice in one day!

Well, sure enough the Jag started and Mr. X tooled it on over to the shop, and the next day I went through the usual drill of checking the fuel system and the sparks and even the electrical connections on the ignition switch to try and locate the problem. Only I couldn't find much in the way of familiar Lucas hardware in the old sparks department, since this particular V-12 had Jaguar's new-and-supposedly-improved electronic ignition. There were no points to look at and see if they'd maybe closed up or anything like that. And the stuff I *could* check (like fr'instance if the sparkplugs made you jump two feet in the air with your hair frizzed out like that guy on *The Mod Squad* when you held them against a valve cover and cranked the starter) was all A-OK.

So I decided to take Mr. X's E-Type on a couple parts runs to see if it would maybe, you know, *do it* for me. But of course it wouldn't. They never do. And, as a matter of general principles, I don't much enjoy driving XKE Jaguars around in Chicago city traffic. There's just too much damn *car* out there in front of you (like you're sitting in the rudder seat of a damn Indian War Canoe, you know?) and to risk street parking one in front of your average Chicago auto parts store or driveshaft or radiator shop is to risk getting uncomfortably familiar with a body and fender man.

Needless to say, Mr. X's Jag ran like a damn champ all day long, and, just like he said, the air conditioner even blew out honest-to-gosh cold air. So I gave it back to him with one of those helpless, shop-owner shrugs and told him I couldn't find anything wrong. Which is why it should come as no great surprise to any *bona fide* Jaguar mechanics in the peanut gallery that I received yet another desperate, rush hour phone call from that same exact booth by the North Avenue overpass on Lake Shore Drive the very next morning. "I'm not *touching* that damn thing!" Mr. X snarled into the receiver. "I'm calling your tow truck guy and it's coming over to you just the way it died."

Sure enough, Mr. X's handsome maroon Jaguar arrived about an hour later, hanging off the back end of a tow truck. And it should again come as no surprise to the true Jaguar *cognoscenti* that the damn thing fired right up and ran like a champ just as soon as we got it down off the hook....

Well, I had to admit I was baffled. The simple, inescapable scientific conclusion was that this particular XKE was either haunted, cursed, possessed by demons, or inordinately fond of the local scenery around the North Avenue beach (which, truth be told, can get very easy on the eyes once the local high schools and colleges let out for their summer vacations).

But I digress. It was obvious that Mr. X's Jaguar had a serious problem, and furthermore obvious that Mr. X believed in his heart of hearts (rightly or wrongly) that I was fully capable of finding it and fixing it. After all, hadn't I kept his old MGB GT and his ex-girlfriend's bright yellow VW beetle in fine fettle over the past several years? And indeed I had. But those were simple cars and I was turning out to be a likewise simple guy. At least as far as complicated automotive devices were concerned. And it was beginning to dawn on me, as I stared, dumbfounded, into that jam-packed Jaguar V-12 engine compartment, that I was maybe a little out of my league. Maybe even more than a little. On the other hand, it *was* a British sportscar, and I *was* supposed to be some kind of British sportscar expert. Hell, it said so right there on my business card....

I was gonna have to figure this out if I wanted to continue looking myself in the eye in my bathroom mirror every morning.

So, with Mr. X's full consent, I drove that maroon E-Type all weekend long. Even took it on a road trip out to the races out at Blackhawk Farms, about 90 miles from Chicago each way. And of course it started on the first twist, ran like a top, and never so much as hiccuped the entire weekend. Hmmm. Which is why I decided to head ever-so-casually over to Lake Shore Drive come rush hour Monday morning and, umm, "reenact the crime," so to speak. And I must admit to experiencing a strange, other-worldly tingling sensation (a little *Twilight Zone* theme music please, typesetter) as the Jag and I inched our way through a massive, heat-shimmering Chicago traffic snarl towards the North Avenue overpass.

But nothing happened. The Jag crawled right over that damn bridge at our allotted, stop-and-go, three-mph dawdle, and I was just getting to think that there was maybe something wrong with Mr. X instead of his car when the engine suddenly cut dead like somebody'd pulled the damn coil wire. Ah-*hah!* No question the sparks had suddenly and mysteriously vanished into thin air. Only *why?* So I pulled over to the side (which is *tough* with the engine dead and no power steering on a V-12 E-Type!), popped the bonnet and ran my eyeballs over all those strange, unfamiliar pieces that made up that Jag's newfangled, high-tech, high-energy, never-needs-no-damn-points-or-condensers ignition system. And the fact of the matter is that I had no idea on earth what I was looking at. So I waited about twenty minutes and tried again—she fired right up, natch—and drove it back to the shop. Whereupon I immediately called my friend and fellow racer Vince Woodfield, who had an authentic British accent and moreover held the position of service manager at a nearby Jaguar dealership. Vince was the guy I inevitably came crawling to with hat in hand whenever an E-Type was getting the better of me at our shop. Which was often.

"Oh, hell," Vince laughed. "It's the amplifier."

"The *what*??!!" Far as I knew, the only things on cars that had amplifiers were the stereo systems. And I didn't understand much about those, either.

"The amplifier," he said again. "The bloody little finned aluminum box down there in the hollow of the vee. Why, we must've replaced a hundred of 'em. I don't know what the bloody factory could have been thinking, putting it there in the first place. Gets too hot when the car's stuck in traffic and the underhood temperatures get really high. You've gotta buy yourself a new one and mount it on the subframe or up on the firewall someplace. Get it the hell away from all the bloody heat."

So that was it! The damn amplifier (whatever *that* was) was getting overheated when Mr. X's Jag got stuck in traffic on a really hot day, and, as fate would have it, the North Avenue overpass was not only the slowest crawl of rush hour but also about halfway equidistant between Mr. X's downtown office and his fancy near north side apartment, allowing precisely enough time for that damn black box to heat soak and crap out in either direction!

In any case, I drove over to the Jaguar dealership later that morning and bought the very last amplifier they had in stock, and I must admit to being thoroughly appalled by the price. Hell, it was enough to feed a family of five for a month. With steak twice a week, even. You could buy yourself a hell of a lot of conventional old plugs-and-points tune-ups for the price of one of those babies. Not to mention that I *understood* stuff like plugs and points and distributor caps and rotors and even a little about condensers, while this nasty little crinkle-finish aluminum box was not only horridly expensive, but arrogantly inscrutable as well.

Far as I was concerned, it was just a home for poltergeists!

READY FOR A TALL, COOL ONE?

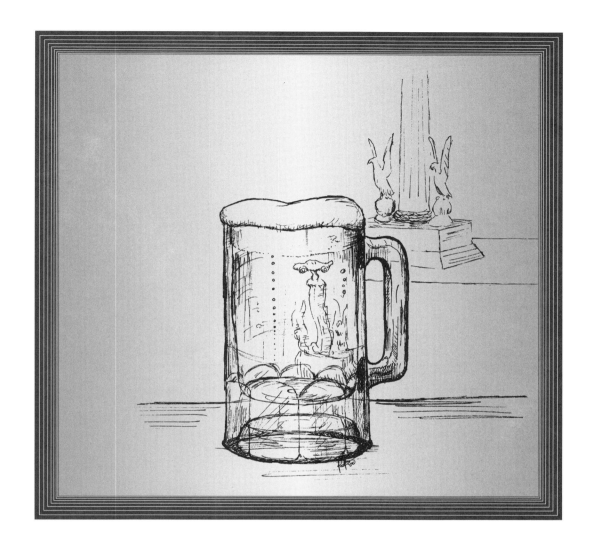

THIS SHORT PIECE ORIGINALLY APPEARED
AS A SIDEBAR TO ANOTHER STORY IN
VINTAGE MOTORSPORT
JANUARY/FEBRUARY, 1989

The latest

and fastest car is the most important thing in professional racing, because you're only as good as your last victory. And that, pretty much, is the general credo in bigtime motorsports. First across and no excuses. Or, as racer's racer Jack Baldwin once put it: *"If you want truth at a racetrack, look at a stopwatch."*

Vintage, God love it, is adjusted somewhat differently. Although the cars are most certainly the stars in our little corner of the sport, once on the circuit, it's not so much *what* you drive as *how* you drive that's important. Because the history has already been written, and if you pour over all those reams of withered paper, totaling up all the winners and losers enumerated in tiny columns of agate type, you come away with the knowledge that glory is both common and fleeting. More important perhaps is the human side of our sport, that special, distilled essence that amounts to so much more than numbers on a page. And where does it come from, this character, this soul, in a sport that measures itself in nuts and bolts and tiny fractions of seconds, culminating in that arbitrary, frozen instant when the checker comes down?

It comes from the people who make it happen, and, if we're lucky enough to be inside the sacred circle, we remember them especially in the moments when they are more than mere appendages to a machine. We always think of the drivers first, because they get to wear the colors, get to carry the ball, get to take the visible risks. But we don't forget the rest of them, the designers and engineers, watchers and wrenches, strategists and stevedores, haulers and beadbreakers, beloved sponsors and dilettante *poseurs,* marketing mavens and promotional pirates and all the rest of the mechanized menagerie that inhabit our circus of thrills, fun, fear and friendships. Beneath every droplet of sprayed champagne on the victory rostrum, every droplet of blood on the emergency room floor, there are so many lives and minds and quick, irrevocable decisions that tie us all into something bigger and nobler than first across the finish line.

At its best, Vintage celebrates this, and does so in the same way and at the same places as those who went before and those who will come after. the racecars grow cold in the moonlight, we gather in unique yet unremarkable rooms to tip a glass and pass some time, recollect history, tell tall tales, and leave our shadows on the walls to mingle with those of the heroes, villains, and marvelous scoundrels who came before us.

It's Siebken's at Road America.

The old Buck's at Mid-Ohio.

The Seneca Lodge at Watkin's Glen.

In fact, there's probably one for every great racetrack. Or at least there should be. Some evening place where you can feel the history of our sport grained into the woodwork and peering out from the yellowed pictures on the walls and filtering like a distant echo through the thick, smoky air. Listen. Listen to the echoes of laughter, lies, psych jobs, schemes and disappointments—and, yes, sometimes tragedy—as you lean against the same bar where maybe John Fitch shared a glass with Phil Walters and Walt Hansgen and a few of the Europeans and talked about the same exact things we do today. Tire pressures. Braking points. Bumps and slick spots. Who showed flair or courted folly on the track that day.

There is a common, comfortable style and a laudable lack of fashion common to these establishments. They promise nothing save friendly surroundings and full measure. And if you want entertainment, you'd best bring it with you.

And so we do.

After all, it's not what you drink. It's where.

And with whom, of course. With whom.

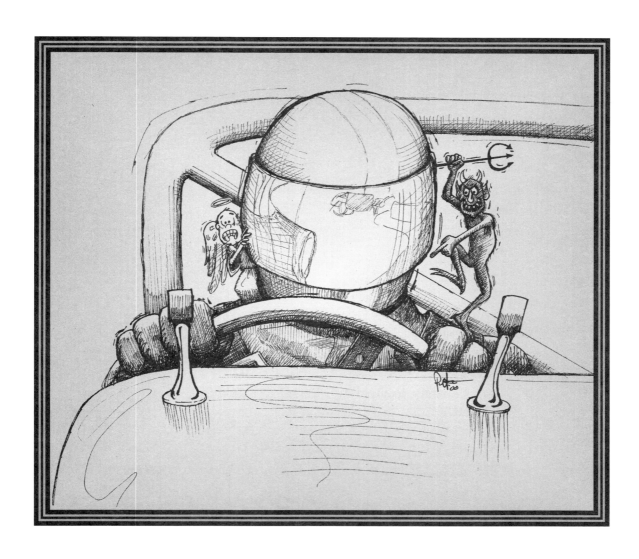

THE AGONY OF VICTORY

*A MARVELOUS EXPERIENCE SPOILED
BY A MOMENT I WISH I HAD BACK!*

ORIGINALLY PUBLISHED AS A TWO-PART STORY IN
VINTAGE MOTORSPORT
NOVEMBER/DECEMBER 1998
AND JANUARY/FEBRUARY 1999

A few years

back my good buddy Steve Weber called to ask if I wanted to be the Honorary Grand Something-Or-Other at the 1998 running of the Pittsburgh Vintage Grand Prix, and while I was flattered (hey, everybody likes an ego fluff now and then, and me more than most) the scheduling gods always put Pittsburgh inconveniently dead opposite my beloved Brian Redman International Challenge (neé Chicago Historic Races) bash at Road America. No way could I envision missing the biggest damn motorized Mazola party of the summer up at Elkhart Lake just to watch a few spindly old East Coast crocks stumbling around some blessed city park in a town I knew only as the home of steel smelters, Three Rivers Stadium, and Mean Joe Greene.

But Steve's an affable and persistent sort, and, what with the coming of the new "mainstream" edition of _The Last Open Road_ and Pittsburgh being a Major Market and all (and moreover having turned over the same old soil in Elkhart since the original version of the book made its debut there in July of '94) I thought, with the most thoroughly transparent of motives, that Pittsburgh might be the way to go. Not that I expected much, even though my longtime friend/enduro teammate David Whiteside (who has seen me through all manner of dodgy and embarrassing scrapes that I would never have gotten into in the first place if not for him!) told me over and over that Pittsburgh was the best damn event on the calendar. But then David's a lawyer by trade and a bit of a crocodile-grinning scoundrel by nature, so who would've guessed he was telling the truth? Fact is, I don't think I've ever trusted him since he bought me that fourth Pusser's Painkiller #5 (or was it that fifth Pusser's Painkiller #4?) during post-race evening devotionals at Pusser's Pub in Port Lacayua during the '87 running of the Grand Bahama Vintage Grand Prix....

So I went to Pittsburgh, expecting little more than a stuffy old museum-on-wheels parade surrounded by an unwashed horde of Local Population gawkers who came because it was free, didn't know a 4CLT from a 4CV, and yearned to be driving Urban Guerrilla 4x4s with huge, knobbly tires and four feet of ground clearance if they could only get the financing. But you know what? There beside the unlikely confluence of the Allegheny, Ohio, and Monongahela rivers, I found a shimmering pearl.

What a fabulous event!

What great cars!

What friendly, enthusiastic people!

And, above all else, what an *incredible* racetrack. Scenic. Sensuous. Dauntingly yet deliciously unforgiving. And oh-so-true to the spirit of the old days. But don't tell anyone. Your mouth-breathing Camaros, over-stimulated Sprites, and disposable Formula Fords are neither wanted nor needed. Sure, the VSCCA comes under fire in certain quarters because they still hold on with brittle, bony fingers to an eligibility cutoff of 1959, don't cotton much to subtly flared fenders, garish newfangled paintjobs, over-pumped powerplants, or calling much attention to yourself, and have no compunctions whatsoever about excluding vehicles they deem overly coarse or common regardless of date of manufacture. While this may not exactly line up with our cherished democratic ideals, the resulting events attract relics and icons you won't see anywhere else, presented and raced very much as they were when new. Or, more accurately, as they were a few years on in their competitive careers. Where else could you find pre-war, supercharged Alfas and Bugattis doing serious battle with flathead-powered oval track racers and the original, one-of-a-kind Ardent Alligator special campaigned by Miles Collier in the early days at Watkins Glen? Or howabout a gaggle of gnarly old Morgan 3-wheelers (no two the least bit alike in typical British *garagiste* fashion)? Or a properly pale blue Salmson, a striking silver BMW 328, and not one, not two, but *three* effing Dellows?

The VSCCA is by far the oldest vintage club in the country (dating back as far as the Mayflower, judging by some of the membership) and over generations has evolved its own ethic, culture and customs, along with a delightfully apt Insider Dialect in which lovely but tiny little under-1000cc machines (mostly of Italian descent) are referred to as "Etceterini." They have their own race group, which includes a lot of the wonderful OSCAs, Bandinis, and Cisitalias that ran at Le Mans and the Mille Miglia and were the wet dream of every young Italian enthusiast's eye, along with cramped little 500cc, motorcycle-powered Kieft and Cooper *monopostos* that amounted to the backbone of British motorsport in the machinery-starved immediate postwar era. They're all up on properly tall and skinny tires, too, which makes for a nice change from the elbowing crowd of suspiciously fat-tired, deep-voiced and high-winding Bugeyes and Minis seen elsewhere on the vintage scene. Plus there's not a Glass Case Job in the bunch, as all the cars are maintained as close to original as possible and have both the perfume and patina of proper hard use.

Which brings up point number two. While the VSCCA doesn't make a big thing of it, it's rather expected that one wouldn't be involved in this business unless one knew how to drive (bloody silly otherwise, eh?) and the general skill level and competitive intensity I observed were up to—and occasionally beyond— anything I've observed elsewhere. Why, I'd pay Cash Money to watch Henry Wessels fling-slide-saw-wrestle his magnificent pre-war Alfa through turn one at Pittsburgh—right on the limit, lap after lap—and the same goes for Jeff McAllister's righteously quick BMW 328, Jim Duffield's ditto Fiat Abarth, Dick Frybarger's double ditto Lotus Eleven, and many, many more. And this on a genuine street circuit with curbs and culverts and stone walls and concrete bridge crossings—scenic, sensual, and enjoyable though it may be—where you are likely only permitted one mistake per car....

Ah, yes. The circuit. To be honest, I'd never before experienced anything so close to the early 50's open road sports car racing I wrote about in *The Last Open Road,* what with narrow, shady, high-crowned public lanes, wonderful and oh-so-natural climbs, dives, sweeps, twists, and turns, strange and unexpected pavement changes, and all manner of steep curbs, deep sluice drains, trees, fire plugs, lamp posts, stone walls, fountains, statues, monuments and concrete bridge abutments hard by the roadway. Sure, they dress it up with a few loads of haybales and stick orange marker cones in the more ominous divots, but the bottom line is that, while the course beckons you on with its delightful flow and rhythm and scenic beauty, you definitely do *not* want to go off, as the scenery looks like it's been solidly planted there for a long, long time.

1998 marked the 16th running of the Pittsburgh Vintage Grand Prix, and the little germ of an idea that floated out of local racer Alan Patterson's garage all those years ago had grown into an enormous annual undertaking for a legion of organizers, sponsors, city workers, PR and media flacks, SCCA and VSCCA types, and a host of local volunteers. It also raised around a million bucks for two very worthy causes, the Allegheny School and the Pittsburgh Autism Society, and every single one of the volunteers I talked to—and the required number to put on an event like this numbers well into the thousands—ranked the night they present the donation checks to the favored charities as the highlight of the whole experience. I was amazed to find that many of them aren't even especially car nuts or racing enthusiasts. "One year a friend of mine asked me what I was doing one night and would I like to help out," perennial volunteer Pete Szymanski grinned, "and I've been here in the trenches ever since. I just love it."

The whole thing starts before they even finish tearing down the barriers from the previous year's race, as there are so many things to do and arrange and promise and promote and beg for. Then, finally, race week arrives, and while one battalion of volunteers and city workers transforms the nifty, narrow, winding, uphill/downhill roads through Schenley Park into a racecourse, another bunch sets up car shows and rallyes to prime the press and pump up the local population. Like fr'instance Thursday evening's thoroughly eclectic car show on Squirrel Hill, a semi-artsy and gentrified old business district not too far from The University of Pittsburgh. Besides the expected lineup of old British Healeys and Jags and TRs and MGs plus some spanking new Porsches and BMWs courtesy of the local dealership, we had a flock of T-Birds and several showroom shiny 60's-era muscle cars, a very original and believable Auburn Speedster, and an absolutely stunning coral pink '59 Lincoln Continental convertible (the one with the razor-edged fenderlines and slanty eyes, remember?) complete with a drive-in burger tray clipped to the driver's-side window, fuzzy pink dice dangling from the mirror, and a drive-in movie sound box hanging off the other side. Hardly Pebble Beach, but just try not to smile....

Come Friday morning, I biked over to watch volunteers unloading several truck loads of donated haybales and endless rolls of snow fencing, observed colorful circus tents popping up like enormous, striped toadstools on the golf course fairways—one for presenting sponsor Buick (G'bless 'em), one for BMW (featured marque, complete with running examples of damn near every significant Bimmer race car from a prewar 328 right through the then current-issue McLaren/BMW Le Mans weapon), and one for the hugely attended British Car Day (held every year on Saturday) plus smaller tents and trailers filled with just about every type of fast food and automotive geegaw vendor known to man. Everywhere you looked, people were building things and hammering nails and moving things into place. And the amazing part was that each seemed to know what had to be done next. It was fascinating, really, like watching a circus take root and blossom in an empty meadow, and I must've biked around the whole 2.33 miles (pant, puff, wheeze) at least a dozen times. And, with every single lap, I became more and more desperate to *drive* it. Why, it was _The Last Open Road_ come to life; an honest-to-goodness 50's-style street circuit like the ones I'd written about (but had never actually experienced) at Bridgehampton, Grand Island, Brynfan Tyddyn, Elkhart Lake, and Watkins Glen! Complete with blind approaches, steep uphills and even steeper descents, no less than *five* 180-degree hairpins, and scenic ravine overlooks bordered by low stone walls where, if you ventured a quick peek over the edge, you found yourself looking *down* on lofty treetops and keen-eyed hawks circling for a meal.

WOW!

So I put aside whatever few remnants of self-respect and dignity I may have left and went into Full Groveling Mooch Mode at the hotel welcoming party that evening. And I was lucky enough to hit pay dirt when my friend and well-respected Connecticut wrench twister and old British car guru J.R. Mitchell offered me his excellent Climax-powered Lotus Seven to run in the Under 2-liter production class (J.R. was running the same car with the other Sevens and Elevens the Sports Racer group) if the organizers would go along with the deal. VSCCA race co-chairman Jake Jacobsen thought it over, smiled, told me to "play nice," and—just like that, can you believe it?—I was *in!*

******

I remember laying awake for hours that night, running the circuit over and over in my mind, the usual buzz of excitement and anticipation underlaid with a nascent flutter of apprehension. Sure, this was a tremendous opportunity to drive a track I'd already fallen in love with in a really decent car (and absolutely everything J.R. runs his wrenches over is guaranteed to be at least that!) but I couldn't escape the fact that you had to be really *careful* here. Like I said before: at Schenley Park, it looked like you only got one mistake per car....

Come Saturday I got my first real crack at the circuit, and right away it was obvious that J.R.'s Lotus was the ideal lump of tin for this particular layout. Sure, its little 1098cc Climax lacked the punch of some of the other cars in our group, but the blessed thing didn't weigh much more than a wad of tinfoil and J.R. had it geared just right (4.88 ring and pinion) for those tight, 2nd-gear hairpins. Plus, like virtually every-thing J.R. prepares, the Seven *worked.* It pulled clean, held good temps and pressures, tracked straight, didn't go all over the place under hard braking, and was a four alarm *ball* to drive. Downside was that finding the quick way around this place was going to take some major learning. Not to mention a few bottles of brave pills. What a devilishly challenging and daunting race track! But what *fun!* Every time I got out of the car I had a helpless grin plastered ear-to-ear across my kisser along with this giddy, adolescent sensation that I'd *gotten away with something,* you know?

Turns out I qualified third in my group, and that made me feel all warm and fuzzy inside until J.R. took the same damn car out and knocked a solid 5 seconds off my time. Oh, my head knew well enough where those five seconds could be found. But it was going to take a bit of convincing to get my heart, right foot, testicular equipment and sphincter muscle to go along. J.R. and I had a little talk about it and, when I went out for warmup the following morning, I finally felt it all coming together. In particular, there was a narrow, bumpy, 3rd-gear sweeper under a canopy of trees that funneled between a curb and a Jersey barrier as it swooped out onto the decaying concrete of Panther Hollow Bridge, and whereas I'd been braking for it the previous day, now I could get by with just a slight confidence lift, and no question somebody with a higher comfort level (i.e.: bigger balls!) would be hard on it and upshifting into top.

To be honest, I'd already come to the conclusion that J.R.'s Lotus was far and away the fastest car in the U2 group (at least on the Schenley Park circuit, anyway) and that meant all I had to do was drive reasonably well and not screw up and we had a pretty decent chance of winning this thing. Yeah. I know. Vintage isn't supposed to be about winning. But I'm not going to lie to myself or anybody else and pretend like it never crossed my mind....

Lunchtime brought a bunch of high school bands and skydivers and such, and I even got to ride around the track in the back of a limo with Grand Marshal/Pittsburgh mayor Tom Murphy, who seemed to be a bright, interesting, enthusiastic and genuine sort even if not all that much of a gearhead. I must've told him a hundred times how impressed I was with everything and how I couldn't believe a city government would not only allow, but encourage and moreover participate in an event like this. "You could never pull something like this off in Chicago or New York or L.A.," I told him. "You should really be proud of this."

He was, too.

******

Have you ever noticed that sometimes it seems to take forever for your race to roll around? Especially if you're thinking you might do really well. But eventually the time came and the Seven and I trundled down to the grid to meet the loyal opposition, none of whom I'd met or shared the same bit of track with during practice and qualifying. On pole was last year's winner and regular VSCCA front-runner Bob Russell in his pretty yellow Alfa Spider, and next to him was Keith Harmer in a raucously well-massaged MGA. So we went through the usual False Grid Introductory Ritual of smiles, handshakes, none too subtle psyche jobs, and the hopefully insidious planting of doubts. All part of the game, eh? And then the time came to climb in and strap up, and, as the helmet comes down over your head, that's when everything always becomes focused, quiet, and intensely personal. At some point, for just the flutter of an instant, you may even wonder if you really want to be there....

Finally the order came to fire up, and, for me, anyway, the engine noise and vibration always seems to shoo the butterflies away. We went around on a really quick pace lap (sure, it was only a Buick sedan, but you can cut a whole lot better line when you've got both lanes to play with!) and things looked pretty ragged and strung out by the time we passed under the green. Then again, maybe that was The Plan. In any case, the Alfa and MG got a good jump and it was obvious right away that they both had a slight edge in the Sheer Grunt department. But the Lotus was so much lighter and nimbler that I was sure, barely halfway through the opening lap, that the race was ours if I just stayed patient and waited for the right opportunities.

I wanted to make sure the Alfa didn't sneak away, but first I had to deal with the wagging back end of the blue MG just ahead. Keith Harmer turned out to be one hell of a driver and more than once made it clear he was not about to step politely aside just because the Lotus might be the faster car. In fact, he slammed the door rather emphatically (!!!) when I made a few half-hearted tries up the inside. But the Lotus had a considerable advantage coming through the awkward, difficult, downhill carousel of a last turn, so I dropped back a length or two, got a strong run through the corner and a momentum advantage, and there was nothing he could do when we arrived at the fast sweeper of Turn One side by side with me in J.R.'s Seven on the inside.

One down. One to go.

It took about a lap to arrive on the yellow Alfa's decklid, and then began one of the most enjoyable cat-and-mouse games I have ever experienced on a racetrack. Again, no question the Lotus was quicker. But the Alfa was *faster,* so I had to plot and pray and plan and weasel about how I hoped to get by. And Bob Russell was driving beautifully; working the car hard, taking a good line, and never leaving so much as a whiff of an opening. But I've had a lot of seat time in Alfas myself over the years, and while they are marvelously smooth and secure around fast sweepers, tight, 180-degree hairpins are hardly their strong suit. Sure enough, Bob's Alfa would wallow over onto its outside front tire through the tight 180's while I could flick and dart my way around in the Seven. It was like a terrier chasing after a golden retriever, and this was for sure a terrier's sort of circuit. It seemed inevitable that we'd find a way by.

But Bob wasn't about to make it easy. Although the flyweight Lotus had a huge advantage under braking for the incredibly tight and narrow haybale chicane leading into that fast, daunting sweeper onto Panther Hollow Bridge, the Alfa could daylight us enough down the straightaway that there was no way I could pull out, pass, and muscle my way back into line before one of us wound up with a face full of hay. So I resorted to harrying the Alfa wherever I could and darting around this way and that in his mirrors—just to get him *thinking,* you know?—and no question we were both giving it plenty of stick and running well below our qualifying times. But I like to think we were also careful and courteous when we started encountering backmarkers, which of course made the distance between us stretch out and draw up like an elastic band. It got pretty hectic there a few times, no lie! And then the Alfa went in a tad deep into the wall-bound, downhill, 180 hairpin on Serpentine Drive, got into a bad push, and had to lift off. I hesitated for a gnat's blink as the Alfa wallowed helplessly out of the way and pulled the trigger.

We were through like a shot.

By the start/finish line the Alfa had recovered and was right on my tail, but I was pretty confident he couldn't get by so long as we didn't get a bad break in traffic. And there was plenty of it, so my lead—like his—tended to accordion from a comfortable five or six car-lengths down to the thickness of a feeler gauge depending on the vagaries of lapped cars. *Geez,* I remember thinking in my helmet, *shouldn't this damn thing be over about now?* After all, here I was leading the blessed race in a car I'd never driven before on a track I'd never seen before and moreover doing so in front of all the VSCCA regulars plus a big old crowd of whooping, arm-waving onlookers.

Anything that changed from here on out could only be bad.

We got the index finger from the flagman indicating *one lap to go* as we blasted past start/finish, and I would be a liar if I didn't admit I was already thinking about how swell this was going to look on my resumé and what I ought to say and who I ought to thank when they shoved a microphone in my face at the end of the cool off lap. And it is at precisely such moments—prematurely drinking the victory champagne before the checkered flag has even waved—that we become such irresistibly delicious targets for the fates and furies.

Last lap. Solid lead. No worries, mate. But ahead is a green Turner running some 30 seconds a lap slower than the Alfa and I. A quick mental calculation indicates I will reach him before the chicane but not far enough ahead to attempt a realistic pass. So

I fall in line. And then have to lock up all four to keep from plowing right into him as the Turner seems to almost park it in the middle of the switchback. The flag man on the corner crew brandishes the blue passing flag at him, wobbling it side-to-side right in his face. But meanwhile the second place Alfa has colosed right up and is once again filling my mirrors to overflowing. I'm angry and impatient. *Damn!* I snarl into my helmet lining, *Why doesn't this idiot get the hell out of the way??!!*

I know that's not a particularly Vintage Correct sort of thought process, but I'm not going to pretend I felt any different. So when the Turner stayed off-line left heading into that fast, bumpy sweeper onto Panther Hollow Bridge—and moreover when I saw, or at least thought I saw, his helmet nod to the right and his finger tip lift up off the steering wheel—I ducked to the inside with my right foot to the floorboards. In that one brief and indelible instant, I was absolutely, positively *certain* that the Turner's driver knew exactly where I was and what I was up to, and had purposely stayed over to the left to allow me and the Alfa by.

I was wrong.

In fact, in all my 30-odd years of racing, I have never been so wrong.

With my left front wheel up to about his right rear, doing nearly eighty around that bumpy, narrow lane, the Turner suddenly turned down across my bows. He simply had *no clue* that I was there! I slammed on the brakes, but there just wasn't enough room and the Lotus' left front wheel tapped the right rear flank of the Turner. It wasn't much of a hit—hardly a tire touch, really—but it was enough to tick the Turner sideways. Whereupon it caught the curbing, flipped high in the air, and, as the whole, horrifying scene passed through my peripheral vision and into my rearview mirrors, I saw the Turner barrel rolling violently down the broken concrete, sending parts and fiberglass and chunks of concrete shattering off in all directions while the driver's head and arms flailed around inside the cockpit like a rag doll.

I cannot describe the sick, helpless hole that opened up inside me. *My God, I've killed this man!* I thought, and prayed desperately that, just this one time, I could snatch that careless instant back from the bottomless pit of eternity. *Why the hell did I DO that?* I demanded of myself. After all, there was no room for the Alfa to get by me there, and the Turner's driver surely hadn't stuck his hand out and made the sort of Unmistakable Point we drum into our fledgling racers over and over again in drivers' school. But I had been so sure he knew I was there. So confidently, impatiently, and arrogantly *sure*. And then I found myself praying from someplace deep inside that the driver was OK. Although I didn't see how he could be, so violent was the wreck and so unforgiving the surroundings.

By then the workers had the red flags out. They only come out when something really bad has happened, and I knew better than anyone how truly bad it was. *My God, I've killed someone,* I kept thinking. *I've murdered him with my own damn vanity.* I pulled over to the side by a corner station and clawed with numb, shaking fingers to get my helmet off. I'm told I was crying, but I couldn't really feel it. It was like my own skin was a million miles away. *"Is he alive?"* I pleaded to the nearest worker. *"Is the driver of the Turner alive?"*

I waited there, suspended in time, while the corner worker listened to his headset. "Driver's out and OK," he said at last, and I felt a warm, syrupy wave of relief go through me. And, just as quickly, fade. He was alive, and that was good. And he seemed to be OK, which was even better. But his car was surely destroyed, and I felt as badly as I've ever felt in my life.

It didn't go away, either.

So they said I won the race and interviewed me a few minutes later down at the start/finish line. I allowed as how I didn't feel all that good about it and how sorry I was about what happened and even that I would've maybe been better off finishing second. I meant it, too. But it's easy to get all humble and noble in hindsight, isn't it? Back in the paddock all these people came up to congratulate me—all they knew is that I'd won the race and that it ended with a red flag, not that I'd had anything to do with the wreck—and I remember feeling hollow and sick inside and wishing everybody would just leave me alone.

Soon enough a flatbed rolled up carrying the remains of the Turner, and that poor car looked like it'd been kicked down the Grand Canyon, all twisted and shattered and buckled and bent everywhere you looked. Thank God it had a good roll bar! I asked about the driver and somebody directed me around to the other side, where I met relative newcomer to the sport Jim Stanco of Westchester, Pennsylvania, for the very first time. He was still in his driver's suit and had an understandably shell-shocked expression on his face. I didn't know what to say, but I told him how very, very sorry I was and tried to explain what I was thinking when I dived under him. Then I shut up and it got terribly quiet and I found myself starting to mumble all over again about how sorry I was. He looked at me kind of sideways at first, but finally reached out a shaky collection of fingers and shook my hand. It didn't fix the way I felt—not hardly—but it was still one of the nicest things anybody's ever done for me at a racetrack.

I guess the bottom line is that Pittsburgh was a fantastic event (Q: *"Outside of that, Mrs. Lincoln, how was the play?"* A: *"Fabulous!"*) where I enjoyed a great drive in a wonderful car on a truly incredible racetrack that unfortunately ended in one of the sorriest episodes I've ever experienced. J.R. and Jake Jacobsen and the rest of the VSCCA people were unbelievably sympathetic and supportive, telling me it wasn't completely my fault and not to agonize over it. "Stuff happens on a race track," was the way J.R. put it (his Lotus was fine except for a quarter-size ding in the left front fender) and Jake said they'd be happy to have me back again, for which I'm very grateful.

But if I look down into that secret little box of truth we all keep hidden deep inside, I understand that there's a terrible distinction between *fault* and *responsibility* in racing and life in general, and further that it is forever the job of those who've been around and know the ropes to watch over and watch out for those who aren't yet—or may never be—on the same page. In my heart of hearts, I know I inadvertently crossed that sketchy line between the ethos of vintage racing and other, less friendly forms of the sport. Had it been a NASCAR race, I could've easily shuffled through one of Dale Earnhardt's patented "I hated that it happened" half-apologies or shrugged the oft-repeated "it was just one a'them *racin'* deals" into the bristling microphones. Only vintage is supposed to be *different.* It's a point I make over and over again when I preach from this pulpit and repeat over and over when I'm teaching newcomers to our sport. And I wouldn't be much on character if I didn't hold myself up to the icy glare of those same, unblinking standards.

Mea culpa.

A tree was felled to make this vacant page....
Think about that whenever you read something really dumb!

NECESSITY IS A MOTHER

*OR: EVERYTHING I KNOW ABOUT PUBLISHING
I LEARNED THE HARD WAY!*

DEVELOPED FROM A TWO-PART ARTICLE REQUESTED BY JAN NATHAN,
EXECUTIVE DIRECTOR OF THE PUBLISHERS MARKETING ASSOCIATION FOR
THE PMA NEWSLETTER
FOLLOWING THE SELECTION OF <u>*MONTEZUMA's FERRARI*</u> AS A
PMA BENJAMIN FRANKLIN "BOOK OF THE YEAR" AWARD WINNER.
IT APPEARED IN AUGUST AND SEPTEMBER, 2000.

I suppose I should start off by plugging my books. *Always* start off by plugging your books. You may never get another chance. So here goes. *The Last Open Road,* is a hopefully funny, worthwhile and entertaining coming-of-age story about a 19-year-old New Jersey gas station mechanic, set against the backdrop of open road sports car racing in the Eisenhower 50's. It was originally self-published (in July of 1994) for one very simple reason. Nobody else wanted anything to do with it. "Oh, it's a *wonderful* story," as one particularly snotty and arrogant young lady in the New York publishing business told me, "but *those people don't read!*"

I disagreed.

So, with my wife Carol's trembling approval, we took out a second mortgage, formed our own publishing company, Think Fast Ink, and published it ourselves in July of 1994. Believe me, our necks were stuck out a country mile! If this thing flopped, our son might not be going to college. Or at least not without a big lottery win or some massive financial aid. Fortunately, the book got great reviews (none, I might add, in the mainstream "book" media—more on that later), received wonderful word-of-mouth support, sold out two hardcover printings (about 12,000 copies @ 25 bucks each), and became something of a cult classic on the car hobbyist/motor sports scenes. Or, to put it less delicately, among those very same people who "don't read" that the know-it-all New York publishing lady warned me about. Ultimately, *The Last Open Road* attracted the attention of bigtime New York publisher St. Martin's Press, who made me a cheap offer for the rights and released a slightly edited and revised version in May of 1998.

Every aspiring novelist's dream, right?

Then why on earth would I want to go *back* to self-publishing when I finished up the sequel, *Montezuma's Ferrari,* and released it in July *(and* October—more on that later, too) of 1999? Simple. It was a much better deal. Now Conventional Wisdom holds that self-publishing fiction is a great way to:

> *a)* Go broke
>
> *b)* Drive yourself to drink
>
> *c)* Entertain recurring thoughts of suicide
>
> *d)* All of the above

But, hey, if all anybody ever listened to was that old Conventional Wisdom, the earth would still be flat, women wouldn't vote, and we'd all head down to the corner barber shop for a good, long bleeding any time we felt poorly. I'm here to tell you that there *are* ways to successfully self-publish fiction. And make money at it, too. But you've got to start by thinking "outside the box" of that old Conventional Wisdom. You've got to identify your core target market—*who the heck is going to want to read this book?*—and figure out how and where you can find and access them. And you've got to treat it as a *business,* too. At least if you like to eat....

But first, a little background. An admission, in fact: I'm a hopeless car junkie. There, I've said it. And probably lost three-quarters of my audience. Or at least that's what that old Conventional Wisdom would have you believe. I really don't know where the attraction came from—certainly not from my parents, who were properly appalled by my addiction to cars and racing—but, from about as far back as I can remember, I was always fascinated by it. Particularly European-style road racing, which has a more upscale, well-educated, and higher demographic following than your average ¼-mile drag race ejaculation or slam-bang Saturday night demolition derby at the local dirt track. Fact is, it's a very technical, cerebral, sophisticated and demanding sport—on many different levels—and addictive as hell once you get the bug.

And that's mostly what I daydreamed about when I was growing up. Becoming a great racing champion. Either that or a great novelist. In fact, I flip-flopped between those two terribly romantic notions the way young girls change outfits before a big date. But the point is, around my folks' house anyway, it was okay to believe in your dreams. In fact, it was encouraged. Although my dad was a pretty successful packaging salesman, he saw himself as something of a free thinker and after-hours philosopher—"a beatnik in a gray flannel suit" was the way he liked to put it—and there are a few things he told me over the years that really stuck in my brain. Like fr'instance:

"If there's something you want to do in this life, you'd better <u>DO</u> it,
because you're a long time dead!"

and:

"There's only one thing you need to know in life,
and that's what you have to do next!"

So I half-heartedly stumbled after my dreams by taking a bunch of creative writing courses in college during the sixties (hey, who didn't?) including one of John Schultz's first—and excellent!—Story Workshop classes at Columbia College right here in my sweet home Chicago. But after a while I got bored with school and dropped out to Head West to experience life, expand my mind (it was all the rage back then), and write one of those Great American Novels that never get much past the first few paragraphs. I eventually wound up in Boulder, Colorado, working as a dishwasher in a restaurant called The Catacombs in the basement of the Boulderado Hotel on Pine Street and living in a tiny garret of a room on the top floor with little more than a bed, a nightstand, a shared bathroom down the hall, and a small desk topped with a huge, 1950's-vintage Royal electric typewriter that I rented from a resale shop with my very first paycheck. Oh, yeah. There was also a cigar box-sized window facing west, offering me a tiny, pygmy-edition view of the mighty Rockies for inspiration.

There was no doubt in my mind that I had the necessary credentials to be a great and successful novelist (shaggy hair, well-worn jeans and denim work shirts, a passing, conversational acquaintance with Yin and Yang, and an overpowering sense of self to name but a few) but, like a lot of young writers, I really didn't have all that much to say. I guess I was more in love with the *notion* of being a writer than moved by any urgent, irrepressible story I needed to tell. So mostly I wrote poetry. And the way I knew it was poetry was on account of no way could any of it be mistaken for prose....

Eventually my hippie odyssey ended (or maybe I just got tired of sleeping on floors and watching hazy, early ayem TV test patterns to see how the plot turned out) and so I came back home and went to work for my dad's packaging business. In return for a sizeable Pound of Flesh in the form of my very first racecar. And, lest you think I'm one of those silver spoon kids who got a shiny new Porsche attended by a crew of white lab-coated mechanics with suspiciously thick German accents, let me assure you that this particular vehicle was the saddest, sorriest, most used-up, piece-of-dogmeat Triumph TR3 racecar in the known universe. Not that I knew it at the time. All I knew is that it took every cent I could beg, borrow, steal and scrape together—some $600 all told—to buy that thankless old destroyer of dreams. And that was just the tip of the damn iceberg as far as begging, borrowing, stealing and scraping together went. Or, as my lovely wife will happily explain to all who may be interested: "The only thing stupider you can do with your money than race cars is to pile it in the street and set fire to it. But at least then it's all over with and you're spared the ongoing grief and agony."

Did I mention that she's one hell of a sport?

In any case, I wanted to go racing in the worst possible way. And that's exactly how I did it. But in spite of all the countless failures, frights, breakdowns, blowups, burnouts and disappointments (I had two wheels shear off—at speed!—in the space of my first three races!) I found myself hooked more than ever. I loved the sensation of going fast, the addictive balance of risk and control, the heady combination of competition and camaraderie, and especially the demand for quick, sure judgement and grace under pressure that racing demanded. People who've never understood or experienced it can't appreciate that racing a good car on a great race course—at least when you and the car are hooked up together and everything's going right—is more like playing music or dancing than anything else. There's a marvelous flow and rhythm to it. Like a Strauss waltz, really. And there's more: a quiet, peaceful, even Zen-like center nestled inside that focused vortex of speed and concentration that nobody on the outside will ever understand. I loved it all....

But it was costing me a freaking fortune.

And that's why I started writing again. To help pay for my addiction and maybe even get a little notoriety for myself on the motorsports scene. Almost on a lark, I'd written a story about the car we had when I was sixteen—hey, *everybody* remembers their first car!—and sent it off to *Road & Track* magazine. They rejected it, and, as I'm sure you can imagine, I was thoroughly crushed. But then I stumbled across it again when I was cleaning my desk a few months later and figured, what the hey, why not send it someplace else? And there's a lesson here:

Be relentless! Never give up!

So I sent it off to *AutoWeek.* And what do you know? They liked it and printed it and even sent me a check and asked me if I had any more. Holy crap, I'd actually gotten *paid* to write about cars! Although I must admit I had some difficulty cashing that check, on account of what I *really* wanted to do was walk around with it stapled to the middle of my forehead.

******

As soon as we were married, my wife and I foolishly quit two solid downtown jobs with decent pay and benefit packages to open a street-corner sports car shop (Mellow Motors at 747 Wrightwood on Chicago's soon-to-be-trendy Near North side) so I could pursue my One True Destiny as a great road racing champion. I told you she's a hell of a sport, didn't I? Either that or the most gullible damn woman on earth! Unfortunately, it turned out to be a total disaster. A veritable gauntlet run of hard lessons, dead ends, teetering financial cliffhangers and cruel comeuppances. But at least we learned a few things along the way. Like that we could survive almost anything together. That was good to know. And also that the first thing you do when you try to turn your passion into your business is you screw up the thing you were so passionate about in the first place. Royally. We also learned that boundless enthusiasm and great people skills are no match for actual nuts-and-bolts knowledge and experience when it came to fixing sports cars. And, like every other employer who has ever hung out a shingle or signed a paycheck, we came to realize that good help is hard to find.

And even harder to keep....

Anyhow, we worked three long, hard, thankless years at it—seventy hours a week and more—and I wound up doing less actual racing than ever before. There was really no time or money for it. Not to mention that, after a ten- or twelve-hour day of thrashing away at other people's cars, the last thing you want to do is start thrashing away on your own. By all rights, we really deserved to go bankrupt. I mean, as much as I loved sports cars—and I loved them dearly—I wasn't all that good at *fixing* them. At least not the wild and undisciplined hodgepodge of mechanical misfortune we gladly accepted in off the street in a vain effort to keep the wolves from the door. *Y'say that rotted-out old Morgan 4/4 you bought needs a total restoration? Have the tow truck driver bring it on in. Your Volvo 142 needs a new exhaust hanger and the lower back shock mounts repaired? Hey, we've seen that before. Pull it up on the lift. Your rusted-out Vee-Dub that you can barely afford gas for and that every cheap, back-alley mechanic in the city has already given up on needs a new clutch and some kind of bargain basement fix on the heater boxes so you won't have to drive with the windows open in sub-zero weather just to keep from being gassed? Hey, your pathetic little story has touched our equally pathetic little hearts. Bring it on in. Y'say your fuel-injected Alfa Romeo won't start in cold weather? Well, we've never actually seen one like exactly that before. But I s'pose we can figger it out....*

Add in that we didn't know pig doots about how to charge properly or run a storefront business and you have a recipe for certain disaster. Hey, scratch the surface and we were just a couple ivory tower kids from the suburbs, you know? But, in the 20/20 clarity of hindsight, I realize that our sorry, stupid, hapless and even scary experiences at Mellow Motors are where many of my stories and characters ultimately came from. When you think about it, humor almost always has its roots in tragedy and adversity. Not to mention that the seeds of success are most often sown in failure.

Amazingly, we managed to sell that albatross of a sports car shop to some other starry-eyed young idiot before we actually went broke, and then I knocked around the motor trade for a few years—hey, I'd be damned if I was going back to my dad's packaging business with my tail between my legs!—working as an assistant service manager at a Lincoln-Mercury dealership and later as a salesman for an upscale imported car dealership in downtown Chicago. At least I was racing again, running an 1974 Alfa Romeo Spider that had already been declared a total by the dealership's body shop before I ever got my hands on it. But it really wasn't that bad and the dealership helped out a little here and there with parts at cost and after-hours work space and a lot of helping hands. And it turns out I must have learned a few things along the way, as eventually, piled atop that mountain of ugly lessons, broken parts, shattered dreams, unpaid phone and electric bills, and assorted other disasters and embarrassments I'd accumulated over the years, I started to win races and even a few bush league local championships. During this period I also moonlighted briefly as a stunt driver extra when the movie *The Blues Brothers* was shooting in Chicago and made the local papers when I was summarily relieved of a 1971 Rolls Royce Silver Shadow convertible at gunpoint on a test drive.

Chalk up two more stories!

******

By 1983 I was back in my dad's packaging business and racing yet another Alfa Spider on the SCCA National circuit—sponsored in part by the dealership—and doing pretty well with it. In fact, we won four of eight races, set a few lap records, and managed to qualify for the National Championship Runoffs at Road Atlanta (sort of the Olympics of amateur road racing in America). But we wound up going through The Week From Hell down there, as one thing after another blew up, fractured, or fizzled out—mostly thanks to my own dumb mistakes and paranoid over-preparation. We wound up stumbling to a dismal eleventh place in the race with a Frankenstein motor built in the dirt and darkness of the paddock the night before, and guys I'd been beating all year long came home second and third. Damn.

I'll never forget that ride home from Atlanta, driving a borrowed van—one of those cheap, bottom-of-the-line "tradesman" models with no sound deadening material, so it was like riding inside a damn kettledrum for fifteen hours—with our sad, vanquished Alfa Spider hitched behind on a similarly borrowed trailer. I owed everybody, every credit card I had was at the redline, and I had absolutely zero prospects for anything better to come. I looked over at my wife sitting beside me and at our 4-year-old son sleeping in the back seat, and I remember thinking there was just No Way I could keep doing this anymore. Not like this....

But you forget all that stuff when you really have the bug—like I said, it's an addiction—and I was ready to try it all over again come spring. Even though *On Track* magazine had rung me up and asked if I wanted to be a race reporter on the Midwestern pro circuit that summer. "Oh, no," I told them, snickering up my sleeve, "I'm a *racer,* not a *writer."* But then my mechanic, Eric, who had been there for me through every long-distance tow and every garage all-nighter, wanted to go through race driving school. With me as his instructor. Only, at the very last minute, the car he was building wasn't quite ready. And so he asked if he could borrow mine....

Why, I remember that night like it was yesterday. My lovely wife was in bed beside me, rotating her head from side to side and silently mouthing the word "no" even as I heard myself saying, *"Yeah. Sure. Okay. Why the heck not...?"*

Visualize my mechanic Eric on his first solo lap in driving school. See him rounding turn six at Blackhawk Farms Raceway in my freshly rebuilt Alfa Romeo. See him getting sideways. See him slide off into the dirt. See the tires catch and spit him back across the track. See the wheels dig into a rut all funny. See the car roll over. And over. And over. Fortunately without injury to Eric. See the crushed and twisted lump of metal that used to be my racecar. See me calling *On Track* magazine again: *"Say, you remember that race reporting deal you guys called me about a few months back...?"*

This turned out to be another of those sneaky Blessings In Disguise deals, as it ultimately led to more stories and feature articles and eventually even regular columns in a couple other magazines. Plus what has certainly been—aside from my family—the happiest and most startling surprise of my life. Almost by accident, I discovered that I could *write* my way into all sorts of nifty, exotic and even priceless old racing cars that I could never even dream of owning! Luckily, vintage racing was just catching on about the time I started getting involved with writing about it, and pretty soon I was racing and track testing everything from spindly old MGs to Le Mans-winning Ferraris to Grand Prix single-seaters to thundering NASCAR stock cars. All under the thoroughly transparent pretext of *"writing magazine stories about them!"*

And I was getting *paid* for it, too!

******

So what has all this to do with self-published fiction? Well, let's start with the first and most basic truth: *You've got to write what you know.* Or, at the very least, you need to be comfortable, conversant and familiar with your subject and genre. Nothing smells worse than bullshit, and people will never pick your stuff up if they catch a whiff. Secondly, *Have a story to tell.* This is so obvious, and yet it's so regularly ignored. Thirdly, and most importantly, ask yourself: *Who is going to want to read this?*

Remember that last one. It'll be back.

So why did I decide to write a novel about automobile racing? And particularly open-road sports car racing back in the early 1950's (when I was personally about seven years old)? Well, to begin with, I pretty much hated all the racing fiction I'd ever read (or, worse yet, seen on the screen) because it just didn't capture that world the way I knew it. The magic of the cars and the skill, thrill, risk and responsibilities of speed. The incredible characters you meet on the circuit, from genuine heroes to even more genuine wankers, fools, con men and idiots. Black sheep heirs of famous fortunes. Long-suffering wives. Dangerous Other Women. And especially the broken down racing bums who can't afford to be there but just can't help themselves. The wild, roller-coaster race weekends and race weekend parties and the long, lonely, gypsy road trips in between. The invisible sea of money running just beneath the surface that it all needs to float on. And, most of all, the secret understanding and singular brand of gallows humor that seals the bond between real racers everywhere and sets them apart from the rest of the world.

This wasn't going to be another lame racing potboiler about some handsome hero driver who can win in almost anything or the aging one who's lost his nerve or finds no meaning in life. No, this was going to be a genuine, historically and mechanically accurate racing story told from the viewpoint of Buddy Palumbo, a blue-collar kid just out of high school, coming of age in the Eisenhower Fifties. A real, three-dimensional kid with family problems and girlfriend problems and the same, incurable and unshakable case of Car Lust I knew so well from my own experience. Buddy's dad is a union shop steward at a big chemical plant over in Newark, and wants the kid to take a nice, safe, solid union job with a secure future and plenty of benefits. But all Buddy wants to do is hang around the corner Sinclair station and fix busted cars. And spend a little time with the station owner's niece, Julie Finzio, a wannabe fashion illustrator who waits tables at the Doggy Shake burger restaurant down the street, cleans up the office at the Sinclair a few days each week, and whose long term prospects aren't much better than Buddy's.

Then one of the station's customers, a big Jewish scrap dealer named Big Ed Baumstein who always drove Cadillacs, sees a new Jaguar roadster—one of the first in the country—and decides he has to have one. Naturally he wants Buddy to take care of it, and so Buddy has to go down to the Jaguar dealership in Manhattan (run by a cheap, conniving, and terminally class conscious British expatriate named Colin St. John) to get parts and advice. There he hears about a sports car race that weekend out on Long Island, he and Big Ed go, and they both get bitten by the bug. Only Big Ed has trouble getting in because the WASPy racing club doesn't accept Jews.

Even lousy Jews like Big Ed.

The story line pretty much follows the 1952 racing season exactly as it happened, only with my fictional characters and the issues of their lives interwoven with the actual people, places, and events of the time. I was very careful with my research (in fact, my original goal was simply to capture a period of racing history in readable, narrative form) but, somewhere along the way, the lives and interactions of my fictional characters got a whole lot more interesting than the era I was trying to capture. I don't know exactly how or why that happened, but it's probably the heart and soul of fiction writing. When your characters start to move on their own—when they *surprise* you!—that's when you know you're really onto something. And also when you need to chain yourself to the keyboard every single day—even when you don't feel like it!—to see how it's all going to come out.

******

It took me almost eight years to write *The Last Open Road,* but a lot of that was giving up in anguish ("I'll *never* get this done!") and then trying all over again a few months later. Or putting the manuscript up on a shelf at the beginning of each racing season, then taking it down again in the fall and starting over from the beginning "to get myself up to speed." The result being that, for the first five years, about all I accomplished was to rewrite the first 200 pages five different times! But, like anything else you do for the first time, the important thing is developing a methodology and learning *how* to do it. How to force yourself to write every day even when you know what's coming out is crap. How to evolve your story while you're working on it and learning how to keep track of time, place, characters, and continuity. And especially how and where to do the necessary research so the narrative rings true.

Hey, if *you* don't believe it, nobody else will.

Most important, you've got to find your voice and style. I tried writing a racing novel in third person omniscient a couple times, and it simply didn't work for me. I was too far away from the action and far too formal with it. In fact, that's where Buddy came from. He's part of the action, but not necessarily one of the stars. I call his style "First Person Barstool," and, if I do it right, it sounds like Buddy's sitting right there on the next barstool, telling you how things are in his life and spinning a few wild racing yarns in the bargain. Off the cuff, you know?

Sadly, anybody with half a knack can load up ream after ream of paper with action, description, and dialogue. The problem is that finally—somehow—you have to get to the end. And that takes persistence, flexibility, continual compromise, realistic goals and rock-solid discipline. Above all, you need encouragement and trust from the people you love and count on. I never could have done any of it without my family. Rightly or wrongly, they believed in me, and that was the fuel that kept me going. Even when I wasn't sure exactly where.

Okay, so I finally finished the damn thing. Now what? Well, like most aspiring writers who figure they've just wrapped up the next _Catch 22,_ I sent it off, unheralded and un-agented, to every major publisher in Manhattan. Then I waited for all those big, fat offers with lots of zeroes to the left of the decimal point to start rolling in. Only instead I got rejection slips. One after another. Some were nice enough to say that they liked it—even liked it very much—but that the subject matter was a major problem. Or, as that one particularly rude young New York publishing lady told me (I believe they must breed them out there): "Oh, it's a wonderful book. But there's just no market for it. _Those people don't read...._"

But I guess you can't really blame her (although I surely did!). Publishing—and especially bigtime, mass market fiction publishing—is a risky business. It takes a lot of money to put a book out, and that's just the tiniest little tip of the iceberg if you're trying to promote a new writer that has no established following and nobody ever heard of before. Especially when damn near every new title from every major publisher springs forth draped in accolades and trumpeted as, surely, "a genuine masterpiece" or "one of the year's ten best." Add to that the fact that the current—and colossally stupid—general marketing strategy in the book biz is to have a _huge_ pile of every hot new title stacked to the ceiling in every damn Borders, Barnes & Noble, and mom-and-pop bookstore across the nation. Just to give the rank-and-file book buying public some inkling of just how scalding, freaking _HOT_ that new title is. So, even on a good, solid Best Seller, you could be talking 40%—or more!—returns when all is said and done. Which is why all the major publishing houses would much rather put their money into More Of The Same from the same established authors. It just makes sense.

But anger and frustration can be tremendous motivators. They can cause you to do things you would never even *dream* of doing if you weren't so damn pissed off. And right at that exact moment, with the phone receiver still shaking in my hand, *that's* when I decided I was going to publish it myself. In fact, *"I'll show YOU!"* was about the total extent of my game plan.

******

Like everyone else who has traveled this steep and rocky path, I discovered that there are an awful lot of things you need to know in order to be a book publisher, and a depressingly large number of them you wind up learning the hard way. After the fact. But that's the nature of the whole learning process, *n'est ce pas?* One of the main things I learned is that *Nobody Cares* ("Oh? You're publishing your own book? How nice. Pass the salad dressing, please....") and the other is that *You pay for everything. Up front.* In fact, that's easily the most difficult and daunting aspect of self-publishing. All the costs—and believe me, there are *puh-lenty!*—are front-loaded. So you've got to have this massive wad of cash sunk into a hole in the ground before you can even attempt to make the first nickel. In our case, we had to take out a second mortgage on our house to get the job done, and there was a very real possibility that our son would not go to college (or at least not without massive student aid) if this swell, self-published book idea of mine fell flat on its rear end. See notes above on what a fantastic sport my wife is. Truth is, her family thinks she's nuts for putting up with me. Hell, *my* family thinks she's nuts for putting up with me.

So there you are. You've got this great book (it's the new *Catch 22*, remember?) and all you need to do is get all those high-toned magazine and newspaper critics to review it and tell everybody how wonderful it is and then get the bookstores to carry it so people will be able to buy it after they read all those stunning reviews. Guess what? You're screwed (see *Nobody Cares* above). For a variety of very respectable reasons, major bookstores only want to deal with master distributors like Ingram and Baker and Taylor. There is no way on earth they could do business with all the tiny, independent self-publisher types of this world, each one clamoring for attention like thousands of hungry, squeaking, squawking baby birds in a nest roughly the size of Soldier Field. Besides, why would they want to? And what about returns? *"Sure, Bub, I know everybody and his friggin' brother is gonna wanna buy this here book of yers. No question about it. But, heh-heh, just for the sake of argument, let's say I got a few left. What then?"*

And therein lies the problem. Unlike any other retail business I'm aware of—and against every known tenet of prudent or practical business practice—virtually everything in the publishing world is sold on consignment. Sure, the bookstores pay for what they put on the shelves. But, if it doesn't sell, you've got to take it back. Regardless of condition. And issue full credit, too. And therein lies the rub. What the heck does anybody—bookstore *or* distributor—want with a credit from you, the whiny little independent self-publisher? After all, you've got nothing else they want to *buy!*

Bottom line, the problem is that your measly little title can't *make* them a significant amount of money, but it can surely *cost* them a significant amount of money (and aggravation) if it doesn't sell. The alternative—offering copies directly to bookstores to put on their shelves on consignment—is a colossal logistical nightmare for everybody involved. Keeping track of who has what in stock and who owes whom how much is a fulltime job for some lame bean counter all by itself. And you need to remember that these businesses have lots of better things to do than keeping track of your particular title. Even if it *is* the next *Catch 22*. Plus it's never going to sell unless you can muster up some sort of media presence and publicity campaign to fuel interest.

Which brings us to *Nobody Cares, Part III:* The mainstream book media is besieged daily—even hourly!—by new titles begging for attention. Many of them come from the big New York publishing houses, some from smaller presses, and countless more—believe me, you have no idea how many—from independent self-publishers. Due to this enormous volume of volumes *(ugh!)* and an understandable desire to keep their lives manageable, the mainstream book media seldom, if ever, considers a self-published novel for review. There are two major reasons for this:

a) They consider the big, established publishing houses as the First Cut. If you can't interest one of them in your story, it mustn't be much good.

b) If they *do* break down and review a self-published novel, they open an enormous can of worms (refer to clamoring baby birds in Soldier Field analogy above) as now every crackpot wannabe novelist in Christendom comes beating on their door and whining about how "You reviewed *his* book, so why won't you do *mine?*" It's much easier to just adopt a general policy against reviewing self-published books and let it go at that. And, believe me, such policies *do* exist. And then you've got the little problem of lead times. All major book media require galleys *at least* three months—sometimes more—before pub date. Do what I did (out of ignorance) and send them something you've already finished and now have a garage full of and would desperately like the world to know about and all you'll get in return is a curt little form letter saying, in essence, *Nobody Cares.*

All of which leaves us in a pretty sorry situation. We've got all our money poured into this big hole in the ground, we own the big stack of books piled up inside it, and, short of hitting the lotto jackpot to fund a monster advertising campaign, we can't get anybody to review it so people know about it and can't get any major bookstores to carry it so people can buy it once they do. And always remember: *Nobody Cares.* Is it time for the stuff about going broke, taking up recreational drinking, and/or possible suicide attempts as mentioned in the opening paragraph?

Or is it time to start looking for a "novel" approach?

******

Let's start off by asking that question again: *Who is going to want to read this book?* And forget about "I gave copies of it to all my friends and they all *loved* it." What else are they going to say? *"Yeah, I tried to read your manuscript, but I kept falling asleep. Honestly, it was like slogging through a damn swamp. You may be the worst would-be novelist in history...So, how about lunch next Thursday?"* The point is this. You need to identify a core target market of people who, because of the genre, setting, era, theme, characters or subject matter just *might* want to read your book. If it's any good, that is. And that's something you'll just have to find out the hard way. Friends and acquaintances will tell you it's wonderful just to get you off their backs. You really need to find objective eyes. And they should be people who can do you some promotional good if they like what you've done.

This is how we did it:

First off, it was pretty easy to define our core market. It was those blessed car people. You remember, the ones who "don't read." Sure, I wanted readers who didn't know or care anything about cars or motor sports to pick up—and hopefully enjoy— *The Last Open Road.* But you've got to start somewhere. And then just hope it spreads. So my wife, son, and I received our first vanload of books, hot off the presses, up at the big, mid-summer vintage race meet in Elkhart Lake, Wisconsin, in July of 1994. About all we had besides the books were some cheap Xeroxed flyers telling people we had them for sale and touting them as "the best damn racing fiction *ever!*" We also offered a tongue-in-cheek guarantee: *"If this book doesn't make you laugh out loud, we'll give you your money back."*

But the key thing is what my wife and son *did* with the posters. The racetrack at Elkhart Lake is huge—over four miles around—and it's situated in sort of a rolling, woodsy, meadow-and-forest state park kind of setting in Wisconsin's scenic Kettle Moraine. It's lovely, really. And a magnificent place to drive a racecar. And while I was busy racing, I'd asked Carol and Adam to "put these flyers where everybody will see them." Only later on I realized that I hadn't seen any attached to the trees or fence posts. Not that they would have done much good there. And then I went to, ahem, "relieve" myself. And there was one of our flyers, taped up over the urinal in the porta-potty. In fact, my wife and son had put them up in every blessed men's room, ladies' room, and porta-john on the premises. And right where you couldn't avoid looking at them. At least not until you were finished, anyway....

Talk about a captive audience!

Besides being one hell of a sport, no question my wife's a genius.

Better yet, our "potty posters" have become rather pleasantly notorious over the last several years, often being the "hook" that interests newspaper or magazine writers who might want to cover our story. Or, as one of my vintage racing friends from California put it: "I can't take a leak at a racetrack anywhere in the country without reading about your damn books!"

In any case, that first weekend at Elkhart Lake was pretty successful. The books arrived at the very last minute (natch!) driven up straight-through by a gypsy trucker the printer had to hire after running into the usual litany of down-to-the-wire production disasters when the binding machine broke down. But they made it—just!—and I couldn't believe what it felt like to finally hold a copy in my hands. In fact, it got me so revved up that I couldn't even think about sleeping. So I took a case over to Siebken's Bar (which, ironically enough, is the setting for several key scenes in the story) and that's where the very first copies were sold. Just before closing time in the wee, small hours of Friday morning. You really couldn't dream it up much better. And we wound up selling over 400 books that weekend, mostly thanks to Carol's potty posters!

Still, printing the thing had about tapped us out, and so there really wasn't any money available for an ad campaign. But I think ads are generally overrated. Or, as the late "Yippie" Abbie Hoffman once put it during his late-1960's flashbulb-pop of media fame: "Don't buy advertising—make *news!*" It's cheaper and far more effective. So, from day one, you've got to be grinding out press releases and calling editors and generally making a pest of yourself and just as generally getting ignored. The important thing to realize is that *the book is just the by-product.* There has to be some other story—about you, about your adventures (or misadventures) in the publishing world, about your posters over the urinals, *something*—to get those media people interested. And remember, you're probably not going to get anywhere with the book review media except for maybe in your own hometown. At least if it's small enough. So you've got to find other types of writers and editors who might be interested in your story.

We were lucky in that there is a pretty large and well-developed selection of Car Nut and Motor Sports magazines on the market (for those people who "don't read," remember?) and we naturally sent books and cover letters off to all of them. Not to mention every blessed car club newsletter, auto writer, and motor sports writer working for every major daily newspaper in the country. And then we followed up with phone calls. And more phone calls. Generally, we got ignored. Sometimes rudely. But that's the nature of the game. You just have to be relentless, not get daunted or discouraged, and accept this simple fact: *For every door that opens a tiny crack, a dozen more will be slammed in your face.* So what?

The good news is that we started getting some results. Thankfully, the car media people were liking _The Last Open Road_. One magazine called it *"the best, most true-to-life, and most utterly hilarious racing story ever written."* Prestigious (and well-read!) *Road & Track* magazine went even further: *"...recalls to mind Holden Caulfield and _Catcher in the Rye_."* In fact, three separate reviewers compared it to Salinger's famous classic. Why, we were even getting rave notices from car magazines in England!

But none of this cut any ice with the mainstream book media. Not one bit. We were patently "beyond the pale" as far as they were concerned, no matter what kind of attention we were getting elsewhere. In fact, when you get right down to it, the book industry—at least as represented by the major publishers and the mainstream book review media—is pretty damn smug and insular regarding "knowing what the public wants." And God help you if your title doesn't hit any of their hot buttons, slander some popular celebrity, or come screaming off the front pages of the tabloids in the grocery store checkout line.

So you're on your own. And you've got to get used to the idea that media deals and news stories that looked *all set* can evaporate in a heartbeat. I'll give you one example. We'd made a deal with a high class bookstore in a huge, upscale shopping center near us (Oakbrook) to do a book signing on Father's Day. When, coincidentally, the center hosted a huge classic car show for all the car-nut dads in the area. Perfect! Better yet, we'd gotten some interest from the local news section of the *Chicago Tribune.* Oh, wow! We'd be in the Sunday paper—bigger and better than any blessed ad!—and then they'd all come out to look at the neat old cars and buy my book. Double perfect! We'd even arranged to borrow an old Ferrari and an even older MG from two of my racing friends to put on display in front of the store....

And then, the night before, it was announced that Chicago's beloved Cardinal Bernardin had pancreatic cancer. It was a local media bombshell that—and rightly so—blew our story right off the pages. Result: no newspaper story, no public awareness, and we only sold about a dozen copies. But there was a lesson in it: *For everything to work right, you need product and publicity to arrive at the same time!* Believe me, writing a book and getting it printed are *nothing* compared to the challenges of marketing and distribution. It does no good to have a great media story and no books available, and it's even worse to have books sitting on the shelf and no media attention.

You'll be getting them back.

******

Which brings us to the ugly and generally misunderstood topic of bookstore distributors. Any time you feel like cursing them as pirates, pillagers, percentage takers and Philistines, just remember that they're in business to make a buck, and that their main function in the overall scheme of things is logistical rather than artistic. Sure, they demand 50% to 55% off, pay in 90 to 120 days, want you to take back all their returns (including damaged merchandise!), and often expect you to pay freight both ways. But *you* need them because the bookstores need them. At least if that's where you plan on marketing your title.

My experience is that there are alternatives. Not so much *instead of* the traditional and established bookstore market, but *in addition to it.* And, once again, it comes down to identifying and focusing in on that core target market that might actually be interested in your book and figuring out where and how you can access them. In our case, we did far better with gift shops and souvenir stands at racetracks and car museums, doing book signings at major races, auctions, and car shows, and getting featured in specialty catalogs that sold everything from car polish to competition brake pads. In some cases, we were the only book in the entire catalog. And always the only novel. But there was a thematic connection between the subject matter in the story and the interest group that ordered parts and equipment through those catalogs. It was just a matter of convincing the companies involved that they could make money selling my books. And it's important that your retailers make a decent profit, because they're not going to want you around if you're not ringing the old cash register.

Like I said, it's *business.*

We also stumbled on other ways to increase visibility. I thought the typeface lettering we used for *The Last Open Road* looked pretty neat. It was just one of those happy accidents where I sat down one day with some good, old fashioned press type and started fooling around. The second one I did was made out of one condensed and one expanded version of the same font, and, as soon as I finished it, I said, *"Wait. Don't do any more. You'll just confuse yourself. It's perfect."* In fact, I liked it so much that we had decals made and gave them away with the books. There were two colors ("cappuccino cream" and "hearty burgundy," to go on dark or light cars) and, pretty soon, we were seeing *The Last Open Road* decals on all sorts of racecars, sports cars, classic cars, motorcycles, tow rigs, tool boxes, trailers and beer coolers—all over the whole damn country. We even started selling them (at, I might add, a decent markup!) so we were actually making a little money on them and simultaneously getting exposure you couldn't buy for a million bucks. That's now expanded into T-shirts, tank tops, jacket patches and even cloisonné jewelry. But I'm getting ahead of my story....

I'd meanwhile sent books and media kits out to several agents in New York—hey, I wanted to be a *writer,* not run a damn publishing company—and finally arrived at a deal with one to try and find me a "real" publisher. This turned out to be another exercise in frustration, as we were heading into fall with Christmas looming and I was running out of copies from the first printing. Although several publishers said they were interested, nothing was getting finalized and meanwhile time was wasting. Eventually it dropped to two houses (although, as my agent gleefully reminded me, that could still mean a bidding war!) and then it all fell apart at the last minute when higher powers inside their organizations decided, once again, that the subject matter was a problem. Not mainstream enough. Nobody's going to want to buy a damn novel about *cars.* And here I always thought Mark Twain did pretty well with that "raft" story of his....

So we went into a second printing on our own (managing to convince our bank to secure the credit line for the production costs with the resulting inventory, but that's another story) and sold most of those in another year. Meanwhile, one of the "real" editors who liked the book a lot had left the publisher he'd been working for and gone back to his old job at St. Martin's Press. I'd kept in touch— even though I'd never met him— faxing over copies of every new review and news story we managed to generate and keeping him abreast of our sales. I was particularly pleased by his interest since he was definitely *not* a "car guy." In fact, he didn't even own a car and had never been to (or had any desire to see) a car race in his entire life. He just liked the story and the characters. So you can imagine how thrilled I was when he faxed me back one day to tell me that St. Martin's would be picking up <u>The Last Open Road</u>.

It was a dream come true.

Or so I thought at the time....

******

The good part is that my editor made me edit <u>The Last Open Road</u>. Oh, I fought and whined and squirmed about it, but I finally caved in and did it. And it was about the best thing that could have happened. To be honest, I hadn't really taken a good, long look at the text for years, and I was properly appalled—as you always are when you look back at your own writing—when I saw some of the things I'd done. And overdone. And hadn't done.

Although it came out a bit shorter, I honestly think the St. Martin's version was probably the better novel (if not necessarily the better "car guy" book). I threw about a half-pound of Excess Fat adverbs and adjectives over the side, added one scene, deleted another, and generally tightened up the narrative. My editor and I were both pretty happy with the way it came out. We figured it was a damn good book. And so then I waited for the big, professional New York media blitz to grind into gear and all that nice, green money to start rolling in.

I'm still waiting.

Turns out the way it works is that big publishers crank out a whole slew of titles every season, and they only have so many hands, feet, bags of gold, and constantly-yapping-into-the-telephone PR-type jaws available in their publicity departments. So they tend to put the muscle and money where they think it will do the most good. Although my editor really liked my book and its prospects, he was apparently the only one—nobody's going to want to buy a *car* novel, remember?—and the total visible evidence of the St. Martin's PR department's efforts was a pleasantly enthusiastic 4-column-inch blurb in *USA Today*. Period. We did get a wonderful 8-page cover story in the *Chicago Tribune Sunday Magazine* (again, more about "how we did it" and "what we'd been through" than about the book itself), but we pretty much generated that out of our own office and efforts. Still, the Trib editors never would've even considered the story if the book had still been self-published. The bottom line was that while St. Martin's had *legitimized* me as a novelist (for which I will be genuinely and forever grateful!), they weren't exactly expending much money or effort trying to sell copies. And this, ironically enough, at about the same time they secured the rights to the Monica Lewinsky story for a paltry $650,000, paid some professional hack another large wad of cash to put it between covers (not that she hadn't been *there* before!), printed a skazillion of them, and watched the vast majority of them march right back home after gathering dust in the book stores for an appropriate period of time.

Yep, those bigtime publishing houses can sure pick 'em.

After all, they know what America wants....

But the point is this. After adding all the numbers up, I realized that we'd sold far more copies of <u>The Last Open Road</u> through the guerrilla, gearhead-oriented distribution network we'd set up than St. Martin's ever did through the conventional book store market. Even of "their" version! So why on earth would I want to go back to them with the sequel, which I was just finishing? Only by contract I had to. Part of every standard new author's contract is an option on your "next work." Whatever it may be. So I sent a cover letter to St. Martin's along with the first manuscript draft of <u>Montezuma's Ferrari</u>, telling them I wanted to bring it out at Elkhart Lake the following July (the fifth anniversary of <u>The Last Open Road</u>'s debut) and asking to see a proposed marketing plan and promotional budget for the new title as part of the deal. There wasn't much in the way of response, and so, once the contract-specified number of days had expired, I found myself back out on my own again.

To be honest, I wasn't real thrilled with the prospect of laying out another large, front-loaded pile of money to publish the sequel. Oh, I knew there was a market—we'd already proven that—but it really wasn't a very good business proposition. Between the cost to print and bind and the costs of freight, warehousing, distribution and marketing and the discounts you had to offer and promo stuff you had to buy and freebies you had to give away, the numbers weren't exactly stunning. Sure, I knew we had a probable loyal customer base for maybe 10,000 copies. Maybe even 15,000. But how do you make any money on ten or fifteen thousand copies?

And then I had a goofy idea. Why not fund all those front-loaded costs the same way professional motorsports have been underwritten for ages: with sponsorships and advertising? And do it in such a way that it fit in with the theme, content and context of the book. To be honest, it was one of those wild, snap-awake-in-the-middle-of-the-night brainstorms that starts sounding a little lame come the dawn. I mean, it was just too *simple,* you know? But then I figured, what the hey, why not give it a try...?

So I made up some solicitation flyers and did a deal with a few of the racing clubs I belong to and magazines that carry my work to piggyback them with their entry forms and new issues for the difference in postage. Fair deal all around, right? And the response—based in large part on the success and status of the first book within the classic car, sports car and motorsports communities—was overwhelming. We got everything from full-page ads from big companies like Mercedes-Benz of North America to smaller ads from more specialized businesses that catered to the classic car, sports car, and motorsports universe. And it made good sense for them. After all, think of the shelf life! Our ads were cost competitive with magazines that wound up in the trash bin at the end of the month. But, in my new book, that ad would be there virtually *forever.* And, if the story was anywhere near as good as the original, each copy would likely be passed around to a large group of friends. It was a pretty good deal. Plus we offered "individual sponsorship" opportunities to people, businesses and racing teams who just plain liked the first book and wanted to participate in the sequel. Which got their names (or the names of people they wanted to honor or commemorate) carved into the headstone granite of our sponsorship page for everybody to see. They also received copies of a limited run, leather-bound and cloisonné-emblemed *Sponsors' and Advertisers' Special Edition* that we promised would never be on sale anywhere. At any price. We called it the world's first "coffee table novel." And it was, too....

In less than eight weeks, we raised over $50,000, paid for all the production costs, and even had enough left to buy out St. Martin's old warehouse and returns inventory of the first book (which are now all but sold out as <u>The Last Open Road</u> heads into its fourth printing!). Better yet, I hired my old friend Art Eastman—who is a World Class genius when it comes to graphics—to help me turn the ad section into something that would *enhance* the value of the book rather than cheapen it. I came up with the idea of formatting the ads into this phony old sports car magazine from the period of the story—like something you might stumble across up in somebody's attic—and mixing in historical racing photographs and actual ads from the fifties, some of them real and some completely bogus. I'm pleased to say some of the advertisers really got in the spirit of it. Particularly my friend Craig Morningstar at Mercedes-Benz, who had somebody dig into their archives in Germany and came up with an old ad from the early fifties featuring the exact same 1952 300SL racecar that figures in a major part of the story.

To top it all off, Art Eastman came up with our outstanding "Prancing Chili Peppers" _Montezuma's Ferrari_ logo, which has unfortunately caught the attention of the Trademark and Intellectual Property weasels at Ferrari (who have recently faxed us all the way from England to kindly "cease and desist" with our chili peppers) but still looks smashing on our shirts and decals. More on this as it develops (but just _think_ of the publicity potential if we—gulp!—get sued by Ferrari).

In any case, we still had to deal with that old marketing/distribution/media lead-time problem and figure out some kind of plan. I knew I wanted to introduce _Montezuma's Ferrari_ at Elkhart Lake in July, because it represented such a perfect fit. Plus I'd be able to sell them at the bigger vintage car meets for the balance of the summer and maybe even start a little media buzz heading into the lead-up to Christmas. But then I couldn't give people like _Publisher's Weekly_ (assuming they'd even look at it) their required early galleys. And that's when we hit on the idea of making not one, not two, but _three_ separate editions. The first was the special, leather bound, limited edition sponsor/advertiser "coffee table" version mentioned above. We made 300 of those. The second was the normal "First Edition," which can be identified by its red binding and the "October 31st" pub date on the copyright page. We printed 7,000 of those. The third, absolutely identical to the "First Edition" except for black cover binding and a few minor words on the copyright page, we called the "Preview Edition." We did 5,000 of those. So we were able to sell the "Preview Editions" at race track and car events for the balance of the summer (believe it or not, they're starting to qualify as collector's items!) while still giving the long-lead book media the timing they required and introducing _Montezuma's Ferrari_ to the mainstream bookstore market as a fresh, new title just in time for Christmas. Not to mention selling as many copies as possible through our own distribution network—at anything from zero to a maximum of 40% discount—before going the 50% to 55% off "distributor pricing" required for the conventional bookstore market.

Best of all, _Montezuma's Ferrari_ started getting some really nice reviews, including one in _Publishers Weekly_ (of all places!) and being picked as Book of the Month by England's prestigious _Classic & Sports Car_ magazine. It's the only novel they've ever selected. The book was also honored as one of the P.M.A. Benjamin Franklin "Book of the Year" award winners (sort of the "Best Picture" Oscar of independent and small press publishing) and, once again, it was the only novel to make the cut. That was pretty exciting for us, and I'm happy to report that sales have been excellent. Plus I'm already hard at work on the content, packaging, and marketing *schtick* for the next title. I guess it's like my dad told me all those years ago: *"There's really only one thing you need to know in life, and that's what you have to do next!"*

Besides, this is *FUN!*

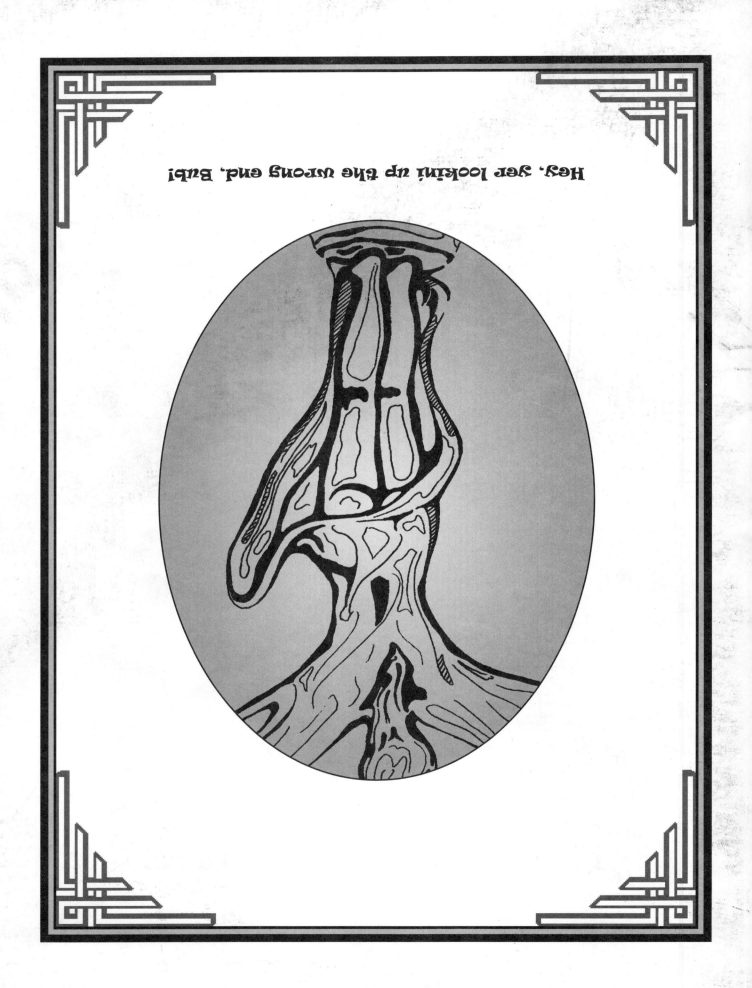